PRAISE FOR

ANGEL

"This book blew me away. It's fresh, imaginative,
hugely entertaining and highly addictive. A stunning read. "
Empire of Books

"A dark and fresh new twist to the celestial beings...
It's a sin to miss a book this good!" *Girls Without a Bookshelf*

"A powerful, dark and hugely inventive thriller that burrows
beneath the reader's skin... This electrifying novel makes a
lasting impression; a must-read." *Jake Hope, teen librarian*

"An extremely compelling idea, so rich and deep and thrilling."
Liz Kessler, New York Times bestselling author

"Forget about vampires, it's all about angels!... Excellent."
Nicole Burstein, Waterstone's Piccadilly

"A brilliant love story...I am hooked."
Rob Welton, Jarrold's bookseller

"Angels are reinvented...in this high-octane action adventure."
The Bookseller

"Compelling...tense, romantic, scary." *Our Book Reviews*

L. A. WEATHERLY was born in Little Rock, Arkansas, USA. She now lives with her husband and their cat, Bernard, in Hampshire, England, where she spends her days – and nights! – writing.

L. A. Weatherly is the author of over thirty books, which have been published in over ten different languages.

www.leeweatherly.com
www.angelfever.com

ANGEL

ANGEL

L.A. WEATHERLY

USBORNE

To my husband, with love

First published in the UK in 2010 by Usborne Publishing Ltd., Usborne House,
83-85 Saffron Hill, London EC1N 8RT, England. www.usborne.com

Copyright © L. A. Weatherly, 2010

The right of L. A. Weatherly to be identified as the author of this work has been
asserted by them in accordance with the Copyright, Designs and Patents Act, 1988.

Cover photograph © Pawel Piatek/Trevillion Images

The name Usborne and the devices ♀ ☺ are Trade Marks of
Usborne Publishing Ltd.

A CIP catalogue record for this book is available from the British Library.

ISBN 9781409521969 02173/1 Printed in Reading, Berkshire, UK.

PROLOGUE

"IS THAT YOUR CAR?" ASKED the girl at the 7-Eleven checkout counter. "The shiny black one?"

Alex nodded as he put a Big Gulp coffee down in front of her.

"Cool," breathed the girl, gazing out at it. It was a Porsche Carrera, and the sunshine was glistening off it like liquid onyx. "We don't see cars like *that* around here very often."

No, I bet you don't, thought Alex, trying to remember where *here* was. Cattle Chute, Oklahoma, or some such dismal place. *Home of the rootin'-tootin' Cowboys!* the bullet-ridden sign outside of town had proclaimed.

"Pump three," he told her.

The girl smiled at him, widening her brown eyes as she rang up his coffee and the gas. "So, are you new in town?" she asked. *VICKY*, said her name tag. She was almost as tall as he was – which wasn't that tall; he was just over five-ten – and her brown hair had been ironed so straight that you could get a paper cut from it.

Saturday job, he thought, pulling out his wallet. *Sixteen or so. She probably goes to that giant high school that I passed just outside of town.*

The thought irritated and amused him in equal measure. He had only seen high school on TV: jocks in their letter jackets, cheerleaders jumping around the field, couples hanging onto each other at the Senior Prom. It was another world, one so stupidly innocent that it was frightening. High school students were old enough to be fighting, only none of them were.

Because hardly anyone actually knew that there was a war on.

"Nah, just passing through," he said. He handed her a couple of twenties.

Vicky's face fell. "Oh. I was just wondering if you'd be going to our high school…but I guess you're sort of old for that. What are you – twenty-one or something?"

"Or something," he said with a slight grin. He was

actually seventeen, but she was right in a way. In all the ways that mattered, he was old.

She took her time getting his change. "How long are you here for? Because, you know – if you're looking for something to do, or maybe someone to show you around—"

There was a beeping sound from his jeans pocket as his cellphone announced a text. Alex's heart leaped. Turning away slightly, he pulled the phone out and flipped it open.

Enemy sighted, Aspen CO. Residence 1124 Tyler St.

Yes! Immediately, Alex felt the fierce buzz sweep over him that he always got when there'd been a sighting. Finally – it had been over a week; he'd been going insane. Putting his phone back in his pocket, he smiled at Vicky. Why not? He'd never see her again anyway.

"Maybe next time," he said, picking up his coffee. "Thanks, though."

"Sure," she said, trying to smile back. "Well…have a good trip."

As Alex pushed open the swinging door, the too-cold air conditioning abruptly gave way to a flat, burning September. He slid into the Porsche. It was low to the ground, and its black leather seats wrapped around him in a dark embrace. It was comfortable as hell, actually, which was good, since he practically lived in it. *Aspen CO,* he punched into the GPS. Estimated time of arrival, 2.47 a.m. Almost nine hours. He'd drive straight through, he decided, taking a gulp of coffee. He didn't need sleep – god, all he'd been *doing* since his last prey was resting.

Pulling out of the parking lot, Alex turned onto Highway 34, heading north out of town. If you could call it a town: there were a few dozen grids of streets with clapboard houses, and a couple of long, brightly-lit shopping strips, where the *rootin'-tootin'* teenagers probably cruised up and down on Saturday night, drinking Bud Lights and shouting at each other. Just outside the town limits it all ended, and became dust and grain silos and oil pumps. Setting the cruise control to seventy, Alex turned on the radio. The Eagles came on, warbling about the Hotel California, and he grimaced. Switching to his iPod instead, he put on some indie rock as the Porsche began to smoothly eat the miles.

And, briefly, he wondered what Vicky would think if she knew he had a semi-automatic rifle in his trunk.

The Rocky Mountains cradled Aspen deep within them, like a giant's palm lightly cupping a handful of diamonds. The road twisted and turned down the mountain as Alex approached the city, his headlights sweeping the dark asphalt in front of him. Startled rabbits froze on the side of the road, their eyes wide, and once he disturbed a buck, sending it crashing and leaping into the woods.

2.51, read his car clock as he crossed into the Aspen city limits. Not bad. The GPS directed him to Tyler Street, a quiet, tree-lined avenue not far from downtown. One of the streetlights was flickering; the rest glowed silently, showing a row of houses with large bay windows and immaculate front lawns. No house lights were on. Everyone was asleep.

Alex parked his car a few doors down from number 1124. Propping his elbows against the steering wheel, he surveyed the house, his dark eyebrows drawn together thoughtfully. Sometimes you could see a sign of them if you knew what to look for, but there was nothing here. It was just an ordinary house, though the front lawn wasn't quite as pristine as the others. A few weeds grew here and there, spiking rebelliously up through the grass.

Letting down the neighbourhood — tsk, tsk, thought Alex.

He'd transferred his rifle to the front seat before he began the descent into Aspen, and now he clicked the magazine into place and sighted along the rifle's length, squinting through the infrared lens at the house. The front door snapped into an eerie reddish focus. He could even read the name on the wrought-iron mailbox that was affixed to the front porch wall: *T. Goodman.*

Goodman. Alex snorted despite himself. The creatures often took human last names to help them blend in; nice to see that some of them had a sense of humour. He screwed the silencer onto the rifle's muzzle. It was state of the art, as sleek and gleaming as the rifle itself. Now all he had to do was wait. He settled back in his seat, gazing at the house. Back in the days when they'd gone out in teams, the other AKs had always hated stakeouts, but they were part of the hunt to Alex. Part of the buzz. Your senses had to be on alert; you couldn't relax for a moment.

Almost an hour later, the front door opened. He had the rifle in place in less than a second, watching carefully through the lens. The tall man on the front porch paused to lock the door, and then jogged briskly down the steps and strode off down the street, his footsteps echoing with purpose.

Alex lowered the rifle, unsurprised that T. Goodman was in his human form – they normally only showed their true nature when they were feeding. He waited until the man had turned the corner, heading towards downtown, and then he got out of his car and softly opened the trunk. Pulling on a black trench coat, he eased the trunk closed again and set off, the rifle safely hidden beneath the coat's long folds.

As he turned the corner he could see his quarry about a block away, crossing the street. He slowed for a moment, letting his gaze drift out of focus. An aura swam into view around the dark figure: pale silver, with a faint blue light flickering feebly at its edges.

Alex quickened his step. The creature hadn't fed in days – which meant that he must be on the hunt now.

Sure enough, the man led him to a bar downtown. *Spurs,* flashed the sign in front. A yellow and pink neon figure of a cowgirl wearing shorts and a tiny leather vest flashed on and off, waving her hat. There was the heavy pulse of music, and a chorus of raucous male cheers.

Recognizing the sign, Alex shook his head in grudging admiration. Spurs was one of those places where the female waitstaff wore sexy clothes and danced on the bar. The men staggering out at this hour would be drunk and rowdy, not paying much attention to their surroundings – ideal if you were on the hunt. It was just the sort of place that he'd have chosen himself, in fact.

A pair of bored-looking bouncers flanked the front door. T. Goodman melted into the shadows nearby, attracting no attention from either of them. Half a street away, Alex took up a position behind a parked Subaru, mentally calculating the fallout distance. He'd be fine, he decided; he'd gone for much closer than this in his time. The bouncers might catch a bit of flak, though.

Just then Spurs's heavy metal door swung open, and a man wearing a dishevelled business suit stumbled out.

"Excellent night, my man," he said, slapping one of the bouncers on the shoulder. "Those ladies are *goo-od*." He shook his head in wonder, as if the power to describe just how good was beyond him.

"Yeah, they're real hot," said the bouncer, looking amused.

"Hope you're not planning on driving, Eddie," said the other one. "Why don't you let us call you a cab?"

Eddie made no reply. He wove off down the street, humming tunelessly to himself. One of his stumbling feet caught an empty beer can, and the sound of it echoed through the night. The bouncers glanced at each other and shrugged. Not their problem.

Alex straightened as T. Goodman detached himself from the gloom and trailed off after the man, a tall, silent shadow. Pulling out his rifle, Alex began to track. It would be any moment now, he was sure of it. They didn't need privacy, just a relatively clear field. Without taking his eyes off Goodman, Alex drew a deep breath to centre himself and then swiftly moved the focus of his energy up through his chakra points, until it hovered somewhere above his crown.

Immediately, he felt a slight shudder pass through him as the creature locked minds with its prey. He had been right – this was it. Wavering, Eddie stopped in his tracks, looking uncertain. Slowly, he turned around.

With a dark ripple, Goodman's human body melted away. A blinding, glorious light grew in its place, until it was like a beacon that shone up and down the street, illuminating everything – the bar, the other buildings, Eddie's small, frightened face. And at the centre of the light was a glowing being, seven feet tall, whose giant, spreading wings were such a pure white that they looked almost blue.

"This…this can't be…" stammered Eddie as the angel drew towards him.

Half a street away, Alex could hear the bouncers laughing with a woman who'd stopped to ask them for a light. If any of them glanced this way, all they'd see would be Eddie standing on his own, wobbling drunkenly on the dark street.

Leaning over the top of the car, Alex squinted through the lens, his hands cool and steady as he aimed the rifle. The angel's face came into focus, magnified several times. As a human Goodman had been as physically attractive as all angels were in that form, though Alex knew that if he'd got a good look at his face it would have seemed slightly weird – too intense, with eyes perhaps a shade too dark for comfort. But now, in his angel form, Goodman's features had an almost otherworldly beauty: proud, fierce. The halo that framed them radiated like holy fire.

"Don't be afraid," soothed the angel in a voice that was

a hundred chiming bells. "I am here for a reason. I need to give you something."

Eddie dropped to his knees, eyes bulging. "I – I—"

The halo. Alex sighted on it, aiming for the deep, pure white at its heart.

"It won't hurt," continued the angel, drawing closer. It smiled then, and its radiance increased tenfold, burning the night. Trembling, Eddie moaned and ducked his head, unable to bear the beauty of it.

"In fact, you'll remember this as the most meaningful experience of your life—"

Alex pulled the trigger. As the pulsing energy of the angel's halo was disrupted by the force of the bullet, the creature burst without a sound into a million shooting fragments of light. Alex ducked behind the car as a shockwave slammed past him, the angel's scream of anguish echoing in his ears. Still in his enhanced state, he could see the energy fields of every living thing nearby affected by the aftershock: the ghostly outline of a tree, of a few stray blades of grass, all of them dancing and warping as if buffeted by a hurricane.

Slowly, everything returned to normal. There was silence. Alex brought his energy focus back to his heart chakra, and the ghostly outlines disappeared. Shoving his rifle under the car for the moment, he walked over to Eddie, who still kneeled trembling on the sidewalk.

T. Goodman was gone completely, with no sign of him left.

"Hey man, you okay?" said Alex easily, crouching beside him. The bouncers had stopped talking and were looking in their direction. Alex raised a casual hand to them. *Everything's fine, dude's just a bit drunk, is all.*

Eddie turned a tear-stained face towards him. "I – there was – I know you won't believe me, but—"

"Yeah, I know," said Alex. "Come on, let's get you up." He put an arm around Eddie and helped him to his feet. *Jeez, the guy could try dieting a little.*

"Oh, my head…" moaned Eddie, leaning limply against Alex's shoulder. *Angel fallout*, thought Alex. Eddie had only been a few feet away, and though most of it had blasted straight back at Alex, he'd still feel the effects for days. It was better than angel burn, though.

Anything was better than that.

"It was so beautiful," mumbled Eddie. "So beautiful…"

Alex rolled his eyes. "Yeah, real beautiful," he muttered. He started walking back towards the bar with Eddie shuffling along beside him. As usual, he felt the mix of pity and contempt that he always felt for civilians. Though he spent his life trying to save them, they were all so clueless that he didn't get much pleasure from it.

"Hey, I think our friend here needs a cab," he said when he reached the bouncers. "Found him passed out on the sidewalk over there."

One of the bouncers chuckled. "Yeah, we'll take care of it," he said, taking the businessman's weight from Alex. "Old Eddie's a regular here, aren't you, buddy?"

Eddie rolled his head, struggling to focus. "Tom…I saw an angel," he slurred.

The bouncers burst out laughing. "Yeah, you mean Amber, right?" said the other one. "She wears those really short shorts while she's dancing around on the bar." He winked at Alex. "Hey man, you wanna go in? No cover charge; our treat."

Alex had been in plenty of places like this in his time, mostly dragged along by the other AKs when he was younger. He thought they were boring as hell, to be honest. And though a drink sounded good, the thought of sitting in a Spurs with his adrenalin still pumping from the kill was a little too surreal, even for him.

He shook his head, taking a step backwards. "Nah, maybe next time. I'd better get going. Thanks, though."

"Anytime," said the first bouncer. Eddie had passed out for real by then, slumped against him like a sack of potatoes. He shifted the man's bulk impatiently. "Hey, Mike, you gonna call that cab company, or what? Sleeping Beauty here is fading fast."

"Yeah, tell him to lay off the hard stuff," said Alex, with a grin. "He'll be seeing pink elephants next."

CHAPTER *One*

"THIS IS *SO* EMBARRASSING," MUTTERED Nina. She was leaning against the driver's side door with her arms crossed over her chest, shaking her head in disapproval.

"Do you want it fixed, or not?" I demanded. My voice came out muffled, because my head was buried somewhere deep in her Corvette's engine. Along with most of my upper body. I was trying to replace her carburettor, only her engine was so filthy that the nuts were practically welded in place with gasket grime. Which is black and gross, in case you're wondering.

"Would you hand me that wrench? The one with the yellow handle."

Nina grumbled to herself as she crouched down to rummage through my tools. "I can't believe you actually have a *toolbox*. I can't believe you brought it to *school* with you." She shoved the wrench into my hand.

"Fine – should I stop? Just say the word." I'd already removed her air filter by then, and disconnected the fuel line and vacuum hoses. We were in the school parking lot, because I had figured it would be easier doing it there than in my garage at home, which is stuffed to the gills with old boxes and bicycles and crap that my aunt keeps meaning to throw out but hasn't got around to doing yet. I had clearly reckoned without the embarrassment factor, though. Story of my life.

"Willow! Don't you dare," hissed Nina, pulling at her brown bangs. "Look, don't get all sensitive. Yes, I want it fixed; I just didn't know that you were going to do it *here*, that's all."

She glanced furtively over her shoulder at the playing field, obviously keeping an eye out for Scott Mason and his gang of swaggering football heroes. The school day was long over with, but football practice was still going strong. Meanwhile the student parking lot was like an empty grey ocean around us, with only a few stray cars dotted about here and there.

"Just be thankful I didn't do it at lunchtime," I told her. "I do have some sense of decorum, you know. Oh, come *on,* you—" I gritted my teeth together as I struggled to turn the wrench, putting all of my weight on it. All at once the nut gave way. "*Ha!* Success." Spinning it free, I pulled the old carburettor out and checked it against the new one. Perfect match. Which was sort of a miracle, given that Nina's Corvette practically belonged in the Smithsonian.

Nina wrinkled her nose. "Decorum, you? Don't make me laugh. Like, what are you *wearing?*"

"Clothes?"

"Willow. You look like...I don't know; I don't think there's even a word for it."

"Really? Cool." I grinned as I wiped my hands off on a bit of wadding. "That means I'm unique, right?" I was wearing a shimmering green 1950s brocade blouse with my favourite pair of battered jeans. My black velvet jacket was draped over the open hood, out of harm's way. I'd bought most of it at Tammy's Attic, which has to be my favourite shop ever.

Nina closed her eyes and groaned. "Unique. Yes, you could say that. Honestly, Willow, Pawntucket is *so* not ready for you."

This was so true that it wasn't even worth debating. Instead I took a screwdriver and started to scrape clean the area where the old carburettor had been, getting rid of all the old dirt and gasket material. Beyond gross. Picture a coal pit that's fallen into an oil slick.

Nina opened her eyes and peered under the hood. "What are you doing now?" she asked warily.

"Getting rid all of your disgusting grime." I showed her the screwdriver, which was now thick with black goo. "Want to help?"

"Eww, no." She sighed and leaned against the side of the car again, twiddling a piece of hair around her finger. "Anyway, what do you have to clean it for? Can't you just shove the new one in?"

A strand of my long blonde hair fell down as I was working, and I tucked it back behind my ear without looking up. "Good idea. Then it wouldn't have a perfect seal, so it would start sucking in air like a dying vacuum cleaner, and—"

Suddenly Nina straightened up again with a jolt. "Oh my god! Here comes Beth Hartley!"

Beth Hartley was one of the stars of Pawntucket High – slim, beautiful, good grades, etc. She was a year older than us, almost eighteen, and a senior. Even apart from that, we didn't exactly move in the same circles. She was on every club and committee there was, and basically lived at school. In fact, I think they'd shut the place down if she ever couldn't come in for some reason. The teachers would all go on strike.

I poured some solvent onto a clean rag and starting swabbing it around the empty space where the carburettor had been. "What was it today, do you think?" I said. "Cheerleading? Prom committee? Saving the world?"

"Willow, this isn't *funny*," moaned Nina. "She's heading right towards us!"

"So? I'm sure she's seen a carburettor before." Nina stared at me. There was a beat, and then I realized what I'd said and started laughing. "Oh. Maybe not, huh?"

She huffed out a breath, looking like she couldn't decide whether to throttle me or join in laughing. "Look, I know *you* don't care, but most people already think you're Queen Weird, you know – this is *not* going to help matters, believe me—" She fell abruptly silent as Beth walked up.

"Hi," said Beth, looking uncertainly from Nina to me. She had long, honey-coloured hair, and make-up that was always so subtle and perfect that you could barely tell she had it on. Which had always seemed sort of a waste of time to me – spending hours putting on make-up that looked invisible once you were done – but there you go.

"Hi," I said back, poking my head out from underneath the hood.

"Hi, Beth," said Nina faintly. "Good drama club meeting?"

"Yearbook," corrected Beth. "Yeah, great." She was staring at the open hood, and me under it. "You're, um…

fixing Nina's car," she said. It was halfway between a question and a statement.

I nodded. "Her carburettor."

"Carburettor. Right," echoed Beth, blinking her wide brown eyes.

There was a pause. I could see Beth mentally shaking her head to clear it, and then deciding that, actually, she didn't really want to pursue the carburettor thing. She cleared her throat. "Um, Willow...I just wondered whether you had the homework assignment for Atkinson's class? I wasn't there yesterday."

I felt my eyebrows fly up. I hadn't realized that Beth even knew we were in the same class. Or in the same school. Or on the same planet. On second thought, scratch that – we probably *weren't* on the same planet. And why was she asking me, anyway? A dozen of her perfect friends were in that class.

I shrugged. "Yeah, sure – it's in my red folder." I motioned towards my school bag, which was sitting beside the open toolbox on the ground. "Would you mind? My hands are all—" I held them up to show her, and she blanched.

"Great, thanks." She slipped the folder out of my bag, quickly opening it and scribbling down the assignment. As she put it back, she hesitated as she glanced at Nina. She started to say something and stopped. Her neck turned bright pink.

The motion of my hand with the rag slowed as I looked at her in surprise. Suddenly I knew exactly what was coming; I had seen it too many times before to mistake the signs. Nina's eyes widened as she realized the same thing. "Maybe I'll...go get a drink of water," she said, taking an ultra-casual step backwards. I could tell she was thinking the same thing I was: *Beth* Hartley? *Really? Miss Perfect?*

Once Nina was gone, Beth edged closer to me, lowering her voice. "Um, Willow..." She took a deep breath, running her manicured fingers through her hair. "I've, um...heard that you do...readings. Like, psychic ones," she added quickly. Her face was bonfire-red.

I nodded. "Yeah, that's right."

Beth seemed to catch her breath. Her expression was trying to be sceptical, but it was suddenly so hopeful and pleading that it was like having a puppy gaze at me. "Well – are you any good?" she blurted out.

I shrugged as I started to install the new carburettor, tightening it into the intake manifold. "I guess so. I mean, not everything I see comes true, but most things seem to. And to be honest, the stuff that doesn't is usually an alternate path."

She was watching me intently, taking in every word. "An alternate path?" she echoed. "What do you mean?"

I thought about it as I tightened the nuts a bit at a time, keeping the pressure on the carburettor even. "It's like...

you know, you have choices in your life. And sometimes I can see several choices unfolding, and what might happen with each one. But they're not all going to happen, because you'll only choose one of them."

Beth nodded slowly. "Yeah, that's exactly what I need help with," she said, almost to herself. "Choices." She glanced back at the school. "Well – would you read me sometime?" she asked in a rush. "Like, soon?"

I blinked at the thought of Beth in my house – the two really didn't seem to go together – but then I shrugged. "Sure, okay. How about tomorrow after school? No, wait a minute – how about Thursday?" I had forgotten for a second that the carer was leaving early the next day, and I'd promised Aunt Jo I'd get home on time to take care of Mom. I gave Beth my address.

"I'll be there," said Beth fervently. Some of her yearbook committee friends had started coming out of the school building behind her by then, and hugging her bag to her chest, she moved off to join them. "And, Willow – thanks," she called softly over her shoulder.

I stared after her, feeling bemused. I guess I should know better than to pigeonhole people – if being psychic has taught me anything, it's that you *really* never know what kind of thoughts people might be thinking, bubbling away like a witch's cauldron under the surfaces of their ordinary lives – but even so…Beth Hartley.

Strange, I thought as I tightened the final nut.

Nina reappeared, her expression practically bursting with *tell me everything!* "She wants a reading," I said, to ward off the inevitable.

"I *knew* it!" exclaimed Nina. "I could just tell, the way she was acting all furtive." She shook her head, looking dazed. "Wow, I can't believe that Beth Hartley even believes in that junk."

Nina is about the least imaginative, most prosaic person in the entire world, and is convinced that anything psychic is a con. Not that she thinks *I'm* a con, necessarily. Just that I'm conning myself. Being dramatic, making things up without realizing it, getting carried away – that sort of thing. She thinks I should be an actress, because I'm obviously so in tune with my inner child. It's sort of amazing that we're even friends, really. But I've known her since I was nine, which is when Mom and I first moved to Pawntucket to live with Aunt Jo, and I guess we've just got to be a habit with each other.

Nina was peering in under the hood at me, shaking her head. "Willow, you do know that you should stop all this psychic stuff, don't you? Half the school thinks you're a witch."

My cheeks grew warm. "Well, that's not *my* fault," I muttered. I was almost finished, which was a good thing, because Nina was really starting to irritate me.

"It *is* your fault," Nina insisted. "You don't have to keep doing readings, do you? No, you don't! Just say no the next time someone asks."

I didn't say anything for a moment. Distantly, I could hear the football team still practising on the field, their shoulder pads thudding against each other like the clash of the Titans. "I *do* have to keep doing them," I said finally. Finishing the carburettor, I wiped my hands clean and started putting my tools away.

"*Why?*" screeched Nina in exasperation.

I spun to face her. "Because people have problems, Nina! All kinds of problems, and I think maybe – I think maybe I help them."

"Oh, come on, Willow, you are *seriously* deluded if you think—" Nina broke off as I grabbed my jacket and slammed her hood shut.

"Here," I said, tossing her keys at her. "You've got to prime it before you drive it again – give the gas a few pumps first." Before she could answer, I had gathered up my things and stalked off.

"Fine, be that way," she called after me. "You know I'm right, though. See you tomorrow. Thanks for fixing my car, you lunatic."

I waved at her without turning around. Getting into my own car, a battered blue Toyota, I piled my stuff in the passenger seat and started the ignition. It purred like a kitten, of course. I might make awful grades, but I am *good* with engines.

I pushed a blues cassette into the deck as I pulled out of the parking lot – okay, so the twenty-first century hasn't quite reached my sound system yet – and headed down Highway 12 towards home. The conversation with Beth tugged at my mind, refusing to let go. What was so urgent about getting a reading done?

Choices. That's exactly what I need help with.

Unease flickered through me and I frowned, wondering why I suddenly felt so apprehensive. Being psychic isn't like everyone thinks – I'm not some all-knowing, all-seeing guru. No, I can't predict the lottery numbers, and ha, ha, yes, I get caught in the rain just the same as everyone else.

The truth is, I get flashes or feelings sometimes, but I don't tend to get anything too specific unless I have some sort of connection, like holding someone's hand. Plus I have to have the mental space to relax and clear my head. If I'm upset or excited then I don't usually get much – and anyway, it's not the kind of thing that you could go around doing all the time, at least not without going seriously insane. So in general I just live my life like the rest of the world, without really knowing how things are going to unfold.

But I do get some pretty strong intuitions at times… and I was having one now, about Beth. I bit my lip as I slowed down for a crossroad.

Whatever her choices were, I suddenly had a very bad feeling about them.

"Pancakes," said Alex, gazing down at the menu. "And scrambled eggs and bacon, with a side of hash browns. And toast." He was starving. It was always like this after a kill; he felt as if he hadn't eaten for a week.

"Coffee?" asked the waitress. She was plump and bored-looking.

He nodded. "Yeah, and orange juice."

The waitress moved off, and Alex put his menu back in the holder and stretched. After he'd left Spurs, he'd cruised around until he'd found an all-night gym downtown. He'd bought a pass and worked out for hours, pumping the weight machines like they were the enemy, doing reps until the sweat poured down his face and shoulders like rain. And slowly, he'd felt the adrenalin that was shrieking through him begin to fade, giving way to a welcome, trembling tiredness.

Finally he'd stopped, his head slumped against the crossbar of the abs machine. "Good workout?" asked an attendant. It was almost six in the morning by then, and the place was starting to fill up. All around Alex was the whir and clatter of the free-weight machines, and the sound of grunts, and feet pounding on treadmills.

He had lifted his head and stared at the guy, hardly knowing where he was for a second. Then he nodded, and managed a smile. "Yeah, great."

Mopping his face with his towel, he stood up. His muscles felt like water. He used to go running after an angel encounter, but it was never enough; it didn't exhaust him. This was good. He might actually manage to get some sleep sometime in the next day or two now.

"Man, I was watching you attack those machines," the man said cheerfully, squirting disinfectant on the seat of a stationary bike. He wiped it down. "You were like something possessed."

Alex had grinned suddenly. "No, that's everyone else," he said. "You know – the ones I *don't* get to in time." And leaving the bewildered assistant staring after him, he'd draped the towel around his neck and gone to take a shower.

Now he took a gulp of dishwater coffee and gazed out the plate-glass window at the Rocky Mountains. Around him, the pancake house was heaving with people – laid-back looking moms and dads wearing jeans and happy smiles, and little kids bouncing on their seats as they scribbled on their Mister Pancake colouring sheets.

He had been to Aspen several times, even before the Invasion. Angels seemed to like it here, who knew why. Maybe it was the fresh mountain air. Alex propped his chin on his hand as he stared out at the snow-covered peaks in the distance. In a strange way, Aspen reminded him of Albuquerque, though Albuquerque was all desert and slanting light; golden stone instead of soaring mountains. It was something about the air – the way you felt so clean and reborn, just by smelling it.

His first solo kill had been in Albuquerque.

Alex's coffee cup slowed on its way to his lips as he remembered. He put it down again without drinking.

He'd been twelve years old. Out on a hunt with Cully and Jake. Martin, his father, had already started getting a bit weird by then – he spent his time stalking around the camp muttering to himself, working his jaw as if he had marbles in his mouth, and when he wasn't shouting at everyone he was obsessively cleaning the guns at all hours of the day and night. Though there'd been a time when Alex could hardly imagine anything better than being allowed to go out on a hunt with his father, now he'd felt relieved when he hadn't come along. And then he'd felt guilty for his relief. His father was a great man, everyone knew that. At least, everyone who counted.

Even so, there had been a jubilant air as their jeep had roared out of camp that time, kicking up clouds of dust ten feet high. Cully, who was from Alabama, had let out a ringing rebel yell, and Jake had punched Alex in the arm, saying, "Hey, little bro, think you can take me? Think you can take me?" Suddenly Alex knew that they both felt the same way he did, and the guilt left him in a happy rush.

"Yeah, I can take you," he'd said, and lunged at Jake, getting him in a half nelson. Gratifyingly – his brother was two years older – it had taken Jake a few seconds to break free, and then he'd launched himself across the seat at Alex with a shout. The two of them fell into the back on top of the mountain of camping gear, scuffling and laughing.

Back then, before the CIA had taken over with their angel spotters and coldly efficient texts, a hunt might take weeks. As well as their camping supplies there were a couple of crates of tinned food in the jeep, and boxes of cartridges. Their guns lay tucked out of sight for now: dependable deer rifles that weren't very flashy, but did the job. Cully even had his crossbow with him. He claimed it gave a cleaner shot, but Alex thought he was just showing off. It was a pain, anyway; they always had to go and find his bolt after a kill.

"If either of you little jerks breaks that stove, I'll kill you," called back Cully in his Southern drawl. He spun the wheel and the jeep skidded around a curve in a shower of sand and pebbles, sending Alex and Jake banging against its side like rag dolls. Once they got into civilization, Alex knew that Cully would drive like a model citizen, but out here it was the end of the world, with only dirt and yucca plants and lizards for company. You could do whatever the hell you liked.

"Up yours," retorted Jake, glancing at Alex with a grin. Jake was taller and stockier than Alex, but he had the same dark hair, the same blue-grey eyes. You could tell they were brothers just by looking at them.

They both looked like Mom.

The thought brought a hard edge to the day. Alex remembered a woman who loved to sing, who used to kick off her shoes and dance along with the radio while she was cooking. When he was little, he used to tug on her jeans to get her attention, and sometimes she'd stop what she was doing and lean down to catch his hands. "Dance with me, lover-boy," she'd laugh, spinning him around.

Mom was the reason they were doing this. She was always the reason. And Alex knew she was also the reason that his father was – maybe – going insane.

The jeep bumped and rattled over the rocky soil. Driving with one hand, Cully lit a cigar, biting off the end and spitting it over the side. He was wearing a black sleeveless shirt, and his shoulders and arms were statue-hard, rippling with muscle. He shook his head as he took a deep puff and glanced at Alex and Jake in the rear-view mirror.

"The Angel Killers, hope of the free world," he muttered. "God help us all."

The drive to Albuquerque took almost four hours, so that Alex felt dull with boredom long before they got there. He perked up as they entered the city limits. Living out in the desert like a bunch of pack rats, sometimes he even forgot that there was a real world out there, but now it all beckoned to him in a sparkling rush – fast food, shopping malls, movies. A billboard with someone called Will Smith on it caught his eye: a tough-looking black guy carrying a gun.

"Hey, Cull, can we go see a movie?" he asked, hanging over the front seat.

"You and Jake can," said Cully. Glancing in the rear-view mirror, he smoothed his blond hair back with his palm and grinned. "I got me some *other* ideas, if you boys catch my drift."

Women. Alex and Jake grimaced at each other. There were several female AKs back at the camp, but Cully said he liked his girls sweet, not wearing combat gear and going out target practising. Women who could shoot as well as he could were a bit off-putting.

The plan was to stop off in the city for one night in comfort before they started roughing it on the long drive up to Vancouver, where Martin had heard rumours of angel activity. But as they pulled into a motel, Cully stiffened. "You know what," he murmured, getting out of the jeep. "I think there's something goin' *on* here."

That meant angels. Alex looked up sharply. The hot afternoon seemed to freeze around them, the whole world suspended.

"Where, Cull?" asked Jake. He seemed older suddenly, more serious.

"Not sure yet," said Cully, his eyes narrowed. "I don't think it's very far, though." He paused for a long moment, gazing around them at the shopping strip. Finally he shook himself. "Come on, let's get checked in and unload. Then I think we're going to have to take a little drive, gentlemen."

Cully got them a room, re-parking the jeep so that it was right outside their door. The three of them worked automatically, carrying their gear in and piling it onto the floor.

They left the rifles in the jeep. When everything else had been unloaded, Cully threw a tarp over them. "Right, come on," he said, climbing back in the driver's seat and starting up the engine. "You both know the drill. Alex, you sit beside me. Jake, in the back."

Alex saw Jake start to protest, and then think better of it. Cully might joke around a lot, but you didn't question his judgement unless you wanted a black eye.

Alex slid into the front passenger seat, his skin prickling with excitement. Though he'd been on perhaps a dozen hunts by now, the thrill hadn't lessened any. And maybe it was petty of him, but he knew that part of the thrill was realizing how good he was. Jake might be older and bigger than him, and just as good a shot, but he couldn't tune in as quickly as Alex, or as strongly. When it came to that side of things, Alex had taken to all the weird stuff their father had taught them just like coming home.

As Cully cruised slowly down the busy Albuquerque street, Alex closed his eyes and relaxed, moving his focus smoothly up through his chakra points. As his consciousness rose above his crown chakra, another world opened up before him. He could feel the energy fields of every living thing nearby – the woman in the car next to them; the guy standing on the kerb waiting to cross the street; his German shepherd, straining at its leash. Their energies all touched his own, and he felt them briefly and then moved on, probing in ever-widening circles.

Distantly, he heard Jake say, "Cully, are you *sure* you felt something?"

"Shut up—" Cully started to say, and then broke off as Alex's eyes flew open and he sat straight up.

"That way!" he said urgently, pointing. "There's a – a park or something, maybe two streets south – I could feel lots of trees. It's in there. It's getting ready to feed." He shivered despite himself. Angel energy felt swamp-cold, clammy. It touched your soul and seemed to leave foul fingerprints on it.

"A park? Excellent," said Cully, turning.

In the rear-view mirror Alex could see Jake looking at him, impressed and a bit jealous. "Good one, bro," he said.

Sure enough, they came to a park a few seconds later. Cully parked the jeep under a line of trees. Glancing around them, he leaned across and opened the glovebox, taking out a pistol with a silencer on its muzzle. He checked the pistol's magazine, and then snapped it shut again and handed it to Alex.

"Go get 'em, tiger," he said.

Alex almost dropped the pistol in shock. "Do *what*?"

"He's only twelve!" burst out Jake at the same time.

"So? You were thirteen when you soloed, and he's better at the chakras than you," said Cully, twisting around to look at him. Jake sank back in his seat again, glowering.

Alex stared down at the gun. He had shot angels before, of course, but never on his own, without back-up. There were more things that could go wrong than he could count. The main one was that the angel might spot him and attack before he managed to shoot it. He'd been on a hunt where that had occurred once, to an Angel Killer named Spencer. Alex swallowed, remembering Spence's vacant stare, his mind completely and forever blistered by the angel's assault.

Or sometimes they just killed you, of course.

Cully was watching him. "Listen to me," he said roughly. "You'll never be of maximum use to us if you can't go out on your own. You can do it; I wouldn't have just handed you a loaded pistol otherwise."

From Cully, this was high praise. Alex licked dry lips. "Okay," he said. Trying to hide his shaking hands, he flicked the pistol's safety on. He wasn't wearing his holster, so he stuck the gun in the back of his jeans and pulled his T-shirt over it.

"Alex…be careful," said Jake, looking worried now.

"He'll be fine," said Cully. He slapped Alex on the shoulder. "And if you're not back in fifteen, we'll call the loony squad to come get ya."

AK humour; you just had to love it. Alex's lips felt stretched over his teeth as he smiled. Then he got out of the jeep and walked into the park.

It only took him a few minutes to find the angel. He didn't even have to open his senses to do it – the moment he saw the young woman sitting under a tree, gazing dreamily up at the clouds, he knew. She was wearing a light summer dress, and her brown hair was loose on her shoulders. Evidently she'd been reading a book; it lay forgotten by her side as she smiled upwards, lost in her own pleasant thoughts.

That was what everyone else would see. Speeding through his chakras, Alex's perception shifted abruptly as a glorious being came into view, over seven feet tall and blinding white. Though its great wings almost blocked out the sun, the angel was far brighter than the sun could ever hope to be. It glowed with radiance, casting pure, dazzling light across the woman's beatific features.

Alex's stomach lurched. He hadn't often seen one actually feeding before. The creature had both hands buried deep in the woman's energy field, which was growing dimmer by the second, twisting feebly as if in protest. The angel had its head thrown back in gluttonous ecstasy as the woman's energy seeped away into its own, like water leaving a draining tub.

And because of angel burn, she'd actually remember the angel as *good and kind.* Just like his mother had, before she'd been killed. Shoving his feelings away, Alex glanced around him. They were in a section of the park away from any paths; the nearest people were a couple of teenage boys about a hundred yards away, throwing a Frisbee around. Shielding himself from view behind a tree, Alex reached behind him and pulled out the gun. Steadying the weapon with both hands, he took aim.

Now that it came down to it, he felt very calm, with a quick excitement throbbing away somewhere underneath. His first solo kill. Cully was right; he could do it. What had he been worried about? He had lived his whole life, just waiting for this moment.

The angel looked up and saw him.

Fear pounded through Alex as he and the angel locked eyes. The creature knew instantly what he was, and it screamed in pure fury, ripping its hands away from the woman's energy field. Useless and forgotten, she slumped to the ground, the peaceful smile still on her face.

Screeching, the angel sped towards him. Alex had a blurred impression of a great rushing and flapping of wings, and of wind tearing at his hair, as if the whole world was whipping past. The pistol began to shake in his hands. *Shoot!* he screamed at himself. But its eyes were so beautiful, even in its rage. He could only stare into them, and know that he was about to die.

No! With the greatest effort of his life, Alex tore his attention away from the angel's eyes and focused on its halo instead. *That's the angel's heart,* his father always said. *Go for the centre.* Alex's hands were so unsteady he could hardly take aim. The angel was shrieking in triumph, its terrible, awesome voice slicing through him. Its halo was the size of a saucer...now a dinner plate...now a ...

Alex shot. The world exploded into shards of light as the force from the fallout blew him backwards, off his feet. He landed in the grass a dozen feet away and for a moment just lay there stunned, the wind knocked out of him.

"Man, if *that* wasn't just about the messiest kill I ever did see," observed a drawling voice. "I was just about to shoot the damn thing myself." Suddenly there was a strong arm around his shoulders, helping him to his feet. Alex staggered, and stared at Cully in confusion. He tried to speak, but the power seemed to have left him for the moment. His head was throbbing as if an anvil had been dropped onto it.

"You're going to feel terrible for a good week, probably," said Cully conversationally, putting away his own gun. "Don't believe in doing things speedily, do you? I thought you were waiting for the son of a gun to fly *into* you."

Alex laughed shakily. Now that it was over, he felt almost giddy with relief – and then his emotions swung to the other extreme, so that he had to clench his fists to keep from bursting into hysterical tears. It had almost got him. It had really almost got him.

Cully squeezed his shoulder. "You did good," he said seriously, dropping the banter. "It's tough when they see you. Stay here, I'm just gonna go check on our lady friend."

He jogged towards the woman, stopping only to pick up Alex's pistol and shove it in the back of his own jeans first. Alex leaned weakly against a tree as their voices floated towards him.

"You okay, ma'am? You look sort of peaked."

"Oh…oh, I'm fine. You won't believe me, but I've just seen the most – the most beautiful, amazing thing…"

Alex closed his eyes. The angel was gone now; he had

killed it – but the woman's words chilled him anyway. Yes, the most beautiful, amazing thing. She'd have a cherished memory now for the rest of her life, and at what cost? Insanity, perhaps? That happened a lot – schizophrenia taking over her life, until she was screaming back at the voices in her head. Or how about cancer? That was always a good one: the angel's feeding touch causing the very cells inside of her to wither up and die. Or MS, so that she'd eventually lose the use of her limbs and end up in a wheelchair, until finally she died of it. Or Parkinson's, or AIDS, or any other ailment you could think of – there was no telling with angel burn; the only certainty was that she'd been inexorably poisoned, and no matter what form the damage would take, the quality of her life would go firmly downhill from now on. And ironically, she would never see the connection between this and the angel. In fact, she'd probably think that the angel had been sent to *help* her, in her time of need.

Cully reappeared. "She's on her way home, happy as a clam – for now, anyway. Come on," he went on, dropping his hand on Alex's arm. "Let's go find your brother, so you can brag you got your first solo kill. Might even brag on you a little myself."

"Why?" Alex asked raggedly. The words felt like sand in his throat. "I did everything wrong! I waited too long to shoot – I looked into its eyes – I—"

His headache threatened to blind him as Cully lightly cuffed the back of his head. "None of that, boy," he said. He draped an arm around Alex's neck as they started walking back to the jeep. "Didn't I just tell you, it's hard when they look at you? You did good. You did good."

Now, five years later in Aspen, Alex stared out the window at the Rocky Mountains, seeing the dry, rugged hills of New Mexico instead. As it turned out, only a handful of angels had ever seen him again; it had just been sheer bad luck that it had happened his first time on his own. But it hadn't mattered. He'd got over his nerves and now he had brought down more angels than he could count – especially since he had long ago stopped bothering to keep track. There hadn't seemed much point any more once Jake was gone, taking with him the friendly competition between the two brothers.

The thought winced through Alex before he could stop it. No. Don't go there.

"Here you are," said the waitress, appearing with his breakfast. The plates clinked against the table as she set them down in front of him. She produced fork, knife and spoon from her apron, and clattered those down as well. "Would you like some more coffee?"

"Thanks," said Alex. She refilled his cup and bustled off, and he eyed the food tiredly, wondering why he had wanted so much. But he needed to eat for the fuel, if nothing else. He might get another text any minute, sending him off to god knew where. Or it could be as long as a week from now. A week full of long, pointless hours that he'd somehow have to fill – which usually meant boxy motel rooms and crap TV shows.

Ignoring the happy families sitting all around him, Alex lifted his fork and began to eat.

CHAPTER *Two*

"HI – COME ON IN," I said to Beth.

It was Thursday afternoon after school, and she was standing on our front porch looking around her with wide eyes. My Aunt Jo lives in an old Victorian house on the south side of Pawntucket, and she very, very kindly (as she keeps reminding us) allows Mom and me to live there with her – which is good, since Mom doesn't have a job and couldn't work anyway. It's a great old house, or at least it used to be, once upon a time. Now it's sort of in need of a paint job. Not to mention all the little deer statues and windmills and tiny flying kites that Aunt Jo has in the front yard.

Beth swallowed, tearing her gaze away from a gnome with a red hat. "Um, it's very…colourful," she said weakly.

I stood back to let her in. The inside of the house looks more normal, apart from the piles of clutter everywhere. Aunt Jo is a hoarder. She saves everything that she ever comes into contact with, only she can never find whatever it is she wants because it's always buried under a foot of mess, so she ends up buying two or three or six of them.

Beth came in hesitantly, clutching her handbag. She looked perfect as usual, in a pair of black trousers and a turquoise top. Her dark honey hair was pulled back in a ponytail, making her brown eyes even larger. I glanced down at her shoes. Prada. Next to them, my purple Converse sneakers looked even more *colourful* than the front yard.

As I shut the door I could hear the TV going in the living room, where Mom and her carer were. Aunt Jo wasn't home from work yet.

"Um – I usually give readings in the dining room," I said, starting down the hallway. "It's back here." Beth trailed after me, gazing silently at the kitten figurines and the bookcases stuffed full of Harlequin romances and floppy sad clowns, and the dozens of dusty decorative plates on the wall. Aunt Jo's a collector as well as a hoarder. She practically keeps the Franklin Mint in business single-handedly. Seeing it all through Beth's eyes, I suddenly realized that maybe the inside of the house wasn't that normal after all.

"Here," I said, motioning for her to go into the dining room. It had two sets of French doors that you could close, separating it from the rest of the house. I slid them shut while Beth gingerly took a seat at the dining table, looking as if she expected the chair to collapse under her.

She cleared her throat, running her hands across the tablecloth. "So, um…how does it work? Do you use Tarot cards or something?"

"No. I just hold your hand." I sat down next to her and rubbed my hands over my jeans. I couldn't believe how nervous I was. It wasn't like I'd never done this before; I'd been giving readings since I was eleven. For the last year or so I'd even been charging money for a lot of them, just to shut Aunt Jo up about how draining it was on the finances to have to support three people all by herself.

Beth took a deep breath and straightened her shoulders. "Okay, well – here," she said, and held out her hand. It was small and neat, with a tiny gold and pearl ring on one finger.

I gazed down at her hand without moving. Somehow, I couldn't quite bring myself to touch it. What was wrong with me? I'd given readings for all sorts of people over the years, and I'd seen plenty of weird and disturbing and even frankly illegal things. Beth Hartley was hardly likely to rank up there with those. But even as I thought it, I knew that wasn't the reason for my hesitation. I was still having that strange…premonition, or intuition, or whatever you wanted to call it.

If I read Beth, it would change everything.

Beth looked anxious. "Is something wrong?" she asked. Her fingers curled under her hand. "Please, Willow, I – I really need help."

I shook myself. "Sorry," I muttered. "I'm just…being stupid."

Closing my eyes, I took her hand. It felt warm, oddly vulnerable. Leaning back in my chair, I let go of everything I thought I knew about Beth, allowing my mind to simply drift. Almost immediately, images started to come, along with things that I just *knew* somehow – facts popping into my head as if whispered by unseen helpers.

"You were walking in the woods last week," I said slowly. "There's a patch of them behind your house. You've always felt safe there – you know these woods really well, and it's a good place to get away from it all, to de-stress."

I heard Beth's faint gasp, her hand tightening in mine. And in my mind's eye, I could see the Beth of last week, idly kicking at autumn leaves as she walked down a worn dirt path. This Beth was wearing sneakers and faded jeans. Her forehead was creased; she was thinking about an

English exam. She thought she had done all right, but what if she hadn't? What if it had affected her perfect 4.0?

Suddenly I knew that Beth was only perfect because she was too frightened not to be. The real Beth wasn't confident at all. She was constantly driving herself, constantly afraid that she wasn't going to get it right. I could actually *feel* her tension, knotting coldly in her stomach.

"You're often worried about things," I said carefully. Half of being a good psychic, I've learned, is not to freak people out by letting them know exactly how much you can see about them. "You can get very stressed."

"That's true," whispered Beth. She sounded close to tears. "But Willow, what I really need to know about is—"

"Don't tell me," I interrupted. "Let me find out for myself." She fell silent. I did too, waiting to see what the images would show me next.

It was the last thing in the universe I ever would have expected.

The Beth in my mind's eye stopped beside a stream; it was a favourite spot. Sinking onto her haunches, she idly stirred the cool, clear water with one manicured finger. *It doesn't matter about my GPA*, she tried to tell herself. *In fact, I've heard that some colleges like it if you don't do perfectly, because it shows that you're better rounded, or something—*

Her thoughts broke off as the stream caught fire. Only it wasn't fire at all, it was light: a bright, hot light that blazed suddenly across the water, dancing on the ripples. Beth looked up with a gasp…and saw an angel.

I could feel my own shock trying to burst through, and I pushed it down, just letting the images come as they would. The angel stood on the opposite bank, a beautiful winged being of light. *Radiant.* That was the word that Beth kept thinking.

It was gazing at her with an expression of great tenderness. "Don't be afraid," it said, and it came towards her, not even stirring the water with its robes.

I opened my eyes in a daze. "You…saw an angel," I said.

"*Yes!*" cried Beth, leaning forward. Her fingers clutched mine. "Oh, Willow, I really did, it was real, I know it! It came right up to me, and it put its hands on my head, and I felt such – such *peace.* I suddenly realized that none of it matters, not my grades, or school, or *anything* that I thought was so important before!"

This all came out in a wild burst. Beth's eyes were intense, fervent. I started to say something else, and then stopped.

The truth was, I didn't know what to say. Were angels real, then? I had never thought so, but then I'd never been very much into religion – probably because so many of the churches around here were the type that held revivals in giant tents and regarded psychics as the spawn of Satan. I bit my lip in thought. Had Beth only *thought* she'd seen an angel? Maybe she'd cracked under all the strain she'd been putting herself under, or even just imagined it, to make herself feel better.

But neither of those felt right, somehow. Even if I was only experiencing all of this second-hand, through Beth… the angel in her memory had felt real.

I swallowed. "Okay, well…let me see what else I can get." I closed my eyes again. Beth's fingers felt tense now, almost quivering with anticipation.

The angel had cradled her head for a long time. As Beth had said, a feeling of immense peace had come over her. Yet there had been something else there, as well. I frowned, trying to put my finger on it. A…a *draining*. The angel's touch had felt wonderful, but it had also left Beth so weak that when it finally departed she could barely make it home again.

Had that been physical, or just emotional? I couldn't really tell; she was trying not to remember that part. She had gone back to the stream every day since, hoping that the angel would return. And frequently, it had. The images became confused in places; sometimes I was seeing an angel, and sometimes a man with the angel's face. Through it all I could sense Beth's joy, her wonder…a swirling of energies as the angel touched her. Unease shivered through me. What *was* this thing, anyway?

"You've seen the angel several times now," I said, trying to keep my voice neutral. "I'm also seeing a man with the angel's face."

"Yes, that's him," said Beth. Her voice was softly ardent, like praying. "Angels can do that – they walk among us, to help us. Oh, Willow, I couldn't believe it when he really came back again. He's promised that he'll always be there for me. I…I'm happier than I've ever been in my life."

And she was, but I could sense that she was also the most miserable. But before I could say anything else, Beth leaned forward, gripping my hand as the words burst out of her: "I just feel like school, and clubs and all that – they don't have any meaning any more, not when all that is out there." She waved her free hand in the air. "Angels are *real*, and that means…well, why am I bothering with anything else?"

I stared at her. "Um…what are you saying?"

There was a pause as Beth gazed down at the dining table, tracing a pattern on the lace tablecloth. Finally she took a deep breath and looked me square in the eyes. "I'm thinking of dropping out of school and joining the Church of Angels."

I opened my mouth and then slowly closed it again, lost for words. The Church of Angels was this massive church that had just sort of sprung up out of nowhere in the last couple of years. More like a cult, really. I was always seeing their commercials on TV: lots of blissed-out looking people going on about how the angels were pure love, and had helped them with practically every problem known to mankind.

"Yes, and helped them empty their bank accounts to boot," Aunt Jo always sniffed.

Beth was still talking. "Now that I know that angels exist, I want to be with people who know what I know, who've seen angels too, who *understand*. And my angel's told me that if I join, then – then we can really be together. But when I think of my parents…" She trailed off, her eyes bright with tears. She fumbled in her handbag for a tissue. "I tried to talk to them about it, you know. Joining the Church, I mean. It was awful. They said I'd be throwing my life away, and that if I was that ungrateful for all the advantages I've had, then they wouldn't lift a finger to stop me." Choking back a sob, she dabbed at her eyes, shaking her head. "I don't know. When I'm away from the angel, it all feels sort of…unreal. But at the same time, it's the most real thing in my life. How can I ignore it?"

She looked up at me, her gaze pleading. "Willow, can you tell me what to do?"

Lost for words is an understatement. I'd never felt so taken aback in my life. "Let me see what I can find out," I said finally.

Closing my eyes, I pushed away my turbulent thoughts and went deeply within myself, searching for Beth's possible futures. They grew before me like a tree, branching and dividing with each choice she might make in her life. Mentally, I blinked. With most people, this map of what might come looked golden and glowing, but Beth's was dull. Stunted. Even worse, her tree had only two main branches to it: a pair of twisted, spindly boughs that grew up from the trunk in a wobbly "V" shape.

A sickened shiver ran over my scalp. How could this be? Beth's future held only *two* likely possibilities…and neither of them looked great. I felt my heart clench as I explored the first branch. Oh my god; poor Beth. Praying that the second one would be more hopeful, I turned to it – and felt a strange chill settle over me. Images flashed past, but they were jumbled; any details just slithered away into a cloud of greyness as I tried to focus on them. Even so, I caught my breath at the sheer, bone-wrenching coldness of this future. Whatever the grey cloud meant, it felt utterly final, like a gravestone with mist curling over it.

My eyes flew open. "Beth, you've got to listen to me; the angel isn't good for you," I said urgently, my words tumbling over each other. "It's hurting you. The best thing you could do is to never go back to that stream again. It might still find you, but there's a chance it'll let you go, and then you could—"

Beth gasped, yanking her hand away from mine. "No!" she cried. "You've got it all wrong!"

"Listen to me! In one path, I see you taking my advice. You try to forget about the angel, and choose school and college. You – well, it's not a bad life," I faltered. "You major in politics, and—" *and suffer on and off from depression for the rest of your life, always wondering whether you made the right choice.* I couldn't say the words. "And make a real difference," I finished weakly.

Beth's face was stone-cold. She stuffed the tissue back into her handbag, not looking at me. "What about the other path?" she asked finally. "Do I join the Church of Angels?"

"Yes, but…it's not good for you. You seem to get sort of sick, and—"

"Sick?" She glanced up.

"Like, tired all the time. Exhausted. You—"

"Does it make me happy, though? Being there?" She leaned forward, her expression very still, very intent.

"I think so," I admitted reluctantly. "It was all sort of mixed up, but – yeah, you seem to encounter your angel again, and then later there are other angels too. You're accepted by the people in the Church. For the first time, you feel like your life has meaning. But—"

Beth's eyes were shining. "Willow, that's wonderful!" she breathed. "That's exactly what I needed to know! It *wouldn't* be a mistake, then—"

"It would!" I snapped. My voice was like a harsh whip, and Beth's eyebrows flew up in surprise. "Trust me, it's *not* a good path. Everything just…felt cold." My heart beat faster as I remembered the slithery grey clouds. Words suddenly seemed so totally, stupidly inadequate.

Beth sat motionless, staring at me. I could hear the TV going faintly in the other room, and the low murmur of the carer's voice, saying something to Mom. Finally Beth cleared her throat. "Well – what do you mean, cold? You mean, like…death?"

I scraped my hair back in frustration. "I don't know! I've seen death before, and it wasn't like that. I don't know *what* it was, just that it wasn't good."

Beth seemed deep in thought, her eyes troubled. Finally she shook her head. "I – I don't know what to think. What you're saying…it goes completely against my own gut feelings. I *know* that the angel is good for me. I can feel it, in here!" She thumped her hand on her chest. "I don't know what you saw, but—"

"There's a part of you that's *not* sure though, or else you wouldn't be here," I broke in desperately.

She looked up, startled.

"What about the tiredness, Beth? It all started with the angel, didn't it? You're still feeling it even now! Your muscles ache, and you feel draggy and worn out and—"

Beth flushed. Without looking at me, she pushed her

chair back and stood up, swinging her handbag over her shoulder. "Thanks for the reading, Willow," she said flatly. "What do I owe you?"

I leaped up. "Wait! Just ask yourself, *please* – if something is really good for you, then it wouldn't make you feel like that, would it?" I gripped the back of the chair with both hands, my voice pleading.

"I don't know what you're talking about," said Beth, keeping her eyes down. "I feel fine. Here, is this enough?" Pulling a leather purse out of her handbag, she thrust a twenty towards me. When I didn't take it, she put it on the dining table, tucking it under the sugar bowl. "Right, I'd better be going now—"

"No!" I clutched her arm. "Beth, please, please listen to me – that thing is killing you!"

Her eyes flashed, and she jerked free. I fell silent, my spirits sinking. I'd gone too far, and now I'd pushed her away from me. Damn it! *Damn* it.

"Thanks for the reading," she said again, her voice cool. "It was really interesting. Don't bother seeing me out; I'm okay." And then she was gone, sliding open the French doors and disappearing down the hallway. A moment later I heard the front door shut, a bit harder than necessary.

I leaned against the dining table as defeat washed over me in a grey sea. Could I have done it any differently? If I had used another combination of words, a better one, then could I have stopped her, somehow? Because I could tell that she had made her decision now; it had been written all over her. She was heading straight for her angel.

What *was* that thing, anyway? I thought back over the reading, trying to get a handle on it. But as far as I could tell, it was exactly what it had felt like: some sort of powerful being, which had somehow set Beth on a path to disaster.

But that couldn't be true...could it? What had I actually seen?

Sinking back into the chair, I gazed blindly at the velvet painting of a sad clown that hung over the sideboard. He was holding a drooping daffodil, and had a big, glistening tear on one painted cheek. Aunt Jo had bought it at a garage sale a few years ago. "Can you believe this for a bargain?" she'd said as she hung it proudly on the wall. "It was only twenty dollars!"

Twenty dollars. My eyes went to the bill under the sugar bowl. I pulled it out and gazed at it, and then gently slipped it back under the bowl and put my head in my hands.

"Look, Miranda, isn't that pretty?" demanded Aunt Jo, pointing to the TV.

It was later that same night, after dinner – which I had

cooked, because I don't like plastic food, and as far as Aunt Jo's concerned, if it doesn't say Hamburger Helper or Chef Boyardee on the label then it's not one of the basic food groups. So I had made a big pot of spaghetti for the three of us, because it's something I can do without really thinking about it. Besides, there's something very soothing about chopping vegetables and stirring a bubbling sauce, and I really needed to be soothed just then. I couldn't stop thinking about Beth.

Aunt Jo had gone on and on during dinner, talking about this woman at her office who she doesn't like. Big surprise; she doesn't like anyone, very much. I kept my head down while we ate, twirling spaghetti around my fork and saying "Mmm," at intervals. Mom had just ignored her, of course. She'd sat stirring the food around dreamily on her plate, and occasionally taking an absent-minded bite. Sometimes I envied her. She didn't even have to *pretend* to listen to Aunt Jo.

Now we were all in the living room, and Aunt Jo was trying determinedly to get Mom to "engage with her", as the therapist puts it. That means actually getting her to pay attention to you for a moment, as if she's still part of the real world instead of off on her own personal planet. Sometimes I'm not really sure why any of us bother. To be honest, I think Mom's probably happier where she is.

"Miranda!" said Aunt Jo again, leaning across and tapping Mom sharply on the arm. "Are you listening to me? Look at the TV. Isn't that tropical beach pretty?"

She spoke a bit more loudly and slowly than usual, as if she were talking to a three year old. Mom didn't respond. She was sitting in her favourite easy chair, gazing off into the distance. The two of us look a lot alike, I guess. She has the same wavy blonde hair that I do, except that hers is cut into a bob so that it's easy to take care of. And she's short like me, though she's not slim any more. Too many years of sitting lost in her own thoughts have left her pale and doughy; soft around the edges.

She's still beautiful, though. She always is. I glanced over at Mom's wide green eyes, so like my own. *Peas in a pod,* she used to say.

Because she wasn't always like this; she used to talk – to me, at least. When I was little we'd play games together, and she'd laugh. Yet even back then, she was so strange and shy around other people that by the time I was five or six I felt protective of her, knowing that she couldn't cope with the world the way I could. And then there was the cloud that would drift over her at times, carrying her far away from me. She'd just sit there, the way she was sitting now, and no amount of crying or yelling would bring her back until she was ready to come. I had to learn to cook my own meals, brush my own hair – and somehow I knew that I could never, ever tell anyone, or else they might take her away from me altogether.

But then as the years passed, what I'd feared so much had happened anyway. My mother had just sort of... slipped away, retreating further and further into her dreams until finally she hardly ever came back from her other world at all.

"Miranda!" pressed Aunt Jo, joggling her arm. "Wouldn't you like to be on that beach?"

Mom sighed, still looking at something none of us could see. "It's so pretty," she murmured. "So many colours...rainbows..."

"No, there aren't any rainbows," said Aunt Jo firmly. "Look, Miranda. Look! It's the *beach*."

Mom didn't answer. Her lips curved upwards in a slight smile.

"*Miranda*—"

"I don't think she wants to engage with you right now, Aunt Jo," I said tiredly. I try a lot with Mom when Aunt Jo isn't around, but I do it my own way, just *talking* to her – not treating her like she's mentally deficient.

"Well, we can't just let her sit there," said Aunt Jo huffily, sinking back onto the sofa. We fell into silence, watching the cheesy TV programme. On the screen, the perky female detective was ordering a Mai Tai in a tropical bar. I hugged a cushion to my chest, gazing at the images without really taking them in. I wanted so much to believe that Beth had only imagined the angel; that she'd just snapped from stress or something. But I knew she hadn't. Whatever that thing was, it was real, and it might have already ruined her entire life. I had to do something, but I didn't even know where to begin.

The doorbell rang. "I'll get it," I said, standing up. "It's probably Nina, seeing if I want to go out or something." Nina was always forgetting her phone, or running out of credit. I sort of hoped it wasn't her, though. I didn't really feel up to dealing with Nina's own special brand of cynicism right then.

Glancing at Mom to see if she'd notice, Aunt Jo switched over to The Shopping Channel – her spiritual home, needless to say. Settling back against the cushions, she nodded without taking her eyes from the screen. "If you go out, get some milk," she said.

But it wasn't Nina; I could tell that immediately from the height of the silhouette that stood on the other side of the front door's glass panes. Whoever he was, he was tall – over six feet, with broad shoulders.

I opened the door a crack. "Yes?"

The man on our front porch had sandy brown hair and a strong, attractive face. He was in his mid twenties, or maybe a bit older – it was sort of hard to tell. "Hi," he said, leaning to one side to peer in at me. "You must be Willow Fields, right? I've heard that you give psychic readings."

My pulse skittered and went cold as I realized: it was the same man I'd seen in my reading for Beth. Oh my god, it was her angel, he was *here*. I wanted to slam the door, but I felt frozen by his eyes – they were so intense, like falling into a well and never finding your way out again.

"I…um, only sometimes," I stammered.

"I see. Well, would you be able to give *me* a reading?"

For a wild moment I wondered if I was going crazy, and if he was actually a customer – one of the word-of-mouth clients who often turned up on our doorstep. A wave of nausea lurched through me at the thought of touching him. My voice came out high, panicked.

"No, I – I don't think so, I'm really busy right now." Wrenching myself away from his endless eyes, I started to shut the door – but before I knew what was happening he'd stepped quickly forward, wedging it open with his foot. At the same moment, his hand shot out and grabbed my own.

The energy from it slapped through me, like falling into water at a hundred miles an hour. I felt my eyes bulge; I couldn't catch my breath. Images were hurtling past almost faster than I could take in. White light, spiralling in a flower. People staring in awe, face after face flashing past. A strange world with gleaming towers and robed beings.

Wings, opening and closing. Someone screaming. *Hunger.*

The hunger roared through me, sapping every other emotion. I needed to feed. *Needed* to. I needed—

The man dropped my hand and I sagged limply against the doorjamb, all strength gone from me. I couldn't speak; I was panting as if I'd just run a mile. "What – what are you?" I whispered finally.

He stared at me without speaking, all pretence of friendliness gone. I could feel menace coming off him in great waves, but there was fear there, too, curling about it like a snake. Not taking his eyes off me, he wiped his hand off on his shirt. Abruptly, he turned and left, jogging down the front steps. Getting into a sleek silver car, he slammed the door shut and drove away into the night.

As the sound of his car faded, I could hear the creaking of crickets, and the faint drone of traffic from the highway. I stood staring down the street, my thoughts in chaos, and then belated fear rocked through me. Banging the door shut, I locked it with shaking hands and rushed back into the living room.

Mom was still sitting in the armchair, still looking absently into space. I stood staring at her for a moment, hugging myself as I tried not to shake – and wishing so much that she'd look up and say, *Willow, is everything all right? Tell me all about it, sweetie. How can I help?*

"Who was that?" asked Aunt Jo, glancing up from the TV.

"No one," I said faintly. Knowing that it wouldn't do any good, I dropped to my knees in front of my mother, clutching her hands in mine. "Mom? Are you there?" I said in a low voice.

Aunt Jo was gaping at me like I'd lost my mind. "What are you doing?"

"Nothing. Just…talking to Mom."

She sniffed. "Well, good luck. I don't think she's feeling very talkative tonight."

I didn't reply as she went into the kitchen. I just kept kneeling in front of my beautiful, broken mother, rubbing her hands between my own. "Mom? Mom, can you hear me? *Please?*"

Briefly, her eyes flickered. "Willow?" she murmured.

"It's me, Mom. I'm here."

Leaning back against the chair, she sighed and closed her eyes. A lock of hair fell across her face and I smoothed it away, stroking her brow. Soon the soft smile returned to Mom's lips, and I knew with a sinking heart that she had left again. She was back in her own world, looking at beautiful, mesmerizing things.

Frustrated, I gazed at her, longing to be able to really communicate. But it would never happen; I would always be the one trying to reach her, and never quite succeeding.

You'd think I'd be used to it, after so many years. And I was, pretty much – only there were still times like now, when I felt a sudden rush of sorrow and disappointment so strong that it almost knocked me off my feet. Even trying to read her didn't help, because her mind was so... fragmented. Full of rainbows and clouds, and snippets of memory. In fact, I found it such a depressing experience that I'd only tried it once.

God, I hated my father, whoever he'd been. I knew from Aunt Jo that before he appeared on the scene, Mom had been normal. *I don't know what that man did to her, but she was never the same after,* she'd told me once. *The doctors can say catatonic schizophrenia all they want, but I know the truth. He broke Miranda's spirit...he broke her mind.* The one time I'd tried to read Mom, I'd caught a glimpse of him in her thoughts, and he'd looked so creepy that the thought of being related to him made me shudder. At least he'd decided to take off and never be involved with either of us. It was the only good thing he'd ever done, so far as I was concerned.

Aunt Jo came back in, carrying a plate of cookies. "Willow, you must have eaten half the pack last night," she said crossly. "You know I like having a bedtime snack in the evenings; it's not very nice to find them all gone."

I let out a breath, still gazing at Mom. "Sorry," I murmured, getting to my feet. As Aunt Jo turned the volume up, I kissed Mom's cheek and went upstairs to my bedroom, holding my elbows tightly as I picked my way around the piles of clutter that seemed to breed on the stairs and landing.

Closing the door behind me, I just stood there for a moment, staring unseeingly at my room – my bed with the swathes of lavender chiffon draped across the bedposts; the purple and silver walls that I'd painted myself. Beth's angel was real. She must have gone straight to it after she left me; she must have told it everything – and then it had come here, looking for me. My thoughts spun in circles. Who could I tell this to? Who could I go to for help? Nina would just laugh at me. Aunt Jo? Ha.

Right, calm. Think this through. Taking a deep breath, I sat on the bed and forced myself to go over the mixed-up images that I'd seen in Beth's second future, trying to remember every last detail. In one of the snippets that had flashed past, this *thing* had been at the Church of Angels, and then later there'd been others like it.

Were they really angels?

A prickle danced across my scalp. Getting up again, I went over to my desk and switched on my computer. It's an old one that I bought with some of my reading-money, and it takes ages to warm up. When it had finally finished humming and whirring to itself, I went onto the internet. *Church of Angels* brought up millions of hits. I clicked onto the first one and a state-of-the-art website loaded slowly onto my screen. There was the familiar pearl-white church from the commercials, awash with sunshine. *Church of Angels. Hope for the millions...including you,* said the text underneath it. I grimaced. I know that plenty of people get a lot from religion and that's great for them, but anything promising "hope for the millions" gives me a pretty bad feeling – and now, after Beth's reading, it gave me an even worse one.

I clicked a button at the top that said, *Find out more.* A video link came on, and suddenly I was watching the Church of Angels commercial. A grey, rain-beaten field; grass moving slowly with the wind. "*Do you feel despairing?*" intoned a voiceover. The camera went into a long shot. A white church appeared in the field, and then as the camera moved further back you saw hundreds of people weaving up a hill towards it – and now the church looked huge, larger than the mightiest cathedral. The sun came out, dazzling on the white stone. The people stopped and gazed upwards, smiling, basking in the rays.

"*Do you feel that God has forsaken you? Well, have faith... for even if there is no God, there ARE angels.*"

"The angels saved my life," said a middle-aged woman to the camera, her brown eyes shining with rapture. "They are pure love, and what they've done for me, they can do for you, too." I felt a twinge of unease.

She looked and sounded exactly like Beth.

Steepling my hands in front of my face, I stared at the monitor as the commercial continued. It played on TV so often that I could have recited every word of it. Usually I just tuned it out, but now I listened carefully, and when it had finished I hit the *play* button and ran it again. It all seemed so slick. So polished.

Remembering that I'd heard there was a Church of Angels in Schenectady, about seventy miles away, I brought up its information…and found myself gaping at the screen in disbelief. This wasn't just a *church*, it was practically a whole town of its own, with apartments adjacent to the church building and even a small shopping centre. The website said that it had over five thousand residential members and growing. Five *thousand*. That was almost a third of the size of Pawntucket. If you joined the Church of Angels then you'd never have to set foot out in the real world again.

Maybe that was the appeal.

I rubbed my temples. *I'll talk to Beth again at school tomorrow,* I decided finally. Okay, her first future wasn't great, but it was a lot better than whatever that coldness in the Church of Angels had meant. If I just tried harder, maybe I could make her see it.

And then somehow, I'd figure out what to do about this being that had latched onto her.

CHAPTER *Three*

RAZIEL STOOD BESIDE THE SWEEPING white railing with his hands behind his back, gazing down at the expansive space far below him. The main cathedral of the Church of Angels, on the outskirts of Denver, Colorado, used to be the largest sports complex in the Rockies. Now, having been bought and transformed by thousands of human devotees, it was a soaring space of worship, with long, gleaming white pews and a graceful domed ceiling. People sitting at the back were mere fly-specks to those in front. Unobtrusive white speakers sat nestled on each of the pink and white marble pillars throughout the cathedral, so that the sermons in praise of the angels could be boomed out to everyone, and ornate stained-glass windows lined the curved walls, displaying angel images almost two storeys tall. Raziel's gaze lingered in satisfaction on one of these. It was in the pre-Raphaelite style; a radiant burst of white and gold showing a trio of angels, wings touching, reaching their arms out towards the viewer. *Come to us.* Yes indeed, thought Raziel with a small, satisfied smile. Please do. And they did, of course, by the millions.

He flexed his fingers. Like all angels, Raziel's human form was unusually attractive, though difficult to pin down as to age – in appearance he might have been anywhere from twenty-five to forty-five, and was tall and slender, with jet-black hair and arresting dark eyes. He knew that his features – in particular, his high forehead with its sharp widow's peak – were seen by humans as being *artistic and sensitive*, which amused him no small amount.

It was between services at the cathedral now; far below, tourists and devotees walked slowly through its vast space, drinking it in and taking pictures, or sitting hunched on a pew praying. Raziel scanned the small, moving human figures, wondering idly if he was in the mood to feed. It had only been a few hours, so it would be somewhat gluttonous of him, but with such a variety of human energies on display, it became difficult to resist. And the things were always so *grateful* to one afterwards. It was rather sweet.

Deciding, he focused his attention onto his body, feeling its molecules begin to tremble as he rearranged his energy, shifting it upwards into the ether. With a smooth, practised shudder, Raziel's human body vanished as he took on the alternate form of his dual nature: a radiant angel of shimmering bluish-white light, seven feet tall.

He merely stood for a moment, dazzling in his beauty as he stretched his wings. In this elevated state of existence he could see the humans' auras: glowing outlines of light that surrounded each person, wavering like coloured soap bubbles as they moved. With a slow shifting of wings Raziel took off from the balustrade and glided lazily about the domed ceiling, scanning them. Mentally, he discarded those that were looking somewhat grey and stunted – they'd been fed on many times already, and their energy wouldn't have the same strong, powerful rush as those humans who were uninitiated to an angel's pleasure. Besides, the stunted ones whom he hadn't fed on himself would have a flavour of other angels to them. At times this held an almost forbidden thrill, but he was in the mood for something pristine at the moment. Pure.

He smiled to himself as he spotted the perfect one: a young boy of twenty or so, whose energy glowed a vibrant blue-green. Circling above him, Raziel reached out with his mind, locking energies. He felt the immediate jolt and capitulation; the boy's expression became a puzzled frown, like someone hearing music that they couldn't quite catch. Turning, he spotted Raziel for the first time, hovering above him. His eyes widened as he stood rooted to the spot, gazing slack-jawed upwards at the angel that only he could see.

Gracefully, Raziel spiralled and landed in front of him. The radiance from his form burst over the boy, lighting him like a spotlight on the stage. "I have come for you," he said, knowing that even *sotto voce,* his words would resonate in the feeble human ears like the ringing of cathedral bells.

The boy began to tremble. "I – I—"

"Yes, you and only you," said Raziel, advancing with a smile. His voice had a light English accent. Like many angels, Raziel often found himself unconsciously taking on aspects of past energy donors. The accent had been with him for years; the energy from that human had been particularly intoxicating. He moved towards the boy, gleaming robes of pure white light swirling gently about his "ankles". A long time ago, they hadn't used to bother manifesting the robes – angels in their light form didn't need them – but humans seemed to place such innocent stock in the detail that it felt heartless to deny them.

With a contented sigh, Raziel stretched out his celestial

hands and touched the blue-green aura for the first time. As other humans trundled obliviously past with their cameras and bags, the young, hopeful energy surged through him, filling him, feeding him. Oh, lovely. As he indulged, images from the boy's life flashed past, along with his hopes, his dreams. They were as pedestrian as most humans'; Raziel disregarded them and focused on the pure pleasure of feeding. The blue-green aura began to shudder as it slowly diminished, greying and collapsing in on itself. The boy, on the other hand, had a wondering, dazed expression as he looked up at Raziel, basking in the angel's beauty along with the soothing serenity that Raziel knew was washing over him from his touch.

"I always knew," he murmured, tears filling his eyes. "I always knew that there were really angels…"

"How prescient of you," said Raziel, withdrawing at last. He could feel his halo glowing more brightly as the buzz of new energy pulsed through him. Smiling at the boy with something almost like affection, he reached for him again, resting his hand on the boy's head. "Stay with us," he said. "We have work for you here." The youth would never be the same again, of course, but once he had recovered a bit Raziel had a feeling that Lailah would appreciate him. Raziel's friend loved young energy, almost collecting it the way humans did bottles of wine.

"I will!" gasped the boy. "Oh, I will!"

As Raziel unfurled his wings and lifted upwards again, breaking the mental connection that allowed him to be seen, he heard someone say, "Tom? What is it?" And the tear-choked response, "I've seen an angel!"

Spiralling once, Raziel caught sight of a slim woman with chestnut-brown hair kneeling on a pew, head bent onto her clasped hands in prayer. Though somewhat damaged, her energy was trying feebly to regain itself; there was a rose-coloured tinge to its greyness. As Raziel watched, she looked up at the stained-glass windows, a euphoric smile on her face. Oh, now *that* was nice, thought Raziel, scanning her body. Was she a resident? He'd have to summon her to his chambers sometime soon, and enjoy pleasure of a different sort. Though not all angels in this world explored the gratifications their human form could offer, Raziel had been a connoisseur for centuries.

As Tom's friend hugged him on the cathedral floor below, saying "Praise the angels!", Raziel soared back to his chambers, gliding neatly through the white stone walls into an office of soft, gleaming wood and grey carpet, with antique books lining one wall. Landing, he focused his mind and drew his energy downwards, bringing it back to the human plane. With a shimmer his physical body manifested itself again, complete with the expensive trousers and crisp white shirt he'd been wearing. Though it took practice, clothes were only molecules of a different sort; it was merely a matter of focusing on them as well when one made the initial shift.

Sitting at his desk, Raziel looked up at a knock on the door. "Come," he said.

The panelled wooden door opened soundlessly and a young man with a tumble of dark curls entered, his footsteps sinking into the rich carpet. He bowed his head. "Sir, Lailah is here to see you."

"Oh, excellent." Pushing aside the tedious Church of Angels paperwork that had awaited him, Raziel leaned back in the leather recliner. "Send her in, Jonah."

Jonah backed respectfully out again, and a moment later Lailah strolled in. In her human form, Lailah had long, gleaming auburn hair, and large blue eyes. Her attributes were, as usual, firmly on display in a tight black suit with a plunging neckline.

Raziel winced as he saw that she was smoking a slender brown cigarillo. Some of the angels felt that Raziel himself had gone disgustingly native, but really – there were limits. "Do you mind?" he said shortly, shoving a pristine crystal ashtray across the desk at Lailah.

With a graceful shrug, his friend extinguished the cigarillo and sat down. "Have you heard?" she asked, crossing her slender legs.

"What, about the Second Wave finally being scheduled?" Raziel relaxed back in his chair, stretching his long legs out. "Good news, isn't it? The Council's little experiment worked out after all. We could have told them so."

Lailah laughed out loud; it was the sound of silver bells. "Yes, I think most of the First Wavers have been surprised that being here isn't exactly a hardship. They've taken to feeding off humans much more easily than they thought."

Raziel smiled. Reaching for a nail file that rested on his desktop, he began to shape his nails. "Well, one does get a taste for the things. Addictive creatures, aren't they?"

"It goes both ways," said Lailah, looking around her at the plush office in satisfaction. She herself had one almost as large. "They seem quite addicted to us, too."

Like Lailah, Raziel was one of those angels who had always enjoyed savouring the taste of human energy. For centuries, angels like them had passed between the two worlds, gorging themselves on the human life force. Though this was tolerated, it was seen as revoltingly base by most angels, who were content to stay at home. But then the Crisis had come, and everything had changed: the angels' own world was dying. When the Seraphic Council's plan to save them had been unveiled two years ago, Raziel and Lailah had volunteered to be included in the first experimental wave of angels who would move to the human world permanently. Why not? Raziel liked the place anyway, and it gave one a certain amount of kudos as a brave, selfless volunteer.

For most of the First Wave angels, though, the move had been a matter of necessity: the angels' resources were dwindling fast, and they needed to feed to survive, even if the majority of angels had never sampled human energy before. Though many issues had been considered before the plan was approved, no one had really thought about – or cared – what the humans' reaction would be when angels suddenly invaded their world on such a scale. They were secure in the knowledge that to do so was almost entirely safe. Not only could angels in their human form blend in easily with the rest of the population, but they couldn't be easily harmed when in that form – and normally, the only people who could even see them in their divine form were being fed off and dazzled by the angel's beauty. The little band of angel assassins that roamed the country was an annoyance, but not a major one; their numbers were pitiably few. Mostly the angels simply knew that to come here was the route to their salvation.

What no one had foreseen was that the locals would be quite so enthusiastic about it. Only months after the first experimental wave of angels had arrived, the Church of Angels had sprung up spontaneously, founded by the humans as a sort of angel frenzy gripped the nation. Though the angels hadn't predicted this outcome, they were quick to take advantage of it. Soon almost every Church of Angels in the country had one or more angels attached to it, basking in the humans' adulation and lazily feeding on whoever they liked. Not all angels were involved with the Church, of course – plenty had discovered that they enjoyed the hunt, prowling the streets and feeding off whoever they might. It was as if something primal in angels, that they hadn't experienced in their own staid world, had now emerged with a vengeance and was greedily indulging itself.

But for a lot of them, the Church had become a cosy refuge, and as an institution it had turned out to be an enormous boon in other ways, as well: as the Church had expanded, it had branched into having its own TV station, a publishing house, a massive internet presence. With angels at the helm, the word of their beneficence had erupted across the country and was spreading fast, bringing more churches and thousands of new devotees daily – all of them eager to experience angelic salvation for themselves, even before they'd ever encountered an angel. When the Second Wave of angels arrived soon – and then others after them – it would be to a very different world than the First Wavers had experienced: one which was loudly enthusiastic about the angelic presence, embracing them at every turn.

The really comical thing, thought Raziel, was how

oblivious the world was to what was happening. Those humans who didn't believe simply thought that those who did were insane. There were a number of sceptics who loudly decried the ridiculous fad that had swept the country; it was always amusing when, as occasionally happened, one of them succumbed to angel burn and publicly changed their tune. Similarly, any organized interference that might have occurred was laughably minimal; feeding from the police and government officials took care of that.

"And *you're* in a rather nice position, aren't you?" said Lailah now with a silky smile. Raziel saw that she was wearing a small Church of Angels pendant around her neck; an ironic touch. "As am I."

Raziel feigned innocence, raising his eyebrows. "Why, I have no idea what you mean. I'm just doing my job at the humans' behest, running their church for them."

Lailah threw her head back as she laughed. "Yes, very noble of you! I can hardly wait to see the Council's expressions when they realize just how much control we have here already."

Raziel smiled. Though the angels had never planned to actually take over the running of the humans' affairs, it was slowly happening. And as an angel intimately familiar with this world, he himself was in a prime position for power. Though more senior angels than he would be arriving as the evacuation continued, by that time he would be thoroughly ensconced, one of the de facto leaders. He'd already wrested for himself the leadership of the main Church of Angels cathedral, which he knew would be the driving force in the brave new world they were forging, rather than the humans' government. And, like many angels, he'd quickly realized that the real power lay in the day-to-day running of things. Leave the preaching to the humans; he was happy to simply indulge in empire building. With fringe benefits, of course.

"It'll be interesting to see how it pans out," he admitted, tossing his nail file back onto his desk. "But if the Council didn't want some of us taking advantage of the situation, then they really should have come across first, rather than hiding at home to see if it worked out."

"Well, exactly," chuckled Lailah. Her gleaming auburn hair shifted on her shoulders as she nodded. After a pause, she said, "By the way, speaking of hiding, I heard that Thaddeus has been taken care of. I felt the ripple myself, a few nights ago. Good, that's a relief."

Raziel grimaced. The subject of the traitor angels wasn't his favourite one. "I don't know what they think they're doing, trying to protect the humans," he said tersely. "It's not as if we have any choice but to feed off the creatures, if we want to survive."

Lailah flashed a grin. "Yes, I think it's just the fact that some of us *enjoy* it so much that troubles them…hypocrites. How many traitors are left?"

"Still a few, but we're getting there," said Raziel. "We came up with quite a tidy solution in the end, you know. Very clever."

Lailah started to say something else, and then stopped as Raziel's cellphone rang from the desk. Leaning lazily forward, Raziel answered it. "Yes?"

"It's Paschar," said a voice.

"Ah, Paschar, hello," said Raziel, dropping back in his chair again. "And how are things up there in upstate New York? Still enjoying your little kingdom?" In the rural neck of the woods that Paschar had settled in, he was the only angel within a hundred miles. At his local Church of Angels he was like a fat, contented bull in a meadow full of cows. Though that would probably change once the Second Wave arrived, doubling the angels' present numbers.

"We've got a problem," said Paschar shortly.

Raziel felt his eyebrows rise at the lack of banter. Paschar was another angel who had spent a lot of time in this world; the two of them went back a long way. "What's going on?" he asked.

"I've been feeding off some new humans in a place called Pawntucket," said Paschar. "It's a bit far afield, but I wanted something fresh…and today I sensed that one of the females has been touched by something angelic. Something that wasn't me."

Raziel frowned in confusion. "And? Are you saying that no one else is allowed to feed off your human?"

"Don't be ridiculous. The energy that had touched her was like our own, but not. It was *human*...but still angelic."

Raziel sat up in his seat. "What are you talking about?" he said. Across from him, he saw Lailah cock her head curiously.

"Listen to me. I went to this creature's house, and touched minds with it. She looks like a human girl, but she's not one."

"What is she, then?" asked Raziel blankly.

There was a long pause. Across the miles, he could hear Paschar take a breath before he said, "She's a half-angel."

For a moment Raziel couldn't speak. Angels didn't breed; they were beings of energy that had existed since before any of them could now remember. Though in their human form they functioned the same as humans, angels were fundamentally different – conceiving offspring with them should be a biological impossibility.

"That can't be," he said at last. "You must be mistaken; such a thing can't happen."

"Raziel, I could sense her angelic form as clearly as my own, but it was tainted, intermingled with her human one.

She's an organic mix of the two; there's no doubt about it. Half human, half angel."

"*How?*"

"How should I know? But somehow, by some fluke… one of us who was here enjoying humans before the Crisis must be responsible for it."

There could be almost a thousand possible contenders, in that case. "Oh, wonderful," murmured Raziel. He sat rubbing his temples, trying to decide whether they could get away with not telling the Council about this. What some angels did in their human form was already controversial enough, without throwing this new complication into the mix.

"But Raziel, there's more," said Paschar. "Something urgent, that needs to be taken care of immediately."

A prickle went up Raziel's spine as he heard the dread in the other angel's voice. "What?"

There was a long pause. "I saw a flash of the future when I touched this…creature's hand. She has it in her to destroy us."

Now I know he's going mad, thought Raziel. But unfortunately, he didn't believe it. "Who do you mean by 'us', exactly?" he asked.

"*Us.* All of angelkind. I don't know how, but it's a possibility that's there within her; a strong one. She will have both the ability and the desire to destroy us all."

Raziel felt himself go cold; distantly, he saw Lailah staring at him, mouthing *What is it?* Paschar was not given to exaggeration, and his psychic skills were as strong as any angel's Raziel had ever known. He had no doubt that Paschar had seen exactly what he said he'd seen.

"She'll have to be done away with, then," he said.

"Immediately," agreed Paschar. "You've got a means for taking care of this sort of thing now, haven't you?"

"Yes, I'll give the order right now."

A few minutes later, Raziel clicked his cellphone off and sat in silence, gazing down at the details he'd just taken from Paschar. A half-angel. Unbelievable; the very thought was obscene. Even if Paschar hadn't had his vision of catastrophe, they'd have to do away with the thing; such a travesty couldn't be allowed to exist. Picking up the bit of paper, Raziel rose to his feet, the leather chair squeaking slightly.

"Trouble?" asked Lailah.

"You won't believe it," said Raziel grimly. "I'll tell you in a minute." Going into the outer office, he dropped the paper onto Jonah's desk. As his human assistant looked up, Raziel said, "This...thing must be destroyed. See to it."

Jonah nodded, his gentle brown eyes worried. "Of course, sir. I'll take care of it immediately."

Raziel gave a curt nod. "See that you do." And going back into his office, he shut the polished wooden door.

On his own, Jonah sat at his desk gazing down at the paper for a moment, feeling troubled. It must be another of the traitors.

Serving an angel was an almost unbelievable honour, and one that Jonah gave thanks for every day. But his position meant that he often knew things that worried him, and the fact of the traitorous angels was one of them. How was it even possible that some of the angels could turn on the others, attempting to put an end to the good works that they did for humans? The idea caused his stomach to tighten anxiously. A world without the angels would be...unthinkable.

Thankfully, a few months ago an efficient means of dealing with the problem had presented itself – a solution so subtle that hardly any of the angelic community knew what was going on, much less the human one. Giving a brief prayer of thanks to the angels for allowing him to be of service to them, Jonah took out his cellphone and carefully texted the address on the paper to the contact number. He felt relief as he snapped the phone shut again. There, problem solved. The traitor would be gone in a matter of days; it would never even know what had hit it. How could it?

Their method was so secret that not even the assassin knew the truth.

CHAPTER *Four*

ENEMY SIGHTED, PAWNTUCKET NY. Residence 34 Nesbit St.

Alex got the text in his Aspen motel room on Thursday night, and was packed and checked out in less than twenty minutes. He spent the next day and a half driving. Finally, in the early hours of Saturday morning, he reached Pawntucket, a sleepy-looking town crouched in the foothills of the Adirondack Mountains. Heading for the main drag through town, he found a GoodRest Motel – there was always a GoodRest; they were as dependable as clockwork – and checked into a room to get a few hours' sleep. The temptation, as always, was to go after the angel immediately, but he knew better. When you were this tired, you were likely to mess up and do something stupid.

He awoke at dawn, instantly alert. Taking a quick shower, he let the hot water beat down upon him, and then got dressed. As he pulled on a T-shirt, the tattoo on his left bicep, an *AK* in black lettering, disappeared under the shirtsleeve.

The motel did a breakfast of sorts – it was food, anyway – and so he went to the main building to grab some donuts and coffee, which he ate back in his room as he checked over his gear. A habit left over from his days out hunting with Cully. *Respect your weaponry and it'll respect you,* the big Southerner had said over and over. Maybe there had been a time when Alex had rolled his eyes a bit, but now he knew that Cull had been right. No matter how prepared you thought you were, it only took one mistake to kill you.

Loading a full magazine into the semi-automatic rifle, Alex clicked it home and sighted along the rifle's length before putting it back into its case. The pistol he tucked into his holster, which was worn under the waistband of his jeans and couldn't be seen at all, if you didn't know it was there. He preferred the rifle, but it wasn't always possible to use it if people were around. Finally, taking the pistol's silencer, he stuck it in his jeans pocket.

He was ready. Gulping down the last of his coffee, he shrugged into his leather jacket and loaded his car, programming the GPS for Nesbit Street. A moment later, he had pulled out onto Highway 12 again, the main road through town.

As he followed the robotic voice's directions, he took the place in with mild curiosity. Pawntucket was like a thousand other small towns he'd seen. The business centre downtown had been slowly eaten away by the shopping malls, leaving everything looking a bit run-down, a bit frayed around the edges. The high school (*The Pawntucket Bears know how to ROAR!* proclaimed the sign) was practically the largest building in the place. And once the students graduated, they'd probably hit the ground running and never look back, thought Alex dryly. The only thing the place had going for it was its backdrop of the Adirondacks, with its autumn splashes of colour looking like a patchwork quilt.

There weren't many angels in upstate New York. The one up here most likely had a clear field, thought Alex. It had probably fed on hundreds of people already.

The GPS directed him to a tree-lined avenue of Victorian houses. Alex passed an early-morning dog walker with a basset hound; apart from that, the street seemed quiet, the grass still damp with early-morning dew. He found number thirty-four, and his eyebrows flew up.

Ohh-kay. So this one was into kitsch, in a fairly big way. That wasn't something he'd seen before – they usually liked to keep a low profile; the neighbour who you knew was there but never caught sight of. Maybe this one had decided that you could hide better by being blindingly obvious. Or maybe it just liked plastic wishing wells a whole lot.

He parked the Porsche a few doors down. Apart from the circus in the front yard, the house just looked shabby: flaking green paint with grey wood showing through. A blue Toyota sat in the drive. Turning off his engine, Alex leaned back in the leather seat and shut his eyes. A few deep breaths later, he had lifted his focus up through his chakras and was carefully exploring the energies in the house.

There were three of them. And they were all asleep.

He examined them further. One of the energies was a middle-aged woman. No, wait a minute – two of the energies were. They were similar. Sisters, maybe? Except that one of them was…odd. Childlike. Someone with mental problems, perhaps. But definitely both human. Okay, disregard those two. The third…

He frowned. Time seemed to slow around him as he checked out the third energy, carefully probing it with his own. "What the hell?" he muttered.

It had the same "kick" that angel energy had; the same

rush of power, but there was no trace of the cold, slimy sensation that he associated with angels. Alex slowly opened his eyes, staring at number thirty-four. Human energy fields had a distinct flavour, an instant recognition that he couldn't even describe. When you touched them with your own, you simply knew that you were touching like with like. This energy just felt...bizarre, as if someone had taken a human energy field and an angel one and mixed them together, somehow.

A slight breeze stirred, and the front yard came alive: tiny kites bobbing, little wooden windmills creaking industriously. The cutesyness of it struck Alex as ominous suddenly. He tapped the steering wheel, hardly even aware that he was doing so. He had to get a look at what was in there, so that he'd have more of an idea of exactly what he was dealing with. And frankly, he'd prefer to do it now, while the thing was still asleep.

Checking the human energies in the house again, he saw that they were both in delta sleep; deeply out of it – good. Reaching under the passenger seat, he pulled out a metal box and took out a set of lock picks. He jingled them in his hand, gazing speculatively at the house. The front door was out – he was too likely to be seen – but there was sure to be a back door. Should he take a chance? Lock picking had never really been his forte; not like it had been Jake's. Still, depending on the lock, he wasn't bad sometimes, and this didn't look like the sort of place where he'd be likely to encounter anything state-of-the-art.

Making up his mind, Alex mentally scanned the houses on either side for dogs, and then got out of the car, closing the door behind him. He didn't bother trying to do it softly – if anyone was watching, trying to keep quiet would look a lot more suspicious than just acting normally. But the street was still, with only the sound of birdsong accompanying his footsteps as he strolled down the sidewalk with his hands in his pockets. The rifle was back in his car, but he could feel the pistol still tucked in his jeans under his T-shirt, there and ready if he needed it.

He turned into number thirty-four's drive. The concrete had spidery cracks running across it, and weeds growing here and there. Edging past the Toyota, he continued around the house to the backyard, creaking open the gate of the chain-link fence. No lock; that boded well. Closing the gate behind him, he took in at a glance the overgrown grass and faded wooden lawn furniture; the pots of greenery that sat on the patio.

To his relief, there was a row of high conifers to each side, blocking the neighbours' view. Good, that made things easier. Going to the back door, Alex eased the screen door open. It had a few holes in it, he noticed; just the thing to keep the flies out. He examined the inner lock and smiled. He was in luck – it was a cheap one. Selecting a rake pick, he inserted it into the keyhole and slid it rapidly back and forth. Almost immediately, there was a faint *click* as the pins fell obediently into place.

Success. Alex opened the back door and slipped inside, tucking the lock picks back into his pocket. Jake had always sneered at him for using the rake; it took a lot less skill than some of the other picks, and was useless against a good security lock. But if it got the job done, why argue?

Glancing around, he saw that he was standing in a pale blue kitchen with white cabinets. An unwashed pot sat on the stove, and there was a meal's-worth of dirty dishes beside the sink. Moving through the kitchen, he edged through a swinging door and found himself in a dining room. His eyebrows rose at the large velvet painting of a sad clown that hung on the wall. Whatever this creature was, it had seriously bad taste, not to mention the precarious-looking heaps of clutter in all the corners — stacks of papers, magazines, cardboard boxes. A white lace tablecloth covered the dining table, with a messy pile of mail scattered across one end. Alex picked up the top envelope. A bill from the Pawntucket Waterworks, addressed to Ms. Joanna Fields.

He froze as a faint snore came from the next room. Placing the envelope quietly back onto the pile, he pulled out his pistol and screwed the silencer onto it before slipping through a pair of French doors into the living room.

A teenage girl lay asleep on the sofa, curled up under a red and black knitted afghan, with one slender arm cradling the throw cushion that was nestled under her head. Long, wavy blonde hair spread across the girl's back and shoulders like a cape. Even though she was sleeping, Alex could see how pretty she was, with her delicate, almost elfin features. He stood in the doorway for a moment, watching the soft rise and fall of her chest. When he was certain that she wasn't going to wake up, he closed his eyes, shifting his consciousness up through his chakras.

As his focus rose above his crown chakra, he breathed in sharply. The human-angel energy was much stronger here, like a tide threatening to sweep him off his feet. This was it, all right; this girl was what he'd sensed from outside. But what was she? Keeping his focus in the ether state, Alex opened his eyes…and saw the radiant form of an angel hovering above the girl's sleeping figure.

His gun was at the ready in less than a second. But even as his finger started to pull the trigger, his mind was balking at what he was seeing. This wasn't right, there was something wrong, something missing—

As he realized what it was, his eyes widened. He stepped around the coffee table, keeping his gun trained on the creature before him. It floated peacefully with its wings folded behind its back, its head bowed slightly, as if in sleep. It wasn't his imagination: the angel didn't seem aware of him.

But more than that, it had no halo.

Alex shook his head blankly. He had to be seeing things. The angel's face was lovely, serene; a magnified version of the girl's own. Yet where there should be a halo framing its head, there was simply…nothing. An angel's halo was its heart; without it, they couldn't survive. His eyes flicked again to the sleeping girl. The image was obviously a part of her; the two of them were linked, somehow. So what did *that* mean, when all his knowledge and training told him that angels couldn't maintain their human form and their ethereal one at the same time?

Alex stared at the girl, troubled. Distantly, he realized that his gaze was lingering on her face, taking in the faint gold of her eyebrows; her eyelashes against her smooth cheeks. His head snapped up as he heard a car pull into the drive. On the sofa, the girl stirred, snuggling deeper into her pillow. Alex moved to the window. Easing the curtains aside the barest inch, he watched an old yellow Corvette park behind the Toyota. The engine fell silent, and a thin girl with brown hair and lots of eyeshadow got out. Alex quickly scanned her. She was wholly human.

As she headed towards the front door, he let the curtain

fall again and slipped into the dining room, pressing himself against the wall to one side of the French doors. The door knocker rapped softly – two short, hesitant knocks. "Willow!" called the girl's voice in an undertone. It sounded like she was looking up towards the bedroom windows. "Hello, good morning...are you awake yet?"

There was a groan from the other room as the girl started to wake up. Craning his neck slightly, Alex watched in amazement as the shining angel-image wavered and began to fade.

"Willow!" hissed the girl on the front porch, knocking again. "Open the door, I forgot my phone!"

The girl – Willow? – lifted her tousled head and peered blearily towards the front door. The angel vanished. Yawning, she threw the afghan off and stood up, heading for the dining room. Alex held himself tightly against the wall, his heart quickening. She shuffled through without seeing him. As she went into the hallway he saw that she was wearing pink pyjama bottoms and a light grey T-shirt. She was petite, only five-three or so, but obviously close to his own age; slim, with a small, perfect figure.

There was no longer any sign of the angel. No indication at all that there was anything non-human about the girl.

He heard the front door open. "Nina, what are you doing here?" she said groggily. "It's hardly even daybreak."

Nina's voice sounded strained. "I know, but I just

couldn't sleep. I kept thinking about Beth – all that stuff you told me yesterday."

There was a pause, and then he heard Willow sigh. "I didn't get much sleep either; I must have fallen asleep in front of the TV. Look, wait here. I'll go get us some coffee."

"Wait here?" Nina sounded surprised. "Aren't I allowed in the house any more?"

"Not at ungodly o'clock, you're not," said Willow shortly. "I don't want to wake Mom and Aunt Jo up, okay? We'll sit on the front porch."

Alex pressed against the wall again as she came back into the house. Thankfully, she didn't turn on the dining room light as she passed through the room a second time, heading for the kitchen, and he remained hidden in the half-shadows. A moment later there was the sound of a cabinet opening, and of running water. Taking a silent step closer to the kitchen door, Alex watched unseen as Willow spooned instant coffee into a pair of mugs. Yawning, she scraped her hair off her face and stretched. She looked so entirely human in that moment; so drowsy and sleep-rumpled.

For a moment Alex just gazed at her, taking in her long tumble of hair, her wide eyes and pixieish chin. Fleetingly, he imagined her eyes meeting his, wondering what she'd look like if she smiled.

Irritated with himself – why was he even thinking about this? – he shook the thought away and quickly checked out Willow's aura. Angelic silver, with soft lavender lights shifting through it: again, like a mix of angel and human. But unlike an angel's aura, there was no bluish tint to its edge; no indication of when she had last fed. In fact, it looked as if she didn't feed at all, at least not in the same way angels did. Drawing his energy back to his heart chakra, Alex regarded the girl in confusion. She was angelic...and yet she wasn't.

A framed photo on a dusty bookcase caught his attention and he moved closer to it, picking it up silently. A small girl with long blonde hair was standing under a willow tree, her face tilted up in delight as its feathery leaves brushed across her face, framing it.

A willow tree. Willow.

Alex stared down at the small photo. If he had needed further confirmation that this girl was something bizarre, then this was it. An angel's human form was always that of an adult – they didn't have childhoods; they didn't breed. If Willow had been a child, then she wasn't an angel of any type he'd ever encountered before.

So what was she?

He ducked into the shadows again as Willow suddenly returned to the dining room. Plucking a purple sweater off one of the piles, she pulled it over her head as she walked back into the kitchen. Smoothing her shining hair with both hands, she tied it into a loose knot at the nape of her neck.

God, she's beautiful. The unbidden thought whispered through Alex's mind as Willow grabbed up the mugs of coffee and headed back outside. "Here you go, Nescafe's finest," he heard her say as she went out onto the porch. The front door closed.

Alex shoved the photo almost harshly into his jacket pocket. Of course she was beautiful, he reminded himself – she was part angel, somehow. He headed quickly through the kitchen again and then out the back door, easing it shut behind him. Jogging across the crumbling patio, he shouldered his way through a pair of winter-smelling conifers and grasped the chain-link fence, swiftly scaling it and dropping into one of the neighbour's backyards. Then from that backyard, he climbed into the next. A few minutes later, he was back on the street again, walking casually towards his car. Glancing at Willow's house, he could see the two girls talking, their heads bent in earnest conversation.

No. He shook his head as he slid behind the steering wheel and started the engine. Not two girls – *one* girl, and one something that he didn't understand at all.

* * *

When the CIA had taken over control of Project Angel after the Invasion almost two years ago, a lot of things had changed. One of the main ones was that each Angel Killer now worked alone, with no contact from the others. Alex didn't even know where the rest of the AKs were now; he hadn't been in touch with any of them for over twenty months. Anonymous texts arrived on his cellphone from unknown angel spotters; there were no names involved, no way for him to link the information he received to an actual person. Though he missed the old days like an ache inside of him – the camaraderie, going on the hunt together, even the boring, endless days at the camp in the desert – he could see that it was necessary. This was war, even if its millions of casualties were too blissed-out to realize it. If he were caught by the angels or any of their human followers, then he wouldn't be able to give them any information.

But it also meant that it was a pain to actually get hold of someone if you needed to.

Alex spent the next five hours in his motel room, trying the emergency number that he'd been given when the CIA took over. He'd been told – on the phone, by an unknown voice – to memorize it, and then to forget he'd ever had it. It wasn't to be used, except in cases of untold emergency.

For a long time, no one answered. He watched the Sports Channel as he hit redial over and over, frowning at the TV screen without taking anything in. "Come *on*, pick up the goddamn phone," he muttered.

Finally, just before noon, there was a click and a woman's voice came on the line. "Hello?"

Alex had been lying on the bed with his cellphone cradled between shoulder and ear, dully channel-surfing with the remote control. He dropped it and snatched at his phone, sitting straight up. "This is Alex," he said.

There was a long pause. "Yes?"

"I need to talk with someone."

"This number is only to be used—"

"This *is* an emergency," he said, his voice tight. "Trust me."

Another pause, this one lasting for almost a minute. "Someone will call you back," said the woman finally. Another click, and the line went dead. Alex swore, sorely tempted to throw the phone against the wall.

It was almost an hour before his cellphone went off. He grabbed it on the first ring. Without preamble, a male voice said, "Are you alone?"

"Yeah," said Alex.

"Good. What's going on?" The voice was accentless, bland. Alex couldn't tell whether it was the same one he'd heard almost two years ago. Briefly, pacing around the motel room with its two double beds, he explained what had happened.

102

"Yes?" said the voice when he had finished. There was too much politeness in the short syllable, implying *What's the problem?*

Alex frowned. "So – I don't know what this girl is," he said. "If there's no halo, then—"

"She's an angel," interrupted the voice. "You're to follow your orders."

Alex felt himself bristle. The CIA had come onto the scene about ten years too late, as far as he was concerned. Where exactly had they been when they were all living out in the desert like refugees, shooting ancient guns and using creaky holographs for training?

"Look," he said, trying to keep his tone level. "She's *not* an angel. I know an angel when I see one, all right? This girl is something else. It's almost like she's…part-angel, part-human." Even as he spoke the words, he knew they were insane. Angels couldn't breed.

"The anomalies are not your concern," said the voice shortly. "Just do your job. She's an angel; she has to be exterminated."

"Did you hear a word I just said?" demanded Alex. He started pacing again, shoving a chair roughly out of his way. "Listen to me: *she is not an angel*. She doesn't *feed*. She had a *childhood*. There's no halo! If she's an angel, then where's she getting her energy from? How does she exist?"

"Again, these aren't your concerns."

Alex heard his voice rise. "You're kidding, right? I'm out there on the front line every day; if there's something I don't understand, I'm *toast*. If this girl's a danger, I need to know how. I need—"

"Trust us," said the voice flatly.

Alex fell silent in disbelief. It was like talking to a robot.

"We have no reason to believe that there are any more like her," the man continued after a pause. "But she must be taken care of. And quickly. She's already caused great harm."

Listening intently, Alex thought he caught a faint English tone to the words. He stiffened as memory traced a finger up his spine. Just like humans, angels had their individual quirks…and one of the few to ever get away from his father had spoken with an English accent. The AKs used to joke that whoever got that angel next time would get bonus points.

"What great harm?" he asked after a pause.

"That's not—"

"Not my concern, right." Alex sank onto the bed. This felt wrong. This felt very, very wrong.

"If there's no halo, then more conventional methods will be fine," said the voice, its English lilt obvious now that Alex was listening for it. "But you're to do it, and do it now. If that creature isn't dead in an hour, you'll regret it." With a click, the voice was gone.

Alex stared at his phone for a moment, and then slowly

flipped it shut and put it on the bedside table. It could just be a coincidence, of course. It wasn't impossible that someone from England could be in the CIA. Except that he didn't really believe in coincidence; it was one of the reasons he'd stayed alive for so long. Mentally replaying the conversation with its evasive, threatening tone, exactly *how* wrong it was struck him forcibly. In his experience with the CIA that wasn't how they operated, at least not with Project Angel. They knew perfectly well that the AKs were the experts, not them – they'd never have said "trust us" to him and actually expected him to buy it. He was being lied to.

His thoughts tumbling, Alex rapped his fist against his jeans. Jesus. Could angels have taken control of Project Angel? The implications reeled through him. And if they had, then why were they so eager for him to kill this girl?

What was she, anyway?

Alex's gaze fell on the photo that lay on the dresser beside his keys. The pretty little girl with long blonde hair, smiling upwards through the trailing leaves. Abruptly, he got up from the bed and began to pack, throwing things into his bag without paying attention to how they were landing. If he was right and the angels were somehow behind this, then he wasn't going to let this girl out of his sight until he knew what the hell was going on.

And meanwhile, he had a feeling that he might have to make a run for it soon.

CHAPTER *Five*

ON FRIDAY I'D GONE TO school early, so that I could catch Beth before classes began. I sat in my Toyota in the student parking lot for over half an hour, watching all the cars pull in one by one, until the parking lot was a sea of glinting metal. Beth's car never showed. I waited until ten minutes after the final bell had rung, and even then I walked into the building slowly, glancing over my shoulder and hoping – but a tight, anxious part of me already knew that it was too late.

Then later that morning Beth's parents must have called the school, because someone overheard Mrs. Bexton talking about it in the office. By lunchtime, Pawntucket High was buzzing with the news: Beth had dropped out to join the Church of Angels.

All that day, I walked around in a daze hoping it was a mistake, and that Beth just had a cold or something; that she'd turn up later, smiling and perfect, the same as always. But of course it didn't happen. Finally, between fifth and sixth periods, Nina showed up at my locker. "You know something about this, don't you?" she demanded. Around us, the hallway jostled with people.

I stared into the messy depths of my locker, suddenly close to tears. "Yeah, sort of," I said softly.

"Come on." Nina grabbed my arm and dragged me out of the school. As we left the building by a side door near the art room we passed a couple of seniors, and I stiffened as I heard what they were saying.

"Well, I think Beth's really brave."

"Yeah, my cousin joined; so did one of my mom's friends. They all say that angels really exist, and that—"

I hunched my shoulders in my jean jacket and hurried out the door after Nina.

Going out to the parking lot, we sat in her car and talked. I told her everything that had happened…apart from Beth's angel turning up on my doorstep. She wouldn't believe me, for one thing, but more than that I didn't really want to think about it myself. Anyway, she was stunned enough. She sat silently for ages, shaking her head. "Willow, this is just…I mean, my god."

"Yeah," I said, and tried to smile. "That sort of sums it up."

"Well – what are you going to do?"

"Do?" I was sitting curled in her Corvette's bucket seat, with my head against the window. I looked up and stared at her. "What can I do? She's already joined; she's not going to *un*-join."

Nina's hazel eyes were accusing. "And you know this how, exactly?"

I scraped my hair back, frustrated. "Because I saw it! She just stays there, getting sicker and sicker, until… something happens." I trailed off, seeing again the cold grey cloud that had drifted over everything.

"Something happens," repeated Nina, drumming her fingers on the dash. "Willow, listen to yourself! It's not like you *know*."

"I do know!"

"You do not. All either of us know is that Beth has joined the Church of Angels, and it's because of your reading somehow, and you've got to *help* her before she ruins her life. Did you know that she was going to try for early admission at Stanford?"

I blew out a breath, wondering why I'd even told Nina.

"Look, I have to go," I said, uncurling myself and grabbing my bag from the footwell.

"Willow, wait! You can't just—"

I was already out of her car by then, heading for my own. But I should have known that Nina wouldn't let go of it.

The next morning, Saturday, she turned up at my house early. "Right, here's the plan," she said briskly, flipping her bangs out of her eyes. "I checked the Church of Angels' website, and the nearest church is in Schenectady. That must be where Beth has gone. There's an afternoon service today at two o'clock; you've got to go there and talk to her."

We were sitting on the ancient glider on my front porch, drinking coffee. With a sigh, I tucked a knee under myself and dropped back against the faded striped cushions. "Nina, I've already told you…it's pointless."

She shoved my leg sharply. "Willow, you *have* to. Come on, do you think your psychic powers are so infallible that it's impossible for you to be wrong?"

Put like that, I didn't really have an answer. I stared out at our street. A few doors down, a car engine started up, breaking the hushed, early morning silence. I sat cradling my coffee mug, listening to it fade away.

"I…don't know," I admitted.

Resting her coffee on her knee, Nina leaned forward to

look me in the eyes. "Please go," she said softly. "You seriously might be the only person she'll listen to."

I could feel myself caving in. I gazed down at the glider's rusting metal arm, picking at a flake of white paint. "I don't know if she'll want to see me, though. She was pretty angry after her reading."

"You still have to try," insisted Nina. "If you're right and she won't leave, then fine. But you have to *try*."

I let out a breath. I couldn't argue with her; she was right. Even though I knew that I hadn't been mistaken about what I'd seen…she was still right. I started to tell her so, and then stopped as a thought slithered coldly down my back. Of course I was going to go to the church. I had always been going to go. I can't psychically read myself – whenever I've tried, I've only seen a sort of greyness. The same sort of greyness that I'd seen in Beth's reading, though without that terrible, graveside coldness.

That was why I couldn't see more to do with Beth's future at the Church of Angels. Because I myself was going to play a part in it.

"What is it?" asked Nina, peering into my face.

I shook my head, draining the last gulp of my coffee and trying to ignore the dread that was suddenly pulsing through me. The last thing I wanted was to even go near the Church now, but it didn't feel like I had a choice. Greyness or not, Nina was right: I had to at least try.

"Nothing," I said. I tried to smile. "Okay, I'll go."

The dread had faded a bit by that afternoon, though the worry hadn't. I stood in front of the oval mirror that sat over my dresser, gazing at my reflection. I was wearing a long purple skirt with lots of sparkly silver threads running through it, and a tight white top. I touched the skirt worriedly. Was it okay? People dressed up for church, didn't they? Not that it mattered, really, but I wanted to blend in if I could.

It'll do, I decided. Quickly brushing my hair, I twisted two long locks on each side and pulled them back, catching them with a small barrette. Putting on my jean jacket and sneakers, I grabbed my bag and went downstairs. I could hear the clatter and splash of Aunt Jo doing the dishes in the kitchen; in the living room, Mom was asleep in her favourite chair. Not a surprise; sometimes I think her sleeping dreams must be as seductive as her waking ones. Asleep, she looked just like anyone else – as if her eyes might light up with recognition if she opened them and saw me. Gazing at her, something tightened in my stomach.

I'm never going to see her again, I thought.

What sort of stupid, random thought was that? I shook it away, ignoring the fear that had suddenly spiked through me. Leaning over the chair, I kissed my mother's sleeping cheek.

"Bye, Mom," I whispered. I smoothed her pale hair back. "I won't be gone long. I love you."

She murmured slightly and fell still again, her breathing soft and even. I sighed. At least she seemed peaceful. I kissed my fingers, touching them to her lips before I slipped from the room. Poking my head into the kitchen, I told Aunt Jo I was going out and then five minutes later I was in my car, heading towards Schenectady.

There wasn't much traffic, even once I got onto I-90. Once or twice I noticed a black Porsche to my rear. I glanced in the rear-view mirror. I'd seen it back in Pawntucket, too, lagging a block or so behind me when I left town. Someone else going to the church, maybe?

If they were, then they didn't need to follow me to find the way. Miles before I even got to Schenectady, huge signs started appearing on the side of the interstate: billboards with sparkling silver lettering saying, *The Angels Can Save You! Church of Angels Schenectady, Exit 8*. My hands tightened on the wheel at the generic image of the huge white church on a hill, so familiar from all the commercials.

When I finally pulled into the mammoth parking lot, all I could do was sit in my car and stare for a minute. I'd been to New York City; I'd seen big buildings before – but nothing quite like this. Maybe it was the way the church sat by itself, rising up from a vast, landscaped lawn, but the sheer impact of it just hit you like a wall. I took in the high, vaulted roof; the stained-glass windows glittering in the sun. On the other side of the parking lot, I could see a complex that looked like a huge shopping mall. There *was* a mall in there, I remembered – plus apartments, a gym, a hairdresser's – anything you might ever need.

It was almost two o'clock; crowds of people were drifting into the church. Getting out of my car, I steeled myself and started heading towards it. With luck, I'd find Beth…but her angel could be in there, too. Fear gripped me like a fist at the thought. I didn't want to see that thing ever again, if I could help it.

I'd only gone a few dozen paces when a nagging *turn around* feeling tickled at the back of my neck. I looked over my shoulder. There was the black Porsche again, a few rows down; a guy about my own age with dark hair was just getting out of it. He wore faded jeans, and a leather jacket hanging open over a blue T-shirt. I let out a breath, glad for the distraction…because the closer I got to that church, the more I seriously didn't want to go inside it.

Half-turning, I slowed my steps so that the dark-haired guy would catch up. For a moment he hesitated, but then we made eye contact and he walked slowly towards me. He had a medium build – slim, but with firm-looking shoulders – and moved like an athlete, confident in his own body. Something fluttered in my chest as I suddenly realized how attractive he was.

"Um – hi," I said, looking up at him as we fell into step together. He was a good head or so taller than me. "Did you just come from Pawntucket?" He glanced down at me, his eyebrows drawn together in a slight frown, and I shrugged. "I noticed your car."

"Yeah," he said after a pause. He cleared his throat. "I'm, um…staying with some friends."

Taking in the strong lines of his face, I wondered whether he was my age after all. He seemed older, somehow. Not his muscles; half the boys at school worked out. But something about his eyes, maybe. They were a sort of bluish-grey, like a storm at sea.

I could hardly look away from them.

I realized I was staring and looked quickly forward, my cheeks warm. I'd wanted a distraction, but not this much of one. What was wrong with me, anyway? There were at least half a dozen boys at Pawntucket High who were almost as good-looking as this guy, and I didn't gape at them like an idiot.

Ahead, the church loomed over us, practically blocking out the sky. We walked without speaking for a few minutes. Once, our arms brushed together; I jerked mine away hastily.

The silence felt stifling. "Are you a member here?" I asked.

The boy gave a soft snort that I realized was actually a

laugh. "No," he said flatly. His dark brown hair was slightly tousled, growing down past the tips of his ears. Gazing at his lips, I found myself wondering what it would be like to trace my finger over them.

Shoving the thought away, I cleared my throat. "So... what are you doing here?"

"Just thought I'd take a look." His eyes flicked over my face. "What about you? Are you a member?"

We had reached the broad white steps by then, merging into a crowd of people climbing upwards, all of us like ants heading for the anthill. At the top, three sets of tall silver doors stood open, waiting. I shook my head as we climbed. "No, there's, um – this friend of mine. Or no, not really a friend, but..." I sighed. "It's a long story."

Watching me, he sort of nodded without answering, as if this actually made sense. I winced, knowing how completely incoherent I must be sounding. Then as the two of us went into the church we somehow got separated in the crowd, and I found myself on my own in the middle of a vast expanse of snowy white marble. Long pews curved in concentric semi-circles, spreading outwards from a white pulpit at the front. I blinked as I got a better look at the pulpit: it was shaped like a pair of angel wings, their carved feathery tips curving upwards. Behind it, a giant stained-glass figure of an angel stood with its arms out, smiling down at us.

Finding a seat at the end of one of the shiny white pews I sat down gingerly, holding my bag on my lap. I bit my lip as I took in the solid mass of humanity around me. The website was right; there had to be thousands of people here. Nina had made it sound so easy, but how was I ever going to find Beth in all of this?

I looked up as a sudden rippling of harp music sounded through the church, its celestial chords echoing. "Praise the angels," murmured the woman sitting next to me. Her eyes were shining, fervent. No, not just her eyes — her whole face, her whole *being,* was lit up with love for the angels. Feeling uneasy, I turned back towards the front as a man in a white robe climbed the short, curving stairs that led up to the pulpit. A preacher, maybe, or whatever you called them here.

"Welcome!" he said, lifting his arms. His voice rang out all around us, amplified by speakers. As he spoke a large screen flickered into life above him, magnifying his image ten times over. He had thinning hair, and round, ruddy cheeks.

"Welcome," responded the crowd in a deep, rumbling murmur.

First the preacher led everyone in a prayer to the angels, asking to be worthy of their love. Then white velvet curtains glided open to either side of the stained-glass windows, revealing a hundred-strong choir. "Hymn 43,

'*The Angels Have Shown Me My True Path*,'" said the preacher into the microphone. The congregation rose. With a crescendo of harp music the soprano choir began to sing, and then everyone else joined in as well, voices resonating like thunder. I fumbled on the shelf in front of me for a white leather book entitled *Angelic Hymns*; flipping it open, I half-sang as I glanced at the pews around me, hoping to catch sight of Beth. I couldn't see her anywhere, but I did see that I was almost the only person who was actually using the hymn book. Everyone else was singing the words by heart, some swaying with their eyes closed.

Suddenly I noticed the dark-haired guy again: he was across the aisle from me a couple of rows back, also at the end of a pew. He wasn't singing at all, just sort of frowning down at his book. I gave a small smile, glad that someone else found this weird, too.

The music ended and the congregation sat down, the notes of the song still vibrating through the church. The preacher gazed silently out at us for a moment. When he spoke again, his voice was throaty with emotion. "My fellow devotees, we are here today for many things, but first...first, we must give thanks to the angels. For today, we have three new residential members of our Church: three blessed devotees all joined together in love of the angels, who have pledged their lives to serving them."

Beth. I caught my breath as thousands of voices intoned, "Thanks be to angels!" The woman next to me looked close to tears of joy. "Oh, praise the angels," she said again, shaking her head slightly and gripping the pew in front of her. "More souls to do their holy work."

My heart beat faster as I shifted on the pew, craning to see. As the harp music quivered around us again, the choir began to sing in their pure soprano notes, their voices lifting up to the high, vaulted ceiling. Slowly, three people in sky-blue robes filed out and stood facing the congregation; two women and one man. I spotted Beth immediately. She was on the left, her honey-coloured hair falling loose on her shoulders. Glancing at the huge TV screen, I saw that she was smiling: a radiant smile that stretched across her face like a beacon. Worry creased through me. She was so pale, with faint circles under her eyes.

Leaving the pulpit, the preacher moved down the short line and greeted them one by one, clasping each of their hands. Finally he turned back to the congregation. On the screen, I could see tears glistening on his round cheeks as he spoke into a hand-held mic: "And now, as our beloved angel blesses our new members, let us all reflect on the angels and give thanks for their eternal love."

Our beloved angel. I tensed, wondering what was about to happen. There was a rustling noise as people seemed to get settled, some bowing their heads, some closing their eyes. Only barely lowering my own head, I peered up through my hair, keeping an anxious eye on Beth. What if she was whisked away again after this, and I wasn't allowed to speak to her?

A deep, waiting stillness fell over the church. Several minutes passed. At the front, Beth was looking upwards expectantly.

And then I saw it.

An angel had appeared; a glorious haloed creature of radiant white light and stretching wings. My breath seemed to vanish in my chest. It was like the being I'd seen in Beth's memory, but *here*, real, right in front of me, shining so brightly that it dazzled my eyes. Its wings moved slowly as it hovered over the new members. From the expression on Beth's face, she had seen it, too. She smiled at the angel above her like a child experiencing all of her Christmases at once. Drifting to the floor, the angel landed beside her.

I stared up at the big screen, and stiffened as I saw the features of its proud, beautiful face. It *was* the same angel that I'd seen in Beth's memory; the same being that had turned up on my doorstep. The angel said something in her ear; she nodded eagerly. And then it reached out to her with hands of light, and—

I froze in my pew, horror gripping me like cold steel. What was it *doing*? As I watched, Beth's energy field slowly came into my view. The angel had its hands buried deeply in it, and it was…draining her, somehow. Beth's energy looked sort of greyish already, with a dim violet light streaking through it; now, at the angel's touch, the violet wilted and died. Her energy field began shrinking in on itself, like a deflating balloon. And Beth just stood there, smiling.

"*No,*" I whispered. I had meant to scream the word. My fingernails dug into my bag as I looked wildly around me. Wasn't anyone going to *stop* this?

The woman next to me was gazing towards the front. "Please come," she murmured. "Please, blessed angel, come and greet our new members."

She didn't see it. Abruptly, I realized that no one else did, either. The congregation all sat there smiling, the same beatific look on each of their faces. I started to shake. I wanted to go pounding up the aisle and yank Beth away from that thing, but what would the angel do to me if I did? For that matter, what would everyone else do? Terror at my own powerlessness swept over me.

Swallowing, I twisted in my seat, looking back at the dark-haired guy. A jolt went through me as our eyes met.; he was watching me. Immediately, he turned his gaze forward, taking in the scene at the front of the church, his expression hard. An odd relief filled me as I stared at him. He could see what was happening, I could tell. I bit my lip, struggling against sudden tears. Neither of us could do anything, I knew that.

But at least he had noticed. At least he saw.

When the angel finished with Beth, it moved on to the next new member. And then the next. Once all three had been touched by it, there was a great movement of shining wings and it departed, vanishing upwards into the brightness of the vaulted ceiling until I lost sight of it. The preacher said something to the three in a murmur; they smiled and nodded. He grabbed up his mic: "Our angel has been here! It has blessed our new members!"

Electricity leaped through the church as the congregation burst into cheers and applause. "Thank the angels!" "Praise be to angels!" The woman next to me was clapping so hard that it must have been hurting her palms. Beth and the others were all beaming; she and the other woman hugged each other tightly, their sky-blue robes wafting together.

"Let us greet our new members!" cried the preacher, his voice ringing through the speakers as he lifted an arm. "Beloved brother and sisters, walk among us now, so that we can feel our angel's love through your touch!" Smiling broadly, the three of them each took a different aisle, slowly making their way up it. People leaned towards them, shaking their hands, patting them on the back, leaping up to embrace them. Joy crackled through the vast room like wildfire.

Beth was in my aisle. I sat up straight as I watched her approach, my pulse pounding in my ears. She looked more beautiful than ever – her face was alight with such a deep, pure happiness. But I could sense her exhaustion; see the slight stagger in her step. *Oh, please, god, I know it's hopeless,* I thought. *But please, please, let me be able to get through to her.*

It took almost ten minutes for her to reach me, and then she didn't even see me at first – the woman to my left was craning past me over the pew, reaching out to Beth. "Bless you. Bless you," she said fervently, clasping Beth's hand in both her own.

"Thank you," said Beth. Still smiling, her gaze fell on me…and she froze.

"You," she breathed. Her eyes widened, and she took a step backwards. "What are you doing here?"

I rose to my feet. "Hi, Beth," I said, gripping my bag. "I – I just wanted to talk to you for a second."

"Get away from me." Her face was white, her lips pinched.

Elsewhere, the church was still filled with the buzz of the other new members receiving hugs and congratulations, but around us it had gone deathly silent. Conscious of everyone nearby watching us, I glanced back at the tall silver doors. "Look, can't we just step outside and talk?" I started to touch her arm, and she jerked away.

"My angel told me you'd be *gone* by now," she hissed. "That they'd taken care of you, so that you could never hurt them."

The church, the pews, the people – all of it seemed to fade away as I stared at her. "*Hurt* them? What are you talking about?"

Beth's face was so full of hatred that something shrank inside of me; her beautiful lips were almost a snarl. "My angel *told* me, okay? You're sick, and twisted! You *hate* the angels; that's why you told me all those terrible things – you're a danger to them; you want to destroy them!"

Her voice rose as she went on, until she was almost shouting at me. I shook my head dumbly, unable to speak. A danger to the angels? Was she completely insane?

Beth's cheeks had gone paper-pale, with a single spot of colour high on each one. "You're never going to hurt them, Willow," she said softly. "I'm going to stop you."

She turned and ran back up the aisle, her sky-blue robes churning over her slim calves. I stared after her in a daze, and then slowly became aware of the low murmurs all around me. "A danger to the angels?" "Yes, our angel said so." "That one, the girl with the long blonde hair." My throat went dry. People were whispering, glaring at me. Not a single face looked friendly. Then up at the front, I saw that Beth was talking urgently to a man with sandy hair, pointing back at me.

It was her angel. He was in his human form again. He was here.

The angel looked sharply at me; I could feel the menace radiating off him even from where I was standing. Trembling, I took an uncertain step backwards, and then suddenly I felt a strong hand grab my arm. "Get out. Now," said a low voice.

The dark-haired guy. I didn't need to be told twice. I turned and ran with him beside me, still clutching my arm. Our footsteps echoed briefly on the pink-veined marble; he shoved open a silver door and we burst out into the sunshine, pounding down the broad white stairs and across the sidewalk that bisected the lawn. Behind me, I could hear the preacher's voice booming out through the microphone: "That girl must be stopped! She's evil; she plans to destroy the angels! On the angels' orders, she must be stopped *now*, before she hurts them!"

"Oh my god, what's happening, what's happening?" I panted.

As we neared the end of the lawn, I glanced over my shoulder and stifled a scream. The angel was in his angelic form again, flying after us, his wings on fire with the sun. The dark-haired guy whirled around; reaching under his T-shirt he pulled out a handgun. The angel let out a furious screech, diving right at me.

And then…and then, I don't know what happened.

The fear left me. It was as if I'd suddenly grown taller. I was up in the air, and I had wings myself – glorious, shining things that gleamed like frost on snow. I felt the autumn coolness on them as I hovered, shielding my human body with its fragile aura below. I watched the approaching angel, looking him coolly in the eye.

He drew back, startled; at the same moment I heard the gun go off and saw his halo waver and buckle. And then he just – vanished, erupting into millions of petals of light.

"Come on!" yelled the dark-haired guy, grabbing my arm again. Abruptly, I was snapped back to myself, running alongside him as we pounded across the parking lot. What had just happened? It had all occurred so quickly; behind us, the crowd was just starting to pour down the stairs. Angry shouts drifted towards us: "There she is!" "Get her, before she hurts the angels!" "Look, she's there!" Halfway across the parking lot, my steps faltered as I glanced back. Wildly, I thought, *Nina, this was a really bad idea.* A man built like a football player was far ahead of the rest of the crowd; he was already at the parking lot, sprinting across to a silver pickup truck. He wrenched open the door.

The dark-haired guy jerked hard on my arm. "*Run,* if you want to stay alive!"

I turned and sprinted as fast as I could, clutching my

bag to my chest and barely keeping up with him. We passed my car and I pulled on his arm, gasping, "Wait – this is mine—"

He ignored me. We got to the black Porsche; he clicked the doors open. "Get in – hurry."

"But—" In confusion, I glanced back at my own car and saw that the crowd had made it to the parking lot; they were surging across, screaming and shouting; I could feel their hatred like a great wave rolling towards me. The man who'd gotten to the pickup truck was half the parking lot ahead of them, so close now that I could almost make out his face.

He was holding a rifle.

As he saw me staring at him, he stopped and took aim, sunlight gleaming on the black metal. I couldn't move. I just stood there, my brain frozen in disbelief. This couldn't be happening. This really, seriously could not be happening.

"*Get in the car!*" shouted the dark-haired guy. Opening the passenger door, he shoved me in; as he ran around to the driver's side door the sharp sound of gunfire echoed past. Flinging himself into the driver's seat, the boy slammed the door shut and started the engine; a second later we were screeching away from the parking lot. Twisting around in my seat, I saw that the man with the rifle had dropped to one knee, still shooting at us.

"He – he was trying to kill me," I stammered as we careened onto Highway 5. "He really wanted to kill me." Suddenly I was shaking so hard I could barely speak.

"They all wanted to kill you," said the boy shortly. He shifted gears.

In seconds, the speedometer had reached seventy and was still climbing. He drove expertly, sending us flying down the highway. For the next few minutes, neither of us spoke. I huddled against the soft leather seat, so cold that I could barely think. The boy kept checking the rear-view mirror, his eyes flicking back and forth. As soon as he could he turned off onto a back road, and then another, and another, flinging us around the tight turns. Finally he'd spiderwebbed his way across to Route 20; he pulled out onto it with a screech and floored it.

Relaxing slightly, he turned and looked at me for the first time since we'd escaped, his eyes boring into mine. "So what are you, anyway?" he said.

My head jerked up, startled. He was serious. "What do you mean, what am I?"

"Part angel, part human. How?"

My jaw dropped as I stared at him. "*Part angel?* I am not!"

"Yeah? So what was that thing that appeared above you when the angel attacked?" His voice was hard.

I licked my lips, suddenly terrified. "I – I don't know what you're talking about."

"There was an angel above you with your face," he said, accelerating as he passed a truck. "It looked like it was protecting you."

I couldn't speak. The wings I'd felt, hovering in the air with the coolness of autumn on them. "I...I don't believe you," I stammered. "I was just hallucinating or something."

"Then you did feel something," he said, giving me a sharp glance.

"No! I mean – it was all confused, I don't really—" I swallowed, pushing the memory away from me. "I am *not* part angel, okay? It's impossible."

"Yeah, it should be." His eyes narrowed. "But you're part angel, all right, and the only way I can think for that to happen is—" He broke off, almost scowling as he tapped the steering wheel. "No way," he said in an undertone. "It can't be."

Whoever he was, he was as crazy as Beth. Sitting up, I shoved my bag into the footwell. "Look, I don't know what you're talking about," I repeated, grating out the words. "I didn't even know that there *were* angels, until a couple of days ago."

"What about your parents?" he asked abruptly. "Who's your father, do you know him?"

I was starting to hate him a bit. "Who are *you*, anyway?" I said, my voice rising. "You're not just some random guy who thought he'd check out the church, are you?"

"Answer the question."

I glared at him. "No, you answer mine."

Though the boy didn't move, I suddenly had an impression of power from him, like a feral cat that might spring at any moment. "I was following you," he said finally. "My name's Alex. And you're Willow. Is your last name Fields?"

I stiffened. "How did you know that?"

His mouth quirked in something like a smile, except that there was no warmth to it. "Because I was in your house this morning."

"You were in my *house*?"

The boy – Alex – sped up to pass an eighteen-wheeler. The Porsche moved like silk on glass. "Yeah," he said, his voice curt. "I was given orders to kill you."

Remembering the gun he was carrying, my throat went dry as I stared at him.

He snorted slightly, catching my look. "Don't worry, I'm not going to do it. I work for the CIA." He grimaced. "Or worked, probably. My job was to hunt down and destroy angels. I was told that you're one. And instead you're..." He trailed off, his eyebrows lowering. "Like nothing I've ever seen before," he muttered.

I could hardly speak for a moment. "You're seriously saying that the CIA ordered you to kill me. And I'm expected to believe this."

Alex shook his head impatiently. "No, I'm saying that I got an order to kill something I was told was an angel. I thought the order came from the CIA, but now I know it didn't, it came from the angels themselves. Anyway, I followed you, to see what was going on."

I opened my mouth and then closed it again, wondering how someone so good-looking could be so delusional. "This is just...completely insane."

He gave me a cold look, his dark hair falling across his forehead. "Really? You saw what that thing was doing to the new members; I was watching you. Angels have been around for centuries, feeding off humans – causing death, insanity, disease. It's called angel burn. That's what they do."

I saw again the scene in the church; Beth's energy subsiding into greyness as the angel drained her. Had this really been going on for *centuries*? My mind balked; it was too much to take in. Looking away, I rubbed my arms, trying to warm myself. "Right. And you think that I'm part angel, for some reason."

Alex's gaze raked over me, his blue-grey eyes startling under dark lashes. "Yeah, let's see. That same angel that appeared above you outside the church? I saw it hovering over you as you slept this morning, too. It looks almost exactly like a real angel, only without a halo. Your aura is a mix of angel and human; so's your energy."

The feeling of flight, of lifting up above my body with wings. No, stop. I was seriously not going to think about this. "Right, so there's an angel that hovers over me as I sleep," I said, my voice shaking. "And you saw this when you were in my house, working for the CIA, even though you're, like, my age. Okay, yeah, I think I've got it now."

The Porsche glided in and out of traffic as Alex changed lanes. "You didn't answer my question about your parents," he said flatly. "Do you know both of your birth ones? You don't, do you? You were raised by a single mother, or adopted or something."

I hugged my knees to my chest. "That's – none of your business."

"Do you ever cause pain when you touch people? How about being psychic?"

"Cause *pain*? Of course not! But—" I hesitated as a small, cold drop of dread darted down my spine. "But, yes, I'm psychic. How…how did you know that?"

His lip curled, as if he wasn't surprised. "It's an angel trait. How did they find out about you, anyway?"

Right, I'd had enough of this. I crossed my arms over my chest and didn't reply.

"*How?* It's important."

I wanted to tell him to go take a leap, but something in his voice made me answer. I glared at him. "Because…I gave Beth a psychic reading. I saw the angel; I saw that it was hurting her. I warned her to stay away from it, and she got angry, and then later the angel showed up on my doorstep, in its…human form, or whatever. It pretended to want a reading and when I said no, it grabbed my hand…" I stopped, remembering the images that had howled through me. "And then it left." I shuddered as I saw again the flying shards of light outside of the church. "What – what happened to it? When you shot it, what—"

"I killed it," said Alex. "Right, so it came and read you. And it saw something that scared it. When was this? Thursday? Late afternoon, early evening?"

He'd killed it. My mouth opened and closed at how matter of fact he sounded, like he did it every day. I let out a breath, trying to marshal my thoughts.

"Um…yeah, Thursday. Early evening. How…"

"That was when I got the order." His jaw clenched; he slapped the steering wheel with his palm. "Damn it, I *knew* it. They really have taken it over."

I frowned as I watched him. Who had taken *what* over? Then all at once I realized that we were heading east, away from Pawntucket. "Hey, where are you going? I have to go home!"

"No way," he said. "You'd be dead in a day."

I felt my eyes widen as I stared at him. He gave me an impatient glance. "Come on, you saw those people; do you really think they're going to just forget about this? They've been told that you're an *abomination* who's planning to *destroy the angels* – they'll tear you to pieces if they ever see you again. What about that girl, does she know where you live?"

Sudden terror splintered within me, icing my veins. "Mom," I breathed. "Oh, my god, I have to get home – you've got to take me home, right now!"

Alex shook his head. "I'm not taking you home."

"You *have* to! My mother needs me, she's sick—"

His voice turned harsh. "Yeah? Well, the best way for you to put her in danger is to go back there. Do you really want an angry mob turning up at your door? Maybe deciding to go for the abomination's mother too, while they're at it?"

"Shut up," I whispered. Nausea rocked through me at the thought. "I – I can go to the police, or—"

"They won't help you. Half of them are C of A."

"Right, well, what do you suggest?" I said, my voice rising. "Are you saying that I'm homeless now? You don't even know me, just take me home! What do you care what happens to me, anyway?"

His mouth twisted. "I don't, except that the angels seem pretty convinced that you're a danger to them for some reason. So if you think I'm going to let you go get yourself killed, you're crazy."

"You have nothing to say about it!" I shouted. "What, am I like your captive now? Take me home!" Alex didn't respond, and I shoved his arm. "Hey! Are you *listening* to me?"

Abruptly, he slowed down, spinning the wheel and swerving over to the hard shoulder. The Porsche rumbled over the gravel, stopping with a lurch. "We don't have time for this," he said. Again I had an impression of barely-sheathed strength, even just in the way his forearm was draped over the steering wheel. Alex's eyes locked onto mine, his expression fierce. "Listen carefully; I'll use small words. If I take you home, you will die. Anyone you care about might also get hurt or die. The only way you can keep them safe is to never go back there."

I felt myself start to tremble. I wanted to believe that he was lying, or crazy, but I couldn't. Everything about him – his voice, his tone, his *vibes* – felt like he was telling me the truth.

"This can't be happening," I whispered. "This just can't be happening." That morning when I'd woken up, things had been almost normal. I remembered the feeling of dread that had shuddered over me when I kissed Mom earlier, and my throat tightened.

"It's happening." Alex rapped a fist against the steering

wheel, glowering out at the passing cars. "I need for you to come to New Mexico with me," he said at last.

For a second all I could do was stare at him. "As in, New Mexico, the state," I said.

"Yeah. The only person I can still trust is there."

"And what does that have to do with me, exactly?"

He gave me a look like he couldn't believe I was really this stupid. "Because if there's even a chance that the angels are right about you, then I'm not letting you out of my sight."

"Oh, you're not," I said, my voice shaking with disbelief. "Well, great. Do I get a choice about this?"

His leather jacket gave a faint squeak as he shrugged. "Sure. You can go home and get killed, and put everyone you love in danger. Go for it."

My chin jerked up as we stared at each other. "I don't even know you," I gritted out. "If you think I'm going to drive all the way across the country with you, you're insane."

The only sound was the traffic passing us on the highway. Alex's dark eyebrows were drawn together; his jaw tense. "How psychic are you?" he asked suddenly. "How do you do it, what do you need?"

Apprehension shivered through me. I shrugged, trying to hide it. "I…just need to hold someone's hand."

He thrust his hand at me. "Here. Go on."

I shook my head, not moving. "I can't do it like this. I'm too upset." Alex kept his hand in the air between us, his blue-grey eyes a challenge. Finally, my mouth tight, I took his hand in my own. It was warm, firm, with calluses on the bases of his fingers. Stupidly, heat flickered through me. Annoyed with myself, I ignored it and closed my eyes, trying to clear my mind.

Jumbled images started flashing past: a camp in the desert, with barbed wire and a burning sky. His brother, taller and broader than him but with the same eyes. Killing angels – the hard, deadly joy of it. Aunt Jo's house, with Alex sitting outside it in his car. He really did work for the CIA. I saw him sensing something strange about my energy – something not angelic, but also not human. Then he was inside, watching me as I slept. I caught my breath sharply as I viewed myself through his eyes, lying curled up on the sofa under our old afghan. There was an angel floating peacefully above me with her head bowed – beautiful, radiant, serene. She had no halo; her wings were folded gracefully behind her back. As Alex moved slowly around our coffee table, keeping his gun on her, her face came into view.

It was me.

With a cry, I dropped his hand. There was a pause.

"Well?" said Alex.

I hugged myself, not looking at him. He wasn't crazy;

his energy had felt clear and strong. The truth of everything he had said, every word, beat through me.

Along with the memory of my wings, gently stirring the air.

"What does this mean?" My voice sounded high, frightened. "These – angel things that you've seen about me. How can I be part angel, unless…" And then I stopped as if the breath had been punched out of me. When I was around eleven, I went through this phase where I really wanted to know who my father was. Since Aunt Jo had no idea I had asked Mom, over and over, whispering the question to her and trying to break through her dream world. *Mom, who was my father? Mom? Do you remember? Who was my dad?*

And once, and only once, she had answered me. Smiling, her eyes had focused briefly on mine as she'd breathed, "He was an angel." I'd given up trying after that.

I felt the blood drain from my cheeks. The image of my father that I'd seen when I tried to read Mom; the man who'd had such a creepy feel to him that he'd made me shudder. He'd had the same strange, compelling eyes as the angel that had stood on my doorstep. And now I remembered: amidst the pretty rainbows of Mom's mind, there had been an angel, too, standing in her old apartment and smiling at her. He'd had the same face as the man. I had thought she was just hallucinating.

I could hardly breathe. I clenched my skirt, bunching the material in my fist.

"Unless what?" demanded Alex.

"You – you said that angels can cause insanity," I burst out. "Do they ever – have relationships with humans? I mean—"

"Yeah," he said, giving me a piercing look.

"What about their eyes? Are they—"

"Weird," he said tersely. "Too intense. Too dark, sometimes. You feel like you can't look away from them."

"No," I whispered. My skirt twisted and writhed in my fist.

"Your father," said Alex, his mouth grim. "I'm right, aren't I? He's one of *them*."

Panic seethed through me, quickening my breath. "I – I don't know. I never knew him – I only saw him once, when I tried to read my mom. But his eyes were just like that. He – he broke my mother's mind; my aunt said that she was normal, before him—" I stopped, the words dying coldly in my throat.

There was a long pause. Alex sat staring at me, his expression battling between *I knew it* and something like disgust. "A half-angel," he muttered finally. "Great." Starting the car again, he merged back onto the highway, punching the accelerator hard. A few seconds later, we were edging up to ninety.

The world was pitching around me like a storm at sea. I knew it was true, even if I didn't want to believe it. I was a half-angel. My father had been one of those *things*; he'd destroyed my mother.

"This should be impossible," said Alex in a low voice. "If angels can breed now—" He broke off, his hands tightening on the wheel. After a pause, he blew out a breath. "Anyway, they think you're a danger to them, and I can't take the chance that you're not. So – what's it going to be? Are you coming with me, or do I have to follow you and try to keep you from getting killed?"

Remembering the sensation of my wings opening and closing, I thought I might throw up. *Don't think of it. Don't think of it.* Letting go of my skirt, I shakily smoothed my hand over it. "Who is it that you want to go and see?"

"A guy called Cully," said Alex. His dark hair had fallen onto his forehead again; he shoved it back without looking at me. "He used to be an AK. Angel Killer. He's the only person I can trust now that they've taken over Project Angel."

What was Project Angel? It sounded like something out of a bad movie. But then, so did being shot at in a parking lot, and that had been real enough to almost kill me. I licked my lips. "Will those people really go to my house? What happens if they do; what if they hurt Mom and Aunt Jo?"

He shrugged coldly, glancing over his shoulder as he took the turn-off for the interstate. "I don't know. They'll be searching for this car before they do anything else. But like I said, if you do go home, you'll die, and so might your family. That's the best I can tell you."

He sounded so brusque, like it didn't matter to him in the slightest. I swallowed hard. "And – and you think this...Cully person might have some answers."

"He's the only person in the world who might."

I was silent for a long moment. *Mom.* I envisioned her sitting dreaming in her chair, her eyes filled with distant, beautiful things. I thought of Aunt Jo's house, of the lavender swathes of fabric draped across my bedposts. And then I saw the screaming crowd at the Church of Angels; felt their hatred again, surging towards me in a dark sea. The beautiful winged being as it swooped after me, shrieking; the barrel of the rifle, pointing straight at me. Maybe Alex didn't seem very friendly, but he had saved my life; I knew it without a doubt. If he hadn't been there, I'd be dead now.

A sickly shiver ran through me. He was right, I couldn't go home. I'd die if I did; I'd put Mom and Aunt Jo in terrible danger. In my mind Aunt Jo's house looked very small suddenly – already distant, moving away from me for ever. If I couldn't go home, then where could I go? I couldn't put Nina in danger, either. There was no place that was safe; those people weren't going to be happy until I was dead.

A half-angel.

The only sound was the humming of the Porsche's engine; the slight whisper of wind rushing past. I hugged myself. If this person Alex knew really did have answers, then I seriously needed some right now.

The words hesitated in my throat. I couldn't believe that I was actually saying them.

"Okay," I whispered, so softly that I could hardly hear myself. "I'll go."

CHAPTER *Six*

FOR THE NEXT FEW HOURS neither of us spoke. I sat staring out the window at the passing trees and farms, hardly able to believe that this had happened. Eventually the traffic got busier and the freeway widened to six lanes, and I woke up out of my daze and realized that we were on the New Jersey Turnpike, heading into New York City. Almost as soon as I thought it, I could see its famous skyline through my window to the right, spiking up at the sky. Alex took the George Washington Bridge across the river, paying the toll in cash. Skirting north of Manhattan, he drove us into the Bronx. After a while we were in a neighbourhood of crumbling buildings and overflowing dumpsters.

I cleared my throat. "I thought we were going to New Mexico."

Alex didn't even glance at me. "Not in this car; they've seen it." His voice was flat. Obviously, he was as thrilled about us going to New Mexico together as I was.

Pulling into a small, run-down shopping centre, he parked the Porsche and got out. I followed him, wrapping my jean jacket tightly around myself. It wasn't dark yet, but nervousness prickled across my scalp as I took in the graffiti on the buildings, the broken glass on the ground. If I'd known that I was going to be coming to a place like this, I'd have worn the baggiest top I owned.

Taking a black nylon bag from the trunk, Alex unzipped it and pulled out a bulky-looking envelope, which he tucked into his inside jacket pocket. Then he went around to the front and swept his hand under the driver's seat, taking out a small metal box. He shoved it into the nylon bag; I caught a glimpse of jeans and folded T-shirts inside. He put in a few things from the glove compartment, too, and then he zipped the bag shut again and slung it over his shoulder.

"Come on," he said curtly.

Shoving down my irritation at having orders barked at me, I started to tell him that he'd left his keys in the car –

and then I realized that that was the idea. Feeling a bit dazed, I followed him across the parking lot with its cracked asphalt, glancing back over my shoulder at the gleaming black Porsche.

"Do you have a cellphone?" he asked as we passed a dumpster. I nodded, and he said, "Let me have it."

"*Please*," I muttered. Digging in my handbag for my little blue Nokia, I handed it to him. He pulled a sleek-looking phone out of his own pocket and tossed them both into the dumpster. They made a clattering noise as they hit the side.

I stared at him. "But—"

"They can track them." He started off again without checking to see if I was following. "They're probably already inspecting your account, to see if you've called home. Don't, not for any reason. We can't risk it."

I started to protest, but the words faded in my throat. This was real. People were actually trying to kill me. "Okay," I said weakly. I trudged along beside him, my thoughts whirling. Aunt Jo and I had never been bosom buddies, but she was still going to be worried sick when I didn't come home tonight. And Mom... I swallowed. Would she even notice? The thought of that felt even worse, somehow.

We came to a subway station and Alex jogged down the cement stairs. He bought us both a ticket, handing mine to me without looking at me. I wanted to know where we were going, but didn't really feel like talking to him any more than he seemed to want to talk to me.

We rode the crowded subway in silence; Alex sat leaning back with his knees slightly apart, tapping his fingers on his jean-clad thigh. Studying him in the darkened window opposite, I took in the slant of his cheekbones, the tense line between his dark eyebrows. My gaze lingered on the shape of his lips. He really was completely gorgeous, I realized reluctantly.

I almost jumped as our eyes met in the darkened window. For a second Alex's face was unguarded as he looked at me, and I caught a glimpse of something – concern, maybe? – that made my heartbeat quicken in surprise. Then the shutters snapped down again, and he frowned and looked away, crossing his arms over his chest. Remembering his expression of disgust earlier, I felt cold suddenly. I shifted as far away from him on the seat as I could.

When we got to Lexington Avenue, Alex stood up without saying anything. As we emerged out onto the streets again the sun was setting; clouds bleeding red against the sky. We were in another run-down neighbourhood, though not nearly as bad as the one in the Bronx. Glancing up at some shops, I saw that the signs were in both English and Spanish. "Um…where is this?"

"Spanish Harlem," said Alex shortly.

He didn't seem to be going anywhere in particular, just wandering from street to street. After a while we came to a residential area, lined with old brownstones and parked cars. The evening still had a tinge of summer to it, and people were sitting outside on the front steps, talking and laughing. Rock music throbbed through the air, something with a heavy beat and warbling Spanish lyrics. I stared around us, taking it all in. I'd never felt so conscious of my blonde hair in my life.

"Bingo," murmured Alex. Following his gaze, I saw that he was looking at an olive-green Mustang Boss parked on the side of the street, maybe a '69 or '70. It was sort of beat-up looking, but still a classic, with hard, muscular lines. There was a sign on it: *$1200 OBO*.

A group of guys were sitting on the brownstone steps nearby, drinking beers. They looked up when Alex approached. "*Hola, ¿qué tal?*" he said. "*¿De quién es este coche?*" He jerked his thumb at the Mustang. His Spanish was quick, fluent.

"*Es mío,*" said one of the men. "*¿Estás interesado?*" He had friendly brown eyes and thick black hair. Rising, he handed his beer can to one of his friends and walked down the steps towards the car.

Alex shrugged, following him. "*Sí, puede que sí. Si me haces un buen precio, podría pagarte ahora mismo.*" I gave him a sideways glance as the two of them walked around the Mustang, talking in quick-fire Spanish. Where had he learned to do that, I wondered? I hardly knew *anything* about him – except that he didn't seem to like me very much. The realization made me feel very lonely. I looked away, leaning against the brick stoop and hugging myself tightly.

About five minutes of bartering later, Alex was counting out some bills from the envelope he'd tucked into his jacket. The guy pocketed the money with a grin, handing over a key ring with a tiny set of fuzzy dice on it. "*Gracias, amigo.*"

"*Gracias,*" said Alex as they shook hands. He tossed his bag onto the back seat and we got in the car. Deep black vinyl seats with cracks in them, a curved sweep of dashboard. "Highway robbery," said Alex under his breath, starting up the engine.

"Why?" I asked faintly. He didn't answer; the car coughed once and then we pulled away from the curb, leaving the men on the brownstone steps behind. I let out a breath, suddenly sick of him ignoring me. "Why was it highway robbery?" I said again, my voice deliberate.

A muscle in Alex's jaw tensed as he drove. Finally he said, "He wouldn't take less than nine hundred, even in cash."

"Really? He must have been desperate," I muttered. Alex glanced at me and I shrugged, slumping against the seat. I wasn't in the mood to explain to him that classic Mustangs were collectors' cars, and that the chassis on this one was in great shape, even with the bodywork needed. The guy could have sold it to an enthusiast for way more than what Alex had paid him.

As we drove uptown, I spotted a Kmart on a corner, with its familiar red sign. I cleared my throat. "Wait, can we stop for a minute?"

"What for?"

"Just – I need a few things."

He looked irritated, but he stopped the car, pulling into a metered space. "We don't really have time to go shopping."

I scowled at him. "Yeah, excuse me for being so frivolous. *You* have your suitcase all packed already; I don't even have any clean underwear. I'll be right back." Getting out of the car, I slammed the door shut. Once inside the Kmart, I found the clothes section and quickly picked out five pairs of underwear in my size. I fingered a T-shirt, wishing I had enough money for it, too, but I didn't – and I wasn't about to go back out to the car and ask Alex for any.

As I waited in line for the cashier, I saw a *News of the World* headline that said, THE ANGELS WALK AMONG US, SAYS WELFARE MOM. I stared at it, the brightly-lit store fading away around me. All of this had really happened. That was why I was here in New York City, buying cheap underwear and about to drive across the country with a boy I hardly knew.

I was a half-angel.

"Can I help you?" called the checkout girl.

Coming back to myself with a start, I walked up to the cash register, clutching the tiny plastic hangers. I slid them across the formica counter. "Um, yeah – just these, please."

When I got back outside, Alex was leaning against the car drinking a Starbucks coffee, his dark hair ruffled from the breeze. Even just standing there in faded jeans and a leather jacket, he gave off a sense of confidence somehow – of being at ease in his own body. A girl about my age gave him a second look as she passed; he didn't seem to notice. For a moment I felt embarrassed that he knew I'd bought underwear, and then I shoved it away. None of this was exactly my fault.

As I walked up, Alex glanced at me. "How did you pay?"

With money, I almost said. "Cash," I told him.

"If you have any plastic, don't use it."

"Do you mind not barking orders at me?" I said tightly. "This is all sort of – difficult enough already, actually."

He gave me a look. Draining the coffee, he tossed the empty cup into a garbage can. "There's an internet cafe across the street; I need to check something out. Do you want to come with me, or wait in the car?" His tone was super-polite. I could have kicked him.

"I'll come," I said.

We crossed the street. The cafe was one of those places where you can buy cans of soda, and sandwiches. "What do you want to eat?" asked Alex as he paid for half an hour's internet time. "I don't want to stop again tonight."

I knew that I should be hungry – I hadn't eaten anything since an apple at lunchtime – but food had never held less interest for me. I shook my head. Alex bought two sandwiches anyway, and handed them to me in their plastic containers. "Here, put these in your bag." Our eyes met as I glared at him. I didn't care how good-looking he was; it didn't give him the right to boss me around. He let out a breath. "*Please,*" he added.

A few minutes later, he was sitting at one of the computer terminals, laboriously typing something into a search engine. The computer next to him was empty. I sat in the plastic chair and watched his screen…and then stiffened as a white church on a broad green hill appeared. The Church of Angels site.

"What are you checking?" I asked.

He didn't respond, scrolling down the main screen with the cursor. "Great," he muttered to himself. "They didn't waste any time."

I stared at the screen. My throat felt like it had sand in it. My own face was looking back at me, with text underneath it that said, *Willow Fields was seen leaving the Church of Angels parking lot in Schenectady, New York, with a dark-haired youth in a black Porsche Carrera. Have you seen her? Please contact your local Church leader urgently for more information and to find out how YOU can help.*

"Oh my god," I breathed. "But – how did they get my photo?"

Alex tapped his mouth with his thumb. "That – book with everyone's picture in it, that you have in high school."

"Yearbook," I said. Was he trying to be funny? But of course he was right; that's exactly where it was from. "Come on, let's get back to the car," I hissed, glancing around us. Suddenly it felt like everyone in the internet cafe was busy going onto the Church of Angels website, scrutinizing my photo.

"Not yet," he said tersely, scraping back his chair. "We'd better get you some sunglasses or something first."

Sunglasses at night, I thought inanely as we headed back to the Kmart, remembering an old 80s song. Nina and I used to do that a lot. We'd quote song lyrics at each other – saying them seriously, like we really meant them in conversation, and then the other one would say, "Hey, I think there's a song about that." My mouth tightened as

I realized that I was thinking about Nina in the past tense. What in the world was she going to think when she heard that I'd disappeared?

"Here," said Alex once we got into Kmart, choosing a huge pair of dark, Hollywood-style glasses from a rack. "And you can shove your hair up under this." He picked up a black cap. His tone was flat, impersonal. He was hardly even looking at me, just thrusting things at me as he spoke. "You'd better get some new clothes, too; they'll probably be circulating a description of what you're wearing."

Even though I knew he was right, I stiffened at the suggestion. "I don't have enough money," I said.

"I'll get them," he said brusquely. I hesitated. I didn't exactly want to take any help from him, not the way he was acting. Alex blew out an impatient breath. "Look, what size do you wear?"

"I'll pick them out," I muttered.

I got a couple of pairs of jeans and a few shirts. I needed another bra, too, and so even though it made my cheeks burn to have to do it, I grabbed one off the rack. I saw Alex glance at it and then quickly away again, his expression stiff. Good, at least I wasn't the only one who was embarrassed.

Finally we were back in the Mustang. Alex started it up, making a face at the coughing noise. "Let's hope this thing makes it to New Mexico," he said in an undertone.

I gazed out the window, not answering. There was a lot of traffic, and it took hours for us to make it out of the city. By around ten o'clock that night, I was watching the New York City skyline grow smaller behind us, all twinkles and stars against the dark sky. I stared back at it, keeping it in sight until the last skyscraper finally winked from view. It was stupid. I had never lived in the city; I had only visited there a few times.

But it felt as if my lifeline had just been cut away.

I didn't think I would ever sleep, but I must have dropped off, finally. The next thing I knew, it was around three in the morning and the car had stopped. Drowsily, I opened my eyes. For a moment I couldn't remember where I was, and then it all came crashing back. I sat up, pushing my hair off my face. We were parked by the side of a road; it was dark.

"Where are we?" I said.

Alex was adjusting his seat so that it leaned back. "Pennsylvania." Lying down, he stretched his legs out.

I gazed at the shadows beyond the car. As my eyes adjusted to the moonlight I could make out pine trees on the side of the road. Everything seemed so still, like we were in the middle of nowhere. I rubbed my arms. "Is it safe to stop?"

He gave a curt shrug. "I pulled off the main road. I've hardly seen any cars for hours."

I could just see his face; he had his eyes closed. His lips looked almost sculpted in the silvery light. "What about angels?" I asked.

"Only you," he said.

It felt as if he had slapped me. "That's not funny," I said in a low voice.

"I wasn't trying to be," he said shortly. "I've been scanning for angels, and each time I did, I saw yours."

Without answering, I lay back on my own seat, covering myself with my jean jacket. My angel. Like it was a part of me. I shuddered, pushing the thought away. Staring up at the Mustang's ceiling, I studied the round plastic dome that sat over the interior light.

"Can I ask you something?" I said after a few minutes.

"Mm," he grunted.

"How come no one else can see these things? In the church, it was like Beth and the other new members were the only ones who even saw the angel, apart from you and me."

Alex sighed; I could feel him rousing himself to answer. "Angels can't be seen in their ethereal form except by the person they're feeding from," he said. "I can see them because I've been trained. And I guess *you* can see them because of what you are."

"You really worked for the CIA, didn't you?" I said quickly, not wanting to think about the *what you are* side of things.

"Yeah."

"How old are you?" I asked, looking over at him. He had his arms crossed loosely over his chest; his dark hair appeared black in the moonlight.

There was a pause; I could feel his reluctance to answer. "Seventeen," he said.

"So – you must have started pretty young," I said, feeling dazed. "What about your brother, does he work for them too?"

It was the wrong question. Immediately, I could sense the tension coming off him, and my own muscles clenched in response. "Would you let me get some sleep?" he said coldly.

Something about his brother. Suddenly I had an awful feeling that he might be dead, and I swallowed, wishing that I hadn't mentioned him. Though actually, I suspected that almost anything I had said would be the wrong thing, with the unfriendly vibes Alex was giving off. Were we going to have to make the whole drive to New Mexico like this, with him barely speaking to me?

I hesitated, but I had to say it. "You, um – you don't trust me, do you?"

A long silence. Finally he said, "I don't trust anybody."

"Yeah, but especially me. Because—" I could hardly get the words out; hardly bear to think them. "Because of what I am."

A muscle in Alex's cheek moved; apart from that he lay motionless. When he spoke again, his voice was hard. "Look, I don't really want to talk to you if I don't have to, okay? You're a half-angel; part of you is just like *they* are. I don't think we have all that much to say to each other."

I was glad that his eyes were closed, because mine were suddenly full of tears. "Fine," I said, feeling more alone than ever. "Sorry to bother you in that case. It won't happen again."

I rolled over onto my side with my back to him, pulling my jacket over my shoulders. I wasn't sure why I'd expected anything different; he'd already made it clear that he didn't want anything to do with me. But even so, it hurt. A lot, actually. My chest ached as I lay there staring out at the faint shadows of the pines, wishing that they were the birch trees outside my bedroom window.

And that I'd never, ever given Beth Hartley a reading.

When Alex awoke it wasn't quite dawn yet; through the car windows he could see that the sky was a pale, pure blue, hovering between night and day. Scraping his hand roughly across his face, he lay without moving for a moment.

Willow was still asleep on the seat beside him. Turning his head, Alex took in the gentle rise and fall of her breathing; the blonde hair that spilled across one shoulder; the slim curve of her body under her jean jacket. He shook his head slightly. Jesus. If he had felt drawn to Willow when he saw her in her kitchen, it was nothing compared to actually being close to her; travelling with her. He tried to remember if he'd ever felt this attracted to anyone before, and couldn't. There had been a few girls in the past — brief encounters while he was on the road — but now he could hardly remember what they looked like. Though he'd barely even touched Willow, he didn't think he could ever forget her face, no matter what happened to him.

And she was a half-angel.

Alex let out a breath. What did that even mean? It shouldn't be possible, and yet here she was, in the car beside him. Looking at her now, curled up asleep, she seemed so completely human. But she wasn't. If he moved his consciousness up to the ethereal plane, he knew that he'd see the image of Willow's angel again, calm and serene as it hovered over her. The same angel that had burst into life yesterday when she'd been under attack...and that looked almost exactly like the beings that had killed everyone he'd ever cared about.

Unbidden, his father's death flashed in his mind; he'd died gasping in agony on a hunt in northern California.

Lost in his madness by then, Martin should never have gone on a hunt in the first place, but he had insisted, striding off on his own with a rifle. The angel had seen him and had attacked before the rest of them even knew it was there, ripping Martin's life energy away with its long, elegant fingers. They had heard the struggle and come running, but they'd been too late; his father had died from a massive heart attack within minutes, clutching his chest and writhing on the ground. Then, just five months later, it had been Jake's death. And his mother's, years earlier, was what had started everything.

He gazed at Willow. The thought of angel–human offspring was repugnant to him; it was just completely wrong. But what really scared him was how drawn he felt to Willow anyway. Simply looking at her was enough to make him forget what she was and want to just…talk to her. Touch her. Get to know her. He seriously couldn't deal with it. She was *half angel*; what the hell was he doing being so attracted to her? What he had told her the night before was true; he didn't want to speak to her any more than he had to – because he had a feeling that if he let his guard down, he'd totally forget that half of her was like the creatures that had killed his family. And he couldn't allow himself to forget that, not ever. It was far easier to keep Willow at a distance; to "bark orders" at her, as she'd put it yesterday.

Anyway, none of this mattered, Alex reminded himself sharply. The important thing was getting them both to New Mexico, and Cully. Though as far as he could tell Willow didn't pose any danger to humans, he knew that the angels must be so scared of her for a reason. He just hoped to god that they were right. The AKs had been slowly losing this war for years; if they couldn't find some way to hurt their invaders en masse, then humanity's days were numbered.

With a murmur, Willow stirred on the seat beside him; her green eyes fluttered open. Alex looked away. From the corner of his eye, he saw her jaw tense as her gaze fell on him. Silence weighed heavily between them as she sat up, smoothing her tousled hair. Obviously, she hadn't forgotten what he'd said to her. Good, it would make things easier.

"We need to find a service station or something, so I can get changed," said Willow stiffly. She was still wearing the sparkly purple skirt and white shirt from the day before; as she pulled on her jean jacket, Alex tried not to notice the flash of smooth skin at her neck, or the way her long blonde hair fell forward onto her shoulders.

"Yeah, okay," he said. And adjusting his seat forward, he started the car.

CHAPTER *Seven*

FOR THE NEXT DAY AND a half Alex drove steadily south-west, crossing slowly from state to state at the tortoise-speed of sixty-five miles an hour. His instinct was to go faster, but he ignored it; the last thing they needed was to get pulled over. Willow sat curled up silently in her seat, hugging her knees to her chest and staring out the window without looking at him. Behind her giant sunglasses he could hardly even make out her features, which was a relief; she'd pulled her hair back, too, twisting it tightly and tucking it up under the cap. They stopped at service stations a few times, to fill up or grab food, with

Willow mostly staying in the car so that she wouldn't be seen. She hadn't been eating very much, and usually just drank water.

She had clearly taken him at his word. They hardly spoke at all, apart from the bare necessities: what kind of sandwich she'd like, or what she wanted to drink. On the rare occasions they did have to talk, her voice was cool, her body language stiff – and he realized how much he'd hurt her, saying that part of her was just like the angels. He couldn't be sorry that he'd said it, not if it kept her at arm's length from him.

Even so, Alex couldn't help noticing things about her, though he was trying very hard not to: the curve of her neck with her hair up; the way she tilted her head to one side as she gazed out the window. Often an expression of sadness crossed Willow's face, and he knew then that she was thinking about the family she'd left behind: her mother, who must have been the damaged energy that Alex had sensed in the house – her mind irreparably scorched by angel burn – and her aunt. For her sake, he hoped they were both okay.

When his thoughts reached this point, Alex realized that he was spending way too much time thinking about her. It was mid-afternoon on the second full day of driving, and they were crossing through the endless length of Tennessee – fully in the South now, where summer was still blazing, rather than the autumn chill of upstate New York. To take his mind off of Willow, Alex switched on the radio, taking a gulp of 7-Eleven coffee. He missed having a port for his iPod; all you ever got on the radio down here was classic rock, gospel or country. He settled for classic rock, and Willow stirred in the passenger seat to glance at him.

"Would you turn the volume down, please?" she said tonelessly.

Without answering, Alex twisted the knob down a notch. Willow turned away again, looking out at the dramatic rise and fall of the Smoky Mountains. He hesitated, glancing at her. Part of him sort of wanted to say something to her, maybe about her family, but he didn't even know where to begin. Grimacing, he took another swig of coffee. Probably a bad idea, anyway.

Just then the Mustang made a loud clunking noise, and started to vibrate. Hastily shoving his coffee in the plastic drinks caddy, Alex peered down at the dashboard. None of the warning lights came on, but then with alarming speed the vibration got worse, the car jolting back and forth.

"Oh, you ancient pile of junk," he muttered. He tried slowing and shifting down a gear. It didn't help any; all it did was add a knocking noise to go along with the clunking. In the passenger seat, Willow had sat up, and looked as if she was listening closely. Suddenly the car lurched, slamming forward; Willow cried out as her elbow hit the dashboard.

Alex pulled over to the hard shoulder as the car groaned and shuddered; he just made it before the rear wheels locked up, bringing them to a halt. Turning off the engine, he looked at Willow. "Are you okay?" he said after a pause.

She nodded curtly, rubbing her elbow. "I'm fine."

"Right." Alex blew out a breath. "I guess I'd better go take a look." Though he knew it would be a miracle if he could actually tell what was wrong. He and Jake had both learned to drive when they were around ten – doing donuts in the jeeps out in the desert – but neither of them had ever been much good with engines.

Popping the hood, Alex got out of the car, immediately feeling the steamy Tennessee heat pressing down on him. He creaked the hood open and propped it onto its stick, gazing down at the Mustang's innards. God, this thing should be in a museum. For lack of any other ideas he checked the oil, wiping the dipstick off on the edge of his T-shirt. Big surprise; it was fine. Ditto for the water. Great, what now? Shoving his hands in his back pockets, Alex glanced up the freeway, trying to remember how far the next town was.

Suddenly the passenger door opened and Willow got out. Coming around to the front she took off her sunglasses and shoved them at him. "Here," she said shortly.

Continuing to the driver's side, she got on her hands and knees and peered under the car. "I need a flashlight," she said, her voice muffled. "Can you see if there's one in the trunk?"

Alex blinked. He started to ask if she knew what she was doing, but the answer was pretty evident. He looked in the trunk, and then came back. "No, nothing."

Willow was silent for a moment, still half-buried under the car. Finally she came scooting out. "I think the prop shaft has come loose somewhere – I can just see it hanging down at the front, at a sort of an angle. If it is, it's not a major repair. I could do it myself, if I had my toolkit and the bolts are all still there. Or else it might be the gear box, which is pretty bad – the whole thing would have to be removed and dismantled."

"You, um…you know about cars," said Alex. And then felt like an idiot. Way to state the obvious.

Willow gave him a cool look as she brushed her jeans off. "Yeah, go figure. I actually do something that isn't freaky half-angel stuff."

Okay, he wasn't going to touch that one. Letting out a breath, Alex looked up the road again. "Well…we'd better see if we can get a lift into the nearest town. And then I guess we'll have to get the car towed."

"Fine," said Willow. She took her sunglasses back from him; her face vanished as she put them on.

Alex put his bag in the trunk. Wordlessly, Willow handed him her jean jacket; he threw that in too and shut the trunk, locking it. He glanced at her. "Look, I—" He stopped, not knowing what to say. Frowning, he turned away, stepping to the side of the road to put his thumb out.

A trucker gave them a lift into Dalton City, about ten miles away. The three of them rode squeezed together up in the cab, with Alex in the middle. He talked to the guy about football, stupidly conscious of Willow sitting so close beside him, her arm and thigh pressed against his. They were both in their shirtsleeves; he could feel the warmth of her bare arm, its light sheen of sweat. *She's a half-angel,* he reminded himself harshly. *Half of her is the same as the creatures that killed your family.*

She felt so human that he could barely carry on a conversation.

Finally the truck rolled to a stop. They were on a giant concrete forecourt on the outskirts of town, with a gleaming service station in front of them. "The garage there'll give you a tow," said the trucker in his Southern drawl, jerking his thumb at it. "And Rose's Diner shouldn't poison you *too* bad, if you want something to eat." A grin flashed through his beard.

"Thanks, man, we appreciate it," said Alex, shaking his hand.

"Yeah, thanks," echoed Willow as they climbed down from the cab. She gave the trucker a friendly wave as he pulled away; then her gaze fell on Alex again, and her smile died.

They went into the garage and Alex arranged to have the Mustang towed in, though the mechanic said that it would be a couple of hours before he could look at it. Great. Back on the forecourt, he and Willow looked at each other. A huge American flag was flying over the service station, rustling gently in the wind. And there was a Church of Angels billboard, showing the familiar white church with an angel hovering over it, protecting it with its wings.

Alex glanced at the billboard, and then at Rose's Diner. There didn't seem much else to do here while they waited, but could they afford to take the chance? Behind her sunglasses, Willow seemed to be thinking the same thing; she was gazing fixedly at the restaurant. "I wonder if any of them are in there?" she said in a low voice.

Alex made a face. Tennessee was part of the Bible Belt; the Church of Angels was big here. "Better not risk it," he said.

Willow didn't respond; she was standing very still as she stared at the diner, apparently deep in thought. "It's okay," she said suddenly. "I just – sort of have a feeling."

Alex hesitated. His pistol was hidden under the

waistband of his jeans, but he knew he'd be loathe to use it on another person – even a Church of Angels fanatic. "Are you sure?"

Still looking at the diner, Willow nodded slowly, the sunshine glinting off her dark glasses. "Yeah. Yeah, I am." She glanced at him, her expression stiff. "Sorry, more half-angel freakiness."

Not wanting to get into it, Alex shrugged. "Okay, well – let's try it." Crossing the forecourt, they entered the diner; a rush of air-conditioned coolness greeted them. Alex slid into a booth; Willow sat across from him. Waitresses in brown dresses bustled about, refilling coffee cups and carrying trays piled high with cholesterol-laden food. Pulling a battered plastic menu from between the salt and pepper shakers, Alex's stomach growled as he studied it. They'd been living off service station sandwiches for almost two days now.

"What's a *fritter*, anyway?" murmured Willow to herself, regarding her own menu. "Or *grits*?"

"A fritter's a sort of fried thing," said Alex, reading about the different burgers on offer. "Grits are for breakfast; they're like oatmeal."

She looked up at him, her face inscrutable behind the sunglasses. "You've travelled a lot," she said after a pause.

Alex lifted a shoulder, wishing he hadn't said anything. They fell back into silence, reading their menus. A red-haired waitress appeared, and set down two glasses of ice water in front of them. "Y'all ready to order?" She took a notepad out from her apron.

"Yeah, I'll have a bacon cheeseburger and fries," said Alex. "And coffee." He shoved his menu back in place.

"Bacon cheeseburger and fries," the waitress repeated, scribbling it down. "How about you, honey?"

Willow started to respond, and then she abruptly stopped, staring at the waitress. "Um...I..." Looking across at her, Alex could see how tense she seemed suddenly; her knuckles on the menu were white.

The waitress gazed at her doubtfully. "Hon? You ready yet?"

"Um – yeah." Willow swallowed, and glanced down at her menu. "I'll have the club sandwich. And a salad."

The waitress's pen moved briskly across the pad. "Coffee?" she asked.

"No, um...just water."

Willow bit her lip, her eyes following the waitress as the woman headed back towards the counter. Catching sight of her profile behind her sunglasses, Alex was taken aback to see the conflicted expression on her face.

"What?" he said.

She winced slightly, glancing at him and then the restaurant around them. Finally she looked back at the waitress again. Letting out her breath, she seemed to make her mind up about something, and started to slide out of the booth. "Um…I'll be right back," she muttered.

"What is it?" he asked.

She shook her head with a quick grimace. "Nothing. I've just – I've just got to talk to that waitress for a minute."

Alex watched in confusion as Willow walked across the diner, slim and petite in her jeans and T-shirt. A moment later she was leaning over the counter, talking to the waitress. She pulled her sunglasses off as she spoke; the waitress's eyes were saucer-large.

What the hell was going on? Unable to just sit there watching, Alex got up and went across to the counter too, propping himself against a red leatherette stool. "Is everything okay?"

"Yes, fine," murmured the waitress. Her gaze was riveted on Willow. "Go on. Please."

The tips of Willow's ears were turning red. Her eyes briefly met his; he saw her embarrassment that he had appeared – and then she straightened her shoulders and turned resolutely back to the waitress. "Well, look, I know that you don't know me and that this might be an intrusion, but I really am psychic. If you could just let me hold your hand for a moment, I might be able to see something."

The waitress hesitated. *Georgia,* said her name tag. A black waitress with dyed blonde hair had been listening, and now she nudged Georgia. "Go on, honey," she said, her expression concerned. "It might be just what you need."

"Please?" said Willow. "I really want to help."

As if she were under a spell, Georgia held out her hand, and Willow took it in her own. She gazed down at the counter without speaking for a moment, frowning. "Your husband died of lung cancer in March," she said quietly. "I see you nursing him for years before that. You had the spare bedroom at home fixed up, so that he didn't have to be in the hospital so much." She looked up. "You loved him more than anything, didn't you?"

Georgia had gone pale, almost swaying with shock. "I – oh, my gosh—"

"That's right!" put in the other waitress, her eyes wide. "His name was Dan, and he—"

"No, don't tell me anything," interrupted Willow. "Georgia won't be able to believe it afterwards if you tell me anything." She went silent again, shutting her eyes.

Alex leaned against the counter, unable to take his gaze off Willow as she continued. "I see pills, on a little shelf in your bathroom," she said slowly. "Diazepam. The doctor gives them to you for stress and you've been hoarding them for months. You've researched it on the internet, and you know just how to do it."

Tears began streaming down Georgia's stricken face. She stifled a sob as her friend mutely rubbed her arm.

Willow opened her eyes. "You mustn't," she entreated, leaning forward. "It's not the way."

"I just – I just want to be with Dan again," choked out Georgia. The other waitress handed her a paper napkin and she wiped her eyes, smudging her mascara. "I – I miss him so much."

Willow's own eyes were suddenly soft with compassion as she held Georgia's hand; her whole being focused intently on the woman. Alex stood without moving as he watched Willow, his thoughts spinning. He didn't know why he was feeling so floored; all angels were psychic to some degree – this was just another sign of Willow's half-angel nature.

Except that somehow, it felt completely different.

"I know how hard it is," Willow went on, squeezing Georgia's hand. "But it's not your time. I see another path for you, a different path. In a few months, you're going to take the insurance money and move home again, back to Atlanta, and you're going to open your own restaurant. It's something you've always wanted to do, but you've felt guilty about the money. You shouldn't. Dan wanted you to have it. It's his gift to you."

"Oh, honey!" murmured the black waitress, putting an arm around Georgia's shoulders. "Can I have a job when you do?" she teased softly.

Georgia laughed through her tears, patting the woman's hand. "You bet, Dora," she said.

"Anyway, that's, um – all I see for now," said Willow. "I hope it's helped." She started to release her hand.

"Wait!" cried Georgia, tightening her fingers around Willow's. "Can you – can you see Dan? Does he have a message for me?"

The hope on the woman's face was so raw that Alex felt a painful twist in his chest. He looked away as memories of Jake gripped him.

"No, I'm not a medium," said Willow gently. "But he's around you, I'm sure of it. And I think he'd really want you to be happy again, if you can."

Georgia nodded, dabbing at her eyes. "I think – I think maybe I can be now," she said wonderingly. "It's been such a weight; you just don't know—" Then she broke off, gazing at Willow in awe. "No, I – I guess you *do* know, don't you?"

Willow gave a small smile of agreement. Watching her, Alex was hit forcibly by the contrast between the elfin beauty of her face and her light green eyes, which looked so much older than the rest of her. All at once he knew without a doubt that she had seen a lot of things in her life that she hadn't wanted to see, just like he had…because that old-before-her-time look was the same that he saw on his own face whenever he glanced in the mirror.

Coming out from behind the counter, Georgia clutched Willow's hand in both of her own. "How can I ever thank you?" she said fervently. Impulsively, the two women hugged.

"That's easy," said Willow with a grin, pulling away first. "Throw away those pills when you get home."

"She will," put in Dora. "I'll make sure of that!"

"Thank you, honey," said Georgia again, touching Willow's face. "I mean it. You've given me my life back."

Willow's cheeks went pink. "I'm glad I could help," she said, suddenly shy.

As Alex and Willow returned to their booth, Willow hooked her sunglasses back on. He stared at her as they slid back into their seats, lost for words. Glancing at him, she self-consciously tucked a stray blonde strand up under the cap. "Sorry, more freakiness," she muttered.

"No, that was—" Alex shook his head, unable to express it. He propped his forearms on the table, studying her carefully. "How did you know?" he said.

Willow regarded him for a long moment, as if trying to work out how sincere he was. Finally she shrugged. "When she came to our table, I could just feel it," she said. "These – great waves of sadness. I could tell she was thinking of killing herself."

Dora appeared, placing Alex's coffee in front of him. "Your girlfriend sure is a wonder, honey," she said to him, squeezing Willow's shoulder. Willow's smile turned strained at the word "girlfriend". He could see her wanting to correct the woman, and then reluctantly deciding to let it pass.

As the waitress moved off again, Alex slowly stirred half and half into his coffee. "So...I guess it was a good thing that the car broke down," he said at last.

Willow had been taking a sip of water; she looked at him sharply as she put the brown plastic glass down. For a moment he thought she might smile, but she didn't. "Yeah," she said. "I guess it was."

When they got back to the garage the mechanic was waiting for them, wiping his hands off on a rag. "Hey, you were right, it's the prop shaft," he said cheerfully. "I'm afraid I don't have the right bolts in stock for it, though – looks like three of them went flying when it came loose."

It was almost six o'clock. Alex sighed. "So...it won't be today, then."

The man shook his head. "No, afraid not. I'll make some phone calls tomorrow morning; I might be able to find some at another garage. Otherwise I'll have to order them in – that would mean maybe two, three days before they get here."

Two or three days. Perfect. Briefly, Alex wondered about just buying another used car. He couldn't, though; he only had about twenty-five hundred left now from the emergency cash he always kept on hand – despite the high wages that the CIA had paid ever since the Invasion, he'd never particularly trusted them – and knew that he needed to save it. He blew out a breath, glancing at Willow. "Um – well, we're sort of stuck here; I mean, we're just passing through—"

"There's a motel just up the road," said the mechanic. "Sorry, I know it's a pain. Check with me tomorrow morning around ten; I'll know by then if I have to order them in or not."

Alex nodded slowly. "Yeah, okay." He glanced at Willow. "Is that all right with you?"

He could see that she had stiffened, even behind her sunglasses. Finally she lifted a shoulder. "I guess it'll have to be."

Taking his bag from the Mustang's trunk, Alex slung it over his shoulder, and he and Willow started walking in the direction the mechanic had told them. It was sunset now, with red and purple streaks billowing across the sky to the west, and a welcome breeze stirring at the heavy air. For several minutes, the only sound was their footsteps on the side of the road, and passing cars.

Alex cleared his throat. "Good call on the prop shaft," he said.

"It was pretty obvious," said Willow, her voice cool. She was holding her elbows, looking down at the ground as she walked. Alex fell silent. Maybe he wasn't psychic, but he could tell that she didn't want to talk to him. They trudged along the road without speaking.

Finally, to his relief, a GoodRest Motel sign appeared, with its familiar blue and white lettering. As they neared it, Alex saw apprehensively how many cars were in the parking lot; it looked like a used car convention. "Um... have you got any feelings about this place?" he asked.

Willow's steps slowed as she gazed at the L-shaped two-storey building. "Not really," she said after a pause. "I think we'll be okay."

Alex hesitated, still looking at the full parking lot. Even if Willow thought it seemed all right, they might be stranded here for several days; they needed to do everything they could to protect themselves. "Listen, we'd better share a room," he said. "I mean, we'll get two beds, but—"

Willow stopped in her tracks, gaping up at him in horror. "Do *what*?"

He felt his cheeks tinge at her reaction, which irritated him; he knew that what he was suggesting was the only sensible thing. "It just looks less noticeable that way," he said. "Plus it's a lot safer if we stick together, where I can keep an eye on you."

"I don't *want* you to keep an eye on me," she snapped. She stalked off ahead of him with long, angry strides, her slender back poker-straight.

He caught up with her easily. "What do you think we're even doing here in Boondocksville?" he pointed out coldly. "People are trying to kill you, remember?"

Willow's mouth tightened, and she fell into an angry silence. "All right," she said finally. "Fine." As they approached the glass door marked *Reception*, Alex started to tell her that he didn't want this either, and then bit the words back – he'd sound like he was protesting too much.

Maybe he was.

At the front desk the clerk shoved a registration card across at him; signing in, Alex showed him some ID – a fake Ohio driver's licence – and paid in cash. Their room was on the ground floor; neither of them spoke as they walked down the concrete path. Reaching number 112, Alex unlocked the door and swung it open, groping for the lights. A motel room just like hundreds of others he'd stayed in came into view – the two large double beds, the round table, the TV hanging from the painted concrete wall.

He dropped his bag onto the table; Willow followed him into the room, shutting the door behind her. She took off her sunglasses and the cap, shaking her hair out and not looking at him. "I think I'll take a shower."

Alex nodded. "Yeah, okay. I'll, uh – take one after you." He knew that he couldn't blame Willow for hating him, and that it was for the best if she did. So why did he suddenly wish that he could go back through time a couple of nights, and take back what he'd said about not wanting to talk to her?

Rooting through her handbag, Willow pulled out a hairbrush and started for the bathroom. All at once she stopped, irritation tightening her face. "I don't have any shampoo," she said. "Do you have some I could use, please?"

Opening his bag, Alex pulled out a tube of sports shampoo and handed it over.

"Thanks." Willow disappeared into the bathroom and shut the door. A moment later he heard the shower starting up, the water hammering against the tiles.

Alex blew out a breath, rubbing his hand across his face. As he picked up the remote control to turn the TV on, his gaze fell on Willow's bag, sagging open on the counter. He could see her wallet lying on top – it was purple, with a stitched flower on it. He glanced at the bathroom, hesitating. Finally, feeling like a thief, he drew out the wallet; it smelled faintly of Willow's perfume. Opening it, he found a New York State driver's licence for Willow Fields, showing that she was sixteen. Nearly seventeen – her birthday was only a month away, on October 24th. He looked at the date in surprise. It was the day after his own, on the 23rd. He was exactly a year and a day older than she was. The coincidence unsettled him slightly, stirring through him like the whisper of a butterfly's wings. In the photo, Willow had her head cocked to one side, her mouth closed in a pursed smile. Her green eyes sparkled, even with the dull, unimaginative camerawork of the New York Department of Motor Vehicles.

Tucking the licence back in the wallet, Alex flipped through the plastic photo holders. There was one of Willow and her friend Nina, with their arms around each other and their heads pressed together. They were wearing funny hats, mugging at the camera. And one that had to be Willow as a little girl, holding the hand of a woman with blonde hair. Her mother?

Alex regarded this photo for a long time. Willow looked very young in it, maybe six or seven. And though her mouth was curved in a polite smile at whoever was taking the photo, the expression behind her eyes was anxious. She stood slightly in front of the woman, her body language protective. And Willow's mother – if that's who it was – had the same wavy blonde hair as her daughter, and stood staring off into the distance. The dreamy smile tugging at her lips was that of someone with severe angel burn.

Slowly, Alex closed the wallet and put it away. He turned on the TV. Lying down on one of the beds with his forearm crossed under his head, he gazed at the screen, still seeing the photo of Willow as a little girl. Her love for her mother was obvious; no wonder she hadn't wanted to leave her.

And now Willow was over a thousand miles away from home, and might never see her mother again…with only some guy she hated for company.

CHAPTER *Eight*

WHEN I GOT INTO THE shower it was like hot needles pounding down on me, sweeping away the grime of the last two days. I lathered my hair, wishing that the shampoo didn't smell so much like Alex. And then I felt irritated that I'd even noticed what he smelled like. The last two days had been difficult enough, without having to deal with him being so stiff and cold towards me, like it hadn't even occurred to him that maybe I was a bit more upset about all of this than he was.

The hot water felt good; vigorous. I stayed in the shower for a long time, savouring it and letting it wash my mind clear of thoughts. When I finally stepped out, I dried myself off and wrapped my hair up in a towel, wiping the steam off the mirror with my hand.

And then I realized that I didn't have any nightclothes to put on. Or a toothbrush. Or toothpaste. I felt like crying in frustration. Great. Now I was going to have to ask Alex for help. For a wild moment I considered sleeping in the towel, and then thought of the logistics of that and sighed.

"Alex?" I called through the metal door.

There was a pause. "Yeah?"

Opening the door a crack, I peered out. "Um – I don't have anything to sleep in. Do you have something I could borrow? And some toothpaste, maybe?"

He glanced at me, and then away. "Yeah, hang on." Getting up, he rummaged in his bag and pulled out a couple of things. Crossing to the bathroom, he handed them to me; our eyes met briefly.

"Thanks." I withdrew quickly inside again, shutting the door.

He'd passed in a pair of black tracksuit bottoms and a faded red cotton T-shirt with long sleeves. They felt soft and worn, the way clothes get with lots of washings. Tossing them onto the counter, I brushed my teeth with a washcloth and then finished towel-drying my hair. When I finally pulled on the clothes, they were so big that I was swimming in them, the sleeves of the shirt dangling past my hands. I started to roll up the right one…and then stopped as sensations washed over me.

There's this thing called psychometry, which is when a psychic can pick things up from objects. Like, you give them dear old Aunt Grace's wristwatch, and they hold it in their hands and can tell you everything about her. I don't know how it's supposed to work; maybe items hold leftover energy or something. Anyway, it's never worked very well for me; the most I usually got when I tried it was just a distant flicker of emotion.

But now, wearing Alex's clothes, I was feeling something more.

I stared at myself in the mirror as I stroked the red sleeve. It felt comforting. I mean, comforting beyond just the normal warmth and softness of an old T-shirt. The energy from when Alex had last worn it was… I closed my eyes, wrapping myself up in it like a blanket.

It felt like coming home.

My eyes flew open. *You're losing it,* I thought. *He hates the very idea of you.*

That was my brain. My hand wasn't paying any attention; it was still touching the sleeve, my fingers running lightly up and down it. The energy that I sensed there felt so familiar, so safe.

I dropped my hand like the sleeve was on fire, and the

sensations stopped. Closing my mind, I rolled up both sleeves almost harshly, shoving them up my forearms. What I had felt was totally crazy. I didn't even *like* Alex. Yet when I opened the door and went into the bedroom, my eyes darted straight to him despite myself. He was lying stretched out on the bed, gazing up at the TV with his arms crossed under his head, and seemed deep in thought.

Glancing across at me as I came in, he actually smiled, his mouth twitching upwards like he couldn't help it. "They're, um…sort of big on you," he said.

"Yeah." I looked quickly away from him, feeling flustered. Sitting on the empty bed, I started to comb out my hair.

"I guess I'll take a shower too, if you're finished." Taking some things from his bag, he went into the bathroom and shut the door. As I heard the shower starting up I tried to forget about the sensations I had felt. Or how much even the slight smile had softened his face.

The local news came on, and my head jerked up, wondering for a second if there might be something on there about my disappearance. But of course there wouldn't be; we were over a thousand miles away. I let out a breath, thinking of home. Were Mom and Aunt Jo okay?

Over the last two days, I'd tried several times to get a fix on them psychically, picturing the house in my mind and trying to feel what was happening there. All I ever got was a sense of worry, and slight irritation – exactly like what I'd expect Aunt Jo to feel if I took off suddenly, and she was left on her own with Mom. I hoped with everything I had that this meant they were both safe, and that no one had come looking for me. I stared unseeingly at the TV screen. Aunt Jo was sure to have rung the police by now, who'd have found out from Nina that I had gone to the Church of Angels, and…then what? Had they found my car? Remembering what Alex had said about half the police being Church of Angels members, I wondered whether they'd say anything if they *had* found it. Or if they were looking for me for reasons of their own, instead.

As if brought on by my thoughts, a commercial started, and suddenly I found myself looking at a familiar pearl-white church. *"Do you feel despairing?"* intoned the voiceover. Oh no, not this. Lunging off my own bed, I grabbed the remote control from Alex's and switched the channel. Another local news programme, this one about a shortage of hospital beds in Knoxville. Good – nice and safe and boring. Tossing the remote back onto Alex's bed, I pulled my pillows out from under the bedspread and settled back, watching.

"Hospital staff are struggling," announced a woman with perfectly styled hair. She was standing in a hospital corridor; behind her, there were beds with patients in them

lining the walls. An orderly bumped against one as he hurried past; there was the sound of someone groaning in the background. *"What once used to be sufficient hospital space for central Knoxville's needs has in recent months become woefully inadequate, as cases ranging from cancer to lesser-known diseases have skyrocketed…"*

Hugging a pillow to my chest, I frowned as I watched, a memory tickling at my mind. This was so familiar, even down to the shot of a news reporter standing in a crowded hospital corridor. Then I remembered: I had watched a similar news story only a couple of months ago, about a shortage of hospital beds in Syracuse.

Hospital beds in Knoxville, Tennessee, and hospital beds in Syracuse, New York. Two cities a thousand miles apart from each other.

The camera went to a teenaged girl in one of the beds against the wall; she was trying to smile, but you could see how weak she was. My scalp prickled as I remembered Beth's reading – that was exactly how I'd seen her looking after she'd been at the Church of Angels for a while. Alex's words rushed back to me, about the angels' touch leaving people hurt, diseased – and all at once I realized that the two news stories weren't a coincidence. There wasn't a shortage of hospital beds, there was an increase in people being sick – and it was because of the angels. This was really happening; not just to Mom and Beth, but to people all over the country. The story ended and another one came on. I sat in a daze, trying to take in the sheer scale of it.

I jumped as the bathroom door opened. Alex came back into the bedroom wearing a pair of navy-blue tracksuit bottoms, his dark hair looking towel-dried. He dropped his clothes on the dresser and moved over to his bag, while I tried not to stare at the sight of him with his shirt off – the toned muscles on his stomach, chest and arms; the smoothness of his skin, still slightly damp from the shower. With a sideways glance, I watched his tanned shoulders move as he rummaged in the bag, taking out a T-shirt. There was a tattoo on his left bicep: a black *AK*, in gothic lettering.

God, he is so good-looking. Heat scorched my face as the unwanted thought whispered through my mind. I really, really did not want to be attracted to Alex. He pulled the T-shirt over his head, and I felt myself relax a bit.

Taking something else out of his bag, Alex said, "Hey, um…this is yours." Turning, he held it out to me. My eyes widened as I saw that it was the photo from home, the one that had sat on the bookcase in the dining room – me and the willow tree.

Slowly, I reached out for it. My throat tightened, remembering when Mom had taken it – one of those brief, wonderful times when she had actually been all there.

See the willow tree, Willow? That's you, that's your name.
I traced my fingers over the glass. "But – how did you—"

"I took it from your house," he admitted. He sprawled onto his bed. Leaning back against his pillows, he stretched a leg out, propping the other one up on the cover.

I stared at him in disbelief, clutching the photo in both hands as if to protect it. "You *stole* it? But why?"

He shrugged as he looked up at the TV, his forearm resting on his knee. "Angels don't have childhoods. When I saw that, I knew for sure that you weren't an angel, so I took it. I thought I might need it, maybe." His blue-grey eyes rested on me for a second. "Sorry."

I started to say something else and then stopped, gazing back down at the photo. "No, I'm...I'm really glad to have it," I confessed. I stroked the frame, and placed it carefully on my bedside table. Suddenly I thought of something. "How did you get into the house, anyway?"

He smiled slightly. "I picked the lock on the back door. Your aunt should get a good security lock; that one's not very good."

I sighed and dropped my head back against my pillows. "Yeah, I wish I could tell her."

There was a short silence, with only the sound of the TV. One of those stupid court shows had come on, where people go and shout at each other in front of a judge. Alex cleared his throat. "Look, Willow..." He paused, and I glanced over at him. He was frowning, tapping his knee with his hand. "I, um...I know that all of this must be really hard for you. I mean, having to leave your family, and...everything."

Oh no, don't be *nice* to me; I'll start crying. I shrugged, clutching the pillows and staring fixedly at the screen. "Yeah, I've had better weeks. Like the week when I had the chickenpox – that was a lot more fun."

He gave a short laugh. The sound surprised me; I realized that I'd never heard him laugh before. But then, I guessed that I hadn't been laughing much, either. We watched the show in silence for a while. A woman was accusing her dog groomer of giving her dog a bad haircut, and wanted hundreds of dollars in pain and suffering. The dog didn't look as if he cared either way.

"When did you first find out that you're psychic?" asked Alex suddenly. He was still gazing at the TV. When I didn't answer, he turned his head to look at me. His dark hair was ruffled, still a bit damp from his shower.

I felt myself tense. I wasn't usually self-conscious about being psychic, but I knew exactly what it meant as far as he was concerned. It was why I'd felt so torn about doing a reading in the diner, right in front of him.

"Why?" I asked.

His shoulders moved as he shrugged. "Just wondering.

It must be pretty difficult – knowing things that other people don't know."

Everything within me seemed to go still. That wasn't what most people said. Most people, if they believed I was psychic at all, just went on about how fantastic it must be. *Wow, you can really tell the future? That is so cool! Can you, like, win the lottery?* Having someone actually realize that it's not always fun was…unusual.

"I don't know," I said finally. "I've always been psychic. It was more a question of…well, realizing that the rest of the world isn't, I guess."

An unwanted memory flashed through my mind: myself at five years old, out shopping for groceries with Mom. There had been a kind-looking lady in the cereal section who'd squeezed my hand and cooed, "Oh, what a pretty little girl!" And that had made me feel good, so that I wanted to do something nice for her, too. So I told her all about the images that I saw. The new house that she and her husband were building. Her teenaged son, who was going to leave home but then return in less than a year. Her new job, which she wouldn't like at first, but—

She'd dropped my hand like she'd been holding a snake. She must have said something before she hurried away, but I don't remember what. I just remember the expression on her face; it had been burned into my brain. A look of absolute horror; of disgust, almost, like—

Like I wasn't even human.

The memory brought a hardness to my chest. What do you know? The woman had been right.

Alex looked back at the TV. "Yeah…realizing that other people weren't must have been tough. Like you were the only person in the world."

"That was exactly how I felt," I admitted. "But then I got to be a teenager, and it stopped bothering me so much. I guess I'd gotten used to being different. Besides, I like helping people, if I can." I stopped in confusion, realizing that we were actually having a conversation – one that wasn't about what kind of sandwich I wanted.

Alex nodded. "I could tell that back at the diner. What you did for that waitress, that was really…" He stopped, seemed to be searching for words. "Really good," he finished finally.

He meant it. I gazed sideways at him, wondering why he was talking to me now…and whether he still thought that part of me was just like the angels. Why did I even care? The memory of how the energy from his shirt had felt flashed through my mind, and my cheeks flushed.

"Um – thanks," I said. On the TV, another court case was coming on: as the dramatic music played, a woman strode towards the defendant's podium, wearing a power suit and lots of gold jewellery.

"Will she get her restaurant in Atlanta?" asked Alex, looking across at me.

I shook my head. "I don't know. It was the nicest of her likely futures, so I hope so, now that I've told her about it."

He propped himself on his elbow, watching me. "Can you read yourself?"

"No. I've tried, but I never get anything. It's always just grey."

"Probably just as well. That would be pretty weird, to see your own future."

"Just being psychic is pretty weird," I said. "Or at least, most people think so."

He lifted a shoulder. "Well, you're talking to someone who kills angels for a living. That's not exactly normal."

I glanced at him, suddenly wondering what his life was like. He was so young to be on his own the way he was, and it seemed like he'd been doing it for years. I shook the thought away, and looked back at the TV set. I wasn't about to ask him any questions, not after last time.

Alex sat playing with the remote control, turning it over in his hand. A long moment passed. Finally he cleared his throat. "Look, um…I'm sorry," he said.

Surprise jolted through me; my head turned sharply as I stared at him.

"What I said, that first night—" He stopped and

sighed, tossing the remote onto the bed. Scraping his hand through his hair, he said, "When I first found out it just threw me, okay? For a lot of reasons. I don't, um — I don't think you're like the angels. And I've been acting like a jerk. I'm sorry."

I felt a smile grow slowly across my face. "Yes, you have," I said. "But apology accepted."

"Good." He smiled back at me. His eyes looked slightly troubled, but it was a genuine smile. It changed his whole face.

Warmth filled me; embarrassed, I turned to the TV again. After a moment, I said, "So, can I ask questions now?"

Alex's dark eyebrows flew up. "You could have asked me questions before."

I shrugged. "I guess. It didn't really feel like it."

He thought about this; a corner of his mouth lifted. "No, I guess it didn't. Yeah, go on, fire away."

I sat up, crossing my legs. "What's this place that we're going to, exactly?"

Alex shifted, pulling one of his pillows out and sitting up a bit. "It's a camp in southern New Mexico, out in the desert. It's where I was trained. I think Cully will probably be there now, training up new AKs."

Angel Killers, I remembered. "And who's Cully, exactly?"

I could practically see the memories flickering across his face. "He used to be an AK, until he lost a leg on a hunt. He knows more about all of this than anyone alive."

Lost a leg. My eyes went to the dresser, where Alex had put his pile of clothes. His gun lay on top, in a holster. Obviously I had known already that what he did must be dangerous, but suddenly it hit me just *how* dangerous. "Does, um…that sort of thing happen often?" I asked.

Alex's expression didn't change, but suddenly I could feel the tension forming inside him, like a coiled wire. "He was lucky," he said shortly. "The unlucky ones either died, or ended up with angel burn."

Had something like that happened to his brother? Looking back at the TV, I hastily changed the subject. "So, you lived at this place?"

"Yeah." Alex hesitated, and then said, "My father was the one who started it."

Him and his father and his brother, all out at this camp in the desert together. I remembered the glimpse I'd gotten from his hand: the barbed wire, the bright, hard blue of the sky. "What about your mother?" I asked.

He gazed at the screen, hardly moving. "It's a long story," he said finally.

"Right, okay." Immediately, I wished I hadn't asked. The subject of his family seemed to be a minefield. We watched TV in silence for a while; I hugged a pillow to my chest. "Listen, the whole…angel problem," I said at last. "It's gotten worse recently, hasn't it? I mean, I don't remember even hearing about them until a couple of years ago, and now it's like – they're everywhere. On TV, in the papers."

Alex seemed to relax a bit. "It was the Invasion," he said, reaching for the remote and tracing it against the bedspread. "They've always been here, but then almost two years ago their numbers just exploded. We don't know why – if something happened in their own world, or what."

I watched him, taking in the line of his neck as he looked down; the slant of his cheekbones. "Where *is* their world?"

"We're not sure," said Alex. I noted his casual use of the word "we", like a team that had been fighting together for a long time. "Another dimension, probably. They seem to be able to cross over into this one."

Another dimension. I had always thought that was just something in science fiction – made-up stories, like angels were. "So they just – live here? The same as humans?"

He drew a knee to his chest, looping his forearm over it. Even when he was at ease, there was a sense of strength, somehow, like a big cat. "Yeah. They have houses, drive cars…they just sort of blend right in, without anyone really noticing them. Mostly they only take on their true form when they feed."

I shook my head, trying to comprehend it all. "What happens if you can't stop them?"

Alex gave a shrug as he glanced at me. "Humanity will die," he said. "Maybe in a few decades, fifty years. The AKs are losing, you know – slowly but surely. We need something big to stop them, or we haven't got a chance."

"God," I whispered. Was I supposed to be the something big, then? I saw again the hospital beds that had lined the corridor in the news programme, and didn't know what to say. "This is just…I can't believe that no one knows about this. Why doesn't the government do something; why don't they *tell* everyone?"

With eerie timing, the Church of Angels commercial came on again. Alex gazed up at the screen, his mouth twisting wryly. "It's not that easy. Most people can only see angels for what they really are when they're being fed off, and by then they've got angel burn; they wouldn't try to get away if you paid them."

I nodded slowly, imagining what Beth would have done if I'd tried to drag her away while that thing was draining her. I think she would have physically attacked me.

Alex was still looking at the commercial. "Plus, the angels seem to make a point of targeting the police, and the government. Quite a few high-ups have got angel burn since the Invasion – that's what first tipped the CIA off that something weird was going on."

"*Really?*" I stared at him, my blood chilling. "Who? Do you mean the president?"

He shook his head. "I don't know, exactly. People who you wouldn't want to have it, definitely."

The commercial came to a close; I watched the final image of the angel with its gleaming halo and radiant wings, smiling serenely out at us. "They're so…beautiful," I said reluctantly.

"Yeah, they are."

Still holding the pillow, I picked at a loose seam in the nylon bedspread. I didn't really want to ask, but I had to know. "So…when someone has angel burn, what happens?"

Alex's dark hair fell over his forehead as he regarded me, looking a bit reluctant. "When an angel feeds off someone, the effect is toxic," he said. "One of the things that happens is that the person perceives the angel as wonderful and kind. Another is that it damages them in some way – causes some sort of disease, or mental illness. MS, cancer, whatever. The more the person's energy is drained, the more severe it usually is."

I thought of Mom, with her vacant, dreamy gaze…and of the vile being who had made her that way. My father. This was a *part* of me; it was inside of me. No wonder Alex hadn't wanted anything to do with me at first; I could hardly blame him. I stared down at the seam, hating myself suddenly.

From the other bed, I could feel Alex's gaze still on me. He cleared his throat. "You know, um…from what I could tell, your mother's one of the lucky ones. I mean, when I checked out her energy, it didn't feel distressed or anything. She must be pretty content."

I nodded. All at once my eyes were leaking; I wiped them with the flat of my hand. "Yeah…it's always sucked for *me,* not having a mom, but at least I know she's happy off in her dream world." I glanced at him and smiled slightly. "Thanks."

A late-night talk show came on; we watched in silence as the host stood in front of the audience, making jokes for the intro.

Hesitantly, I said, "So, um, my angel – the one you saw over me – it doesn't feed, right?"

"No, it doesn't," said Alex.

I looked quickly up at him, biting my lip. "You're sure?"

He kept his voice matter-of-fact, but his eyes looked like they understood how I was feeling. "I'm positive. Your angel doesn't have a halo, and that's an angel's heart; it's where the energy is distributed from as they feed. Plus your aura doesn't show any signs of feeding, either – an angel's aura always does."

"So…that means I don't hurt people? Like, when I touch them, or anything?"

"I don't think so," said Alex. "I mean, a half-angel is something new, but I really don't see any reason why you would, Willow. Angels only hurt people when they feed. And, you know, if you haven't noticed anything in sixteen years, then I'd say you're probably pretty safe."

I let out a breath. Thank god for that. This was already nightmarish enough, without the thought that maybe I was somehow damaging people the way angels did.

On the TV, the talk show host was sitting behind his desk with a cardboard skyline of New York City behind him, interviewing an actress in a tight red dress. It felt so unreal, that angels were here in our world, hurting people, and that everyone was just going about their business, oblivious. Alex must feel like this all the time, I realized.

"Can I ask you something, now?" he said suddenly.

A slight wariness came over me, but I nodded.

"Your, um…your angel," he said. He sat cross-legged on his bed, turning the remote control over in his hand. "I know you weren't aware of it before a few days ago. But now that you are, can you feel it there?"

I stiffened. "No," I said flatly.

Alex nodded, rapping the remote against his knee. "I just…wondered whether you could make contact with it, if you tried."

My muscles felt rigid. I stared at the TV. "I have no idea, and I'm not going to try. I wish it would just go away."

A commercial came on; when it ended the actress was gone and a comedian came onto the stage. I was aware of Alex studying me. "I don't know if ignoring it is going to work," he said. "I mean it was there, protecting you. It's a part of you, somehow."

"Well, I don't want it to be," I said. Abruptly, my voice was shaking. "Alex, you've got to be kidding – one of those things destroyed my mother's mind; one of them has ruined Beth's life. I *hate* it that I have something like that inside of me. So, no, I'm not about to contact it, or make friends with it, or whatever. No way."

"Okay," he said. "Sorry."

I didn't answer. I gazed at the screen, listening to the audience laugh at jokes that didn't seem remotely funny to me.

Alex glanced at me, his blue-grey eyes concerned. "Listen, I didn't mean to upset you, or anything. This all must be—" He shook his head. "I can't even imagine what this must be like for you."

And it helped, somehow, just knowing that he had thought about it; that he realized how hard it was. I sighed. "The thing is…I feel so completely human. I know I'm not, I *know* that. But inside of me, I just feel normal. I mean, okay, maybe I'm sort of weird, but I still feel normal."

Alex smiled slightly. "You're not weird."

"Oh, please." I rolled onto my side to face him. "Listen, when you saw the – the angel hovering over me..." I trailed off, not even really sure what I wanted to ask.

"What?" he asked. His dark hair was almost dry now, looking soft and tousled.

I shook my head quickly. "Nothing."

He hesitated, studying me. "Look...do you want to change the subject?"

"To what?"

"I don't know." He motioned to the TV. "We could talk about this comedian; he's supposed to be getting his own sitcom soon."

I snorted and rolled onto my back again, propping myself up onto the pillows. "Yeah, if anyone's here to see it. Alex, doesn't it drive you insane, knowing all of this when the rest of the world doesn't?"

He shrugged as he leaned back against his own pillows, resting an elbow behind his head. His eyes were thoughtful as he looked up at the TV. "Sure. But, you know – it's just how it is. If I thought about it too much, I'd go crazy, so I don't."

That actually seemed like pretty good advice. I stared back at the screen, and felt something relax a tiny bit inside of me. "What's his sitcom supposed to be about, do you know?" I asked finally.

We watched the rest of the show, chatting occasionally

about the guest stars and the jokes. When it was over, we went to sleep. It felt weird sliding under the covers with Alex in the next bed – so intimate, even though he was about ten feet away. Once we were both settled he switched out the light, and the room plunged into black.

We lay there in silence for a while. The absence of light was so total that I couldn't even see his bed. "Alex, do you think the angels are right?" I said softly. "Do you think I really can destroy them, somehow?"

His voice sounded deeper in the darkness. "I hope so. God, I really hope so." There was a pause, and then he said, "Goodnight, Willow."

"Goodnight," I echoed.

I lay awake for a bit, listening as his breathing grew slower, more regular. As I fell asleep, my hand seemed to creep up of its own accord to touch my arm, stroking the softness of his T-shirt. I drifted off feeling the warmth of Alex's energy again, wrapping gently around me.

CHAPTER *Nine*

THE NEXT MORNING ALEX AND I started back for the garage to find out about the car. Though it was only ten o'clock, the day was sticky with humidity already; my hair up under the cap felt damp and heavy. As we walked the half-mile or so, we talked about the heat; whether the car would be ready that day; the too-sweet motel donuts we'd had for breakfast. Neither of us mentioned how things had shifted between us, but it was there anyway. Things just felt a lot more relaxed, like we didn't actually hate each other now.

But then, as we started to cross the concrete forecourt

to the garage, sudden prickles scattered across my neck. I stopped. "Wait a minute," I said, lightly touching Alex's arm.

He glanced down at me. He was wearing a burgundy T-shirt, and the hair at the nape of his neck was curling slightly from the heat. "What?"

I shook my head slowly, still gazing at the garage with its bright sign and plate-glass windows. It had seemed fine yesterday, but today I had the weirdest feeling about it – nothing I could put my finger on, just a really strong sense that I shouldn't go inside. "I – I'd better go back to the motel," I said, taking a step backwards. "I'll wait for you there, okay?"

Alex's eyebrows drew together. "What's wrong?"

I swallowed. "I don't know. Just – I don't think I'd better go inside there."

He glanced back at the garage, frowning. "Okay, here," he said, digging in his jeans pocket for the plastic room key. "I'll be as fast as I can."

"Thanks." I took the key. "Um – have them check out the Mustang's air filter while they're at it, okay? I think it might need a new one." Then I turned and started walking hurriedly back up the road, glad for the sunglasses that covered half my face.

The blue and white GoodRest Motel sign grew gradually closer. It was so quiet, with only the occasional car speeding past. After I'd been walking for about five minutes, I heard a new noise: rhythmic footsteps striding behind me on the concrete. Hugging my elbows, I peered nervously over my shoulder. It was Alex. I felt my shoulders relax; I waited for him to catch up.

"You were right," he said as he fell into step beside me. "There was a guy in there checking about his car; he was wearing a Church of Angels cap."

I heaved out a breath. "Oh, god. Do you think he saw me?"

Alex shook his head. "I don't know. I don't think so; he was talking to the mechanic when I went in. The Mustang won't be ready until around noon tomorrow," he added. "He's found a garage that has the right bolts, but he won't be able to get them until this afternoon."

Tomorrow. I rubbed my arms. "So...I guess we'll just wait in the motel room, then."

"Yeah, I guess," said Alex. His legs were so much longer than mine that he took two steps to my every three. He smiled slightly. "It's not really safe for us to be doing any sightseeing, is it?"

We got the motel room for another night and headed back to it. As Alex swung open the door to the room, something occurred to me. "Hey, um – what's your last name, anyway? I just realized I don't know."

The corner of Alex's mouth lifted. He took his wallet

out of his jeans pocket; opening it, he pulled out a few pieces of ID and handed them to me. "Here, take your pick."

I stared at them in amazement as I flipped through them. A California licence for Alexander Stroud...a Michigan licence for Alex Patton...an Ohio licence for William Alex Fraser... I started to laugh. "Wow, you're like James Bond," I said, handing them back to him. "What's your real, actual last name?"

"Kylar," he said, tossing the wallet onto the dresser. "I don't have any ID with that on it, though. I don't really exist, so far as the system's concerned."

My jaw dropped. "What – really?"

He looked amused at the expression on my face. "Yeah, really. My bank account was under a fake name; it was set up by the CIA. I never got a social security card or anything. Or a real driver's licence."

I really couldn't think of much to say to this. I had thought I was joking about the James Bond thing; apparently I wasn't. I sat down on my bed and pulled my shoes off. "Do you have a middle name?"

Alex grinned. "Yeah, it's James, actually." Taking his own shoes off, he sprawled back onto his bed, reaching for the remote. As he switched the TV on, another talk show flickered onto the screen.

"You're just making this up now," I said after a pause.

"Your middle name is *not* James, as in James Bond."

"No, it's James as in James Kylar, my grandfather. What about you, have you got one?"

"No, just Willow Fields," I said, stretching out. "I always wanted a middle name; I was the only girl in my class who didn't have one."

Alex looked over at me, his eyes interested. "So, um… what was it like? Going to school?"

I glanced at him in confusion, and then suddenly realized. "You never went."

He shook his head. "No, I grew up at the camp, pretty much. I've only seen school on TV. Is it really like that – with homecoming, and proms and stuff?"

So that's why he hadn't known what a yearbook was called. Feeling a bit dazed, I said, "Yeah, it's exactly like that. Prom is a *very* big deal, actually. Some of the girls even go into New York City to get their dresses. They spend, like, thousands of dollars on them."

"Did you?"

I barked out a short laugh. "Uh, no. I never went."

He rolled onto his side, facing me. "Why not?"

I could feel my cheeks heating up. I stared at the TV, where the talk show host was sitting next to a guest, both of them dabbing at their eyes with tissues. "Because no one ever asked me."

Alex's dark eyebrows rose. "Seriously?"

"Yeah, seriously. High school is…" I shook my head. "There are all these ruling cliques, and if you don't belong to one of them, then – that's sort of that for you. I never really fitted in; I was always just Queen Weird."

His eyes were narrowed slightly as he regarded me.

"What?" I said, feeling self-conscious.

"I'm just having a really hard time picturing this," he said. "Prom is like the big dance, right? At the end of school? And you're saying that *nobody* ever asked you to it?"

I would have been a bit irritated, except that he sounded so honestly surprised that I found myself laughing instead. "Alex, I've never even had a date. You're really not grasping the extent of the 'Queen Weird' thing here."

"Queen Weird," he repeated. "Why – because of the psychic stuff?"

I pretended to be deep in thought. "Well, let's see; there was the psychic stuff, and the way I dressed, and fixing cars…"

"What's wrong with the way you dress? You mean like that purple skirt thing?"

I held back a smile at "purple skirt thing". "Yes, exactly. It's not in fashion; I bought it at a thrift shop. Most of my clothes were like that." I thought of a World War I era jacket I had loved, and a pair of high-button shoes from the twenties that I'd worn until they literally fell to pieces.

And Nina had threatened to disown me when I'd turned up to school in a bomber jacket once.

Alex was starting to look seriously confused. "Okay, so…maybe girls would notice that kind of thing, but you're saying that this actually mattered to the *guys*?"

"In Pawntucket, it did," I said. "The girls who were popular were the ones who all wore the right thing, and had perfect make-up. I hardly even *owned* any make-up. I mean, I think I literally had one tube of mascara, and it was about two years old."

"Why do you need make-up?" he said, sounding bewildered.

"I don't know," I said. "I've never really understood it, either. I guess that's why I'm Queen Weird."

"Right," said Alex after a long pause. He gave his head a brief shake, like he was clearing it. "Well…if you want my opinion, the guys in Pawntucket are idiots."

"I always liked to think so." My cheeks tinged with heat as I glanced at him. "Thanks."

He smiled, looking a bit embarrassed. "Okay, take me through a typical day," he said, straightening up.

"You're really interested?"

"Yeah, go on."

I shrugged. "Okay. It's pretty boring, though." Sitting cross-legged on the bed facing him, I described everything about Pawntucket High – classes, and bells ringing, and homework, and GPAs, and shuffling through the hallways in a crowd, and final exams and lockers, and the cafeteria, and skipping classes sometimes when it got so boring I couldn't stand it any more.

Alex listened intently, taking in every word. When I finally finished, he shook his head slowly. "That all sounds so strange. I can't really imagine it – having to do homework, and actually caring about what grade you get."

I laughed. "*My* life sounds strange? Yours is like something out of a movie." And then it hit me – really hit me – that I might never go to high school again. I had always sort of hated it, but it was a bizarre thought anyway; it made me feel so adrift, somehow. What was going on there now, I wondered? Everyone must be talking about me, trying to figure out what had happened.

"What?" said Alex, watching me.

I managed a smile. "Nothing."

We watched TV for a while after that, ordering a pizza from Dalton City when we got hungry. Alex turned out to know the plots of half the soap operas that were on. "I can't believe you actually watch this stuff," I said. It was mid-afternoon by then and I was lying on my bed, feeling too-full and a bit stir crazy.

On his own bed, Alex was stretched out on his side looking totally relaxed as he stared up at the TV, like a sleek panther lying in the sun. He shrugged as he took a bite of pizza. "There wasn't much else to do when I was waiting for a text," he said. "I get pretty sick of the Sports Channel sometimes, when they're just showing golf or whatever."

I found my gaze lingering on him, just taking him in. "So how did it work?" I asked, trying to imagine what his life must have been like. "Who sent you the text?"

"Someone at the CIA. The information came from angel spotters."

"Okay, so you'd get a text, and then what?"

Tossing the crust back into the box, Alex shut the cardboard lid. "I went to wherever it said. And then did a bit of surveillance, checking the angel out and waiting for it to try to feed. That's when you have to attack, when they're in their angel form. You don't have much time."

Remembering how quickly he'd reacted when the angel had come after me, I didn't have much doubt that he was very good at it. I thought of the shards of light, falling against the sky. "So...how does a bullet kill them?" I said slowly. "I mean, they look like they're just made of light."

He stretched, flexing his arms. "You have to get them right in the halo. Like I said last night, that's their heart, basically. We're not totally sure how it works, but when the bullet hits, the halo's energy sort of jumps off the rails. It sets off a chain reaction that their bodies can't handle, and then it just blows them apart."

And my angel didn't have a halo. What did that mean?

I slammed the thought away. I didn't want to think about it, didn't want to know. After a pause, I said, "It's so weird that something so small can destroy them."

Alex snorted. "Yeah. Not very good planning; I guess they don't have bullets in their own world."

"Does it always work?"

"Usually. Sometimes if you nick the edge of their halo, they just pass out in their human form. That's only happened to me a couple of times, but it's a pain when it does – you have to trail them for days for the chance to get them again. Plus they're aware of you then."

I couldn't help staring at him. It all sounded so incredibly dangerous. "And…you've been doing this for how long now?"

"Which?" he said, glancing at me. "Hunting angels, or getting texts with their location?"

"I don't know. Either."

"I've been hunting angels since I was eleven," he said.

"*Eleven?*"

Alex shrugged. "I had already been in training for years by then. Besides, it was a lot different back then – a bunch of us would go out hunting together, following leads. A hunt might take weeks. We'd be out on the road together, staying in different places. Camping sometimes." A brief, wistful look crossed his face, and suddenly I knew just how much those times had meant to him.

I shook my head slowly, the wheels of my mind still spinning over him being an Angel Killer since he was eleven. "Okay. What about the texts?"

He lay back on his pillows, propping them up under him. "Well, ever since the Invasion, the CIA took things over. After that we each worked completely on our own, with no contact from any of the others. Angel spotters would send us the details, and we'd just go after them."

I gaped at him. "You mean you've been by yourself since the Invasion? But you said that was almost two years ago."

"Yeah," he said shortly.

I felt my heart chill. I couldn't even imagine it. Maybe I wasn't the most sociable person in the world, but being alone for that long in awful motel rooms like this, with only my own stupid thoughts for company? I'd go insane. "So you got a text with my address on it," I said after a pause.

He nodded, staring up at the TV like he wasn't really seeing it. "I was in Colorado. It took me about a day and a half to get to Pawntucket, and then I went and checked you out."

"Broke into my house and followed me," I corrected him.

Alex gave me a sideways glance. "Well, the orders I got were just to shoot you. Following you for a while seemed like a better idea."

"I'm not complaining," I said. I studied him, noticing the toned muscles of his arms, the contrast of his dark hair against the white pillows. "You, um…you're in danger too, aren't you?" I said suddenly. "I mean, the angels want to kill me, but you can't be very popular with them, either. You rescued me from the church – and you know that they've infiltrated Project Angel."

He shrugged, linking his hands under his head. "Yeah, I'm probably not their favourite person."

How could he sound so calm? I swallowed, not knowing what to say. "You, um…you really did rescue me, you know," I said finally. "I'd be dead now, if it wasn't for you. Thank you."

Alex looked quickly at me, his eyes surprised. I smiled, and after a beat he smiled back. "That's okay," he said.

The rest of the day passed. An old movie came on, something called *The Ghost and Mrs. Muir*; then a couple of game shows and sitcoms. We watched sometimes and talked sometimes – mostly just about what was on TV, but it felt nice. Relaxed. Finally, around nine or so that night, Alex got up and stretched, yawning.

"I think I'm TV-ed out for now," I said, yawning too. "Much more of this, and my eyes are going to fall out."

"Yeah, me too." Reaching for the remote control, Alex turned the TV off. "Hey, do you know how to play quarters?"

I shook my head. "What's that?"

"We just need a glass." He got a plastic one from the bathroom and sat down at the round table, moving his bag off it. Swinging my legs off the bed, I joined him, taking the chair next to him.

"Right, it's usually a drinking game, but it doesn't have to be," he said, digging in his jeans pocket. He took out a quarter. "All you do is throw it flat against the table, like this—" His forearm flexing, he tossed the quarter sharply against the wood; it jumped up in the air, kissing at the plastic lip of the glass and then spinning back onto the table. "Almost," he said. "You're supposed to get it in the glass."

"Okay, let me try," I said, reaching for the quarter. It was harder than it looked; on my first attempt it hardly even bounced at all. Finally I got the hang of it, and sent it flying up into the air and into the glass, almost knocking it over.

"Good one," said Alex with a grin.

We started keeping score, using a GoodRest pen and a sheet of stationery. Alex wrote both of our names at the top; his handwriting was quick and spiky. After an hour or so, he was ahead seventy-two to fifty-seven, but then I started to have a run of luck and leaped ahead of him.

"Are you sure you're not cheating?" he asked, marking down my latest goal.

"How could I cheat?" I snapped the quarter against the table again, and it went straight in. "Yes!" I cried, lifting my fist.

He quirked a dark eyebrow at me. "Maybe you're psychically making me think that you're winning, when you're really not."

I burst out laughing. "Yes, I have psychic mind control, you're right… Look, dude, I don't need to cheat; this game is easy." I tossed the quarter again, missing it this time, and slid it across the table to him. "See? Not cheating."

"Hmm," he said, picking up the quarter.

I propped my chin on my hands, watching him. "Do you, um…think that the psychic stuff is really weird?"

"Stop trying to distract me," he said. "Just because you're in the lead." His blue-grey eyes were narrowed as he aimed, bouncing his forearm slightly as he prepared to throw the quarter.

"Sorry." I sat back in my seat with a smile as he threw; the quarter went in.

"No, I don't think it's weird," he said, adding it to his score. He glanced up at me. "We trained in all kinds of strange stuff at the camp. Not that, exactly, but stuff that most people would think was just as strange – auras, chakra points, all kinds of stuff."

I pulled a knee up to my chest. "So even though being psychic is an angel thing, you don't think it's weird?"

He shrugged. "Well, the angels would never use it to help anyone," he said, getting ready to aim again. "So I don't think you have much in common with them there."

Warmth flowered within me. "That's...a nice thing to say. Thank you."

Without answering, Alex snapped his arm and threw. He missed and rolled his eyes, pushing the quarter back at me. "That's what I get for talking to you."

He won in the end anyway, a hundred to ninety-four. "Best two out of three?" he suggested, jiggling the quarter in his hand.

"You have *got* to be kidding," I said. "I'll be seeing quarters in my sleep."

He laughed. "Yeah, I'm kidding." He tossed the quarter into the glass; it made a rattling sound. "I think I'll quit while I'm ahead."

Getting up from the chair, I dropped onto Alex's bed and opened the pizza box; there were a couple of pieces left. "Do you want one of these?"

"Thanks." He stretched across from the table, and I handed one to him. I wasn't even hungry, really; there's just something about cold pizza.

For the rest of the night we watched a movie that was on. Halfway through it, Alex moved to the bed, stretching out on his stomach a few feet away from me. It was an action film, and he kept rolling his eyes, muttering things like, "Man, you would *never* do that...is this guy trying to get killed, or what?"

I was sitting cross-legged, with my elbows on my knees. "Would you be quiet, please? I'm trying to watch this."

Shaking his dark head, Alex fell silent as the hero got ready to confront the bad guys, sliding his gun straight into the waistband of his trousers. "Hey, he's not using a holster," I said, glancing at Alex's on the dresser.

He laughed out loud. "Yeah, I guess he must want to shoot something off. It'd be so great if these things were true to life – the next scene would show him at the hospital, like, clutching himself in agony."

I laughed too, imagining it. "Okay, it's a pretty stupid movie. But we've still got to see how it ends."

When it was finally over, Alex yawned, reaching for the remote control. "Good, the world's been saved and the guy's still in one piece, somehow...maybe we should go to bed; it's after midnight."

I started yawning too. "Stop that, you're setting me off," I said. I stood up; my legs felt stiff and creaky.

"Sorry, I guess it's contagious." He snapped the TV off and then looked down again, fiddling with the remote. "You know, um...it sounds stupid, but this has been a good day," he said. His cheeks reddened slightly. "I'm usually in these places on my own; it's sort of nice to have someone to hang out with."

My heart tightened. It sounded as if his life had been so incredibly lonely, these last two years. "It's been nice for me, too," I said shyly.

And amazingly, it was true. Even though I'd been sitting in a motel room in Tennessee, today had somehow felt – well, not normal, exactly, but a really welcome reprieve from everything that had been going on. Like I'd been able to just put my thoughts on hold for a day. And I knew a lot of that had simply been being with Alex. I'd never really been alone with a boy like this before; I'd never dreamed that it could feel so natural.

"I'm, um...I'm really glad that we're talking now," I said.

Alex didn't look up for a moment. When he did, he smiled at me, and I saw the same faintly troubled look in his eyes as before. "Yeah," he said. "Me too."

That night, the dream came back.

"*You got my back, bro?*"

"*Got your back.*"

He'd recently turned sixteen, and was on a hunt with Jake and a couple of the other AKs in Los Angeles, City of Angels. The jokes always abounded when they were in this place, and in fact, angels did seem to like it there – on this latest trip, they'd spent over a week getting fixes on them and hunting them down, killing ten so far. It was a lot, even for Los Angeles…for, although no one realized it yet, the Invasion had just occurred. Everything in Alex's life was about to change, like a spinning coin.

At the time though, it had just seemed like an unusually busy hunt. The tenth angel they'd brought down had been right outside of Grauman's Chinese Theatre; the angel had been about to feed on a tourist taking a photo of Marilyn Monroe's famous prints in the cement. Even with a silencer, Alex would have balked at pulling his weapon on the crowded street, but Juan, who'd taken over as lead when Cully had his accident, had a genius for somehow not being spotted in plain view. In a matter of seconds, the angel was fragments of light, gently drifting away on the air. The tourist, unsuspecting, snapped his shot and then moved on to Charlton Heston.

"Now *that* was just pure class," said Jake as the four of them moved away through the crowd. He slapped Juan on the shoulder, winking at Alex and Rita. "So that's ten – time to celebrate, right?"

Juan gave him a sideways look. He was short, but built of solid muscle, with brown eyes and thick black hair. "What's this? Celebrate how? You mean miniature golf or something, right?"

Alex laughed out loud. "Miniature golf? Come on, Juan. *Sé realista.*"

"You're both underage," said Juan, shaking his head. Unlike Cully, he actually seemed to care about this.

Alex and Jake rolled their eyes at each other. Alex hadn't been seriously challenged in a bar in almost a year, and Jake was hardly ever even questioned. It wasn't only their fake IDs; the two brothers just looked older than they were. They both worked out all the time back at the camp, so that they were hard with muscle, and apart from that, Alex knew that years spent on the hunt had given them a look that simply didn't belong to teenagers.

"Underage, right," he said, shouldering his way through the crowded sidewalk. "But not too underage to give us guns."

"Yeah, seriously," said Jake. "You mean we get to put our lives on the line and we don't even get a beer for it? *Eso no está bien,* man. I mean it."

"Oh, why not, Juan?" said Rita. She was in her thirties, tall and lanky, with a no-nonsense ponytail. "We're heading back tomorrow anyway. And you know what it'll be like then – no real fun for a hundred miles."

Finally Juan blew out a breath and shrugged. "What can I do with you all twisting my arm? But if you two are arrested, I am just leaving you in the jail to rot. *Los zopilotes podrían limpiar tus huesos. ¿Entiendes?*"

"*Sí, sí,*" said Alex with a grin.

"Now, that's more *like* it," said Jake. The two brothers

gave each other a high five, clenching hands briefly. Though Alex wasn't as into bars as Jake was, the thought of a night out on the town was still a welcome one. Things had felt pretty grim ever since their father's death five months before; this would be the first time since then that either of them had really relaxed.

As it turned out, the night was a good one, though the next morning Alex felt like death as Rita nudged him awake. "Hey. Move it," she said, shoving him with her foot. They had only gotten one motel room to save money; he and Jake were both sprawled out on the floor in sleeping bags.

"What?" Alex peered blearily up at her. She was dressed, her hair damp. A few feet away, Jake was snoring, still wearing the clothes he'd had on the night before.

"Juan's just been out doing a final scan, and he thinks there's some more activity up in the canyons – we're going to go check it out before we leave." Rita shook her head with a slight smile as she glanced at Jake and then back to Alex. "You two look terrible, you know that?"

"Yeah, yeah," yawned Alex.

After a shower and some coffee, he felt better. He and Jake sat in the back seat of the truck as Juan drove them up through the winding hills above Los Angeles. Jake stretched his legs out. "Hey, did you see that girl last night? The blonde in the pink T-shirt?"

Alex's head was leaned back against the seat, his eyes half-closed. "Hard to miss her, the way she was stuck to your mouth half the night."

"Yeah, she totally wanted me...I told her I was a marine on leave. I wanted to go outside with her or something, but she wouldn't leave her friends."

"Right, so she didn't want you *that* much," said Alex, holding back a yawn. Through the window, Los Angeles was spread out below them in a sea of houses and buildings, fading off into the distance.

Jake laughed. One of his knees bent and fell sideways, tapping against Alex's own. "Yeah, you're just jealous... didn't notice you getting any action."

After half an hour or so, Juan pulled over to the side of the road. They were up in the canyons now, in a quiet, wooded area. They climbed out of the truck; Alex checked his pistol briefly before tucking it into the holster under his waistband. Around him, the others were doing the same.

"Okay, I think there's at least two up here, maybe more," said Juan, glancing around them. "Jake, you and Alex make a team; so will Rita and I. Check in with me every thirty minutes till we're done."

"Got it," said Jake, pulling out his cellphone to check the time. As Juan and Rita headed off down a wooded path, he looked at Alex. "You scanning, bro?"

"I'm on it," said Alex, closing his eyes. Lifting his consciousness up through his chakra points, he explored the area around them, feeling the various energies nearby. There weren't many. A lone walker in the woods; a dog; Juan and Rita... He felt the chill of angel energy heading towards the walker, but disregarded that one; Juan and Rita would take care of it. Scanning a bit further out, he picked up another one.

"That way, a quarter of a mile or so," he said, opening his eyes and nodding up the road. "I think it's near one of the canyons."

They started walking along the road. The fresh air felt good, clearing his head. Beside him, Jake had his hands stuck in his back pockets, a habit they both shared. "Hey," he said after a pause. "Can I ask you something?"

"What?" asked Alex.

His brother lifted a muscular shoulder. "Do you ever... think about doing anything else?"

Alex was startled. "What? You mean, not hunt angels?"

"Yeah," said Jake, glancing at him. His eyes were like looking in the mirror.

It had hardly ever even occurred to Alex. He went silent for a moment, considering it. "Not really, I guess," he admitted. "I mean, we sort of have to, don't we? It's not like there's that many people around who can fight them."

"Yeah, I know," said Jake, looking down at the road as he walked. "But all the other AKs got a choice, didn't they? They had other lives first. You and me never did; Dad just told us it was what we were going to do."

Alex nodded slowly, knowing what he meant. "Yeah," he said. "It just – feels like me, though. Who I am. I mean, I don't know what else I'd even do." He thought of the tattoo on his bicep. Jake had a matching one; so did most of the AKs.

As they passed a line of oak trees, a steep canyon opened up to their right; Jake gazed out at it without speaking. "No, me neither, really," he said finally. "I guess I just wonder about it sometimes – what it would have been like if Mom hadn't been killed. Like, talking to that girl last night – her life was just so totally different from ours. I could hardly even imagine it."

"Wait a minute," said Alex. "This is you, right? You're saying that you *talked* to her? You found out things about her *life*?"

Jake grinned. "Yeah, okay, I didn't find out that much…"

Alex stopped suddenly, putting his hand on Jake's arm. "It's getting close," he said. They cut across the road to a wooded glade, crouching behind some trees. Soon a woman with brown hair appeared a few hundred yards away, strolling down the road. She stopped every so often, leaning against the low stone wall that separated the road from the canyon and gazing out at the view. Scanning her, Alex got a jolt of angel energy; her aura was pale silver with hardly any blue. She was ready to feed, probably hoping to come across a hiker or walker.

"Trawling," said Jake, watching her. "Great, this could take hours."

A tickle of anticipation went up Alex's spine. He nudged Jake's arm. "Hey. Are you thinking what I'm thinking?"

Jake looked at him and groaned. "Oh, man, you've got that stupid gleam in your eye."

"Come on, let's do it," said Alex, not taking his eyes off the angel in its human form. "It'll take for ever otherwise."

Jake shook his head, starting to smile. "If Cully ever found out that we did this…"

"I know, he'd kill us." Alex glanced at him with a grin. "Do you want to lure it, or should I?"

"I'll do it this time," said Jake. "I know how much you love springing into action, hotshot."

Alex laughed. "Yeah, you know it…" As his brother got up, Alex took his gun out. Digging into his jeans pocket, he screwed the silencer on.

"Right," said Jake, slapping him on the shoulder. "You got my back, bro?"

"Got your back," said Alex.

"Cool," said Jake. "Then let's go get us an angel."

And as Alex kept his gun trained on the woman leaning against the wall, Jake stood up and started casually across the road.

Alex awoke with a jolt, hearing his dream-voice echoing in his ears, screaming his brother's name. Oh, god, the dream again. The same stupid dream. Breathing hard, he swallowed and covered his eyes with his forearm. He had thought he was over this – seeing those last twenty-four hours replayed, over and over in his head. It had been almost two years now; why couldn't he just accept that Jake was never coming back? That he was gone for ever, and it was all Alex's own fault?

On second thought, maybe there were some things that you could never accept, no matter how long it had been.

Letting his arm drop to the pillow behind his head, Alex opened his eyes. It barely made a difference; the room was almost pitch-dark, its curtains showing only the faintest sliver of light. In the other bed, he could hear the soft sound of Willow's breathing. As his eyes adjusted to the dimness, he could just make out the small curve of her body as she lay curled under the covers. He hesitated for a long moment, gazing at her – and then shifted through his chakras, lifting his consciousness up through his body until it hovered outside of himself, above his crown.

The angel appeared over Willow: life-sized, radiant white. As before, her lovely face – a mirror image of Willow's own – was bowed in repose, her wings folded behind her back. He could see the glowing outline of every feather; could see every fold of the robe that fell from the angel's shoulders.

Alex lay looking at the angel for a long time. The halo-less image didn't move, and neither did he. He took in the long spill of her hair, her lips, her downcast eyes that looked as if she'd be smiling if she glanced up. And slowly, he could feel the dream releasing its hold on him. As the images of Jake slowly faded, his breathing calmed; his heart stopped thudding.

When Alex finally closed his eyes once more, it was Willow's face that he saw…and he knew that he'd be able to sleep again.

CHAPTER Ten

RAZIEL LEANED BACK IN HIS leather chair, drumming his long fingers irritably on the armrest. "Any news?"

Jonah nodded, shuffling his papers as he sat perched on the chair on the other side of the desk. "Yes, um...our police in New Jersey stopped the Porsche, but the passengers weren't them. It appears that they dumped the car in New York City with the keys inside, and someone stole it."

Raziel rubbed the bridge of his nose. "So we don't even know what they're driving now. Or if they're driving."

"Er...no," said Jonah, his brown eyes blinking.

Raziel dropped his hand onto his thigh with a slap. As if the half-angel's escape from the Schenectady Church of Angels four days ago, along with her would-be assassin, hadn't been enough. "What about the remote viewers?" he asked.

Jonah licked his lips. "Well…several of them have gone to Schenectady to read that girl, Beth, and see the half-angel in her memories – but they say it will take time, if they get anything at all."

Raziel grimaced. He had thought as much. Most angels' psychic skills didn't extend to picking up specific information without physical contact, and even with those few who could view things remotely, it was often hit and miss.

"Time," he muttered, tapping his fingers on the desk. With the Second Wave planned for barely over a month away, time was the one thing he seriously didn't have. Anger swept over him again at the thought that the assassin had killed Paschar. Apart from the ripple of pain, of incompleteness, that every angel felt at the death of another, Paschar had been the only one of them to have actually had contact with the half-breed – the only one who could possibly have found her more speedily.

"What about the aunt?" he asked. "Is she still asking questions?"

Jonah's brown curls moved slightly as he shook his head.

"No. The police investigation has been closed already. She's been told that the, um….girl…had a secret boyfriend, and that she ran away with him. She seems to believe it. She's grateful to the Church for putting her niece's photo up; she thinks we're trying to help find her. The friend isn't convinced, but no one's taking her seriously."

"Good," said Raziel shortly. It wouldn't have troubled him to have to dispatch either the aunt or the friend, but it would have been an aggravation that he didn't need. "What about our person in New Mexico?"

Jonah swallowed. "Well, he's watching for them; he's in contact with the Albuquerque branch. But he thinks that they should have arrived by now, if they were coming. So maybe they're not. He doesn't know where the assassin might go, in that case. He says that he's very, um… resourceful."

Raziel hissed out a breath from between his teeth. He'd gathered that much on his own, by now. He fell into silence, cursing the decision to retain this particular assassin in the first place. Someone who was that good at killing angels obviously had a few brain cells in his head; with hindsight, they should have seen trouble brewing with this one. And now he and the half-angel actually seemed to have joined forces. The thought that the creature was still out there, with the Second Wave about to occur, was deeply unsettling.

Jonah shifted in his chair. "There have been a few possible sightings from Church members," he offered.

Raziel's assistant was ideally suited for his job, being devout to the angels without having been damaged by them – the boy's energy simply wasn't very compelling. However, at times Raziel wanted to throttle him.

"*Yes?*" he said sharply. "Do go on, Jonah; don't hold back."

Jonah cleared his throat, looking down at his papers again. "Well – actually there have been thousands of possible sightings since we put the information up, but only a few that seem like they may be onto something. One is a girl in Madison, Wisconsin who matches the description; Church members there are checking her out. And there's been a possible sighting near Toronto…and another one in Brooklyn… one in Eugene, Oregon…one in Dalton City, Tennessee…one in—"

Raziel could feel his hold on his temper slipping. "Jonah, do you actually have any good news to tell me?" he interrupted, his voice icy calm. "Or just a long list of places where teenage girls with long blonde hair have been spotted?"

Jonah ducked his head down; there was a rustling noise as he rifled through his papers again. "Um – well, the one in Dalton City was a bit different; the Church member there saw a girl in sunglasses who he thought looked a bit suspicious."

A girl in sunglasses. Was this really the best they had? Raziel rubbed his forehead again, wishing that he couldn't feel headaches in his human form. "I presume they're checking it out."

"Yes, the Church members there are on it. They'll let us know."

"Right." The chair squeaked as Raziel sat up. "I want them found, Jonah. We can't have that thing still at large when the Second Wave arrives."

His assistant nodded. "I understand," he said fervently. "We'll find her – every Church member in the country knows how important it is that she's stopped."

And there were no people more rabidly committed to a course of action than Church of Angels members, thought Raziel – surely the creature would be found soon; the half-angel and her protector couldn't have simply vanished. "Very well," he said heavily. "On to the Second Wave, then. I've had some further news. The plan is that the opening is going to be created here, in the main cathedral."

Jonah's eyes grew wide. "*Here?* The Second Wave of angels is really going to arrive here? Oh, my gosh, that will be – such an incredible honour—"

"Yes, so the Council wants a bit of a welcome to take place," broke in Raziel. "Something low-key, I should think."

"Oh, no!" gasped Jonah. As Raziel looked at him in

surprise, his assistant's cheeks flushed. "I just meant – sir, you have no idea how much this is going to mean to everyone. The whole Church should be allowed to celebrate! A Second Wave of angels, blessing our world with love and peace – my gosh, we should fill the place to the rafters. We should have choirs, and a special service – we should decorate the cathedral with acres of flowers; we should—"

"All right, I get the idea," said Raziel. Jonah went quiet, his face alight. Raziel sat for a moment, playing with a silver letter opener as he mulled it over. It did have a certain appeal – thousands of cheering Church members would show the Second Wavers just how popular the First Wavers had been, just how successful at paving the way for them. On the other hand, the logistics of it seemed nightmarish.

"Could you organize something?" he asked his assistant.

"*Me?*" Jonah went pale. "I – oh, it would be an honour – I mean, I've never attempted anything like this before, but I – I would do my utmost—"

"Yes, all right, then," said Raziel. "I'll leave it all up to you. Do whatever you like; I know that you'll arrange something appropriate." He bestowed a smile on his assistant. "Good idea, Jonah. The angels are most grateful."

"Thank you," breathed Jonah. "Thank you. I'm – I'm honoured to be of service."

"You are very welcome," said Raziel. "You may be excused now."

After his assistant had left the room, still murmuring his thanks, Raziel sat back in his chair again, thinking grimly of the half-angel. *Willow* – what a ridiculous name for something half-divine; it seemed to highlight the travesty that was her very existence. Stretching his arm out, he tapped the mouse to his computer, bringing up the Church of Angels website that had already been on his screen. Once again, he studied the thing's face: the wide green eyes, the slightly pointed chin, the long blonde hair. Such an utterly normal-looking girl – pretty, but nothing special. And yet, according to Paschar's vision, she somehow had the means to destroy them all.

As Raziel gazed at the thing's image, it niggled at him, not for the first time. There was something vaguely familiar about the shape of her face, her eyes. He shrugged the thought away. She was half-human, and many humans looked similar; it was hard to even tell them apart at times. Moving the mouse again, he closed down the site, and the girl's photo vanished. Regardless of what she looked like, the important thing was that *Willow Fields* did not have long to live.

And once she was found by the Church's devoted followers, she was going to wish with all her heart that her assassin had followed his orders to shoot her.

* * *

In the outer office, Jonah sat praying at his desk for a moment, giving thanks to the angels for this immense honour that they'd bestowed upon him. When he raised his head, his face was radiant; he sat gazing around him, drinking in his surroundings – the tidy desk, the soft, off-white carpet, the small Michelangelo painting of an angel hanging on the wall.

When he compared his life now to how it had been eighteen months ago, he could hardly believe it. He'd been struggling in college, hating the degree he was doing, with hardly any friends and a family that had always been remote at best and actively unsupportive at worst. His future had seemed swathed in shades of grey – a career he didn't want, nothing to look forward to, nothing to really care about. Reading Eliot in his English class, he'd thought that if he had any courage, he'd just end it all – then at least he could go out with a bang, rather than the whimper of continuing on with his mediocre, pointless life. He used to idly plan how he might do it, knowing that he would never actually have the guts, but it made him feel better. It cheered him up, in a strange way.

And then one day he had seen an angel.

He'd been walking through the campus, glumly worrying about his biology class. He had to do at least one science requirement for his degree, but he had no aptitude for it and was slowly failing, and now it was too late to try to switch to geology or something else a bit easier. Jonah had sighed, staring down at his feet as he walked. Maybe it was better if he *did* fail; it wasn't as if he even wanted the degree anyway.

All at once a radiant flash of light had stopped him in his tracks. And, looking up, he had seen an angel flying slowly towards him – a bright, glorious being of such utter radiance, emanating such love and peace, that Jonah had simply stood there, frozen with wonder as the angel drew closer.

Do not be afraid, she had said. *I have something to give you.*

White light had burst around Jonah as the angel rested her shining hands on him, and he had felt something flowing into him – a strength, a resolve, that he had never known before. The angel's face was pure beauty, her features peaceful and kind. When she finally flew away, her wings shining in the sun, his world had been changed for ever.

He had dropped out of college; he'd never felt such freedom in his life as the day he drove away from campus. He'd gone straight to Denver, where the new Church of Angels cathedral was being built. There he had encountered other angels, just as glorious and shining as the first – and though none of them had ever touched him more than fleetingly, he still basked in the glow of their serenity, their peace. When he realized that angels lived among people in human form, the knowledge had simply confirmed to him that the world was not a grey, sodden place; it was beautiful and shining, full of magic. And somehow, he had actually lucked into this job where he served an angel himself.

Jonah sat at his desk, wondering at his good fortune. Shaking his head with a smile, he forced himself to focus: he had work to do. Opening up a new document on his computer, he began to make a list of ideas for the celebration of the Second Wave of angels. Suddenly another thought came to him: perhaps they could get TV and news coverage. Excitement tingled at his scalp. Yes, of course – surely they should let the whole world know about this? His mind buzzing with plans, he quickly got up to ask Raziel about it.

Crossing the room, Jonah started to knock on Raziel's office door…and then stopped, his fist in mid-air, as he heard the angel's voice on the phone.

"Yes, Lailah, I know they won't be feeding the moment they arrive, I'm just saying that we'll have the cattle all here on display for them… Yes, that's right, a big celebration, everyone cheering and happy to see them – it'll be a nice little welcome, don't you think? They can see all the blissed-out faces, realize how happy the humans are to be fed off by us..." There was a pause, and then Raziel laughed. "Now now, don't be greedy... You know you have to be in your human form for that..."

Jonah backed away from the door slowly, his head spinning in confusion. Angels feeding off humans? Obviously, he hadn't heard correctly. The idea of angels taking anything from humans was ridiculous – unthinkable. He had seen for himself the good that they did, what they gave. The angels had changed his life. They had *saved* his life. Perhaps Raziel had simply been joking. The angel had an acerbic sense of humour sometimes, and Jonah knew that he didn't always catch the nuances of it.

He had just got it wrong. That was all.

Sitting at his desk, Jonah gazed at the open document on his screen. Hearing the word "cattle" in his mind again, he somehow didn't feel quite as enthusiastic about organizing the celebration as he had a few minutes ago, even if Raziel had only been speaking in jest. Slowly, he saved what he'd done and closed the screen down, logging onto his e-mail instead. It was a relief to see that he had several new messages that needed to be taken care of.

He began to type:

From: Jonah
To: LHGrimes
PSullivan

Hi, thanks for copying me in on this. We'll look forward to hearing what the outcome is in regards to the couple staying at the motel. If it's them, please don't hesitate; take appropriate action immediately.

Blessed in the angels,
Jonah Fisk

I was flying.

Even in my sleep, I smiled to myself in wonder. What an amazing feeling, to be so weightless, so free. Spreading my gleaming wings, I hovered above my sleeping body in the motel room. Alex was asleep in the next bed, lying on his stomach. I could see the light of his energy; his tousled dark hair; the tattoo on his bicep as he lay with his head on his wrist. Part of me just wanted to gaze at him for a moment, but I knew that I couldn't wait – I had something I needed to do. Slowly, moving my wings, I started to lift. Going through the ceiling was like passing through a ripple of water. I passed through the room above, too; it was empty, with unmade beds. Travelling faster now, I soared through the motel roof.

It was mid-morning; I burst out into strong sunshine. Spiralling once, I glided downwards, feeling the warmth on my wings.

And then I saw him.

There was a man looking in through our motel room window, wearing tan trousers and a short-sleeved plaid shirt. He had a camera. He was trying to take photos, but I could feel his frustration; it was too dark in the room. He didn't know who was in there, and he needed to find out. As I watched, he aimed the camera again at the inch or two of open curtain.

In a dizzying rush, I flew back to my body.

I woke up with a jerk under the crisp motel sheets. I was in the room; it felt like morning. Relief swam through me as I exhaled. It was just a dream. I'd been flying, and I'd gone outside—

I stiffened as I heard a noise: a slight shifting, like someone standing nearby. Slowly, hardly daring to breathe, I rolled my head sideways on the pillow. The curtains were open a crack. I could see the dark outline of a man, standing on the walkway outside.

Oh god, it wasn't a dream; it was real. I lay there, my pulse echoing in my ears. Could he see us? Could he see who I was? I watched, too scared to look away, as the man's head moved, trying to peer in. Finally I heard the sound of a car approaching, and he abruptly left. The room lightened a bit as a slit of sunshine angled in through the window.

Flinging my covers back, I lunged across to Alex's bed, shaking his shoulder. "Alex! Alex, wake up!"

"Mm?" He stirred, lifting his head from the pillow. "What is it?"

"There was a man, looking in our window."

He came awake in a second, sitting up. "When? Just now?"

I rubbed my arms; I felt cold suddenly. "Yes, I saw him. He was looking in through the crack in the curtains. Then a car came, and he left."

Alex swore, glancing at the window.

"I'd better close the curtains—" I started off his bed; he stopped me with a touch on the arm.

"No, don't – then he'll know we saw him." He sat silently, gazing at the window and tapping his fingers on his knee. "Right, whoever it is can't know for sure it's you, or else he wouldn't have been trying to look in. But he's going to be watching the room now – we've got to get out of here without him seeing you, somehow."

The fact that Alex already seemed to be planning what we should do helped my own mind to clear a bit; my panic to fade slightly. "The bathroom window?" I suggested.

His dark eyebrows rose as he considered it. He nodded. "Yeah, maybe – I could kick the screen out—"

We both jumped as the phone rang.

Our eyes met, startled, as it shrilled through the room again. Finally Alex leaned across the bed and picked it up. "Hello?" I couldn't believe how relaxed he sounded, like he'd just woken up and was still half-groggy. There was a pause; I could hear a man's voice. "Okay," said Alex finally. "Thanks. I just got up; I'll be there in about an hour."

He looked at me as he hung up. "The garage, supposedly. They said that the car's ready."

My eyes flicked to the gap in the curtains again. "It – it could be someone trying to lure us out of the room, though."

"Yeah, it could," he said.

We both stared up at the digital clock on the TV. It was ten-twenty.

"He said around noon, but…" Alex trailed off; his face was intense, thinking. "It sounded like him, though. And you thought he was okay, didn't you?"

I shrugged, not really wanting our lives to depend on this. "As far as I could tell, but…"

"Right, I think we're going to have to take a chance," said Alex. He moved suddenly, throwing his covers back and getting out of bed on the other side from me. "Keep out of sight while I get dressed, okay?"

He grabbed his things and went into the bathroom. Shakily, I went and sat down at the table; it was close enough to the outside wall that no one would be able to see me. I heard Alex take what had to have been the fastest shower in history, and then a few minutes later he was out again, his hair damp, dressed in jeans and a grey T-shirt.

I watched as he moved swiftly around the room, throwing clothes into his bag. Finally he took his handgun from the dresser and tucked it into his holster; I caught a glimpse of toned, flat stomach.

"I'll go get us some breakfast," he said.

I stared at him. "What? Alex, I'm not exactly hungry right now."

He smiled slightly. "No, me neither. But if he sees me coming in with breakfast for both of us, he'll think we're staying in here for a while." He looked at the window again. "Get dressed while I'm gone, okay? But make sure you're not seen."

I rose from the chair, feeling shaky suddenly. "Alex, be careful."

"I'll be fine. No one's going to do anything until they know whether it's you or not. Just keep out of sight, all right? Dead bolt the lock again once I'm gone, and check the peephole when you hear me knock."

I nodded, determined that I was going to at least pretend to be as calm as he was. "Yes, all right."

Alex's gaze lingered on me for a moment. "Don't worry, we'll be okay," he said softly. And then he left, his body language casual as he went out the door and closed it behind him.

Locking the door, I grabbed my clothes from the day before and scurried into the bathroom. Knowing that he'd be gone at least five minutes, I jumped in and out of the shower and then got dressed, twisting my wet hair up under the cap. Then I quickly finished packing, shoving my clothes and our bathroom things into Alex's bag as well. When I came to the picture that Mom had taken of me, I wrapped it carefully in tissue paper, tucking it into my handbag.

Just as I was fastening my bag shut, a knock rapped through the room. Even though I knew it was probably Alex, my heart leaped into my throat. I edged over to the door, craning up on my tiptoes to look out the peephole. "It's me," said Alex's voice at the same time. I could see him standing outside, balancing two cups of coffee and a napkin full of donuts.

I undid the lock, shutting the door hastily after him as he came in. "Did you see anyone?"

He nodded as he dumped the food onto the table. "Yeah, there's a guy at the far end of the parking lot, sort of hanging around outside his car." He took a quick slurp out of one of the coffees, glancing at me. "Are you ready?"

I swallowed hard. "Yeah, I think so." I looked at the small pile of white-powdered donuts, and thought that I'd never felt less hungry in my life.

"Good, then let's get out of here."

I followed Alex as he went into the bathroom again.

The window there was only half the size of the ones in the bedroom, but still large enough to climb through. Beyond, there were some pine trees and then a road; I could hear cars going past. Alex slid the window open and climbed up on the toilet. A short, hard kick to the screen, and then another one. It fell out with a clatter, landing on the ground below. And even though it wasn't the time to be noticing it, for a second I found myself just...admiring the way he moved. His muscles were so fluid, so confident.

Jumping down, Alex went and got his nylon bag, lowering it towards the ground outside and letting it drop. My bag followed after it. "Can you climb out?" he asked me. The window was sort of high up, almost at chest level.

"If you help me up."

Now that we were actually getting out, I felt almost calm. I put my hands on the sill and Alex gave me a boost, lifting me up by the waist. I went through the window and twisted round. Holding onto the sill, I dangled my legs down and then dropped to the ground, stumbling a bit as I landed on the screen. I shoved it out of the way, along with our bags. The window was more of a squeeze for Alex, but a few seconds later he had squirmed out, jumping down beside me.

"Can you close the window if I lift you up?" he said, looking back at it. "Just in case he gets in – he might think that he missed us going out the front somehow."

I shook my head, almost smiling. "You think of everything, don't you?"

The corner of his mouth lifted slightly. "I try. Here, get on my shoulders." He bent down. Resting a hand on the hardness of his shoulder, I straddled his neck; a second later he had lifted me up as lightly as if I didn't weigh a thing. He looped his arms over my legs and I stretched upwards, sliding the window shut and trying not to notice how it felt to be so close to him.

When I was on the ground again, Alex glanced out towards the road. "Right, you'd better not come with me while I go for the car. Are you going to be okay, waiting here?"

We were in a small grove of pine trees, partially hidden. I nodded. "Yeah, I think so."

He hesitated as he gazed down at me, his eyes concerned. "I don't suppose you'd take my gun if I gave it to you, would you?"

The thought sent chills through me. My eyes flickered to his waistband, where I knew the gun lay under his grey T-shirt as it hung loosely over his jeans. "Uh – no. I seriously couldn't use a gun on anyone, Alex."

He sighed, shoving his hair back. "No, I didn't think so. Look, just – keep out of sight, okay? Keep safe. I'll be back as fast as I can."

"Okay," I said. My throat felt dry suddenly. "Be careful,

Alex. I mean – please, be really careful."

"I will." He turned and walked out towards the road, his hands shoved casually in his back pockets. A few minutes later, he had turned the corner and was gone from sight. Abruptly, the trees felt very still. I put on my sunglasses and sat leaning against the outside wall of the motel, wrapping my arms around my knees and trying to make myself as inconspicuous as possible. It was warm, even here in the shade; I could feel the back of my neck growing damp.

The minutes passed, stretching out. I tried to count them, wondering if Alex had had time yet to reach the garage. Oh god, please let him be okay. Please let whoever was watching us think that we were still sitting in the room, eating too-sweet donuts and drinking awful motel coffee.

After a while, my legs started to feel stiff. I stood up, pressing against the rough grey bark of a pine tree as I stared out at the road. He must have gotten there by now, surely? What was taking him so long? Across the road, a woman sat waiting for a bus, wearing a bright yellow sundress. There was a baby stroller next to her; as I watched she peered into it, laughing and shaking her head, and then reached in like she was adjusting her baby's blanket. She looked so happy that I felt my nervousness fade slightly.

Suddenly the woman glanced up, her expression startled. Following her gaze, my heart faltered.

There was an angel flying towards her.

The bark dug sharply into my cheek as I stood against the tree, my heart thudding. I didn't want to watch, but I couldn't stop. The angel was a female, her long hair flowing past her shoulders. Her halo shone brightly, and her robes swayed around her legs as she landed, her glorious wings spread. She folded them behind her back and started forward. She put her hands on the woman, who was gazing up at her with wonder. And she began to feed.

The woman's life energy came into my view. I could see it draining, collapsing in on itself, fading from a vibrant pink and violet to a dull grey. The woman just sat there on the bench, staring up at the angel with an expression of such love and gratitude that I had to duck my head away, screwing my eyes tightly shut. Distantly, I heard her baby begin to cry.

The sound of a car approaching, then slowing down. I forced myself to look. It was Alex, pulling over to the kerb. Across the street behind him, the angel was still feeding, her wings gently opening and closing. She had her head tilted back, and she was smiling, her halo shining brightly.

Move! I shouted at myself. *You have to!* My legs felt wobbly and unsure of themselves. Ignoring them, I grabbed our bags and ran for the car. As I came out of the shade, the angel seemed to explode into brilliance, sunshine bursting off her white wings. Alex leaned across the seat, opening the door for me; I shoved the bags in and he swung them into the back. Flinging myself into the seat, I slammed the door shut. "Hurry, let's get out of here," I said, my voice shaking.

He pulled away from the kerb, looking sharply at me. "What is it? Did you see someone?"

I shook my head. And I didn't want to, but I had to – I twisted to look over my shoulder. The angel was gone; there was a woman standing in her place with long black hair and a pretty white top. As I watched, she touched her victim lightly on the shoulder and drifted off down the sidewalk. The woman blinked, looking dazed. As we rounded the corner, I could see her reaching for her baby, and then she passed from view.

"Willow? What is it?" asked Alex.

"Nothing," I managed faintly, turning forward again. "So, um…you made it to the garage okay."

He nodded, shifting gears as we came to a stoplight. "Yeah, it was fine. I think we got away clear – I saw the guy still standing there watching our room as I drove past."

Relief rushed through me, and I let out a breath as I slumped back against the cracked vinyl seat. A surge of guilt followed, that I could feel relieved for myself after what I'd just seen.

Alex was still watching me, frowning in concern. "Willow, come on, talk to me. What's wrong?"

I was silent for a moment, not wanting to say the words. "There…was an angel, feeding on a woman across the street from the motel."

He winced. "Oh, god. No wonder you looked so upset. Are you okay?"

"*I'm* fine. I doubt that the woman is."

"Yeah, I know," he said in a low voice.

There was a pause. I gazed out the window, still seeing the angel's wings moving back and forth; the woman's life energy fading away into greyness, as she sat there smiling. "How come I've never seen that before?" I asked woodenly. "Up in Pawntucket?"

He shook his head. "There aren't that many in upstate New York. I don't know why; there seem to be some regions they like better than others."

"But – the Church of Angels in Schenectady is huge."

"It only had one angel, though, from the sounds of it. They kept mentioning *our angel* during the service."

I went cold. "One angel, and…all those people?"

Alex glanced at me. Sounding a bit reluctant, he said, "Some of them really like variety. They might feed on a dozen different people a day." The light changed to green; we started forward. I sat in silence, and after a moment I felt his gaze on me again. "Listen, I know how hard it is when you see it happening, but...try not to think about it, okay? There wasn't anything you could do."

"Right, and how exactly am I supposed to not think about it?" I asked thinly. I hesitated. "Alex, do you know how I knew there was someone outside our room? I was having a dream that I was flying, and I knew I had to go outside, and I saw him – I had wings, just like that *thing* back there. Except that it wasn't a dream at all, was it? I did have wings. I—" I broke off, my mouth tightening hard. No, I wasn't going to cry. I was not.

We came to the turn-off for the interstate and Alex got onto it, accelerating as he merged. He shrugged. "If that's how you found out, then I'm pretty glad it happened. If you hadn't seen what you did, we might both be dead right now."

And I knew he was right, but that just seemed...too easy, somehow. I shook my head, my thoughts too tangled to put into words.

For a few minutes neither of us spoke. I sat curled up with my head against the seat, staring out at the passing cars and the high green hills. Then Alex looked across at me. "Hey," he said. "You were right about the air filter too, you know. It needed to be replaced."

"Yeah?" Was I actually supposed to care about this?

He nodded, his fingers lightly tapping the wheel. "So, um...how come you know so much about cars, anyway?"

I grimaced. "Alex, I don't feel like—"

"Come on, tell me. I'd like to know," he said. His eyes met mine, and abruptly, my throat tightened at the understanding I saw there. He knew exactly how I felt; he was trying to help. "Did you take a class on it in school or something?" he went on.

A few billboards flashed past. I stared dully at them, still seeing the woman. Finally I said, "No, it wasn't offered."

"How, then?"

I sighed, and then shifted in the seat. "Do you really, seriously want to know this?"

He smiled. "Yes, I really, seriously want to know this."

"Okay." I sat up, trying to marshal my thoughts together. "It was because of my Aunt Jo. See, um…Mom and I have lived with her from the time I was nine. And she's always been sort of horrible about it. I mean, she helps take care of Mom, but she's always complaining about how expensive it is, having us both there. Anyway, one day her car broke down, and she just wouldn't stop talking about how much it was going to cost. So I went to the library and got a book on do-it-yourself car repair, and…I fixed it."

Alex laughed out loud, and I felt some of my tension ease, like something hard and tight loosening in my chest.

"Really?" he said. "That's completely brilliant."

"Yeah." Despite myself, I smiled at the memory, too. "She took a taxi to work that day, and I played hooky from school and I fixed it. It was just the alternator; all I had to do was go to the dump and get a new one. You should have seen her face when she got home – I think she'd really been looking forward to complaining about it for a few weeks."

"I bet." He gave me a considering look, his eyes warm. "How old were you?"

I thought. "Thirteen? Anyway, then I just got really into it. I like engines. They're not actually that complicated. There's a real...logic to them."

"Well, it's about all I can do to check the oil," said Alex, changing lanes as he passed a truck. "So I'm pretty impressed."

"Yeah, but you're James Bond," I said. "James Bond doesn't have to fix his own car."

He grinned. "True. Plus I used to have a car that was actually from this century, which helped."

His Porsche. I thought of it sitting in the parking lot in the Bronx. Except that I seriously doubted whether it was still there any more. "Did it bother you much, having to abandon it?" I asked, pulling a knee to my chest.

Alex shook his head. "Not really. It was a great car, but getting killed would have bothered me a lot more."

"And anyway, the Mustang's a great car, too," I said after a pause.

His eyebrows shot up. "You're joking, right?"

For a second I thought *he* was joking. "No, I'm not, actually. It's a complete classic."

"Um, yeah. Is that another way of saying it's a broken-down wreck?"

I felt my jaw drop. "Alex! Come on, this is the classic American muscle car. A '69 Mustang is *iconic*. I mean, think of *American Graffiti*. Would George Lucas have put *Porsches* in it? No, he would not."

His face twisted as he tried not to laugh. "Right, I sense that I'm losing this argument."

"Well, at least you admit it." Suddenly I felt a lot more like myself again; it was a huge relief. We had got away, we were safe for now. Maybe the dream that had saved us had been more half-angel freakery, but I didn't have to think about it right this second; I could choose to put it aside. And Alex was right — as horrible as it had been to see the angel feeding, I couldn't have done anything to help the woman.

I gazed across at him, studying the sculpted lines of his face; his bluish eyes and dark hair. And though I never would have believed it those first few days together, all at once it struck me how kind he was. How really, truly kind.

"Thank you," I said.

His eyes narrowed slightly as he glanced at me. "You're welcome. What for?"

"You know what for," I said. "That, um…it really helped. Thanks."

Alex shrugged, looking embarrassed. "You just can't let it consume you when you see something like that," he said finally, running his hands along the wheel. "It's hard, but you have to let it go."

Outside, Tennessee glided past, the dramatic hills becoming gentle and rolling. We skirted around Memphis and by six o'clock we'd crossed the Mississippi river, curving wide and vast below us. Halfway over the bridge we were into Arkansas, where the land suddenly flattened, turning into broad fields dotted with trees.

In the driver's seat Alex shifted, flexing his shoulders.

"You know, I could drive for a while," I suggested.

His eyebrows lifted as he glanced at me. "You want to?"

"Yeah, I would, actually," I said. "It'll give you a break, and get us there a bit faster if I help. Besides, I've never driven a Mustang before."

He grinned. "Well, I know you won't believe me if I say you're not missing much. But yeah, thanks – I'll take you up on that." He pulled over to the side of the road and we got out to switch sides. The late afternoon sun beat down on us. It was so strange that it was still practically summer here, while back home we'd all be wearing sweaters and jackets.

I paused in front of the car, looking out at a field of

crops. Short, twiggy-looking bushes, with heavy balls of white on them, like snowfall. I did a double take as I realized what they were. "Is that actually cotton?"

Alex stopped beside me, his hands in his back pockets. A slight breeze ruffled his dark hair. "Yeah, you get a lot of it down here. Rice, too."

I gazed at him, thinking that even if he'd never been to school, he knew so much more than most of the people I'd ever known. "Where did you learn to speak Spanish?" I asked. "Was it at the camp?"

He nodded. "A couple of the AKs were Mexican...I just sort of picked it up. Plus we weren't far from the border; we used to go over into Mexico sometimes." He glanced down at me with a smile. "Hey, are you trying to get out of driving?"

His eyes were warm, full of laughter. Suddenly I had an insane urge to just step forward and slip my arms around his waist. I shook it away. "Nope," I said, holding my hand out. "Here, give me the keys."

Slowly, we crossed through Arkansas. The Mustang was great to drive. The tracking was a little off, but the wheel under my hands just felt amazing, like holding a piece of history. Soon after I started driving, the sun vanished below the horizon. A few hours later, we were in Oklahoma; it was so dark that I couldn't make out the countryside at all.

I peered out through the windshield as I drove. "Another state that I've only heard about before, and now I can't even see it."

Alex was lying back in the passenger seat, his eyes half-closed. "This part of it's just like Arkansas, pretty much," he said. "Don't worry, you're not missing anything exciting."

From what I could see in the headlights, he was right. "What do you think will happen when we get to the camp?" I asked.

He sat up a bit, stretching his arms. "We'll need to get all the AKs together and regroup, and then set up on our own again without the angels knowing. I don't know how many AKs there are out in the field now – hopefully Cully will have some idea, so we can work out what our next move is."

I really wasn't sure how I was supposed to fit into this, or why the angels were so certain I was a threat to them. It didn't matter, though – for as long as my family might be in danger, there was no way I was going home. Mixed feelings swirled through me: a sharp stab of sadness at the thought that I might never see Mom again, but also a sense of relief that whatever the future held, it sounded as though I would be with Alex. I swallowed as I realized just how important that had become to me. When had that happened?

"Do you want me to drive for a while?" asked Alex, glancing over at me. "You've been at it for hours now."

"Yeah, okay," I said after a pause. And I pulled over so that we could change sides.

CHAPTER *Eleven*

IT WENT FASTER WITH BOTH of us taking turns behind the wheel. By around noon the next day, we'd passed through Oklahoma and were heading across the Texas panhandle. I stared out the windshield in awe. I had never seen anything to compare with the absolute flatness here – the sweeping, empty expanses of burned-looking grass, stretching out for miles to the unbroken line of the horizon. The sky soared above us, looking about ten times larger than usual, and grain elevators peppered the landscape. Every dusty little town seemed to have one, though often there wasn't a single person in sight. As I drove, I gazed at an abandoned elevator that stood beside a boarded-up house, wondering if the owner had finally become so fed up with all the flatness that he'd just left.

Both of us were getting hungry, so I pulled into a service station with a shop. "Would you drive for a while now?" I asked, tucking my hair up in the cap.

"Yeah, sure," said Alex. "Are you going in?"

"Just to use the Ladies'."

"Okay, what kind of sandwich do you want – ham and cheese, right? And water to drink?"

"Yeah, thanks. And you'll be getting your coffee," I teased. "You're a complete caffeine addict, you know."

"Hey, I've got to have at least one vice," he said with a grin. He started off across the pavement, his stride loose and relaxed.

Smiling, I got out of the car and went around to the side of the service station, where the restrooms were. When I'd finished, I splashed my face with cold water and went back out into the blinding heat. Alex hadn't returned to the car yet, and as I headed towards it, I saw a payphone to the side of the parking lot.

My steps dwindled to a stop as I stared at it. They couldn't track a payphone, could they? I had some change in my purse; I could ring Nina and find out whether Mom was okay. The temptation was almost unbearable. I had actually started to walk towards the phone when

I hesitated, wondering if they might have tapped Nina's cellphone. Could you do that?

No, I thought. *I can't; it's too risky.* But almost doing it and then not was worse than never having spotted the payphone at all. Ridiculously, I felt tears clutch at my throat. Angry with myself, I pulled off my sunglasses, swiping at my eyes with the heel of my hand.

"Hey. You okay?" said Alex. He was just walking across the parking lot towards me, carrying our food. He frowned, his eyes on mine. "What's wrong?"

I shook my head. "It's stupid. I was just really tempted to call Nina, and see how Mom is. I didn't," I added hastily. "But I just – really wanted to."

He looked like he understood. "I'm sorry," he said. "I hope she's okay."

I managed a smile. "Thanks. Me too." Taking my sandwich from him, we walked back to the Mustang. I could feel my hair about to slip down from the cap, and before I got in, I put my sandwich on the roof and quickly started to redo it. Pulling my cap off, I tossed it onto the roof too, smoothing my hands down my hair.

Just then a gleaming silver pickup truck swung in to the space next to us. I glanced up at it. There was a couple sitting in the cab. The man had a bushy brown moustache; the woman, frosted blonde hair that was stiff with hairspray. As I started to twist my hair up again, the woman looked over at me and our eyes met.

Time seemed to slow down. Her face slackened in shock. I saw her mouth fall open, and then it was moving, forming words: *It's her.*

Panic burst through me. I didn't have my sunglasses on; I'd hooked them into the front of my T-shirt as we were walking back to the car. I leaped into the Mustang and slammed the door. "We've got to go," I said, my words falling over themselves. "That woman saw me." Shoving my sunglasses on again, I saw her talking urgently to her husband, pointing at me. He was leaning over her, squinting down into the Mustang.

Alex didn't wait to be told twice; he backed us out in a rush and then floored it, squealing out of the service station. I twisted around in my seat, looking back. My sandwich and cap were bouncing over the concrete; the man had got out of the truck and was staring after us. There was a Church of Angels sticker on the pickup's bumper.

And a rifle hanging in the cab.

"How could I have been so *stupid?*" I breathed. I was shaking, my fingers cold. The man had to have noticed the New York plates on the Mustang; he'd know. The last thing I saw before the service station disappeared from view was him climbing back into his truck. My pulse was slamming through my veins. Were they coming after us?

A turn-off was coming up; Alex took it, taking us onto Highway 83. I watched out the back window. The truck didn't appear. "Maybe we've lost them," I said tentatively.

"Maybe," said Alex, glancing in the rear-view mirror. "Except that they probably know every road around here. It wouldn't take a genius to figure out that we'd leave the interstate."

My hands clenched; I couldn't stop trembling. "I'm so, so sorry," I said. "I was being so stupid—"

He shook his head briefly. "Stop it – it's not your fault the Church of Angels is full of whackjobs."

I huddled in my seat. The highway took us through a small, dusty town called Jasper. Miles passed, and then there was another small town called Fonda. Nobody seemed to notice us, and I started to hope that we'd really lost them. But then, a mile or so after we left Fonda, Alex looked in the rear-view mirror again, his eyes lingering on something.

"I think we've got company," he said.

"Is it them?" My throat tightened as I whipped around. And there was the silver pickup truck, cruising along behind us. For a single wild moment I hoped it might be a different one, but then it got closer and I saw that there were two people sitting in the front; a man and a woman. And the woman had blonde hair.

Alex floored the accelerator and the Mustang shot

ahead, its engine roaring. It was miles between towns out here; we were out in the middle of nowhere, with only flat, scorched land and endless skies. The highway was a run-down road, almost empty of traffic. Behind us, the silver pickup accelerated too, eating up the distance between us.

Fear pummelled through me. "Oh god, Alex, keep going, whatever you do."

"Yeah, don't worry, that was sort of my plan," he muttered.

Staring behind us, I watched in sick horror as the pickup drew closer, gaining on us with almost comical speed. Then they were right on our tail, their bumper nearly touching ours. My eyes met those of the woman. She was gripping a pendant around her neck, glaring right at me. Her husband was at the steering wheel, his expression fixed, intent, like a hunter with a ten-point buck in his sights.

Suddenly the pickup rammed us from behind. The Mustang jolted forward with a metallic crunching noise. Swearing, Alex spun the wheel, careering over the yellow line. Its engine roaring, the pickup pulled up beside us on the passenger's side. The woman was leaning over her husband and holding the rifle, pointing it right at me.

Alex saw it in the same moment I did. "*Get down,*" he shouted, swerving. He shoved me towards the floor just as there was the sound of gunfire, and then my window burst into thousands of fragments of glass. I screamed, throwing my arms over my head. I could feel the pattering of glass all around me; in my hair, on the back of my T-shirt.

"Stay down," ordered Alex's voice. Shaking, I peered up from under my arms and saw him grab his gun from the waistband of his jeans, flicking the safety off. But before he could fire back I heard tyres squealing, and saw from his gaze that the pickup had pulled in front of us. There was the popping sound of gunfire again.

"Jesus!" He ducked low in his seat as the windshield exploded.

Safety glass flew all around us; a sudden rush of wind howled past. The Mustang veered wildly, but somehow Alex managed to keep control. The sound of the rifle, still firing, became more distant and then stopped altogether. Alex pulled onto the shoulder, did a screeching three-point turn, and headed back in the direction we'd just come from, wind whistling through the car. I stayed with my head down, not daring to move. A few minutes later I felt the car turn. There was a rough bumping, and then we jolted to a stop.

In a daze, I sat up, glass falling from my back and shoulders with little clinking noises. Alex had pulled off the highway; we were on a dirt road in the middle of a field. There was a cut on his cheek where a piece of glass must have struck him – a thin trickle of blood, like a red teardrop tracing down his face.

"Are you okay?" he asked urgently, gripping my arms. "Willow, are you hurt?" His eyes were wide, almost frightened.

Numbly, I wondered why. Alex faced danger all the time; it didn't seem like him to get scared by it. I was still trembling, but I nodded. "I'm – I'm fine." Reaching out, I started to touch his cheek, and then swallowed and pulled my hand away. "Your, um…your face is bleeding."

Alex's shoulders relaxed; he let out a breath. Brushing at his face with the flat of his hand, he glanced down at the blood, and then swiped at his cheek with a paper napkin. "Yeah, it's fine. Come on, let's get the hell out of here before they come back."

He started the car again with a lurch. Rumbling over the dirt road, we came to a T-junction; the road intersecting our own was paved. Alex turned right, and the Mustang gained speed, the wind rustling past us. He pushed a hand through his hair, shaking the glass out. "Right, we've got to ditch this car and find another one, like *now*, before they find us and decide to try again."

"You mean steal one," I said.

"We don't have a choice," he said, shifting gears. "I know it's not a great thing to do, but—"

"No, it's okay," I interrupted, my voice unsteady. "In fact – I can probably help."

Alex glanced at me, startled, and then amazement spread slowly across his face. "Oh, man. You know how to hotwire a car."

"I know the theory," I said, hugging myself. "It's, um – not very difficult."

He gave a short nod. "Right, we've just got to find one, then."

I sat stiffly in the glass-strewn seat, frightened of every car that we passed. Thankfully, there were only two, and neither of them slowed down when they saw us. After a couple of miles, we came to a sign that read *Palo Duro Park Rd.* "Palo Duro," muttered Alex. "Wait a minute, that sounds familiar." He took the turning.

"What is it?" I asked.

"A canyon," he said. "A really big one. Cully told me about it; he used to come camping here. People go hiking here a lot – we might be able to find something." We were on a paved road that twisted and turned for a mile or so; there was dry, open grassland to either side. And then suddenly...there wasn't. "Oh!" I breathed, straightening up as the canyon came into view. Like a film I'd once seen of the Grand Canyon, it was suddenly just *there,* the land opening up before us into a soaring, silent expanse of depth and space and red rock.

Alex's expression had hardened as he looked out at it, as if he was thinking about something. Before I could wonder about it too much, we went around a wide curve in the road, with the canyon sloping steeply away from us in a scrabble of dust and loose rock. "There," I said suddenly, pointing. "That one'll do; it's old enough." Parked just off the side of the road was a boat-like grey Chevy, its owners presumably hiking on the dirt path that wound downwards.

Alex pulled in behind it and killed the engine. "Right, be careful. I'll keep an eye out for cars."

I nodded and got out of the Mustang, shaking bits of glass off me. Going over to the Chevy, I could see that the windows were open a few inches to let in the air. "Do we have a coat hanger or something?" I asked, cupping my hands around the driver's side window. In the back, I could see a blue and white plastic ice chest. Alex found some wire in the trunk of the Mustang, and brought it to me. Making a loop in one end, I managed to get the old-fashioned push-button lock on almost the first try.

I slid in behind the wheel, terrified that someone was going to come driving along any minute. "Okay, I've just got to see whether…" I peered under the steering column, and unclipped a plastic lid. "Ha, we're in luck. The wires we need are right here. Do you have a knife? I need to strip some of this insulation off."

Digging in his jeans pocket, Alex handed me a metal pocketknife with *Yellowstone National Park* on its handle. I pulled the blade out, and a moment later I had trimmed off about an inch of insulation on two of the wires. I twisted their exposed ends together.

Alex stood casually to one side keeping an eye on the road, as if we had just stopped to take in the view or something. Glancing over at me, he shook his head. "Have you considered a life of crime?"

"Very funny," I said. "Right, now I just need the ignition wire..." Finding a wire wrapped in brown insulation, I stripped it like the others. Stroking it against the other two, I heard the engine begin to spark and took it away again. "There, that's it." Getting out, I brushed my hands off on my jeans. "All you have to do is touch this wire to those two, and then rev the engine enough so you don't stall."

He didn't move; he just stood there for a moment, gazing down at me. "You're really amazing, you know that?"

I felt my cheeks turn red at the warmth in his voice. "Yeah, well...a misspent youth, I guess."

We glanced back at the Mustang. It looked even worse when you were standing at a distance, like it had been a demolition car at a fairground. "Come on, we've got to push this thing off the road," said Alex.

"No way!" I protested in alarm. "Alex, come on. Whoever owns this car is *hiking* down there. We could kill them."

"No, look," said Alex. He pointed downwards a hundred yards or so, to where a dense line of trees and brush rose up from the scrabble. "See, that should stop it, so that it won't hurt anyone. And meanwhile it might buy us a little bit of time; no one will know we've been here until it's found."

I pursed my lips, gazing down at the treeline. "Yeah, okay," I said finally.

We grabbed our things from the Mustang. Alex put it into neutral, and we started to push. A few minutes later, the car was rolling down the steep slope with an almost eerie grace, gathering speed as it went, tyres crunching against the rocky earth. When it hit the treeline it jolted and came to a sudden stop, with much less noise than I would have expected. Silence wrapped around us again, with the car nestled down among the trees like a strange piece of art.

I stared down at it, feeling a pang for such a great car being treated this way. "I'm sort of expecting it to burst into flames, like in the movies."

"Let's hope it doesn't," said Alex. He tossed his bag into the back seat of the Chevy. "Come on, we've got to get out of here."

The car's engine burst into life as he touched the wires together. "Nice one," he said, revving the engine. Doing a quick three-point turn, he pulled away from the shoulder and headed west. I found a map in the side of the door and unfolded it, trying to figure out where we were. "Good, we can take back roads all the way now," said Alex, glancing at it. "We'll be in New Mexico soon, and then I'll know where we are."

I nodded. Remembering the ice chest, I turned in my seat and looked at it. Slowly, I pulled off the lid and saw Cokes, sandwiches, a few cans of beer. My mouth twisted. It was stupid, but I felt almost as bad about stealing these people's lunch as I did their car. They were going to have a really terrible day now, because of us.

"We didn't have a choice, Willow," said Alex, watching me from the driver's seat. "I know that doesn't make it right, but – it really was life or death."

"Yeah, I know." I hesitated, and then decided it would be silly to waste the food. I pulled a couple of Cokes out of the ice chest and put the lid back on. "Here, do you want one? Since your coffee just went over the rim with the Mustang."

He smiled. "Thanks." Our fingers brushed as he took it. His hand felt warm, and for a fleeting moment I imagined just leaning against his shoulder; him putting his arm around me. It would be so nice. It would be so really, really nice.

Quickly, I shoved the thought away…but found my gaze resting on the dark scab on Alex's cheek, where the glass had hit him.

Life or death. And I had thought that I was calm, but I wasn't; suddenly I was shaking. Putting a hand to my hair, I could feel that there was still glass caught in it. Trying to control my trembling fingers, I propped my Coke between my legs and slowly picked out a few pieces – bright, hard shards that caught the sunlight.

Just like an angel's wings.

Even in the moonlight, the ground looked dry, dusty, as though it hadn't rained in a thousand years. They'd crossed over into New Mexico a few hours earlier, criss-crossing their way on remote back roads – which, once they'd got out of Texas, had abruptly turned to dust. The Chevy groaned along at about thirty miles an hour, with the wheels spitting up a steady stream of dirt and pebbles as they rumbled over the uneven ground. Occasionally one would *ping* against the windscreen, nicking it. Alex had frowned as he drove, concentrating on steering them around the ruts and dips. Finally it had gotten so dark that driving had become too risky in the Chevy, and he'd pulled off the road and they'd stopped for the night.

They hadn't seen another living soul in hours.

Now Alex sat leaning against the car, drinking one of the Coors they'd found in the cooler. Willow sat a few feet away with her knees pulled to her chest, staring out at the desert. It had always reminded Alex of the ocean, in a weird way – so endless, and utterly silent. And cold, now that the sun was gone. He had his leather jacket on, and Willow her denim one. Draining the beer, Alex crushed the can between his hands and looked down, playing with the crumpled aluminium. Ever since they'd pulled off the road, his mind had been replaying over and over again, like a bad dream, the moment when he'd seen the rifle pointed at Willow – the split-second instant when he thought she might die.

His heart had almost stopped.

Alex turned the can over in his hands, watching it glint in the moonlight. In that moment he hadn't cared whether she was a threat to the angels, or about anything at all apart from saving her. The thought of her being hurt was like something inside of him being torn to pieces. He swallowed hard. When had the fact that Willow was a half-angel stopped mattering to him? He didn't know. Maybe it had been the reading she'd given the waitress in the diner, or their time in the motel room, or maybe just sometime on the road with her. But at some point over the last few days, its importance had melted away. The idea that Willow was in any real way like the invading parasites was laughable to him now. Her angel aspects were simply a part of who she was – and who she was, was just…amazing. Though Alex didn't like what had happened to bring Willow into being, he was still very glad that it had. He didn't really care what she was, so long as she existed.

In fact, he could hardly imagine being without her any more.

The thought stunned him; he felt his hands grow cold. What the hell was going on? Being attracted to Willow was one thing, but this was… Alex's thoughts trailed off, lost in confusion. It wasn't just how she looked; it was Willow herself, everything about her. He hadn't had this depth of feeling towards anyone since Jake had died. And he didn't want to be having it, not ever again. It wasn't worth it; being close to people just meant pain, eventually. For the second time that day, an image of his brother's death flashed through his mind, and Alex's jaw tightened.

"Is everything okay?" asked Willow. Glancing up, he saw that she was watching him, her blonde hair almost silver in the moonlight.

"Yeah," said Alex, shortly. "Just kind of tired."

She hesitated, her eyes scanning his face, but she didn't pursue it. "How long will it take us to get to the camp from here?" she asked.

Alex scuffed his shoe across the sandy soil. "Four or

five hours, probably. We should be there by noon or so tomorrow, if we don't run into any trouble."

Silence fell. In the distance, a long, wavering howl sounded, and Willow started. "What's that?"

"Coyote."

She stared at him, her face alight with amazement. "What, really?"

He had to smile. "Yeah, really. They're not just in the movies, you know."

Willow shook her head. "It's so strange. I grew up hearing robins and bluejays, and you grew up hearing coyotes." Touching her hair, she made a face as she plucked out a piece of glass and tossed it onto the sand. "Oh, honestly...I thought I'd gotten all of these before, but there seems to be an endless supply." With a frown, she ran her hands through her hair again, searching.

Alex said the words before he could stop himself. "Do you, um...want some help with that?"

Willow's head snapped towards him, her expression startled. He shrugged, trying to ignore the sudden pounding in his chest. "It's just that I can still see some of them, right at the back. They're sort of...shining in the moonlight."

"Okay," she said after a pause.

Getting up, he moved over to sit beside her; she turned her back to him. His breath felt tight as gently, he ran his fingers through her hair, finding bits of glass and pulling them free. Her hair was soft against his searching fingers, and the desert lay vast and empty around them as he worked, neither of them speaking. There was the faint almost-noise of glass on sand as he tossed pieces aside, and the sound of their breathing. Willow sat very still, hardly moving.

Finally Alex stroked her hair slowly, all the way down its length. He dropped his hands and swallowed. "I…think that's all."

"Thanks." Willow's voice came out in a whisper. It was all Alex could do not to encircle her in his arms and pull her back against his chest. *Don't,* he told himself harshly. *If you get close to someone again, you'll regret it.* He rose hastily to his feet.

Willow got up too, hugging her elbows and not looking at him. "I, um…guess we should get some sleep," she said.

"Yeah," said Alex. It felt like he was standing on the edge of a cliff. He took a step back. "I'll just…" He motioned into the desert.

"Yeah, me too," said Willow, with a quick, embarrassed smile.

She went behind the car while Alex went off in the other direction a few dozen paces. By the time he heard Willow emerge again he was looking up at the stars, his hands shoved in his back pockets.

He turned and saw her face, etched in the moonlight. He managed a smile. "Right, well – we're probably better off in the car. It gets pretty cold out here at night."

Willow nodded, and a few minutes later they were in the Chevy, lying back on their separate seats. Willow covered herself with her jean jacket.

"Are you going to be warm enough?" asked Alex.

"I think so," she said.

"Here." Shrugging out of his leather jacket, he draped it over her. The gesture was much more intimate than he'd meant it to be, with her gazing up at him. Abruptly, he let go of the jacket, and leaned back into his own seat.

"But you'll be cold," said Willow, touching the jacket's sleeve.

"I'm fine."

"Here, you take this, then." She stretched to hand him her jean jacket, and then stopped. "I mean – it'll be too small for you, but—"

"That's okay. Thanks." He took the jacket, his fingers closing over the softness of its worn fabric. As he spread it over his chest, he caught a faded whiff of Willow's perfume.

Wrapping the leather jacket around herself, Willow closed her eyes. "Well…goodnight," she said finally.

"Goodnight," echoed Alex.

He didn't go to sleep for a long time.

CHAPTER *Twelve*

EVER SINCE HE'D BEEN GIVEN the responsibility for organizing the celebration, Jonah had been so busy he could hardly think. He'd put together a team of devotees to be his assistants, and had them measure the available space inside the cathedral, estimating how many flowers were going to be needed. Over fifty florists in Denver had to be hired to fulfil the order for long garlands of calla lilies and violets to wrap around the cathedral's pillars, not to mention the massive standing displays that were to go on either side of the space where the gate was to open. He liaised with the cathedral's musical director, who was ecstatic over the coming celebration; together, they planned a choral programme truly fit for the angels. New robes of a shimmering silvery blue were ordered for the soprano choir, with dozens of Denver seamstresses put to work to rush the order through. There was to be a procession of acolytes from churches all over the country; just coordinating their details was a nightmare in itself. Thousands of fliers were ordered; tickets for available spaces in the cathedral were arranged; extra crowd accommodation planned for the day.

It had been decided not to directly involve the media apart from those run by the Church, but already word was spreading like wildfire, with Jonah receiving hundreds of e-mails a day begging for tickets. Soon he had to put another few devotees solely in charge of ticket sales, or else he wouldn't have had time to get anything else done. And there was so much else he needed to think about: lighting, programmes, refreshments. He wanted to make sure that he considered every conceivable detail, so that the celebration would, rightly, be the most spectacular event the young cathedral had ever seen.

But meanwhile, even through the daze of details that surrounded him…he had begun to notice things.

Just little things at first, such as how often Raziel vanished from his office, and how satisfied with himself the angel often seemed on his return. And the residential devotees: how common it was to see one of them gazing up at nothing, smiling. Jonah knew that they were communing with the angels at these times, and prior to the vague sense of unease that had now come over him, he had never even questioned this. But it happened so often. And the devotees usually seemed so tired afterwards. Once, passing a woman staring up at nothing in a corridor, Jonah spoke to her and received no answer. Gazing at her radiant, unseeing eyes, he hesitated, feeling awkward, and then continued on his way. When he glanced back over his shoulder, he saw her standing slumped against the wall, her face pale.

Jonah wavered. Finally he went back, his footsteps hardly making a sound on the thick carpet. "Are you all right?" he asked.

The devotee's eyelids came open. Her expression was shining, joyful. "Oh, yes! One of the angels has just been with me. Praise the angels!"

"Praise the angels," echoed Jonah.

But the woman staggered slightly as she started down the corridor again; he saw her touch the wall for support. She looked so drained. So weak.

In fact, so did many of the devotees.

How could he have never noticed it before? It seemed incredible to Jonah, as if he was now viewing cathedral life with a new pair of eyes. Thousands of resident devotees lived in nearby accommodation; they took care of every need that the flagship Church of Angels centre had, from cleaning to cooking to paperwork. They had a gym, a movie theatre, a hairdresser's…but their most popular port of call seemed to be their doctor's office. Glancing through some of the personnel files on his screen, Jonah felt a chill. Not a single resident seemed to be healthy.

Yet surely it was just a coincidence. Or not a coincidence, exactly, but simple cause and effect: if you were having health problems in your life, then wouldn't that be the natural time to turn to the angels for help? Of course so many of the devotees didn't seem to be well; it was why they'd needed the angels in the first place. Jonah felt a rush of relief at this theory, but it was short-lived: further delving into the records showed that many of the devotees appeared to have been just fine on their arrival. Until they'd been at the cathedral for a while.

Pulling up the Church homepage, Jonah gazed at the photo of the half-angel, Willow, with her long blonde hair and elfin face. And for the first time, he wondered exactly what sort of danger she constituted to the angels.

It was late afternoon. Raziel had disappeared to his living quarters; Jonah was alone in his office. He sat looking at the phone. It would be a simple enough call to make, and surely once he'd done so, these terrible doubts would go away. Suddenly he felt that he'd give anything to return to the time when he'd had no reservations at all.

Flipping through his Filofax, he found the number he needed and dialled. It was after business hours in New York, but he knew someone would pick up in the residents' quarters.

"Hello, Church of Angels Schenectady," said a man's voice.

Jonah sat up. "Yes, hi – this is Jonah Fisk, from the Denver main office. Could I speak to Beth Hartley?"

"Beth? I think she's still on cleaning duty."

"Would you mind getting her, please? It's important."

Jonah sat tensely in his chair as he waited. His office was very still, very quiet. The small painting of the angel hung across from him, softly illuminated by a dimmed light. He took in the fluid lines of the angel's wings, its gentle, loving face. Its very beauty seemed to taunt his suspicions, tingeing him with guilt.

"Hello?" said a girl's voice finally.

Jonah explained who he was. "I'm sorry to bother you," he said. "I just, um…need to ask you about Willow Fields."

Beth sounded cautious. "What about her?"

Jonah cleared his throat. "Well…what happened, exactly?" Beth went silent. Hating himself, he added, "Please, I need to know. It's important – the angels have asked. Was she a friend of yours, before all this happened?"

"No!" said Beth, her voice startled. He heard her swallow. "Um, we were mostly in different classes; she was a junior. She was always pretty strange, but seemed nice enough. And she was supposed to be psychic, so…I went to her for a reading."

Jonah sat without moving as Beth described the encounter, finishing with: "She saw my angel; she knew exactly what had been happening. But she – she told me horrible things. I mean, really horrible things." He could hear tension running through the girl's tone, like a thin steel wire.

"Can you tell me what?" asked Jonah. Reaching for a pencil on his desk, he fiddled with it nervously, tapping it against a yellow legal pad.

"I don't really like talking about it," said Beth finally. "But if the angels have asked…" She took a deep breath. "She – she said that my angel wasn't good. That he was… killing me, and that I should get away from him. She got really insistent about it, in fact. She said that if I joined the Church, I would keep getting sicker and sicker."

Jonah cleared his throat, his thoughts whirling. "Right, I see. And…you haven't, of course."

"No, of course not!" said Beth. "I mean – yeah, I'm pretty tired sometimes, and my muscles ache, but I think I might just have the flu or something. I'm fine. I couldn't be happier. Do you know if she's been found yet?"

"No, not yet," said Jonah.

"Oh," said Beth. "I was hoping—" She sighed. "I just really hate the thought that she's out there, and that she might hurt the angels."

"We'll get her soon," said Jonah distantly. "Thanks for your help, Beth. The angels be with you."

After he hung up, he sat at his desk for a long time, looking at Willow's smiling photo and trying to take in what he had just found out. Willow had thought that Paschar was a danger; she'd tried to stop Beth from joining the Church because she was worried about what it might do to her. Far from being an evil threat, it sounded as if Willow had actually been concerned about Beth, and trying to help her.

And now the angels wanted her dead.

Jonah stared blindly at the screen, hating the thoughts that were icing through his mind. The angels had saved him. They had *saved* him; there was no doubt at all about that. Yet he was starting to wonder if maybe he was the exception.

Who could tell him what was really happening? Who could he go to for answers?

A thought came to him; he stiffened. Slowly, he clicked his mouse a few times and pulled up an e-mail on his screen. Since the assassin's disappearance, Jonah himself was no longer responsible for dealing with the problem of the traitor angels – but when information came to Raziel by e-mail, he was still often copied in on it. Now he sat gazing at the three-line e-mail with its brief contact details, his heart thudding. The very idea was repugnant; to actually *talk* to one of them? Yet if he really sought answers…this might be the only place he could find them.

I can't, thought Jonah wretchedly. *I'm just getting it all wrong. I've got to believe in them; what else do I have?*

But there were Raziel's laughing words. The woman slumped against the wall, her face drained. And the smiling girl on the website, who had tried to warn someone that an angel was hurting her.

It felt as if the whole world was ringing in his ears.

Hardly able to believe he was doing it, Jonah reached for his pencil and the legal pad. His hands shaking slightly, he glanced back at the e-mail and wrote down a phone number.

The camp lay in the southern part of the state, twenty miles out in the desert – a hard, scrubby land with bare, flat-topped mountains rising up from the horizon. There were no signs or roads, but Alex knew the way like he knew his own face in the mirror – though he'd never imagined making the drive in a stretched-out Chevy that belonged back in the eighties with disco music and Space Invaders. He kept the speed low as the Chevy moved slowly over the rough ground, watching the temperature gauge and praying that the radiator wouldn't overheat. It already felt like it was nearing a hundred outside. And, just to make things even more fun, the car seemed to be out of Freon now. Even with the windows rolled down, it was stifling.

The tension from when he'd picked the glass out of Willow's hair had thankfully faded with the morning, and he and Willow talked easily on the journey. Her slim arms were glowing with a faint sheen of sweat as she sat with her bare feet propped up onto the dashboard. "I wish I had a pair of shorts," she said, fanning herself.

"We can probably get you some at the camp," said Alex. "Someone should have something you can wear."

Her green eyes looked thoughtful. "Are there female AKs?"

Alex nodded. "Sure, some really good ones. In fact, the women tended to take to the chakra work better than the men." He went silent as they came to a dried-out riverbed, concentrating as he guided them slowly over the rocky ground. A lizard sat on a nearby boulder, observing them with a contemptuous stare. *Do you really think that thing's going to make it? Good luck, sucker. Hope you enjoy being buzzard-meat.* All they needed was to break an axle out here. Not even Willow could fix that.

Straining, the Chevy groaned as it struggled up the riverbank, and Alex winced, wondering if they were going to have to walk the rest of the way. Then with a sudden heave, the car made it up and over. He let out a breath.

Willow pulled her long hair off her neck; twisting it into a coil, she knotted it back in a bun. She cleared her throat as she finished. "You know, um…I'm sort of nervous about this."

"What? Going to the camp?"

She nodded, tapping her hand against the open window. "With all the Angel Killers there, when I'm…what I am. They're all going to hate me, aren't they?" Her voice sounded strained.

Stupidly, this hadn't even occurred to him. He thought about it as he steered them around a series of ruts. "I guess some of them might be pretty taken aback at first," he said. Like he had been; he didn't say this, but he knew they were both thinking it. "But, Willow, it's not like you're on the angels' side – they want you dead; they think you can destroy them. That's what everyone will be interested in, not what you are."

Her chin moved slightly. "I hope so."

The urge to touch her was overwhelming. Alex gave in to it, resting his fingers fleetingly on her arm. "Hey, don't worry. It'll be okay."

Willow's face relaxed a fraction. She shot him a small smile. "All right. Thanks."

They drove in silence for a while as the Chevy wheezed and moaned across the desert. Spiky yucca plants dotted the dry soil, and lizards scuttled out of their way. Finally, wavering with heat lines in the distance, Alex could see the camp's chain-link fence coming into view. "Guess what, I think we made it," he said.

Willow sat up straight. "Is that it?"

"That's it." Viewing the camp through her eyes, he saw a cluster of low white buildings in the middle of nowhere, surrounded by a chain-link fence with razor-edged wire curling at its top. There were no trees; no ornamentation of any kind. It was sparse and functional; completely featureless.

It was the only home he'd ever really known.

Willow pulled her shoes on, not taking her eyes off the camp as they neared it. "It looks just like what I saw." She swallowed, glancing across at him. "How many people will be there, do you know?"

He shook his head. "No idea. The most that were ever there when I was there was thirty-seven."

"That's all?"

Alex shrugged. "It varied," he said. Varied, depending on who had gotten killed that week, and whether Martin, his father, had managed to recruit anyone new. They had gotten a lot of crazies out there – people who couldn't handle the energy work and ended up drifting around in a dreamy haze, or psychos who just wanted to shoot up everything in sight. The core number of AKs that you could actually count on had been more like twelve.

As they neared the gates, he slowed the Chevy almost to a stop and untwisted the wires under its steering wheel. Obediently, the car died.

He stepped out into the baking sun, shading his eyes as he gazed into the camp. Apprehension crawled across his neck. It was much too quiet; there wasn't a single other vehicle in sight. On the gate in front of them, the sign that said *Private Property, Keep Out at Risk of Physical Harm* was hanging sideways, dangling loosely from one screw.

On the other side of the car, Willow had gotten out, too, staring in at the buildings beyond the fence. She looked quickly at him, not saying anything.

Alex had a very bad feeling about this. Walking up to the gate, he saw that the lock that had always hung there was missing; there was only a latch in its place. He lifted it, and the gate pushed open easily at his touch. Inside, the building that they'd used as general storage stood with its metal door open, obviously vacant. The other buildings looked similarly abandoned. God, it was like a ghost town in there.

Willow moved to his side, hugging her arms. "Um…so what does this mean?"

"It means I'm an idiot," said Alex. He slapped his hand against the chain-link fence; it trembled and rattled. "*Damn* it. The CIA must have moved the whole operation after they took over. The training camp could be anywhere now."

Willow bit her lip. "Oh." She looked back at the buildings. "Do you think Cully is definitely where the camp is?"

"I don't know. I just assumed he'd be training new AKs, but…" Alex pushed roughly at the *Private Property* sign, so that it swung on its remaining screw. "I don't even know how to get hold of him. None of us have any of the others' cellphone numbers; we all had to work completely solo."

Willow looked deep in thought. "Well – what if he's *not* training new AKs?" she suggested finally. "Where would he be then? Maybe we could start with that, and see if we can track him down."

Her reasonable tone calmed him, made it easier to think. "Yeah, maybe…we could try Albuquerque, I guess. I know most of his old hang-outs. If he's not with the AKs, he's probably there, somewhere."

"Okay," said Willow. "Albuquerque it is."

She gave him a smile, and after a moment Alex managed

a rueful one back. Relief washed through him that she wasn't blaming him for his stupidity – he was blaming himself enough already for both of them. He started to head back to the car, already dreading the thought of trying to get that thing back across the desert again.

"Could we, um…have a look around before we go?"

Alex looked at Willow in surprise. She was still standing at the fence gazing into the camp, the sun casting chain-link diamonds across her face.

"What for?" he asked.

She hesitated, glancing back at him with a smile. "I'd just…really like to see where you grew up."

"This was the canteen," said Alex.

They were in a long, low building with a counter to one side. The metal folding tables and chairs were still there, the chairs sitting scattered about the tables as if everyone had just gotten up and trooped off to the rec room to play poker, or go out to the range for some target practice. Alex shoved his hands in his back pockets, gazing around him. It was like seeing two scenes at once, one overlaid on the other: there were Cully and some of the other AKs, sitting laughing at a table. *Man, what is this slop?* Cully had demanded at practically every meal. *Where's that lowlife cook, so I can shoot him?* Alex smiled slightly, remembering.

There had been no cook; they'd lived off canned goods and stuff in plastic packets.

Willow drifted slowly around the room. Her fingers lingered on the back of a chair as she passed it. "What was it like, growing up here?"

"I don't know. It just seemed normal, to me." Walking over to the counter, Alex picked up an empty coffee mug, turning it over in his hands. "We didn't have a TV, because they used up too much power, so I didn't really know how weird it was. I mean, I sort of knew that the rest of the world didn't live like this, but..." He shrugged, putting the coffee mug back.

"How old were you when you first came?"

"Five," he said.

"So young," she murmured. "Where are you from originally?"

"Chicago. I don't really remember it, though."

There was a light dusting of sand on the floor. It made a scraping noise under Willow's sneakers as she moved to join him. "So what did you learn here, if you didn't go to school?"

He laughed suddenly. "Hey, we had school – we did target practice, and how to spot angels, and taking care of your weapon, and reading auras, and manipulating chakra energy—" He raised an eyebrow at her. "I was probably busier than you were."

Willow shook her head, looking dazed. "Yeah, you probably were. When I was five, I was still trying to colour in the lines." She leaned against the counter beside him, gazing around the empty room. Alex saw that her hair had slipped slightly from its knot, resting on her neck in a loose coil. Against his will, he found himself remembering the softness of it against his fingers the night before; the silkiness of its long strands.

"And your father started this place?" asked Willow, looking up at him.

Glad of the distraction, Alex pushed himself away from the counter. "Yeah. Come on, I'll show you the bunkhouse." The sunlight dazzled the white buildings as they went back outside, nova-bright. "My dad worked for the CIA," he said as they walked through the wavering heat. "I guess he specialized in some pretty strange stuff – before he joined the CIA he spent a few years in Asia, learning about human energy fields, how to work with them."

Their shadows wavered ahead of them on the concrete. Walking silently at his side, Willow glanced up at him as she listened.

"He travelled a lot when I was little," went on Alex. "Then when I was five, his assignment changed or something, and he was home a lot more. And…that's when he first found out about angels."

They had come to the bunkhouse. The door was partly

open; Alex pushed it with the flat of his hand and stepped inside. It was relatively cool in here, with shadows painting the walls. The metal bunk beds were still in place, though the mattresses and bedding were gone. "Here's where I used to sleep," he said, going over to the second bunk on the right. "My brother Jake always took the top bunk, and I got the bottom."

Willow went still. "Your brother?"

Alex nodded, recalling a hundred fights of, "*Jake, you dipwad, you just stepped on my face*" – "*Hey, you like my smelly feet, don't you, Bro? Here, you want 'em again?*"

"Yeah," he said. "He was two years older than me."

Willow came over to stand beside him. She touched his arm. "Alex, I'm, um…I'm really sorry."

She already knew? Alex's muscles tightened as surprise jolted through him. He kept his eyes on the bunk as images of the Los Angeles canyon flashed past, as quickly as a shuffling deck of cards. Finally he said, "Do you know the details?"

Willow shook her head. "No. I didn't see it when I read you, I just sort of guessed. I meant to tell you I was sorry before, but – well, I didn't like you very much then." She gave a small smile.

Alex felt himself relax a fraction. Thank god; having her sympathy for what had happened would have been like torture. "I don't blame you," he said after a pause. "I

wouldn't have liked me very much either, if I were you."
Glancing down at her, he managed a wry grin.

Their eyes locked, and held. Willow's hand felt warm
on his arm, slightly damp from the heat. All thoughts of
Jake faded; Alex felt his pulse beat faster as he looked down
at her upturned face. The moment froze, neither of them
moving. All at once Willow seemed to realize how close she
was standing, and she dropped her hand and stepped back,
looking flustered.

Alex cleared his throat, his thoughts tumbling.
"Thanks," he said. "About Jake, I mean. It was a while ago,
what happened, but...thanks."

"You, um...were telling me about your father, and how
he first realized about the angels," said Willow. She sat on
the metal frame of the bottom bunk, leaning against the
support post. Alex sat on the other end, careful to keep a
few feet between them.

"Yeah." Suddenly he didn't feel like dwelling on this.
His voice turned curt, impersonal. "See, my mom had
been acting really distracted, leaving the house at all hours,
that kind of thing. So my dad got suspicious. He thought
she was having an affair or something, so one day he
followed her when she said she was going running. And he
found her in the middle of the running path, just sort of
standing there, smiling up at the sky."

"Oh no," whispered Willow.

"He tried shaking her, slapping her – nothing. Finally, because of all the energy work he'd done, I guess he sensed something strange and he moved his consciousness up through his chakras. And he saw the angel right there, feeding off her."

There was utter silence around them.

"The angel was – pretty startled when it realized it had been seen by someone it wasn't feeding from. It turned on my dad and he managed to fight it, using his own energy. That's not something we do any more; it's too dangerous. But meanwhile my mom was screaming and crying, telling Dad to stop, that he didn't understand. She got in between them, and the angel just...ripped her life energy away, all at once."

Willow's green eyes were large. Her throat moved as she swallowed.

"The angel disappeared, and my mom – had a massive stroke. She went into a coma and died the next day." Unbidden, another memory came: himself and Jake, standing at the side of their mother's hospital bed with their father behind them, gripping their shoulders. Alex remembered feeling more confused than sad, not understanding why she wouldn't get up.

"Oh, Alex," breathed Willow. "I am so sorry."

He gave a brusque shrug. "It was years ago. Anyway, the CIA probably thought Dad was crazy when he started talking about angels killing people, but he had been with them for a long time, so they gave him some funding and let him do what he wanted. Nobody took it really seriously, though, back then. Except for the AKs."

"And…then the Invasion happened," said Willow.

Alex nodded. He had one arm looped around the support post, and he rubbed its warm metal with his thumb. "Yeah. And suddenly the CIA was a lot more interested in whatever it was that Dad had been doing out here all these years. They took over the whole operation, like I told you. And I guess they improved it, in a lot of ways. We got better weapons, better cars. And decent salaries, for a change."

Willow looked as if she knew how much he missed the old days, when the AKs had all worked together. "Where's your father now?" she asked. "Is he still an AK?"

"He's dead, too," said Alex. "He died about five months before the Invasion." He glanced at her, the corner of his mouth twisting. "Hey, aren't you glad that you asked about all of this? It's such a cheerful topic."

Willow shook her head mutely, looking stricken. "Alex, I…"

"Come on, this is depressing," said Alex. He stood up. "So, you want to see my English textbook?"

She hesitated, and then tried to smile. "You had an English textbook? I thought you didn't do normal subjects."

"Yeah, let's see if it's still here." Crossing to a metal bookshelf that stood against one wall, Alex squatted onto his haunches, scanning the rusty shelves. "Yeah, look, here you go." He held up an old Sears catalogue.

Her smile became genuine. "You're kidding!" she laughed.

"Nope." Alex flipped through it. "This was English, math...there's even a map in the back, so we got a bit of geography. Plus the lingerie section was pretty cool. The only girls Jake and I ever saw were always wearing combats." Standing up again, he tossed the catalogue back onto the shelf.

"Were you two the only kids here?" asked Willow. She had turned on the bed to face him, drawing one knee up to her chest.

"Yeah. And every so often, someone would realize, hey, these boys aren't in school. We'd better educate them! And then the catalogue would come out for a few days. We liked target practice a lot better."

Willow started to say something, and then abruptly fell silent as they both heard it: a vehicle was approaching.

Immediately, Alex's expression turned taut, alert. He drew the gun out from the waistband of his jeans and flicked the safety off. "Get behind the door," he ordered softly.

Willow did so without argument, moving quickly across the room. Keeping close to the wall, Alex edged towards the open doorway, flanking it on the other side. He listened intently as the vehicle came to a stop, and then the slam of a car door echoed through the air. Only one. Good, he thought, pressing against the warm wall. If one of their friends from the panhandle had somehow caught up with them, then they were in for a surprise.

Slow, uneven footsteps were approaching; they seemed to hang in the air. At the sound of them, Alex's eyes widened. If he didn't know any better—

"All right, who the hell's here?" bellowed a familiar voice. "I don't like surprise visitors, so you better come on out and show yourself. 'Cause I've got a gun, and I am not happy."

A grin burst across Alex's face as joy and relief leaped through him. "It's *Cully*," he said to Willow. "Cull!" he called through the doorway, putting his gun away. "Cull, it's me, Alex!"

Cully was peering into what used to be the rec room, a rifle held at the ready; he wore jeans and a sleeveless T-shirt. At Alex's voice he spun awkwardly, surprise crashing over his broad features. For a moment he simply stared, looking startled...and then he started to smile. "Alex? God damn, it *is* you!"

Leaving the bunkhouse, Alex strode towards him, smiling broadly. He and Cully embraced, pounding each other on the backs. The big Southerner was as muscular as ever. Pulling apart, Cully squinted his blue eyes as he pretended to appraise Alex. He shook his head. "You've got even uglier, boy. How is it possible?"

"Hey, I'm just trying to be like you," said Alex with a grin. "Cully, what are you doing here? We thought—" Suddenly he remembered Willow. Turning back to the bunkhouse, he saw her standing in the doorway, watching them with an uncertain expression on her face.

Cully turned too. His eyebrows flew up. "Well, lookie here," he drawled. "Who's *this* pretty little thing?"

Willow came forward with her arms crossed over her chest, blinking in the sunshine. "Hi," she said, lifting a hand. "I'm Willow Fields. It's nice to meet you."

"*Willow Fields*...now, isn't that a pretty name," said Cully. He glanced appreciatively at Willow's figure. "You sure have got yourself a looker here, haven't you, boy? Now, ma'am, what are you doing with this reprobate? He'll lead you down the road to ruin, I promise you."

Alex felt heat creep across his face. "Um, we're not—"

"We're friends," said Willow. Her smile was a bit strained. Remembering her concerns about the AKs hating her, Alex wasn't surprised.

"Friends," repeated Cully, nodding his head as if tasting the word. "Gotcha. Well, in that case, why don't we three friends go and sit down for a bit, have something cool to drink?"

"Great," said Alex. "You got one of the generators going, then?"

"Yeah, I'm staying in your dad's old house," said Cully as they started down the road. He walked stiffly, swinging his prosthetic leg with every step. "Can't really be seen from outside the enclosure, even when I've got my truck inside."

"How come you're out here on your own, instead of training new AKs somewhere?" asked Alex. "We thought the place was abandoned."

Cully's rifle hung from his hand, moving in time with his steps. "It's seen better days, and that's a fact," he said. Walking beside Alex, Willow remained silent, her arms still crossed over her chest. As Cully spoke she turned her head to gaze at him, taking him in.

"As to what I'm doing out here, me and the CIA don't get along," Cully went on. "So I'm just holding down the old fort. Somebody's got to." They reached the house that Alex's father had lived in – one of the smallest buildings in the enclosure, but the only one that had had any real privacy. Cully opened the door and switched on the light. Alex stepped inside the main room. It was like stepping back in time; the place was exactly the same as it had been the last time he'd seen it – the scuffed table and chairs; the beat-up sofa that doubled as a bed. His father's maps on the wall were still the only decoration, with red pins showing suspected angel locations from over two years ago. The generator hummed faintly in the background.

"Home sweet home," said Cully, propping the rifle against the cement block wall. "So what are y'all doing here, anyway? I had just gone on my monthly supply run; I swear I couldn't believe it when I got back and saw Grandma's Sunday car sitting there. Good gravy, how'd you even get that thing out here without blowing it up?"

Alex laughed. "It wasn't easy. I thought we were going to be buzzard-food a few times." He dropped onto one of the scuffed wooden chairs. Willow sat hesitantly next to him, watching Cully.

"And as for what we're doing here…" He shook his head, not really sure where to begin. "It's a long story."

"Well, in that case we need a drink to help it along," said Cully. "Lemme see what I've got to wet our whistles." He lurched his way into the small kitchen, humming to himself.

The moment he was out of sight, Willow leaned towards Alex. "Something's not right," she whispered urgently, her breath tickling at his ear. "I know that he's your friend, but—"

"What is it?" Alex whispered back in surprise.

She shook her head anxiously. "I don't know. He's planning something, but I can't—"

She sat quickly back again as Cully reappeared, holding

a bottle and two glasses. There was a clinking noise as he set the glasses on the table. "You're in luck, my friend, I still got some Mr. Beam. And how about you, ma'am, you up for a drink?"

Willow gave a small smile. "Just water for me, thanks. Or a Coke, if you've got one."

"You sure?" He waggled the bottle enticingly. "Old friends and new friends, all together – deserves a bit of celebration, don't you think?"

"No, that's okay."

Cully heaved a pretend sigh. "All righty, let me get you a Coke, then. But we'll have you cuttin' it with that bourbon before the day's over, won't we, boy?" He winked at Alex, and headed into the kitchen again.

"What do you mean, he's planning something?" muttered Alex. In the kitchen, there was the sound of the small fridge opening.

Willow's face looked strained. "I'm not sure. He's glad we're here, but…it's not because he's happy to see us. There's something going on that he doesn't want us to know."

Alex felt unease ripple through him. "Willow, I've known him for almost my entire life."

Sitting back in her seat, she nodded, her expression far from convinced.

A few moments passed. Glancing towards the kitchen, Alex suddenly realized that Cully had been gone for longer than he should have. Then he hated himself for even having the thought. Not looking at Willow, he quietly pushed his chair back and went into the kitchen.

"Hey, Cully, do you want any—"

He broke off. Cully was leaning against the kitchen counter, looking down at his cellphone. "Just textin' my momma," he said cheerfully, tucking the phone into his breast pocket. He gave Alex a grin. "Funny how the service out here improved once the CIA poked their nose in, isn't it?"

Apprehension stirred through Alex. In all the years he'd known Cully, he'd never known him to keep in touch with his family. Hiding his thoughts, he picked up the cold Coke from the counter as they headed back into the other room. "Yeah...remember how everyone used to nag Dad to move the camp?" He handed the Coke to Willow; there was a hissing sound as she popped it open.

Cully chuckled as he settled himself stiffly into a chair. "Boy, do I. Folks got a little tired of trying to call base and just getting static. Then here comes the CIA, and boom – we got service!" Pouring splashes of bourbon into both of the glasses, he pushed one across the table to Alex. "So what's your news, boy? You gonna tell me what's going on?"

Stalling for time, Alex took a swig of the bourbon, tasting its smoky burn as it went down. He never drank much when he was on the road – you never knew when you were going to get a text sending you halfway across the country – but back before the Invasion, there had been countless poker games with Cully and a bottle of Beam.

Alex had never thought, then, that he would ever have reason to doubt the man.

He gave a casual shrug, keeping his expression neutral. "Nothing's going on – I just don't get along too well with the CIA, either. So I thought I'd take a break. Willow and I met in Maine – she felt like taking off for a while, too."

"You're not a runaway, are you, Miss Willow?" asked Cully, propping his muscular forearms onto the table with a grin. He swirled the golden liquid around in its glass.

"No, um – my parents don't really care what I do," said Willow with a tight smile. "They probably haven't even noticed I'm gone, yet."

"Well, I don't blame you about the CIA," said Cully to Alex. He drained half his glass in one gulp. "Cellphone service, yes; running an outfit like this, no. Buncha yahoos, if you ask me. What we need is your old man back, god rest his soul."

The words seemed to hang in the air as a memory came back to Alex: they had just buried his father out there in the blistering desert, a mound of rough, sandy soil the only marker. Cully had dropped his hand heavily on Alex's shoulder as they trudged back to the jeep. *I know how you feel, boy,* he'd said. *I had to bury my momma when I was just a few years older than you. Hurts like hell.*

Now, sitting at his father's old table, Alex nodded at Cully's comment – but he could suddenly feel the adrenalin surging through him. Cully's mother was dead. Who had he been texting, then?

"So what's your plan?" asked Cully. "You wanna stay out here for a while, show Miss Willow the sights?" He winked at her. "Man, we got some good ones. We got lizards, and buzzards…coupla coyotes…plenty of sand, if you like to sunbathe…"

Willow's hand clenched the Coke. "Maybe. I, um… I don't know what our plans are yet."

"Ah, you can't come out here all this way and not stay a while," said Cully easily, sloshing another few fingers of bourbon into Alex's glass. "'Sides, be nice for me to have the company. Gets a bit lonesome out here, and that's a fact."

"Yeah, I bet." Alex took another swig of his drink, leaned forward on his elbows. His voice sounded like it was echoing in his ears as he said, "So how's your mom doing?"

Cully shrugged. "Oh, you know, the old gal's still going strong – plays bridge like a fiend down there in Mobile. Think I'm gonna have to sign her up to Gambler's Anonymous. Or else take her to Vegas, let her clean up on the slot machines." He grinned.

"I thought your mother was dead," said Alex.

There was a beat. Cully's mouth was still curved in a smile, but the laughter had left his eyes. "No, that's my stepmomma. She died of cancer when I was about sixteen; cut my old man up plenty."

Cully's father had been a Baptist preacher; Cull had often made jokes about how he himself had broken practically every one of the Ten Commandments by the time he was a teenager. Alex remembered him laughing, shaking his head: *My poor old daddy, I almost drove him to drink. There he was, a preacher who lived by the good book; had been with the same woman his whole life – and somehow he got a hellraiser like me for a son. Man, he almost used to cry as he was whalin' on me with the flat of his Bible.*

The same woman his whole life. There had been no stepmother.

Hardly able to believe he was doing it, Alex reached for his gun. In one fluid motion, he'd pulled it from its holster and flicked the safety off. He pointed it at Cully. "Who did you text, Cull?"

A hard wariness came over Cully's face. He lowered his glass. "Now, Alex—"

Alex stood up, never taking his eyes off him. "Answer me."

His gaze narrowed, Cully hefted himself out of his chair. "Alex, bud, there's some sorta mistake here…"

"Get your hands up," said Alex. Cully did so in slow motion. Alex's eyes stayed locked on his. "Willow, reach into his breast pocket and get his cellphone. Cully, if you move an inch, I swear to god I'll shoot you."

Swallowing hard, Willow pushed her chair back and did so, her hand fumbling in the pocket. She got the cellphone and moved quickly away as she fiddled with the buttons.

Her face paled. Her eyes flew to Alex's face. "It says, *They're here. I'll hold them till you arrive.*"

"You want to explain that, Cull?" said Alex quietly.

Cully gave a slight shake of his head. "Now, Alex, I've known you for a lot of years. Hell, you're like a brother to me. So you've got to believe me when I say this is for the best."

Alex motioned for Willow to start towards the door. Snapping up Cully's car keys from the table, he shoved them in his jeans pocket. "What are you talking about?"

"You," said Cully. He jerked his head towards Willow. "You and that – *creature* you've picked up. Alex, listen to me, you don't know what you're doing. The angels say that girl's gotta go, and so she's gotta *go*."

"The angels, right." Trepidation pricked at Alex's arms. He moved a few steps backwards, still holding the gun on Cully as he grabbed up the rifle from where it stood against the wall. He handed it to Willow. "Cully, we *kill* angels, remember?"

"Not any more," said Cully. He started to take a step forward.

"Stop right there," said Alex in a low voice. "Don't make me shoot, Cully."

Cully stopped. His hands moved in supplication. "Alex, truly, I thought I was doing the best thing all those years, but I was wrong – we all were. You gotta listen to me, boy. The angels have a plan for us. They *love* us. We gotta do what they say, so that we're deserving of their love—"

No. Not angel burn; not Cully. Alex felt sick. "What are you really doing out here?" he interrupted.

"I live here, like I told you. I'm doing the angels' work, Alex."

"What the hell does that mean?"

Cully shrugged, his hands still up. "There might be a couple of AKs still left outstanding; if they turn up here I can hold them till the angels come, to show them how they've gone astray. And as for right now—" He shook his head. "Boy, every Church of Angels member in the country's been keeping a lookout for y'all. I've been thinking you might turn up here for days. I wouldn't have budged an inch, if I hadn't been flat out of food and water."

Alex stared at him, his thoughts reeling. A couple of AKs still outstanding? So what had happened to all the rest of them? But he had a terrible feeling that he knew.

"Who's left?" he said in a low voice.

Cully shook his head. "No one, probably; I've been here for months. Now, I'm begging you, bud, you've gotta shoot that thing like they want, before she hurts the angels. Just do it now, and this'll all be over with. Hell, I'll even do it for you; just give me the gun. I can tell you've got feelings for her—"

Alex had heard enough. "Come on, Willow. Let's get out of here."

Standing near the door, Willow seemed frozen, staring at Cully with her arms wrapped tightly around herself. At Alex's words, she turned towards him – and suddenly Cully reached under his T-shirt and yanked out a pistol. He aimed it at Willow. *No!* Alex fired at the same moment Cully did, their shots echoing through the room like the backfiring of a car. Time slowed, sharpened. Alex heard Willow cry out. Cully staggered and fell backwards, his gun clattering to the floor; a red bloom of blood burst from his shoulder.

Alex sprang across the room; time snapped back to normal speed as he grabbed up Cully's gun. The man was struggling to sit up, grimacing as he clutched his shoulder. "Lemme finish her off!" he gasped out. "By the angels, lemme finish her off!"

Turning quickly back to Willow, Alex's heart constricted as he saw her sitting slumped against the wall, her face the colour of paper. There was blood on her arm, and on her lilac-coloured T-shirt.

"Willow!" He was at her side in a moment. Fear pounded through him as he crouched beside her, scanning her anxiously. "Where have you been hit? Are you—"

"I'm okay," she said, her voice trembling. "It's – it's just my arm." She held it out.

Relief rushed through him, leaving him weak as he saw that the injury was minor – the bullet's head must have just missed her; its body had trenched into the side of her forearm as she'd put it up to defend herself. The wound was small but deep; it had to hurt like hell.

He squeezed her other arm tightly. "Is that the only place you're hurt?"

She nodded, her lips pale. "I think so."

"Then come on, let's get out of here before his friends show up." Helping Willow to her feet, Alex picked up the rifle that she'd dropped. Cully's cellphone was lying on the floor beside it; he stomped it hard a few times, until the display screen cracked and went blank.

Cully had staggered to his feet, clutching the back of a chair as he gripped his shoulder; blood twined over his fingers. "Alex, I swear to you – you're making a big mistake," he panted.

His eyes were bright blue, almost as familiar to Alex as his own. A hard pain clenched in Alex's chest as they regarded each other. Brothers, he had said. The man had been more like a father to him; he had looked up to Cully more than anyone he'd ever known.

"Yeah, I know I am," he said softly. "I should kill you – the old Cully would have thanked me for it."

CHAPTER *Thirteen*

WE RAN FOR THE GATE, our footsteps pounding on the baking concrete. With every step, pain burst through my arm; blood was streaming down it in ribbons. I gritted my teeth, shoving the pain aside. I was *not* going to slow us down.

A dusty black 4x4 truck sat parked outside the gate beside the Chevy; in the back through its tinted windows I could just see stacks of boxes. Alex helped me climb up into the passenger's side, his hand strong under my good arm. Jogging to the Chevy, he grabbed our things, flinging them in the back, and then jumped into the driver's seat.

A second later we were roaring off, bouncing and jolting over the rough earth as clouds of dust swirled up behind us. My arm was so bloody now that I could barely see the skin. Swallowing hard, I leaned back in the seat, feeling like I might pass out.

A few minutes later, the truck stopped. My eyes flew open – and then widened as Alex yanked his white T-shirt over his head. "Give me your arm," he said. Taking out his pocketknife, he started a tear in the shirt and then tore it in half, folding the material into a long strip.

Shakily, I held my arm out. "What are you doing? Alex, we don't have time—"

"We've got to stop the bleeding," he said. "As soon as we're safely away somewhere, I'll dig out my first aid kit." Bending over me, he started wrapping the makeshift bandage around my arm. His head was bowed, his dark hair tousled.

My pulse pounded as I stared down at him. Even through my pain, I had to resist the urge to stroke my fingers through his hair, or touch the smoothness of his bare shoulder. His hands as he worked were deft and sure, but so gentle – he was being careful not to hurt me any more than he had to. I sat very still, hardly daring to move.

I was in love with him.

The knowledge swept through me, truer than anything I'd ever known. Oh my god, I was in love with him. And even though we were friends now, he had never said that what I was didn't matter. How could it *not* matter to him? He'd been trained to kill angels since he was five years old.

Alex tucked the end of the shirt in, securing it. The *AK* on his bicep flexed slightly. "There," he said.

I glanced down at my arm, hiding my face. "Thank you," I said as I touched the soft white cloth. It had the same energy as from his T-shirt in the motel room; that same comforting sense of coming home.

I could feel his blue-grey eyes on me; for a second I thought he was going to say something, but he didn't. Then he started up the truck, and a moment later we were hurtling through the desert again. After creeping along in the Chevy, the truck was like flying. We came to the dried-out riverbed, rocked across to the other side. Finally we were swinging onto a dirt road, heading north.

Put it aside, I ordered myself harshly. Yes, I was in love with him. I had been for days, I realized – that moment on the side of the road when I'd wanted to hold him, and last night, when just feeling his fingers in my hair, his closeness, had made me want to faint.

But it didn't change anything. He didn't feel the same way about me; he couldn't.

I took a deep breath. "So – what do we do now?" I asked.

The muscles of Alex's bare arm moved as he shifted gears. "I don't know," he said. "If it's true that the rest of the AKs are gone, then—" He broke off, shaking his head. "Christ, I really don't know."

We sat in silence for a while. Finally, twisting in his seat to look over his shoulder, Alex reached behind him and pulled a bottle of water from a cardboard case. Unscrewing it, he took a deep, thirsty swig, and then offered it to me. I started to reach for the bottle – and then something caught the corner of my eye, and I turned to look behind us.

In the distance, five angels were heading towards us, flying in a starburst formation.

"Alex," I said in a low voice.

Following my gaze, Alex glanced sharply at me. "How many?"

"Five of them." I couldn't take my eyes off them. They shone against the blue sky with a bright, burning white light, their glorious wings stroking the air. Even knowing what they were, what they did to people…I had still never seen anything so heart-achingly beautiful in my life.

Then I cried out as the truck jolted. There was a squeal of brakes as Alex pulled off the road, bringing the 4x4 to a sudden sideways stop. "What are you *doing*?" I cried.

"We can't outrun them," he said. "And I can't fight them from a moving truck." He grabbed the rifle he'd taken from Cully from the back seat; checked it for ammunition and snapped it shut again. Jumping out of the truck, he ran around to my side; I was already climbing down. Behind us, the angels were growing larger and larger in the sky.

Pressing against the side of the truck, Alex sank to his heels. He took a deep breath, closing his eyes for a moment as he centred himself; I felt his energy shifting, changing. Opening his eyes again, he took up a position behind the hood, sighting along the rifle's barrel.

"Yup, five of them, all right," he murmured. I could tell that he'd handled a rifle since he was a child; he held it as though it was a part of him.

Without taking his eyes off the approaching angels, Alex pressed the car keys into my hand, squeezing it briefly. "Right, Willow, just – keep down, okay? With any luck, your angel will make an appearance again and protect you."

I stared at him. "But what about you?"

He shook his head impatiently. "Don't worry about me. If anything happens, take the truck and get away from here."

My heart started thudding. "I thought you said we can't outrun them," I said faintly. The angels were very close now, only a couple of hundred yards away.

"I can't; they'd catch up with me and tear my life energy

away. You might have a chance, though, if your angel's there." Alex was crouched over the rifle, his body both tense and relaxed at the same time. He shot me a glance, and I saw the worry in his eyes, the concern for me. "I'm serious, Willow. If it's looking bad, just get away from here."

I'm not leaving you, I thought. *There is no way that I'm leaving you.* I gripped the keys hard; they dug into my palm.

I started as Alex shot, the echo booming across the desert like thunder. In the air, one of the angels vanished into falling petals of light. I pressed tightly against the truck. They were almost near enough now to see their faces; I could hear screams of rage, see the flurry of shining wings. Alex shot again and missed as one of the angels darted to the side; tracking it, he got it as it moved. It burst into pieces, confetti on fire with the sun.

Suddenly the remaining three angels were on us, their wings filling the sky. Alex started to fire again, and then ducked as one of them surged forward and swooped at him, trying to swipe him with its wing; the others were just behind. Fear pummelled through me as I realized: Alex could never fight this many when they were so close. They were going to kill him.

All at once there was a shifting, a stirring. I felt myself growing taller, and then I was in the air, hovering over my human body as it crouched on the dry, scrubby ground below. I had an angel's body, pure white, brilliant in the sun. There was no fear, only determination.

They were not going to kill me, and they were not going to kill Alex.

The other angels attacked in a frenzy, going for my vulnerable human aura below. One dove straight for it, swiping at it with her wing. The desert turned sideways, rose up to meet me as I whipped smoothly in front of her, our wings glinting like sunlit mirrors. Her blow deflected harmlessly; she screeched in fury. "Get away, half-human *thing*," she hissed.

I didn't answer; I was already whipping away to block the other one, cutting sharply in the air and then back again, wings flashing, faster than light.

Only seconds had passed. Alex fired again; the angel that had been on him exploded into fragments of light. Screeching in fury, the remaining two dove at him in a spiralling chaos of wings and radiance. I saw his jaw tense as he realized there was no way he could get them both; one of them was going to kill him.

The low mountains on the horizon seemed to shift sideways, straightening again as I darted above him, spreading my wings.

Alex's eyes widened as he saw me; I saw him lower his rifle slightly, staring upwards. The two angels banked sideways, in opposite directions; the world turned this way and that as I swooped through the air above him, blocking them, keeping him safe with my wings. With a howl of anger, one of the angels veered back towards my human figure. Alex started to shoot; the other one, momentarily getting away from me, dove right at him. He looked up, startled; hit the ground and rolled as her wings strained for him. She was on him; she was going to get him.

I didn't even hesitate. I went for the angel that was on Alex first, swooping in and forcing her back with my wings. I don't know how I knew how to fight, but I did, and she screeched in fury, flapping and snarling at me. Dimly, I was aware that my human form was vulnerable, that the other angel was almost on it. I didn't care. This angel was not going to hurt Alex.

A shot sounded as Alex fired. Light erupted around us like fireworks as the angel attacking my human form vanished.

The final angel howled in rage. She beat at me with her wings, trying to push me aside; then suddenly she twisted backwards, spiralling towards Alex, wings shrieking through the air. The desert turned as I dove to protect him again, but it wasn't needed. From the ground, he rolled and shot – and the final angel's halo buckled and trembled. A second later it was gone.

The sudden stillness was like a clear mountain pool. I hovered for a moment, gently moving my wings as shock and relief coursed through me. We were still alive. Somehow, we were both all right. I saw Alex stagger to his feet and look up at me, his expression dazed – and then I slowly drifted downwards, merging with my human body on the ground.

I was me again.

Alex came over to me; dropped to his knees. He was breathing hard, his torso streaked with grime and sweat. We stared at each other. I'd been trying so hard not to really think about it…but now I couldn't ignore it any more. I started shaking as the reality of my otherness roared through me. This hadn't been a brief flash, or something that might have been a dream – it was utterly, achingly real.

I wasn't completely human.

The words tore out of me. "Oh god, I don't want this, I don't want it—" All at once I was clutching my forehead, crying; great sobs that racked helplessly through me, shaking me like a terrier does a rat.

"Willow! Willow, don't – please don't—" Then Alex's arms were wrapped tightly around me; he was holding me, rocking me. I slumped against his chest, crying as if I would never stop. "It's okay," he whispered, his voice ragged. He cradled me to him, dropped his head onto mine so that I felt his lips moving in my hair. "It's okay."

I cried for a long time, wetting his skin with my tears,

so that his chest turned warm and slick under my cheek. Slowly, I became aware of the strength of his arms; the faint smell of his sweat. His heart, beating firmly against me.

I sat up, pulling away. I could hardly look at him. "How can you bear to touch me?" I wiped my eyes with my hand. "When you know I have this *thing* inside of me that's like them?"

"No!" Alex's voice was fierce. His hands clenched me by the shoulders as he forced me to look at him. "Willow, listen to me. You are *nothing* like them. Nothing."

I gulped, wanting so much to believe him. Biting my lip, I stared at the hard, bare mountains on the blue horizon, remembering how they had shifted as I flew. "It's never going to go away, is it?" I whispered.

Alex shook his head slowly. "No," he said. His eyes were full of compassion.

Glancing down, I ran a finger across the scrabbly soil; it felt dry and gritty to my touch. Around us, the desert seemed to stretch out for ever, the sun beating down on us like an oven. "Okay," I said finally. "I sort of knew that." I cleared my throat, embarrassed suddenly. "I'm – I'm sorry. I didn't mean to freak out."

"Don't apologize." He helped me up, his hand remaining briefly on my arm. "Are you all right?"

I nodded, not really looking at him. "Yeah. I think so." But as I remembered what had happened, heat stroked my cheeks. My angel had protected him, my love for him as obvious as if I'd blurted it out.

Alex blew out a breath. "Right, well – we'd better get away from here. Try to figure out what we're going to do."

We climbed back into the truck; my legs felt strange and wobbly. And belatedly, my arm was hurting again, throbbing dully under Alex's T-shirt. He spun the steering wheel as we lurched back onto the dirt road. A second later we were speeding through the desert again. I leaned back against my seat, closing my eyes…and tried not to remember the sensation of having wings, glittering in the sunlight.

We came to a rest stop about an hour after we got back onto the highway – a brown-painted building with vending machines standing on its porch area, and a few empty picnic tables scattered about. Alex pulled over behind the building, out of sight from the road.

In the ladies' room, I changed my T-shirt for a fresh one and then stood at the sink, splashing water on my face. Some of it got on my hurt arm, turning streaks of dried blood a pale, runny red. The mirror was one of those metallic ones that you can hardly see yourself in, but I could see enough to realize that I looked like something out of a horror film. My hurt arm had red snaking down it like the zombies had just attacked. I smiled faintly as I imagined Nina: *Look, it's Willow Meets the Zombies! Somebody get Steven Spielberg on the phone!* Then my smile faded. What would she say if she knew the truth about what I was? Trying not to think about it, I wiped the blood off with a moistened paper towel, working around the square of Alex's T-shirt. Then I dug my hairbrush out of my bag and combed my hair back, tying it up into a knot.

"Hey," said Alex's voice. I glanced up; he was standing in the doorway holding a small first aid kit. "Can I come in? We should probably get your arm fixed up."

I could hardly meet his eyes. "Yeah, sure."

He had pulled on a blue T-shirt, and looked like he'd splashed water on himself too; his arms and neck were slightly wet. So was his hair, as if he'd stuck it under the tap. The urge to touch the dampness of it where it lay against his neck was almost overwhelming. I glanced away.

Coming over to the sinks, Alex gently took my arm; I winced as he unwrapped the strip of T-shirt. Once it was washed off, the wound didn't look that bad, though it was sort of deep. Alex cleaned it with a tube of antiseptic from the first aid kit, and then wrapped gauze around it. His hands were skilful, efficient.

"Um…you really know what you're doing," I said.

He shrugged, his dark hair falling across his forehead. "We had to do everything for ourselves at the camp. There wasn't a doctor for miles." He secured the gauze with tape, firming it in place with his finger. His finger lingered for a moment, and then he dropped his hand. "Right, I think you'll live."

I touched the bandage. "So…what now?"

Alex shook his head as he put the first aid things away. "I don't know," he said. "It sounds like there aren't any AKs left now, apart from me. Even if there are, I don't have any way to find them. Cully—" He stopped, pain creasing his face. "Cully was the one person I thought I could trust," he said finally.

I didn't want to ask, but I had to know. "Alex, do you still…do you still want to stay together? You don't have to, if you'd rather not. I could go off on my own, or something."

His head jerked up. "What are you talking about?"

"You're in so much danger with me, and—" I looked away, hugging myself. "And after what you saw today, I wouldn't blame you. I mean, I know you've seen my angel before, but not like that. It must have been—" My mouth tightened; I couldn't continue.

"Willow." His voice was very soft. "What I saw was your angel protecting me. When I was in trouble, she protected me even before she protected you." He hesitated. "Did you know she was doing it? Or was she – something separate from you?"

I didn't want to answer this; it felt too exposing, too raw. But I couldn't lie about it, either; it would be to deny everything I felt about him. "No, it wasn't separate," I whispered. "I didn't know it was going to happen, but once it did…I was the angel. I – I didn't want anything to hurt you."

Alex stood without speaking for a moment, just gazing at me. My heart clenched at the expression in his eyes. Finally he said huskily, "Jesus, Willow. You shouldn't have done that, not for me. If anything had happened to you—" He broke off.

"I know." I let out a breath. "I wouldn't be able to defeat the angels."

"That's not what I meant." His throat moved as he swallowed. "Yes, I still want to be with you," he said.

I felt tears start. "Really? You really trust me, even though I'm a half-angel?"

He stared at me in confusion. "I've known you were a half-angel since the day we met."

"I know, but—" I swiped at my eyes. "It just feels a lot more real to me, now. Do you trust me?"

Slowly, Alex shook his head. "How can you even ask me that, after what you did? I'd trust you with my life."

I almost sobbed out loud; I tried to turn it into a laugh. "I thought – I thought you didn't trust anyone."

"I'll make an exception in your case." Reaching out, Alex touched the side of my face, gently cupping my cheek with his hand. "Willow, that was the – nicest, most wonderful – *stupidest* thing that anyone's ever done for me."

I did laugh then, wiping my eyes. "So you really want to hang out with someone this stupid?"

His own smile faded. "Yeah, I do," he said softly, his hand still touching my face.

The world went very still around us. Distantly, I could hear the sound of a car passing by on the highway; my heart thudded crazily as we stared at each other. Alex hesitated. His head moved a fraction, so that for a wild moment I actually thought he was going to kiss me.

Then a look that I couldn't read flickered through his eyes. Letting his hand fall from my face, he cleared his throat and smiled. "If, um – you still want to hang out with me, that is."

I nodded, my cheeks on fire. "Yeah, I think I can deal with that," I said, managing to smile back. Embarrassment was pounding through me. How could I have imagined, even for a second, that he was about to kiss me?

"So...what now?" I said after a pause, trying to sound normal.

Silently, Alex finished packing his first aid kit. "Come on, let's get something to drink," he said.

Standing outside, he fed coins into the vending machine, buying us each a Coke. I hadn't thought I wanted anything, but suddenly it tasted wonderful, like the most fabulous nectar, and I took deep gulps. We were alive, that was the important thing. And we were still going to be together. Warmth filled my chest at the thought.

Leaving the porch area, we went back out into the sunshine, heading towards the truck. Alex was frowning, looking down as he walked. "To tell you the truth, I think our options are pretty limited," he said finally. "I was counting on Cully to know how to reach the other AKs." He sighed. "What we really need is for the CIA to find us, if Project Angel still exists."

"Could they?"

He shrugged. "Yeah, in theory...if there's anyone left in Project Angel without angel burn, then they've got to be looking for us – they must have spies in the Church of Angels who'll have heard what's going on."

I thought about this as we reached the truck. I could feel the heat coming off it, just standing next to it. "That doesn't help us, though, does it? Even if they are looking for us, we don't have any way to contact them."

Alex shook his head as he drained his Coke. "No...we're on our own." He pitched the empty can into a metal garbage can nearby; it made a metallic ringing noise. "Look, I think that just keeping alive is probably a pretty good goal for now. What do you think about going to ground for a while? It'll give us some breathing room, so we can try to figure out what to do."

"Going to ground," I repeated. "You mean – hide out somewhere?"

His eyes met mine. "Yeah, what do you think? I know a place we can go."

Just the thought of being somewhere alone with Alex, not on the run or driving all day, sounded incredible. Remembering the warmth of his hand on my cheek, my heart quickened. "Yeah," I said. "It, um…it sounds good."

"Okay," he said, nodding. We climbed back into the truck. Replacing the first aid kit in his bag, Alex tapped the steering wheel, looking deep in thought. "Right, with any luck, those were the only angels in the area – if we get away fast, it might take a while for the others to figure out what's happened. The place I'm thinking of is up in the mountains, so we'll have to stop and grab a few things we might need. And check out whatever Cully's got in those boxes back there; make sure we have enough food."

I started to smile. "You mean we're going shopping?"

Alex laughed. "Don't get too excited; we're talking sporting goods." He started the truck. "Right," he said. "It's 106 miles to Chicago, we got a full tank of gas, half a pack of cigarettes, it's dark…and we're wearing sunglasses."

I felt my mouth quirk at the *Blues Brothers* quote. And I thought, *even if he's never going to feel the same way about me, it doesn't matter*. I still wanted to be with him.

I never wanted to be without him.

"Hit it," I said.

A few hours later, they had crossed over into Arizona, keeping to minor roads whenever they could. Coming to a small shopping mall outside of Phoenix, Alex pulled into the parking lot, finding a space that was half-hidden behind a dumpster. Checking the boxes that held Cully's supplies, they looked over the stacks of canned food. "Do you think it'll be enough?" asked Willow, craning over her seat.

"I'd better get some more," said Alex, looking across at the supermarket that sat at one end of the mall. "I want us to be able to hide out for a long time, if we need to."

Willow glanced over at the supermarket too, her brow furrowed. "Well – I guess I'd better stay in the truck while you get whatever we need. I don't have a cap to hide my hair any more."

Alex knew that she was right, but he didn't like the thought of leaving her alone – not when a description of the truck had probably already been e-mailed to every Church of Angels member in the country. "I'll hurry," he said. "Here – take this, okay?" Reaching under his T-shirt he took out his gun and held it out to her; her green eyes widened.

"Alex, you know I don't—"

"Please," he said.

Gingerly, she took it, looking as if she expected it to grow teeth and bite her. "I could seriously never use this," she said.

"Fine, just wave it threateningly at someone if you have to. But I'd feel better if you had it." Taking his wallet out, he glanced inside it, counting his cash.

Willow's eyebrows rose at the number of bills. She placed the gun carefully in the storage bucket, keeping her fingers well away from the trigger. "Are you sure you're not a drug dealer?"

Alex laughed. "No, I just never really trusted the CIA. I always kept some cash on hand, in case I needed to take off." He glanced at the clothes she was wearing. "You're going to need a few things; it'll be colder where we're going. What size do you wear? Shoe size too, so I can get you some hiking boots."

Willow told him, looking apprehensive. "You're going to do my shopping for me?"

He grinned. "Don't you trust me?"

She bit her lip. "Um…only get solid colours, okay? I hate prints. And could you get me a toothbrush?"

"Solid colours, no prints, toothbrush – got it. I'll be back as soon as I can." Alex paused before he got out, concern creasing through him. "Look, keep down, okay? Pretend you're asleep or something."

She nodded, her eyes warm on his. "Don't worry. I'll be fine."

Alex did the shopping as quickly as he could, loading a cart with everything he thought they might need. At the sporting goods store, he bought them both hiking boots and thermal sleeping bags; a camp stove; canisters of gas. He didn't start to feel really out of his depth until he checked out a clothing store to get things for Willow. He did the best he could, taking a pile of clothes to the counter.

"Shopping for your girlfriend?" said the girl at the cash register.

"Sort of," said Alex. As she rang up his purchases, his attention was caught by a display of silver jewellery on the check-out counter. One of the necklaces had a chain so slim it was almost invisible; a faceted crystal teardrop hung from it, catching the light. Lifting the necklace up on the display rack, Alex turned the pendant over in his hand. It reminded him of Willow. The crystal was the way her angel had looked, as she hovered in the sky above him.

"That's pretty, isn't it?" said the girl. "I bet she'd like it." She dimpled at him.

Alex hesitated, not sure whether it was a good idea. But the memory of Willow's angel lingered: the way it had protected him, keeping him from harm. He'd never been so moved by anything in his life. Besides, he thought, they'd probably still be in hiding when their birthdays came up in a few weeks; it would be nice to have something to give to her.

He unhooked the necklace from the rack. "Could I get this?"

The girl placed the necklace in a small white box padded with cotton. "You are going to get so many brownie points for this," she smiled. She started to put it in the large plastic bag with the rest of Willow's clothes.

"Here, I'll, um – keep that separate," said Alex. Paying her, he stuck the box in his pocket. "Thanks."

He headed back to the truck, feeling confused with himself. The moment in the washroom came hurtling back; he had only barely stopped himself from kissing Willow. What the hell had he been doing, anyway? He *knew* better. Even just as friends, he didn't want to be as close to anyone as he'd somehow already managed to get to Willow. It wasn't worth it; caring about people simply meant that he lost them.

Yet it felt as if there was no way back. He didn't want to be this close to her...but the problem was, he didn't want to be without her, either.

When Alex reached the truck, to his relief Willow was curled up asleep, hardly even visible from outside. He stood gazing at her for a moment, thinking how peaceful she looked.

"Hey," he said softly, leaning in and touching her shoulder through the open window.

She stirred drowsily awake, blinking up at him. "Oh, wow, I really *did* fall asleep." Getting out, she helped him load some of the lighter boxes into the truck.

"Careful of your arm," he said, glancing at the bandage.

"It's okay now, just a little sore. I had a good doctor." Spotting the shopping bag with the clothes, Willow peeked inside. "Hey, a red sweater...that's really pretty."

Alex had thought the colour would look great with her hair, though he was too embarrassed to say so now. He shrugged as he stacked boxes. "I got you another cap, too – you'd better put it on."

She did so, tucking her hair out of sight and putting on her sunglasses. As they finished loading the supplies, she said, "Do you want me to drive for a while?"

"That's okay; go back to sleep if you want."

Willow had her head to one side, taking in the truck's lines. "No, I'm fine," she said. "I don't mind, really."

Alex grinned suddenly. "Oh, I get it. You just want to drive a big 4x4 and see what it's like, right?"

Her eyes sparkled with laughter. "Well..." she admitted.

"Go for it," he said, tossing her the keys. She snapped them smartly from the air, and a moment later was perched on the driver's seat, moving it forward. She looked incredibly cute behind the wheel. Trying not to think about it, he settled beside her, stretching his legs out.

Starting up the truck, Willow checked the rear-view mirror and manoeuvred them out of the parking lot. "Which way am I going?"

"Take the interstate north for now," he directed. "We'll get off it soon, and use back roads instead."

She pulled out onto the main road. "This is great," she said, downshifting as she slowed for a stop light. "Nice and smooth."

"No way. Is it really better than a Mustang?"

"You know, it's so sad how you just don't get it." She glanced at him with a smile.

They rode in companionable silence for a while. Willow snapped on the radio, twirling the dial to a classical station. The floating, buoyant sound of a violin concerto wrapped around them. "Is this okay?" she asked.

Alex had his eyes half-closed, his hands linked over his stomach. "Yeah, I like classical. Dad used to play it sometimes."

Between the music and the motion of the truck, he

almost drifted off to sleep himself. Then Willow's voice said, "Um, Alex…can you wake up?" He opened his eyes groggily. She was peering into the rear-view mirror, looking anxious. "Okay, tell me I'm being paranoid," she said. "That green Pontiac back there. Is it following us?"

Immediately wide awake, he twisted in his seat. The Pontiac was cruising along behind them, about ten car lengths back. "What's it been doing?" he asked.

"Keeping exactly that same length behind us, no matter what I do. I've tried speeding up a little and slowing down, and it always stays right there." She looked in the mirror again. "I mean, I know it's the interstate, so it's hard to tell. I've just…sort of got a feeling about it."

Willow's "feelings" were more than good enough for him. "Right, move to the outside lane," said Alex. She did so. A moment later, the Pontiac followed, gliding across the lanes.

"Just keep going at this speed," he said, keeping an eye on the Pontiac. "Then when you get to the next turn-off, throw the wheel hard and get onto it."

Willow nodded, her hands tensing on the wheel. An exit came up a few miles later; waiting until the last possible moment, she spun the wheel sharply to the right and swerved across three lanes of traffic. Horns blared; the 4x4 lurched as she bounced up the ramp, spinning the wheel to right them. Behind them, the Pontiac quickly changed lanes, but didn't make the exit in time. Alex watched as they sailed fruitlessly past.

"Okay, as soon as you can, get back onto the interstate again, still heading north."

Willow's eyes flew to his. "*Back?* But—"

"It's okay. Trust me."

With a worried look, she took the next turn-off, returning them to the interstate. About ten minutes later, Alex spotted the green Pontiac speeding down the interstate in the opposite direction, having obviously taken the next exit off to follow them. He let out a breath. "Good. They fell for it."

Willow swallowed. "Do you think we lost them?"

"For now, anyway," he said. He glanced at her. "Hey, pretty good driving."

"Pretty good trick," she said, trying to smile. "Did you have high-speed chase lessons in school?"

Alex hesitated. "Cully told me about it," he said finally. "He used to bootleg, back in Alabama. You should have heard the stories he used to tell." He fell silent, pain knifing through him.

Willow was watching his face. "I'm sorry," she said in a low voice. "He was a good friend of yours, wasn't he?"

Memories flashed past – Cully smoking his cigar with a grin, shaking his head in the rear-view mirror at him and Jake. And then later, Cully's arm firm around his shoulders, steadying him, saying, *You did good. You did good.* Alex cleared his throat. "Yeah, I've known him for most of my life. He was just – a really good guy." He tried for an upbeat tone. "Wow, look, another depressing topic."

"I don't mind depressing topics," said Willow softly.

"I do." He leaned back in his seat again, stretching his legs out. Deliberately, he changed the subject. "Do you want to stop and grab something to eat soon, if there's a drive-through or something?"

"Okay," said Willow after a pause. Then she smiled at him, giving him an arch look. "It's time for a coffee break, that's what you're really saying, isn't it? You need your caffeine fix."

The warmth of her smile flowed through him, easing the pain over Cully. Suddenly all Alex wanted was to reach across and touch Willow – to link his fingers through hers as her hand rested on her thigh, or gently stroke the hair back from her temple.

He pushed the thought away harshly and crossed his arms over his chest. "Yep, definitely time for a coffee break," he said, closing his eyes. "You see right through me."

CHAPTER *Fourteen*

THEY SLEPT IN SHIFTS THAT night, driving steadily north-west. The states changed from California to Nevada and then back again as they danced with the border, leaving the desert behind them and entering the Sierra Nevada mountains. By around six a.m., the route had grown so steep that Alex had to keep changing gears as he steered the truck up the twisting roads. Hidden in the pre-dawn shadows, he knew that there was a drop of several hundred feet to one side, with only a flimsy guard rail between it and the truck. In several places, the sweep of their headlights showed skid marks, where cars had crashed into it.

Finally, on the mountain side of the road, he spotted the hard, rocky scrabble that he remembered from the camping trip with Jake, when they'd first found this place. Engaging the four-wheel drive, Alex steered them off-road and the truck obediently started up the hill. A moment later they'd rounded a bend, taking them out of view from the main road.

Willow stirred, lifted her head. "Where are we?" she asked sleepily, her blonde hair tousled. Glancing at her, Alex's gaze lingered for a brief moment; she looked so soft and vulnerable.

"Not there yet," he said. "Go back to sleep if you want."

Instead she stretched and sat up, peering out the window. "The place is up here?"

"Yeah, about fifteen miles back in the mountains." He concentrated as he drove; the way was even worse than he remembered, even in a truck like this. They moved slowly, rocking from side to side as the 4x4 crawled upwards.

After over an hour, they finally came to a high, stony valley, with grass and shrubs growing resolutely between the rocks. Alex parked the truck. They were in a sort of bowl in the middle of the mountains; around them, the morning sun tinged the peaks with a golden light, as if they were glowing from the inside.

"This is...beautiful," said Willow, shaking her head with awe. "Are we camping?"

"Sort of." Climbing out of the truck, Alex suddenly felt happier than he'd felt in a long time. The air was so fresh up here that it hit you like a rush of adrenalin, waking you up and making you feel alive. He grinned at Willow. "Come on, it's time for the hiking boots."

They got their boots on, and Willow pulled the bright red sweater over her head. He had been right; it looked great on her. "This is so gorgeous," she repeated softly, taking in the early morning mist that curled about the valley, and the evergreens that spiked towards the sky. Then she glanced at the truck. "Um, wait a minute… do we have to carry all this stuff?"

"Yep. It's not far." Alex grabbed one of the boxes, and Willow did the same. There was a thin deer trail leading steeply up through the rocky underbrush to the north. They started climbing, winding their way through the pine trees.

About a hundred yards up, they came to a clearing with a stream running through it. A small, dilapidated cabin sat nearby, leaning slightly to one side. "Oh!" gasped Willow, stopping short. "Alex, what *is* this place?"

Shifting his weight to open the door with one hand, Alex entered the cabin and went inside, dumping his box on the table. Willow followed him, wide-eyed. "Jake and I built it, sort of," he said.

"You – *really?*"

He nodded. "Sometimes we used to go off camping on our own for a couple of days, on the way back from a hunt. When we found this place it had half-fallen down. We came back here a couple of times, fixed it up some." Glancing around him, Alex realized that he'd forgotten how basic the cabin actually was. There was greenish moss growing on one of the walls, and the ancient camping bed looked like something had been nesting in it. Still, it was better than being shot at.

Willow's eyes were shining. "You're a genius," she said fervently, dropping her box down beside his. "Nobody will ever find us here."

He smiled. The cabin was pretty much their only option, but he was glad that she didn't mind it. "Just don't breathe too hard, or the roof might cave in."

They started moving the rest of their things inside, hiking back and forth from the truck. Willow took her sweater off again, tying it around her waist. "I wonder who used to live up here, anyway?" she said as they started up with another load. Her cheeks were pink with exertion.

"Probably a prospector," said Alex. He was carrying a box on his shoulder as he moved up the trail. "There's a sort of wooden contraption behind the cabin, like you'd use to pan for gold."

"What, like the forty-niners? Do people still do that?"

"Yeah, I guess...just drop out of life, and go off

panning." Out here in the middle of nowhere, with only the mountains and the sky around them, Alex could see the appeal. If there weren't any angels in the world, he'd be tempted to do something like it himself.

When all their things were finally in the cabin, Alex got the camping axe from one of the boxes and they went back down to the truck, where Willow helped him camouflage it so that it couldn't be seen from the air. Hacking off slim, prickly branches from the surrounding pine trees, they wove them together into a sort of screen on the truck's roof and hood, securing it all in place with twine.

"Do you think it'll hold?" said Willow finally, taking a few steps back and regarding their handiwork.

Alex replaced the axe in its leather case. "Should be okay. We'll keep checking on it, to make sure."

She shook her head, her green eyes admiring. "You know, I really don't think camouflaging the truck would even have occurred to me."

He laughed. "Yeah, but if it breaks down, you're the one who gets to fix it – I bought you a toolkit, just in case."

They climbed back up the narrow trail to the cabin. Inside, the small space was overflowing with boxes and bags. Alex started shifting them into some sort of order, glad to have something else to do. All at once he was very conscious of the fact that he and Willow were out here alone together, sharing the same small, intimate space.

Willow helped him stack the food boxes at one end of the cabin. She had fallen silent since they got inside, and he saw her give him a troubled glance when she thought he wasn't looking. After several minutes, the quiet felt like it might choke him. He cleared his throat. "I got a camping stove and some gas for us to cook with...I mean, it won't be great, but—"

"No, it's perfect," said Willow. Her eyes flashed to his and then away again, her face reddening. Turning quickly, she put her clothes bag in the corner, rolling down its plastic top. Alex started to say something, and then stopped as the realization thundered through him:

She felt the same way about him.

He hadn't been sure. Even when he'd almost kissed her, he hadn't really known what she was feeling – apart from that somehow, she liked him, even after he'd been such a jerk to her to start with. But now...

It doesn't change anything, Alex told himself dazedly. *It's still a really bad idea.* Even so, he stood frozen, staring at her as the world seemed to shrink around them.

Straightening, Willow self-consciously tucked a strand of hair behind her ear, not meeting his gaze. "Listen, is it possible to...I mean, I'd sort of like to get washed off and changed, but—"

Alex came abruptly back to himself. "Uh, yeah – there's the stream, but it's pretty cold. And...I didn't bring a towel." Damn. Why hadn't he thought of that?

"That's okay," said Willow. "I can just use a T-shirt or something to dry off with."

Alex grabbed one of his old ones from his bag. "Here, use this."

Their fingers touched as she took it from him. "Thanks."

He turned away as she rooted through her shopping bag for fresh clothes, pretending to be fiddling with the camping stove. There was nothing to fiddle with; all you did was hook up the gas lead to it. Finally Willow hesitated by the door. She was holding a neat pile of clothing with a motel bar of soap perched on top of it; his T-shirt was under her arm, along with one of the rolls of toilet paper he'd bought. At least he'd remembered that much. "I guess the...facilities are outside, right?" she said awkwardly.

"Yeah, um...sorry," said Alex, rising to his feet.

"No, don't be sorry! This place is amazing. You're amazing." Red swept her face again. Ducking her head away, she said hurriedly, "So, anyway, I'll just go to the stream." And then she was gone, the door shutting softly behind her.

Alex let out a breath. Somehow, he found himself rearranging the cardboard boxes, so that some that had been on the bottom were now on the top. He thought he'd give anything for some really hard, physical work right then – about ten miles on the treadmill would do it, or a hundred reps of the biceps press.

After twenty minutes or so, the door opened and Willow came in again, her green eyes dancing. "Oh my gosh, you weren't kidding. That was *cold*!" She was wearing jeans and the red sweater; a pale blue T-shirt peeked out from the bottom of it.

Alex grinned, relieved at the easing of the mood. "Hey, don't say I didn't warn you."

"I hung your shirt over a branch outside," she said, tucking her things away in her bag. "It can be our designated towel, okay?"

"Sounds good."

"So, um…" She stood up again, and gave a small, smiling shrug.

It was only about ten a.m.; they had a whole day to fill. Eager to avoid that sort of tension building again, Alex said, "Hey, do you play cards?" He dug in one of the boxes. "I bought us a deck."

Willow raised an eyebrow at him as she sat down at the table. "Are you sure you want to risk this, when I almost beat you at Quarters? I play Go Fish, does that count?"

"Go Fish?" He held back a laugh. "Yeah, I think I'll risk it." There was a box resting on the other rickety chair. Taking it off, he pulled the chair around to her right – the only place in the crowded cabin where there was room. He slipped the cellophane wrapping off the cards; the plastic made a crinkling sound as he put it aside. "Is Go Fish all you play? How about blackjack? Or canasta?"

She shook her head with a grin. Her hair was still loose, falling past her shoulders. "Sorry. I think I must have had a disadvantaged childhood."

"Gin rummy?"

"Barely."

"I'll teach you blackjack first," he said, thumbing through the deck and pulling the jokers out. "It's really easy." The deck rattled as he shuffled it. He dealt them two cards each, flipping them expertly across the table.

"So, why am I not surprised that you're a card sharp?" Willow picked up her cards.

He shrugged as he looked down at his own hand, trying not to notice the way her face lit up when she smiled. "We used to play a lot, back at the camp. There wasn't much else to do at night without a TV, apart from listening to the coyotes howl… Okay, I'm the dealer this round, so you're trying to beat me. The goal is to get as close to twenty-one points as you can, without going over. Wait, we need something to bet with—"

Scraping back his chair, he delved into one of the grocery boxes and found a large bag of M&Ms. Cully had always had a sweet tooth, he remembered with a pang.

"Great," said Willow when she saw them. "That can be breakfast, too."

She had a point; suddenly he was starving. Opening the bag, Alex scooped out a handful and then slid it across to her. "Right, the face cards are ten points each, the ace is worth either one or eleven, and the rest are what they say they are." He popped a brown M&M into his mouth.

Willow seemed to think this over, munching a few of the candies as she gazed at her cards. "And we're supposed to be going to twenty-one, right?"

"Right."

"Cool." She laid down her hand. Alex groaned, laughing, as he saw that she had a king and an ace. "I'd like the ace to be worth eleven points, please," she said, dimpling a smile at him. "What do I win?"

"Okay, you asked for it. What you win is me taking my gloves off and wiping the floor with you." Scraping the cards across the table, Alex shuffled the deck again and slapped it on the table in front of her. "Your deal. Though I'm not really sure why I keep putting myself through this with you."

She gave him an arch look as she picked up the cards. "Glutton for punishment, obviously."

They played for hours, sometimes stopping to talk. As if by mutual agreement, neither of them mentioned anything about angels. They just talked, sharing stories from their lives. Alex found out that Willow liked to cook, and that she even made home-made jam in the autumn; he told her about his own secret love of astronomy, and how in the camp he used to lie on the desert ground at night and stare up at the stars. After a while, they heated up a couple of cans of chilli for lunch, eating straight from the cans with metal camping forks. Remembering that there were a few six-packs of beer in one of Cully's boxes, Alex went outside to put one of them in the stream to chill.

"We've got a fridge," said Willow, drifting out after him.

"Yeah, all the modern conveniences." Alex straightened up from the stream and stretched, feeling stiff from sitting still for so long. "Do you want to go for a walk?"

Putting on their hiking boots, they explored the area around the cabin for the rest of the afternoon, following the different deer trails. Willow was very relaxed company; easy to talk to when either of them felt like talking, or just as happy to stay quiet, lost in her own thoughts as they climbed. Glancing at her profile as they sat on a boulder gazing out at the view, it suddenly struck Alex that he'd never felt so comfortable with anyone in his life. It felt as if he'd known Willow always.

No. It felt like she was a part of him.

He was silent as they hiked back to the cabin. When they got to the stream, Willow walked ahead of him, bending down and touching the beer cans. "You'll be happy to know that the fridge works," she said over her shoulder with a grin. "Do you want one?"

"Yeah, thanks." She handed him a cold beer, and then carefully nestled the rest of the six-pack back into the stream, resting it against a rock. "You don't want one?" he asked as they headed into the cabin, stopping to take their boots off.

She shook her head. "I don't really drink; it just makes me fall asleep. I might have a few sips of yours, though."

They went back to playing cards, heating up another meal when they got hungry. As it started to get dark, Alex lit the camping lantern he'd bought, putting it in the centre of the table. Slipping outside to use the "facilities", Willow returned wearing a pair of navy blue sweatpants instead of her jeans.

"A bit comfier," she explained. She dropped into her seat again, to his left at the small table. They had turned to gin rummy by then, playing for matchsticks after the M&Ms were all gone. Picking up her cards, Willow settled back into her chair and drew a knee up, her bare foot curled over the edge of her seat as she inspected her hand.

Alex gazed at her. Her mouth was slightly open; she ran her fingernail against her lower teeth as she thought. She'd knotted her hair at the nape of her neck again, and a strand had slipped loose onto her shoulder, gleaming in the lantern light. Suddenly all of his objections seemed meaningless. *Don't,* he thought. *You'll regret it.*

He didn't care any more.

Slowly, unable to stop himself, he reached over and cupped his hand around her foot.

Willow's eyes flew to his, startled. They stared at each other. Her foot felt small under his hand; he rubbed lightly with his thumb, feeling the silky heat of her skin, his pulse hammering through his veins. He felt like he was falling. All he could see was her.

She looked close to tears. "Alex—"

Leaning across the corner of the table, he cradled her face in his hands and kissed her.

Her mouth was soft and warm. With a sob, Willow returned the kiss, throwing her arms around his neck; he felt her hair tumble down around his hands. Happiness burst through him, exploding through his chest. Willow. Oh god, Willow.

She started to pull away. "Alex, wait – are you sure about this? I'm a half-angel, I can't change that—"

He almost laughed. "Shut up," he whispered.

It was awkward with the table between them. Scooping an arm under Willow's knees, Alex pulled her gently onto his lap, holding her close as they kissed again. Her body felt small, perfect, meant to be in his arms. Her long hair tickled around his face and he stroked it back, twining his fingers through its softness, feeling his heart pounding against hers.

At last they came apart, staring at each other in wonder. Alex knew that he was smiling; he couldn't stop. "You are so beautiful," he said in a low voice.

Willow shook her head dazedly. She touched his face; he shivered as she traced his eyebrow with her fingers. "I never thought this would happen," she said. She swallowed. "I've, um...sort of been wanting it to."

Alex couldn't stop looking at her; it was as if he'd never seen her before. Slowly, he ran his hand up her arm. Just the feel of it made his breath catch in his throat. "Me too," he said. "Since practically the first time I saw you."

Willow's eyes widened in surprise. "But – you hated me then."

He couldn't help himself; his lips brushed her neck, her cheek. "No, I didn't," he murmured against her warm skin. "I never hated you. Even when I thought I should, I was so attracted to you that I could hardly stand it. I've been going insane, these last few days."

She leaned back slightly. "You – *really*? I couldn't tell – I – at the rest stop, I thought I must have just imagined it."

All Alex wanted to do was keep kissing her, but she seemed so stunned that he started to laugh. "You're supposed to be psychic; you really couldn't tell what I was feeling?"

"No!" Willow gave a short laugh, looking dumbfounded. "I was too – I could hardly even breathe when you were touching me, hardly *think*. I thought you were just…comforting me, and that you only wanted to be friends."

He linked his fingers through hers, gripping her hand tightly. "Believe me, being friends was the last thing on my mind just then. I wanted to kiss you so much that it hurt."

She hesitated. "Why didn't you? Because I'm a half-angel?"

Alex shook his head. "I haven't cared about that in days. It was because…" He could hardly even remember now why this hadn't seemed like a good idea. "Because I'm an idiot, I guess."

Willow sat very still. Around them, there was only the glow of the camp lantern, and the velvet silence from outside. "It really doesn't bother you, then? What I am?"

Emotion tightened Alex's chest. Taking her head in his hands he kissed her deeply, his lips lingering on hers. "Willow, all I care about is that you're you, and – and that you're with me. That's all that matters."

"Really?" she whispered, her eyes bright with tears.

He laughed suddenly, smoothing her blonde hair from her face. "Hey, *I'm* the lucky one, don't you know that? You are so – absolutely incredible. Everything about you."

Willow swallowed. "I'm pretty lucky too, actually." Touching his hair, she leaned hesitantly forward and he wrapped his arms around her, sinking into sensation again. The warmth of her lips on his; the slight weight of her on his lap; the smell of her. He glided his hands down her back as they kissed, feeling the gentle dip of her spine through her sweater. He could never get enough of this, never.

Finally Willow pulled back. "Wow," she said weakly. "That's – even more amazing than I thought it would be."

Alex's arms were still looped around her waist; it took a serious effort not to draw her back to him and start kissing her again. He managed to control himself, and grinned. "You mean with me, or just in general?"

"In general," she said. "But I have a feeling it's especially amazing with you." She leaned back in his arms; her smile turned wondering as she studied him. She reached out and stroked the line of his cheekbone. "You are so…completely gorgeous, do you realize that?"

What he realized was that he was happier than he'd ever been. He gazed at Willow, drinking in her face, feeling amazed that this was happening – that she was here with him, and that she actually felt the same way.

"Come here," he said softly. And pulling her towards him, he simply held her, cradling her against his chest.

* * *

I sat there with Alex holding me for a long time, listening to the steady rhythm of his heart beating through his shirt. Around us there was absolute silence, broken only by the distant hooting of an owl somewhere out in the night. I was still trying to comprehend that this was true – that I was really here, with Alex's arms around me. My heart felt so full that it was almost like a pain in my chest.

Finally Alex shifted his weight slightly, and I realized how long we'd been sitting in the hard wooden chair. I sat up on his lap. "Maybe we should go to bed," I said softly. Then I realized what I had said, and my cheeks flamed.

Alex went very still.

I swallowed. "I mean…it's late, and we're both tired…"

"You're right," he said. He took my hand, rubbing his thumb against my palm, and I felt myself go weak at his touch. "I'm not sure how much sleep I'll get with you in the same room, but – yeah, okay. Do you want to take the bed? I can crash on the floor."

I hesitated, glancing at the camp bed. "Um…okay, that sounds good." I didn't want him to stop touching me, not even for a few hours, but I didn't know how to say it. I almost laughed at myself, at how disappointed I felt – already, touching him was like some drug I couldn't do without. Reluctantly, I started to slip from his lap. His arms tightened around me, and he pulled me back for another kiss.

"Hey, not so fast," he whispered with a grin. I smiled too as our lips met, happiness bounding through me like a coursing stream. *I love you, Alex,* I thought as we kissed. *I love you so much.*

"I can't believe that I can just do that whenever I want to now," he murmured as we drew apart. The look in his blue-grey eyes was exactly how I felt – so warm, and so full of wonder that this had actually happened between us. "You may not be getting much done for the next few weeks. Or months, or years."

Years. My heart skipped, hoping that was true. "That sounds pretty good to me," I said shyly.

As Alex went outside to get changed, I took one of the sleeping bags from its nylon case and flopped it over the bed, wishing that he was going to be sharing it with me. Just imagining what it would be like to feel Alex close to me all night, holding me in his arms, tinged my face with heat. Letting out a breath, I shook the thought away and pulled off the red sweater he'd gotten me, leaving me wearing the sweatpants and T-shirt. The bandage on my left arm looked stark against my skin. Sinking onto the bed, I touched the gauze, remembering how Alex's fingers had lingered when he'd put it on.

I almost jumped when the door opened. Alex came back inside, wearing black sweatpants. I swallowed as I saw his chest was bare.

"Forgot my T-shirt," he said sheepishly. His bag was on the floor near the bed; I watched the lantern light play on his skin as he crossed to it. Squatting by the bag, he rummaged for a shirt. I sat mesmerized, taking in the movement of his back and shoulders as the golden light caressed them. His dark hair lay ruffled against his tanned neck; the curved line of his spine lay half in shadow.

I couldn't stop myself. In a dream, I slowly reached out and touched the black *AK* on Alex's arm.

His skin was warm. Electricity coursed through me at the feel of it. Time stopped; the air felt suspended in my lungs as I gently traced the letters of his tattoo, the firm swell of his bicep. Of its own accord, my hand glided its way up his shoulder, savouring the different textures of him – hard muscles, smooth skin. Still crouched by the bed, Alex barely moved as I touched him; it was as if he wasn't breathing. His eyes met mine, and I dropped my hand and tried to smile, my pulse pounding. "Sorry. I've um…sort of been wanting to do that ever since that first night in the motel room."

His eyebrows shot up; he sat on the bed next to me. "You have? But – you hated *me* then."

I shook my head. "No, I – I really wanted to hate you, but I think I knew even then that—" I broke off as fire swept my cheeks. I had almost said the words; I'd almost told him I loved him.

"What?" asked Alex. The dim light made his eyes look darker; his hair almost black.

I couldn't meet his gaze. Tucking my hands under my arms, I stared at the nearby table – the mess of cards on it, the lantern giving off its quiet glow. "When you gave me your shirt to wear that night, I could feel you. I could feel your…essence."

The world went still. We were sitting only inches from each other, not touching. Outside, I could hear the faint murmur of the wind blowing through the trees.

"What did it feel like?" he asked in a low voice.

"Like…coming home," I admitted.

My chest clenched as I looked up at him. His eyes were locked on mine. "Willow…you know that you said you couldn't tell how I felt at the rest stop?"

I nodded, and he took my hand, laying it flat on his chest with his own hand resting over it. "Can you tell now?" he asked.

His heart beat firmly under my hand; my own pulse was hammering so hard that I could barely think straight. Closing my eyes, I took a deep, steadying breath, and then another as I tried to clear my mind, to feel what he was feeling. For a moment there was just the softness of our breathing – and then all at once it washed over me in a great wave.

He was in love with me, too.

I opened my eyes. Alex was still holding my hand to his chest, watching me, his expression more serious than I'd ever seen it. Unable to speak, I slowly dropped my hand and wrapped my arms around him. His own arms came around me as he rested his head on my hair.

"I really do, you know," he said, his voice rough.

"I know," I whispered back. "I do you, too."

We held each other, our hearts beating hard. My eyes were closed, my face pressed against the warm dip between his shoulder and neck. Alex. I felt a happiness so great that it was like a deep stillness within me; as if something I'd been looking for my entire life had just slotted into place, making me whole.

After a long time, I opened my eyes and realized that we'd almost fallen asleep. Alex was leaning against the wall of the cabin, holding me. As I stirred, he did too. "I guess I'd better go to bed," he said, kissing me.

"No, don't go," I murmured, my arms tightening around him. "Stay with me."

I could feel his smile against my lips. "Okay. I'll just turn out the light," he said softly.

I kept my arms around his waist as he stretched out of bed, resting one foot on the floor as he craned for the lantern. A moment later the cabin lay draped in darkness. We curled up under the sleeping bag together, lying in each other's arms and listening to the soft sounds of the wind outside. The bed was narrow, so that it was almost like trying to balance on a diving board – but I'd never felt so comfortable or protected in my life than there with Alex's arms around me, my head on his chest.

He touched my hair as we lay in the darkness, smoothing its long strands across his torso. "Is it bothering you?" I asked.

"No, I love it; it's so soft." I felt him running his fingers through it, playing with it gently. "I was right, you know," he said eventually. "Those guys in Pawntucket are complete idiots."

I smiled. "So would you have taken me to the prom, if you went to Pawntucket High?"

"Yeah, definitely," he said. "I bet you'd look so beautiful…even more than you usually do."

Warmth filled me. I straightened up slightly, trying to see his face in the darkness. "You really think that, don't you?"

"What, that you're beautiful?" Alex sounded surprised. "You are. The first time I saw you, you were wearing these pink pyjamas and a grey T-shirt, and you were making coffee…and I just couldn't take my eyes off you."

I swallowed hard at the tone in his voice. I couldn't believe that he actually remembered what I'd been wearing. "And the first time I saw you, all I could think of was doing this." I traced his lips with my finger; he took my hand in his and kissed it.

We lay there without speaking for a while, Alex gently stroking my hair. His arms felt so warm and safe around me that I found myself starting to get sleepy again. Stifling a yawn, I nestled against him and felt him kiss my head.

"*Te amo,* Willow," he said quietly.

I came awake slightly, smiling into the darkness. "What does that mean?" I whispered.

I could almost hear his own smile. "What do you think it means?"

I hugged him, kissing his collarbone and wondering if it was possible to actually die of happiness. "*Te amo,* Alex."

You'd think that a cabin in the middle of nowhere, with no TV or electricity, would be a place where you'd start to go pretty seriously stir-crazy soon. But it was the exact opposite. Being with Alex, in a place where we could simply relax and forget that half the country was after us, was just…magical. That first morning, I woke to find him lying on his side with his head propped on his hand, looking down at me and smiling.

Tingles swept over me; it was like waking up and remembering that it's Christmas. "Good morning," I said, drinking him in. His eyes looked almost pure blue in the morning light; there was a faint hint of stubble on his jaw.

"Morning." The muscles on his chest moved as he leaned over and kissed me. Long, slow, deep. He smelled of sleep, and a warm smell that was just Alex. I felt myself falling.

"That…is such a nice way to wake up," I breathed when the kiss ended.

Alex stroked my cheek with the backs of his fingers. "Not as nice as just waking up and seeing you there, lying beside me. I thought for a second I must be dreaming."

"Was it a nice dream?" I asked. I couldn't stop smiling as I looked at him.

He grinned; his dark hair was rumpled from sleep. "Oh, yes. It was a very, very nice dream." We lay smiling at each other, with the sleeping bag soft around us and the sound of birdsong outside. Sunshine angled in through faint cracks in the cabin wall.

"So what do you want to do today?" said Alex after a while.

"Be with you," I said promptly.

He tickled my face with a strand of my hair. "Yeah, as if you've got a choice."

"Even if I had a choice, that's what I'd choose." Relishing being able to just reach out and touch him, I stroked my hand across his chest. "That's what I'd always choose."

We ended up going hiking that day, exploring further above the cabin. The view up there was spectacular –

mountains upon mountains, stretching out before us like we were up in an airplane. We sat on a small ledge, gazing out at the sun playing on the peaks and the shadows of the clouds down below. "It's beautiful, isn't it?" said Alex quietly. "I love places like this."

"Better than the desert?" I leaned against him; he put his arm around me.

"It's different. The desert's so empty, but it's beautiful too – you should see it when there's a storm, with lightning coming down. This, though...I could just look at this all day."

His expression as he stared out at the mountains made my heart turn over. I twisted sideways, kissing him, and felt his other arm wrap around me as he kissed me back. Then I laughed in surprise as he suddenly hauled me onto his lap, grinning. "Of course, I could look at you all day, too," he murmured as he bent his head down again.

It was so peaceful up at the cabin, with only the mountains and the sky, and the occasional wheeling hawk for company. We both knew that we couldn't stay there for ever, but as the days passed, I think we both wanted to believe that we could – that there weren't any angels in the world; no Church of Angels fanatics who were trying to kill us. And sometimes, I could actually forget all of that. It was as if the cabin existed outside of all our problems.

Alex and I spent almost every moment together – going for long walks, playing cards. We spent a whole afternoon having leaf-races in the stream; we spent another one checking out the prospector's device behind the cabin. It worked by dumping silt from the stream into a cradle and then filtering it out; you could still see where whoever had originally lived there had dug big chunks out of the bank in places, searching for gold.

"I wonder if he ever found any?" I mused, touching one of the cradle's legs. It was half-rotting, its wood a soft grey.

Alex was crouched on his haunches, examining the rusty screen that you sifted the silt through. "It'd really be too bad if he didn't, after going to so much trouble." Then he glanced up at me, raising an eyebrow. "Hey, how come we're both calling him 'he'? It could have been a girl prospector."

I laughed. "I guess you're right. Wow, I never thought *I'd* be sexist."

He shook his head. "You'd better be careful about that. They'll kick you out of the girl mechanics' club if they find out."

"You won't tell them, will you?"

"Hmm, let me see..." Standing up, Alex brushed his hands off on his jeans, shooting me a considering glance. "How much is my silence worth to you?"

I wrapped my arms around his neck, pulling him down slightly so I could kiss him. Around us, I could hear the trickling of the stream, and the faint, faraway cry of a hawk. "Is that enough?"

"Ha. In your dreams." Drawing me back to him Alex kissed me again, his lips warm and lingering on mine. When we pulled apart, he looked at the cradle and laughed. "You know, it was probably some grizzled old guy with a beard, who chewed tobacco and smelled bad."

I still had my arms around his waist, smiling as I looked up at him. Being with Alex made me so completely happy, in an easy, uncomplicated way that I hadn't felt since I was a small child. "I love you," I said. In the four days we'd been there, it was the first time I'd said the words to him in English; they just slipped out.

Alex's expression went very still as he looked down at me, his dark hair stirred by the slight breeze. I picked up a sudden wave of his emotions, and they almost brought tears to my eyes. Gently, he took my face in his hands, kissing me.

"I love you, too," he said against my lips.

CHAPTER *Fifteen*

As the days passed, Alex and I spent so much time just talking – it felt as if there weren't enough hours in the day for all that we wanted to say to each other, all that we wanted to discover. And then sometimes I'd find myself just looking at Alex, still hardly able to believe that this had happened; sometimes I'd glance up and see that he was looking at me the same way. Sleeping in his arms at night felt so incredibly warm and safe; waking up beside him was like a sunrise inside of me every morning.

He was so easy to live with. We just *got along*, on the most minor things, like how often we wanted to clean the cabin (which was every couple of days or so, when the mess started driving us crazy), and who was going to do which chore. Not that there were that many of them. Mostly I cooked – which was just heating up cans – and Alex cleared up afterwards.

Then there was kissing him, touching him, being touched by him. Simply being near Alex was enough to make my pulse shoot up. I knew that he felt the same way about me, but whenever he held me, I could sense it so clearly – he wanted to take things at my pace, and not go any faster than I was ready for. I loved him so much for that; for understanding that I needed a bit of time to get used to all of this. It was funny, though. That side of things all made me feel so completely, totally human: Alex's arms wrapped strongly around me; the heat of our mouths together as we kissed, so that I was plummeting, soaring – what could be more human than that?

But that moment in the desert when the truth finally hit me had blasted away any tiny thoughts I might have had about this angel thing being a mistake, or not quite real. It was real, all right – the only reality that I'd ever have from now on. I was a half-angel, and that would never change; I had this *thing* inside of me which would never go away. And even though the memory of the desert horizon turning around me so effortlessly as I flew was sort of... magical, the reality of what it actually meant was anything but that. No matter how human I felt when I was with Alex, I wasn't. It wasn't a boy with a girl; it was a boy with something half-human.

The thought made me feel so wistful sometimes, like gazing out of a rain-streaked window. It was as if something I had never fully appreciated before was now gone for ever. And because of it, I couldn't even wonder about a future with Alex, not really. For whatever the thing was inside of me, it meant I might be the one to destroy the angels...and that they wanted me dead. How much time did either Alex or I actually have?

I hated thinking about all of this; I wanted it just to go away, for ever. Alex seemed to sense that it wasn't my favourite subject, and mostly, we didn't talk about it very much; we just savoured being together. And despite all of the danger we were in – or maybe because of it – the fact that we were in love felt like the most important thing that there could ever be. No matter what the future might hold, right now we were up here together, with long days filled solely with each other.

I never wanted this time to end.

Jonah glanced around him nervously as he entered the cafe in Denver's Lower Downtown district. He didn't go into Denver much, spending most of his time at the cathedral, and had never been to LoDo, with its Victorian houses and art galleries, at all. It had taken him several wrong turns to even find the cafe, much less somewhere to park. More than once he had been tempted, strongly, to just forget the whole thing and go back to his apartment at the cathedral.

But somehow he hadn't.

Now, as he ordered a cappuccino at the counter, he heard someone say his name. "Jonah Fisk?"

He turned sharply, and saw a tall man with broad shoulders and blond hair standing there. He had the same intense eyes as Raziel. Jonah swallowed. "Yes, um… that's me."

The angel held out his hand. "Nate Anderson. Thanks for coming."

Jonah nodded, still unsure whether he should have done so. When he'd gotten his coffee, he followed the angel to a table at the rear of the cafe, half-hidden by a large ficus tree. A woman of about thirty or so with shoulder-length brown hair was already sitting there, wearing a tailored suit. She half rose as Jonah approached.

"Hi, Sophie Kinney," she said, offering her hand. Her brown eyes weren't angel-intense, but they were still pretty intense. Shaking her hand, Jonah sat down hesitantly, suddenly feeling as awkward as he'd felt back at college.

"Well, first of all, thanks for the tip-off," said the angel.

There was a half-drunk coffee in front of him; he took a sip. "I thought Sophie and I had got out in time; I didn't realize that they were onto me."

"That's okay," said Jonah, his voice faint. It hadn't really been his intention to tip the angel off that the others were aware of his traitorous activities; he had just needed to talk to him. But of course in doing so, the effect had been the same. Already, just by doubting the angels, he may have caused irreparable harm to them. His stomach clenched at the thought.

Gazing down, he stirred his cappuccino. "Look, um – I'm not sure I should be here. I mean, I just wonder if all of this is a mistake. The angels helped me, they really did."

"You've seen one?" asked Nate. "In its divine form, I mean?"

"Yes, it changed my life." Jonah described the encounter.

As he finished, Nate sat back in his seat, a look of surprised pleasure crossing his handsome face. "One of the marshallers," he said to Sophie. "How about that for luck, with the Second Wave about to come – that Jonah ended up as Raziel's right-hand man?"

"Um…what?" said Jonah.

Sophie leaned towards him. "Listen, it's not a mistake, I'm afraid," she said crisply. "Angels are here because their own world is dying; they're feeding off humans. They cause death, disease, mental illness. We've been trying to fight them covertly, but now that the department's been taken over—" She sighed.

"What about the angel *I* saw, though?" said Jonah. "She was..." He trailed off. The angel who had come to him was one of his most cherished memories; he didn't want anything to change that.

"She was on our side," said Nate. "Not all of us believe that angels have the right to destroy humanity; a few of us are trying to stop it. She didn't feed from you, she was doing something called marshalling – placing a small amount of psychic resistance in your aura, to make you unpalatable to other angels. It can sometimes be passed from human to human, too, in the right conditions, through auric contact – it's our hope that if we do enough of this, it might start to make a difference."

Unpalatable to other angels. Jonah froze in his seat. His words stumbling over themselves, he said, "I – I've seen other angels in their divine form since then, at the cathedral, but – they never touch me for more than a moment. I just sort of get glimpses of them, and then they're gone." Dizzily, he remembered the woman in the corridor, the long moments she'd spent gazing upwards. The angel touching her had clearly been taking its time.

Nate nodded. "It worked, then – good, it doesn't always."

"Which means you don't have angel burn," added Sophie.

"Angel burn?" Jonah raised his coffee cup, holding it in front of him almost like a shield. As Sophie tersely explained, he felt himself go pale. "You're saying that it's true, then; the angels really are feeding off people. Literally feeding off them, hurting them. And that – that the people just see them as good and kind."

"That's about right," said Sophie. "Apart from the physical damage, it pretty much fries the human brain. You get sort of obsessed with them – everything is '*Praise be to angels*.'"

Jonah winced at the familiar phrase.

Nate rested his forearms on the table. The angel was built like a football player, and seemed to have an easy grace in his own body. "Look, the thing is, it's about to get a lot worse," he said. "And you're in a unique position to help us, if you'll do it."

The bustling cafe noise seemed to dim around him as Jonah's heart pounded with apprehension. "Um…what do you want me to do?"

The pair explained. By the time they had finished, Jonah's coffee had long grown cold, and the funky LoDo cafe with its worn tables and posters of movies on the walls had taken on the feel of a nightmare. "I – I don't know if I can do that," he stammered. "I mean, it's true that I'm in charge of the celebration, but…"

"It all depends on finding the half-angel," said Sophie. "She's the only one who might be able to succeed." She let out a short breath. "We were close, but we lost them; now they could be anywhere."

"But even if we find her, we'd need your help to actually pull it off," said Nate. "We couldn't do it without you, in fact."

Jonah stared down at his cup and saucer. His previous unshakable faith in the angels felt like a pain inside of him – something beautiful and precious that had been sullied for ever. He didn't want to believe this; he wished that he could just get up and walk away and pretend that none of it had ever happened. But even if he did believe it, how could he possibly do what they were asking?

I can't, he thought. *I just can't do it.*

They were both watching him, waiting for him to speak. Finally Jonah cleared his throat. "I'll, um – I'll have to think about it," he said.

Dimly, he was aware of Sophie's mouth pursing with frustration; she started to say something and Nate put a hand on her arm. "Do that," he said. "Jonah, I think you know that we're telling you the truth. The situation is… pretty bad. And it will just get worse. Humanity as you know it isn't likely to survive this."

"You, more than anyone, know the sheer scale of this thing," said Sophie tightly. "So yes, think about it – but don't take too long; we're running out of time." She took out a business card and a pen; scratching out the phone number on the card, she wrote a new one. "Here," she said, handing him the card. "Call me the second you decide."

Jonah nodded, gazing down at the card. *Sophie Kinney, CIA.* He'd throw it away when he got back to his apartment, he thought. Even if every word they had said was true, there was simply no way he could do this.

"Thanks for coming," said Nate. His chair scraped against the floorboards slightly as he stood up. "We'll leave you in peace now. And Jonah…"

Jonah looked up, and the angel smiled at him – a sad, understanding smile, his eyes burning into Jonah's. "Sophie's right," he said. "Don't take too long."

The days slowly turned into a week, and then slid past two. It started to feel as if Alex and I had always been up at the cabin; as if we had all the time in the world. Except that sometimes, underneath the lazy rhythm of our days together, a bolt of pure fear shivered through me – a foreboding, as if something was on the horizon waiting for us. I couldn't tell whether it was something I was actually sensing, or just my own concerns. I held back from mentioning it; there was no point unless I got something more definite. Alex and I both knew that we were in danger, and that our days up here couldn't last for ever. Apart from anything else, just the weather turning colder was a clue. The air bit at us with the threat of winter now; I often had to wear two sweaters when we went outside. Before too much longer, we were going to have to decide our next move, and face whatever was coming next. I knew that Alex was aware of it, too – there were times now when he fell silent, looking deep in thought. I didn't question him about it; I didn't really want to bring it out into the open, just yet. Though I knew it wasn't true, in a way it felt as if our days up there might never end, if only we could put off talking about all of this long enough.

Even with these worries, though, our time together was still so full of joy. And, though I wouldn't have really believed it was possible, Alex and I grew even closer, until it seemed like we were two sides of the same coin.

"He was just...incredible, actually," said Alex. We had finished eating dinner a while earlier, and were now just sitting talking, with the camp lantern casting a golden glow on the table between us. "I mean, no one else even knew about angels, much less how to kill them. Dad had to do it all on his own at first. He'd go out hunting to find them, testing different ways to destroy them – he should have gotten himself killed a hundred times over, but he didn't, somehow."

I was listening with my chin propped on my hand. "Where were you and Jake while he was doing this?" I asked.

"At home, at first. In Chicago. He hired someone to watch after us."

I swallowed. After their mother had just died? It sounded awful, for such young children. "Okay, go on," I said after a pause.

"Then about six months later, when he'd gotten his funding and was ready to start training other people, we moved to the camp with him. He was still travelling a lot then, though – he had to recruit new AKs, follow leads, that kind of thing. It was a few years before things really got off the ground." Alex smiled wryly, playing with a camping fork. "And then another few years after that before he started to lose it."

"Lose it?" I stared at him in surprise. "I didn't know that."

Alex tapped the fork lightly against the table. "Yeah, didn't I tell you? For – I don't know, five years, maybe – Dad was the best of the best. I mean, *nobody* was a better AK than him. And it wasn't just that, it was strategy too, and training, and organizing all the hunts. But then he just…got obsessed."

"Obsessed how?" I asked.

Alex's face was bathed in shadow as he gazed down,

accenting his lips and cheekbones. He shrugged. "Killing angels was all he could think about. After a while he wouldn't let any of the AKs take any time off, ever. Everyone at the camp was going stir-crazy, ready to kill each other. That's when people started sneaking time after a hunt, just a day or two to take a break."

I shifted on my chair, watching him. "Like you and Jake, when you fixed up this place?"

He nodded as he glanced at the walls around him. "Yeah, that was good," he said quietly. "That was a really good time. People used to sneak down to Mexico a lot, too. Or up to Albuquerque. Anywhere where they could just have some fun." The corner of his mouth lifted. "Fun had gotten to be a concept that Dad didn't really get any more."

I watched the fork as he tapped it against the table, not sure whether I should ask. "How did your father die?" I said finally.

The fork kept the same rhythm as before. "An angel ripped his life force away. He died of a massive heart attack."

"You were there," I said, feeling it suddenly. I reached for his hand, gripping it hard. "Oh, Alex, I'm sorry."

He nodded, his jaw tensing. "Yeah, it was…bad. But I don't know, he died fighting, I guess. He would have liked that."

"You must be really proud of him," I said softly. "And he must have been proud of you, too."

Alex laughed suddenly. "He used to say I was too cocky for my own good... Yeah, he was, though. He was pretty proud of me." He glanced up at me and smiled, squeezing my fingers. "Okay, enough about me for now," he said, leaning back. "Your turn. What's something I don't know about you?"

All at once I really wanted to tell him about my mother. I pulled one of my knees up to my chest. "Well – you don't know how Mom and I first came to live with Aunt Jo."

Alex shook his head. "No, how did you?"

"We lived in Syracuse," I said, tracing my hand across the worn wood of the table. "And Mom was on welfare. Everyone knew that she had mental problems – I mean, she'd been diagnosed, and all that – but no one knew how bad it was, except for me. She was able to – to put on a facade for a long time, when other people were around."

I told him about how Mom had gotten gradually worse and worse, so that by the time I was seven or eight, I was having to cook for us both, and do all the cleaning and laundry. "I always made sure that I kept the house really nice," I said. "So, in case anyone ever came in, they wouldn't know anything was wrong. I got myself off to school every day, and – everything." I was silent for a moment, remembering sitting in the back of the school bus gazing back at our dinky little house, so worried about Mom, about leaving her there on her own all day.

"What finally happened?" asked Alex in a low voice.

"I got home from school one day when I was nine, and Mom wasn't there." I looked at him, tried to smile. "I waited for hours; I didn't know what to do. I didn't want anyone to know that anything was wrong, but – I was really scared. So finally I called the police, and they came over. It turned out that they'd picked her up that afternoon; she'd been just – walking around in a daze. Wandering into traffic, not knowing who she was."

Alex reached across and took my hand, gripping it wordlessly. I let out a breath. "So, they put her in the hospital, and they put me in a foster home, and it was – horrible. I was there for almost a month."

"What about your aunt?" said Alex. His fingers were warm against mine.

I shrugged. "I don't know. I didn't know where she lived, but I think they probably found her pretty quickly. It just – took a while for everyone to figure out what they were going to do, I guess."

His voice hardened. "So...what? You're saying that she just let you sit in a foster home for a month?"

Slowly, I nodded, remembering the tiny bedroom that I'd shared with a girl called Tina – how she always wanted me to talk to her and I wouldn't talk to anybody.

I used to lie on my bed for hours staring at the wall, hating everyone there.

"Yeah," I said finally. "I mean, I don't know what was going on in her life or anything, and I guess it was – a pretty big disruption, to suddenly have this nine-year-old foisted on her." Alex didn't say anything, and I went on. "Anyway, after a while she came and got me, and I went back to Pawntucket with her. And then a few weeks later, Mom came to live there, too. The doctors thought she should be hospitalized full time, but there wasn't enough insurance for it. I guess that sort of thing is – pretty expensive." I looked down. "You know, I always hated my father anyway, for doing that to her. Knowing that he was an actual predator, and that he never even cared about her at all, just…makes it ten times worse, somehow." Not to mention that I had come from him; that I was a part of him. I didn't say the words.

"I know," said Alex. And I could tell from his voice that he did know. He understood exactly how I felt about all of it, even the parts I'd left unsaid. He squeezed my hand as we sat in silence for a moment. "You're not your father, though. You're nothing like him. You were there for her; you cared about her more than anything."

I swallowed hard, seeing so many memories. "She's my mom. I love her. I just…wish I hadn't let her down, back then."

"Willow." With his other hand, Alex touched my cheek. "You know that's not true, right? You did better than some adults could have done, and you were only nine years old. You did everything you could."

Letting out a breath, I closed my hand over his, leaning my head against it. "Thanks." I managed a smile. "I've never, um…told anyone about that before. Thanks for listening."

He smiled slightly. "I've never told anyone about my dad before, either," he said. He leaned forward and kissed me, and I stroked my other hand around his neck, feeling so grateful that we had somehow found each other. That even with everything that had happened, even with all the danger that we were in…we had still found this amazing thing together.

"Hold still," said Alex.

"I can't!" I gasped. I was leaning over the stream, my hair a slithering mass of shampoo. I shrieked, half-laughing, as Alex poured a canful of water over it. "*Oh! That is so cold!*"

Alex started laughing too. "You're the one who wanted to wash it."

"I had to, it was getting disgusting… Is all the shampoo out?"

"Nope. Not even close."

I screeched as he poured another can over my head, and then another. Goosebumps scattered up my arms; my scalp felt like it was on fire with cold. Finally – just when I was about to tell him to forget it, that I didn't care any more whether I still had shampoo in my hair or not – he said, "Right, I think that's all of it." I felt him wrap the T-shirt around my hair, squeezing the water out.

I straightened up cautiously, shivering as drops of icy water darted down my neck. "I'm never washing it again; I don't care how disgusting it gets."

Alex rubbed my arms briskly, grinning. "You say that every single time."

"It's *true* this time. I swear that water's twenty degrees colder than it used to be."

Back in the cabin, I sat on the bed combing out my hair; trying not to get the sleeping bags wet. It was such a relief to have clean hair again, even if it felt all tangled after that. Alex sat next to me, leaning back against the wall and watching with a smile.

"Your nose is all red," he said.

"Yes, that's how it gets when I'm dying of hypothermia."

Bending forward, Alex kissed the tip of my nose lightly. Then, getting up from the bed, he went over to his black bag, crouching down beside it on the floor as he unzipped an inner pocket. He came back and sat beside me again. "Here," he said, handing me a small white box. "Happy birthday."

Slowly, I took the box, feeling stunned. I had lost all track of time up here. "Is it my birthday? But – how did you know?"

Alex gave a sheepish grin. "Um – I sort of looked at your driver's licence, when you were taking a shower that first night in the motel."

I was holding the box with both hands. "You didn't! That's not even fair – you don't even *have* a driver's licence with your real details on it." I looked down at the box, touched its slightly dimpled top. "What is it?"

"Open it and see."

Carefully, I pulled the lid off. And then just sat gazing downwards for a moment. There was a necklace inside – a slim, shimmering silver chain with a crystal teardrop hanging from it. "It's beautiful," I breathed, drawing it out. The faceted pendant winked in the sunlight, turning slightly on its chain. "Alex, this is so…" I trailed off, lost for words.

He smiled at my expression. "It, um – reminded me of you," he said. "Of your angel's wings."

My heart seemed to stop. We hardly mentioned my angel; I didn't like thinking about it. And usually, I didn't have to. For whole long days at a time up here, I had been able to just shove it to the back of my mind, and almost forget that I wasn't wholly human.

"My angel's wings?" I repeated.

Alex nodded. "The way they shone in the sun."

"But…" I stared back at the pendant, my thoughts spinning. "But you must have gotten this before we even got together."

"Yeah, when I was buying your clothes." He ducked his head down slightly, peering at my face. "Hey. What is it?"

I could hardly put it into words. The pendant with the light hitting it was so clear, so shining. "You don't just *not mind*, do you?" I said slowly. "About me being a half-angel. You really…accept it."

Alex gave a gentle laugh, and tapped my forehead with his fist. "Hello. Have you just figured that out?"

I knew that I wasn't expressing this well. "It's just that you couldn't see something like this, and think of my angel, unless you really…" I broke off, feeling stupidly inarticulate.

There was a long pause. Finally Alex cleared his throat. "You know…back in the motel room in Tennessee, I woke up from a nightmare once. A really bad one, that I used to have a lot. And I looked at your angel." He scanned my face. "She's beautiful, Willow – she looks just like you, only more radiant. And just seeing your face, I was able to go back to sleep again."

My throat went tight. All the way back in Tennessee, he'd felt that way? "But all angels are beautiful," I said after a moment. "And they're still deadly."

"You're really not getting this," said Alex. He touched my face. "Yes, all angels are beautiful, but it's just how they look. Your angel is you; she's a part of you. She's beautiful like you are, and that means she's…everything I love."

I sat very still, staring at him. "Alex…"

He smiled softly, shaking his head. "Willow, I thought you already knew that."

I stared down at the necklace again, almost too moved to speak. "I love it. Thank you." I stroked my hand under the pendant, watching it catch the light. Carefully, I undid the clasp and put it on; I could hardly even feel the chain around my neck. Looking down, I touched the pendant, seeing the way it sparkled against my skin. I knew that I'd never take it off.

I felt almost shy as I looked at him. Finally I cleared my throat. "So…when's your birthday?"

He grinned suddenly. "Yesterday."

I stared at him. "What – seriously?"

"Yeah, October 23rd. I turned eighteen."

"Why didn't you *tell* me?"

"What for? I already have everything I want." He reached across and fingered the pendant; I felt it move against my skin. "Willow, look," he said slowly. "We haven't talked much about what might happen, but you know that I always want to be with you, right? I mean – no matter what."

And I had known it; I felt it every time he held me – but even so, actually hearing the words made my heart catch. I nodded hard. "I want that, too," I said. "Always, Alex."

The look in his eyes melted me. Cupping his hands around my face, he kissed me, his lips warm on mine. As we drew apart, he put his hand on the side of my face; I nestled my cheek into it. "Okay, then," he said softly, rubbing the corner of my mouth with his thumb.

"Okay," I echoed.

We just sat there for a moment, smiling at each other. Finally Alex picked up my hairbrush. "Here, let me finish this for you."

"Are you sure?"

"Yeah, turn around."

With a quick kiss I turned my back to him, and a moment later felt him gently combing through my damp hair, working through the tangles. I touched the pendant as it sparkled against my skin. And I knew that I had never loved Alex so much, as right at that very moment.

* * *

That night I lay awake for a long time, curled up against Alex's chest as he slept, his arms wrapped loosely around me. The cabin was dark and still around us, with only a faint rectangle of moonlight shining in through the outline of the doorway. Reaching up, I touched my pendant, running my finger across its faceted smoothness.

For the first time, I thought about my angel – I mean, really thought about her, instead of slamming a door on the idea the moment it came to mind. I remembered the feeling of flying, of seeing the desert turn and dip around me as I swooped through the air. Alex had told me that full-blooded angels couldn't take on both a human and angel form at the same time, but it seemed like I could – my human form had remained while my angel one took flight, taking my consciousness with it. She emerged when I slept, hovering above me, and had once warned me in something I'd thought was a dream. So far she had emerged when angels were around, too, if I needed her.

Apart from that, where was she usually? Was she somewhere inside of me?

I felt a stirring of curiosity about the idea, remembering that Alex had once suggested trying to contact her. Could I? Did I even want to?

Maybe, I thought tentatively.

The cabin was very still around me. Alex's breathing was slow, steady; his chest warm and smooth under the circle of my arm. I closed my eyes. Hardly knowing where to begin, I took a breath to relax myself and then started drifting slowly, searching.

Hello? I thought. *Are you there?*

Faintly, I became aware of a flicker of energy deep within me: a small, crystalline fire that pulsed with a heartbeat of its own. In my mind, I drew slowly forward. The light sparked like a diamond on black velvet. I felt a swirl of energy drift gently towards me, exploring me just as I was exploring it.

A jolt of recognition; I felt myself smile in wonder. The energy was so like my own, but different, more charged: a shining rush of power that knew me and was happy to see me. Suddenly all I wanted was to simply be in the light. I moved forward and it grew larger, stronger; it dazzled my eyes but didn't hurt them. I let it envelop me and there was an explosion of brightness, like sunshine in a crystal cave. Its energy swept through me, almost making me laugh with joy. I felt its pulse become my own.

And then I saw her, so clearly in my mind's eye: the angel who was me.

She stood gazing at me, her shining robes falling from her shoulders, and I thought dazedly – *Alex is right. I am beautiful.* Because this serene face held such a pure, deep beauty that I felt my throat tighten. She had no halo, but her bright wings were spread out behind her, moving gently, flashing like sunshine rippling on water. Her long hair fell loosely past her shoulders, like mine often did. Her eyes shone; I could feel her love for me cradling around me as we regarded each other.

I never knew, I thought in wonder. All my life, there had been this whole other part of who I was, and I had never even realized it was there. Suddenly I knew that I could simply shift my consciousness into hers, if I wanted – that I would still be me, but I would be her, as well. We were two; we were one. She was the twin I had never known, there for me whenever I might need her. The knowledge glowed warmly, like a small ember inside of me.

But not yet. For now, this felt like enough – just to know that she was there, and that she wasn't something to be afraid of. Gently, I withdrew. My angel smiled after me, understanding. As I moved away she faded, and there was only the small, bright light – and then that, too, vanished as I brought my consciousness back to the cabin.

I opened my eyes.

The darkness of the small room, with its faint tinge of moonlight. I was still lying in the sleeping bag in Alex's arms, with my head nestled between his shoulder and chest. He felt so warm and solid, so safe. Love for him rushed through me; turning my head I softly kissed his chest, hugging his waist with my arm. He had known. Somehow, Alex had known long before I had – the angel side of me wasn't anything like the angel who had hurt my mother, or the ones who had hurt his family. She was a part of me; I could trust her just as much as I trusted myself.

For the first time since I found out what I really was, I felt the hard knot inside of me ease. It was such an incredible relief, like sinking into a warm bath on a chilly day. I didn't have to hate myself any more. I could just…be me again, even though "me" was so much more than what I'd once thought.

Deep within me I could still sense the flicker of energy, like a tiny, welcoming candle. Smiling, I snuggled closer to Alex and felt him stir slightly, his embrace tightening around me. We lay in each other's arms, our breathing rising and falling at almost the same time. Around us, the night was so still, so utterly peaceful.

I was a half-angel – and for the first time, that seemed like something that might, just possibly, be okay.

"We're expecting at least sixty thousand people on the day," said Jonah. "I've arranged for security to help with crowd control, and we've got permission to use the fields to the south of the cathedral as extra parking. I've got a team of devotees who are going to help with that, guiding people in." He put a plan for the extended parking areas onto Raziel's desk, pointing out the location. "All the other details are coming together, too. We're having a full dress rehearsal on Friday night, and then the flowers are being delivered early Saturday morning, and—"

Raziel sat listening with his head propped onto his hand. He wore dark trousers, and a crisp white shirt open at the neck. Idly, he picked up the plans and glanced at them, tossing them back onto his desk. "Fine, it all sounds like it's in hand," he said. "And what about the half-angel? Is there any news?"

Jonah swallowed. "She…hasn't been found yet," he said.

Irritation creased the angel's face. He tapped his silver letter opener against his desk. "Yes, I'm aware of that. Almost a month now with nothing at all. Are you saying you have *no* updates?"

Slowly, Jonah drew the parking plans back across the desk and put them with his other papers. For a wild moment he wasn't sure what to do – and then, his heart thudding, he told the truth. "No, um…there was something this morning. One of the remote viewers thinks he's close to finding them; he's picked up the half-angel's energy in the Sierra Nevadas. They just need to pinpoint the exact location. A day or two at the most."

Raziel stared at him. As always, Jonah felt slightly dizzy looking into the angel's eyes, though it had never really bothered him before. Now his muscles tightened, and he glanced away.

"We finally have news, and you sat there dribbling on about *parking plans*?" demanded Raziel scathingly.

"I, um..." Jonah trailed off, his cheeks hot.

"A day or two," muttered the angel, running a finger along the letter opener's blade. "Finally, we're getting somewhere. All right, the moment their location is pinpointed, get someone out there to dispose of them, do you understand? The Second Wave will be here practically any moment. I want them both destroyed by then, is that clear?"

Jonah nodded. His fingers felt icy. "Yes, sir. I'll – I'll make it happen."

Raziel dismissed him, and Jonah went back to his own office, shutting the panelled wooden door behind him. Slowly, he sank down into his chair and buried his head in his hands. It was true; the half-angel was close to being found. And when she was... Jonah felt his stomach swing with dread.

He still didn't know whether he had made the right decision.

CHAPTER *Sixteen*

"HOW ABOUT THAT ONE, IS that a constellation?" I asked, pointing upwards. We were down in the small valley where the truck was parked. Alex sat leaning against a rock; I was between his legs with my back against his chest, his arms around me as we both stared up at the stars.

"Which one?" he asked.

"That little cluster up there. See?" I pointed, my hand framed against the glittering night sky.

"Yeah, that's the Seven Sisters...the Pleiades." Alex's head lowered, and his warm mouth brushed my neck. I caught my breath. We had been here for over three weeks now, and I wasn't even remotely used to how good it felt to be kissed by him. Twisting towards him, our mouths met.

"It's so sexy how you know all of this," I murmured after a moment.

He grinned against my lips. "Yeah? I know about the summer constellations, too. Will that get me bonus kisses?"

"I think it might, actually." I kissed his jaw, nuzzling its slight stubble. Alex's arms came around me again as I settled back against him, and we were silent for a while, staring at the stars. There were even more here than there had been back in upstate New York; you could just feel yourself falling into them. Gazing upwards, I shivered slightly as a cool wind brushed my face.

"Are you cold?" asked Alex.

"A little. I'm okay."

He arranged his leather jacket so that it was wrapped snugly around me, and then folded his forearms over my stomach, holding me close. I leaned back against him, warm and safe in his arms, feeling his chin resting lightly against my hair.

"So, um…I sort of wanted to tell you something," I said finally. "I did what you suggested that time. I contacted my angel."

Alex bent sideways, looking down at me. An amazed smile lit his face. "Really?"

"Yeah, the night of my birthday." I felt a small ember of pleasure inside of me, remembering. "I just...wanted to keep it private for a while."

He nodded, looking as if he understood. "Do you want to tell me about it now? Or not?"

"No, I really do," I said. Shifting over his thigh so that I could face him, I sat cross-legged on the ground, describing everything that had happened. "It was just so amazing," I finished finally. "I know that I don't have to be afraid of her any more now. That I don't have to — hate myself, for having something like that inside of me."

Taking my face in his hands, Alex kissed me softly. "Are you going to contact her again?" he asked after a pause.

"Yeah, I will. I sort of — well, I sort of want to try flying again." My cheeks heated.

He shook his head, a wondering smile on his face. "I would too, if I were you." He hesitated, and then said, "Why don't you try it now?"

"Now?"

"Yeah, why not? I'd really like to see. I mean, unless you'd rather be on your own."

The more I thought about it, the more I liked the idea. Excitement tickled through me. "Um — okay, I will," I said. Holding his hands, I closed my eyes. I could feel Alex centring himself as well, preparing to rise up through the chakra points. Taking a breath, I went deeply within myself, searching for the light that I now knew was there.

I found it at once – a pure, crystalline fire, waiting for me. I sped towards it this time; it enveloped me almost immediately. A burst of light, and warmth. There was my angel, smiling at me – radiant, shining white, like sun on snow, her face just as lovely and serene as before. I regarded her for a moment, drinking her in, amazed that she was really a part of me. And then, with a slight mental flick, I moved my consciousness to hers.

I was lifting; I was growing taller, leaving my human body behind. But at the same time, I was still seated on the ground, with Alex's hands holding mine. I opened my eyes in a daze and saw my angel hovering just above us, her wings moving gently. And at the same time I *was* the angel – I was up in the air; I could feel my wings stretching; I could see myself and Alex both gazing up at me.

"Alex, I can see her," I whispered from beside him. "I mean – I *am* her, but I'm here, too."

He glanced at me, startled, and then back at the angel. "But how—"

"I don't know," I said, not taking my eyes off her. "I think – I think before, she just took over and came out, because I was in danger and she could help. But I've bonded with her this time, and so it's different, somehow." Closing my eyes, I became my angel as she turned and soared over the valley.

The stars shifted, came to meet me as I flew up and up. I could feel the wind stroking across my wings; feel it stirring my hair. Far below, I could see the energy forces of every living thing in the valley. The plants were all turned into something magical, with gleaming white outlines that moved softly with the wind. Creatures that I hadn't even known were there suddenly appeared: a mouse crouching in the grass; a pair of deer moving through the pine trees. On the ground, I could see Alex's life force – a rich, vibrant blue, with flashes of gold. And I could see my own beside it: bright angelic silver, with lavender lights shifting through it. The two energies were so close that they mingled like smoke; they looked completely right together. I wheeled in the night sky, sending the stars turning on their axes.

As I sat on the ground I opened my eyes again, staring upwards as my angel flew. "She's so beautiful," I murmured. "Alex, I can feel everything she's feeling."

He put his arms around me and I leaned against his chest, still watching my angel as she soared against the stars, her snowy wings outspread.

And then, in the air, I stiffened.

It felt as if icy water had been flung over me. Something was there; what was it? Gliding for a moment, I craned desperately to listen to something that I couldn't quite catch – a probing, a *thinking*. Fear slammed through me, cold and ominous; the foreboding that I'd felt before was only a shadow compared to this.

Something was coming.

Turning on my wing, I dove back through the stars towards my human body; with a bright flurry, I had merged. At the same time, I was clutching Alex's hands, my words tumbling out in a panic. "Alex, I felt something!"

His hands tightened in mine; his voice sharpened. "What?"

"I – I don't know. Something's on its way. Something dangerous."

"A person?"

I shook my head helplessly; I felt almost tearful with panic. "I don't know – a person, or a situation, I don't know! But it's coming here, and soon."

Alex's face was tense. "When's 'soon', can you tell?"

"I…" I swallowed. "I don't know. I don't think it's instantly – I mean, not right this second. But…soon."

"Right, we've got to get out of here," muttered Alex, dropping one of my hands and scraping his hair back. "Damn it – it won't be light for hours; we'd break an axle trying to get down that mountain in the dark." He blew out a breath; I could practically hear his mind working. "Okay – we'll get packed tonight and leave as soon as we can, the moment it's dawn."

I swallowed hard. "And – and go where?"

"I've been doing some thinking about that," he admitted. His eyes met mine. "How would you feel about Mexico?"

"Mexico?"

He rubbed my palm with his thumb as he nodded, his dark eyebrows drawn together in a troubled frown. "From what Cully said, it sounds like I might be the only AK left – I've got to get more people trained, or else humanity won't even stand a chance. But meanwhile, we need a base where you can be really safe, and the Church of Angels isn't as organized down there. We could find someplace secure to hole up, while I put some feelers out. There were some good AKs from Mexico – I think with luck, I could get something going there, and start up operations again. What do you think?"

I felt slightly dazed; I hadn't picked up on any of this from him. Slowly, I said, "It – it sounds really good, except…it's all going to take time, isn't it? I mean, starting things up again, and training people."

"Yeah, but what choice do we have?"

I didn't want to speak the words, but I had to. "Alex, you told me once that the AKs were losing the war. That you needed something big to stop the angels."

He didn't say anything.

The night air felt cold and still around us; the stars above were thousands of piercing lights. I took a deep breath. "I'm the something big, aren't I? I can't just hide away for ever. I'm supposed to be the one who can defeat them."

Alex gave a short, humourless laugh. He tossed a pebble into the undergrowth; it made a short rustling noise. "Yeah. You know, it's funny, but I'm really not as crazy about that idea as I was at first. Willow, if anything ever happened to you—" He stopped abruptly.

I moved closer, leaning against his chest and hugging him. He put his arm around me; I could feel the tension in his muscles. Fumbling over my words, I said, "Alex, you know I feel the same way about you – I'd die if anything ever happened to you. But if I really can destroy the angels somehow, so that no one else is hurt by them…" I trailed off.

His other arm came up around me too, holding me tightly. All at once his emotions washed over me, as clearly as my own: fear of losing me, determination that he wouldn't. And, so deep down that he was hardly aware of it himself, he was thinking about his brother. I stiffened as sudden images flashed in my head: a boy who looked like Alex, but taller and stockier; he was lying on the rocky ground, staring blindly up at the sky. Alex screaming his brother's name, his voice ragged with agony. It was his fault, all his fault.

He hardly ever mentioned Jake – I still didn't know

exactly how he had died. And I couldn't find out this way; it felt like eavesdropping. I slammed the images away as quickly as they'd come.

"I love you," I whispered into his neck, wishing desperately that I could take it all away, somehow – all of the deaths that he'd been through; all of the pain he'd suffered.

"I love you, too," he said. Slowly, I felt him relax. Pulling away a bit, he kissed me, stroking my hair back, and then dropped his forehead onto mine. "Look…this is the best plan I can come up with for now. I've got to keep you safe, Willow. If you really are the one to destroy them, then – we'll deal with it when the time comes, okay?" He drew back, searching my face.

"Okay," I said finally. It wasn't as if either of us even knew why I was supposed to be such a threat. And allowing myself to imagine Mexico with Alex, I liked the sound of it. I liked the sound of it a lot.

I just hoped that whatever was coming wouldn't follow us there.

I pushed the thought away with a shiver and pressed against Alex, wrapping my arms around him. It felt as if I could never be close enough to him. He cradled me to him, rubbing my back, our heartbeats thudding together. Finally he kissed my head and said softly, "Right, come on, half-angel chick – we'd better start packing."

"Half-angel chick?" I burst out laughing, my tension fading slightly as I pulled away to look at him. "Did you really just say that?"

He smiled and smoothed back a strand of my hair. "Yeah, there's this half-angel chick I've been hanging out with. She's pretty cute...I think she's got a real thing for me."

I smiled too. "Gosh, how did you know that? You must be psychic."

"Hey, you're not the only one with talents." There was a slight scrabbling noise as Alex stood up; holding my hand, he helped me to my feet. "Come on, we'll get the truck loaded up tonight, so that we can leave the second it's light enough."

We started across the valley, holding hands, picking our way across the rocky ground in the moonlight. It was so bright that I could see the deer path clearly, snaking up through the rocks ahead of us like a vein of silver.

"I'm glad that you can see your angel like I do," said Alex suddenly. I stopped, looking up at him. The faint light bathed his face, lingering on his cheekbones and lips. "Seeing her flying like that, against the stars...she's so beautiful, Willow."

"So are you," I murmured, reaching up to touch his cheek. We kissed, his mouth warm on mine, and he held me close for a moment.

"It's going to be okay," he whispered in my ear. "It's all going to be okay."

When Alex woke up a few hours later, he could tell that Willow wasn't lying beside him even before he opened his eyes. He sat up. She wasn't in the cabin, either; the small space was almost empty, most of their things already packed and loaded in the truck. After her premonition the night before, worry creased through him. Getting out of bed, he hastily pulled on his hiking boots and went outside.

Willow was standing in front of the cabin. She had her boots on too, and a sweater on over her sweatpants as she stared down at the mountains below. Her smile was etched with sadness when she saw him. "Isn't it beautiful? I just – came out to say goodbye."

Letting out a relieved breath, Alex wrapped his arms around her from behind; she crossed her arms over his and leaned against his bare chest. He kissed her neck, and looked out at the mountains. They were lit purple and rose with the first faint fingers of dawn, wraiths of mist curling around their bases like smoke. It was time for them to leave, as soon as they got dressed.

"We'll come back someday," he said.

"I'd like that," said Willow softly. Turning, she stretched

up to kiss him; as their mouths met, Alex pulled her closely against him.

And then he froze. There was a distant chopping sound carrying towards them on the air.

Willow heard it at the same moment; she stiffened and spun around. "What's that?"

"Oh, *Christ*, it's a helicopter," breathed Alex. Adrenalin surged through him. Ducking back into the cabin, he snatched up the rifle; he was back outside in seconds. "Come on." He grabbed Willow's hand and they ran across the clearing for one of the deer trails, scrabbling quickly up the rocks behind the cabin. The rotary noise was growing louder, beating through the air. As they climbed, Alex cursed himself – why hadn't they left hours ago, the moment Willow told him her fears? If the truck had broken down, then they could have just hiked the rest of the way; at least they would have been gone from here.

Willow slipped slightly. He steadied her arm with his and they kept climbing. She had gone silent, her face pale but resolute. Finally they reached a small, rocky ledge, with the cabin below it in clear view, looking almost toy-like. And there was the helicopter – sleek and black, swinging slightly in the air as it touched down in the valley near the truck.

"Oh, no," whispered Willow.

"Get down," said Alex quickly. He lay flat on the

ground, ignoring the small, sharp stabs against his chest, and sighted along the rifle, peering through the telescopic lens. Willow lay beside him, her eyes fixed fearfully on the scene below.

The helicopter snapped into sharp focus. It was unmarked, with tinted windows. As its blades slowed, a man and a woman climbed out of it. The woman had shoulder-length brown hair and was wearing grey trousers and a fitted jacket; the man was blond, in jeans and a bulky fisherman's sweater. Closing his eyes, Alex moved quickly through his chakras, scanning to check out the pair's energies. They were too far away for him to sense, but when he opened his eyes again he could see their auras clearly through the lens: the man was an angel; the woman human. As Alex watched, they started climbing up the deer path towards the cabin. The woman was carrying a briefcase.

"What can you see?" asked Willow in a low voice.

Tersely, he told her. The man and woman had reached the cabin now; they knocked on the door and then looked inside. Knocked on the door. Alex stared through the lens, frowning. Why were they bothering with being polite? They must know that their helicopter had been heard; he'd expect them to go in with all guns blazing. In fact, if they were Church of Angels, he'd expect a small army, not these two. Who the hell were they?

As he watched, the woman took a small hand-held amplifier from her jacket. Looking up at the mountains around her, she spoke into it; her voice echoed around them. "Alex Kylar and Willow Fields. Special Agents Kinney and Anderson here, CIA."

Alex's shoulders stiffened with surprise. "They must be from Project Angel," he muttered. Did the woman have angel burn, or was she unaware that her colleague was one of the enemy?

Down below, the female agent was still gazing upwards, turning slightly as she spoke. Her next words rocked him: "We're aware that you can read auras. Special Agent Anderson is an angel; he's on our side. It's imperative that we speak to you."

Beside him, Willow stifled a gasp. "Alex, can that be true?" she whispered.

An angel, on their side? Slowly, Alex took his eye away from the lens and shook his head. "I doubt it. It's exactly what I'd expect them to say, to lure us down there."

Willow hesitated. "If I got closer, I could try checking them out psychically."

For a moment he thought she meant climbing down again, and then he realized. "He's an angel; he'd see you."

"Yes, but I don't think he could hurt me. I'm not like them – my life force is in my human form, not my angel one. It might be the only way we can find out."

Alex didn't like the idea, but thinking about it, he knew she was right. "Yeah, okay," he said finally. "Be careful." He put his eye back to the lens; if Willow's theory was wrong and her angel looked like it was in danger from either of the agents, they'd regret it.

Willow shut her eyes, going very still for a moment. Gradually, her angel took form above her, its wings gleaming in the rosy morning sun. Flying upwards, the angel went into a long, slow glide, heading towards the cabin. Alex crouched over his rifle, watching the man and woman intently as the angel approached, flying over the stream.

"He's seen me," murmured Willow beside him.

"Yeah, I can tell," said Alex. The blond man's eyes had widened in momentary surprise as he spotted Willow's angel; now he was saying something to the woman, his expression urgent. Alex tensed as Willow's angel swooped close to them and hovered, her wings moving gently. But the man made no threatening gestures. Instead, he turned to face Willow's angel, his arms slightly out from his sides; the woman imitated him, though she clearly didn't know quite where to look.

"They're both...mentally opening themselves to me," said Willow softly. There was a long silence; the wind rustled around them. Alex glanced at Willow at his side, taking in her furrowed frown. Finally she opened her eyes, looking deep in thought. "Alex, I think they're what they say they are. They're both from Project Angel; they believe they're the only agents left who haven't been contaminated. He's an angel, but...he really is on our side. He hates what the others have been doing here."

Alex put his eye back to the lens. "Yeah? Ask him what he's been feeding on," he said, scanning the angel's aura again. It looked sated, as if the being had recently indulged.

Willow closed her eyes again. There was a pause, and then Alex saw the man's lips moving. When Willow opened her eyes again she looked saddened. "I – I thought the question at him, and he heard me," she said. "He feeds off people who already have angel burn. He hates doing it, but he says it's the only way he can survive to try and stop what's happening."

"Do you believe him?" asked Alex, glancing at her.

Slowly, Willow nodded. "Yeah, I do," she said. "I believe both of them."

Alex looked back at the scene below. Neither the man nor the woman had moved as Willow's angel hung in the air above them, her wings as white as pieces of clouds. He shook his head in disbelief. He had complete faith in Willow's psychic abilities, but even so...an angel that actually cared about what it fed on?

"Okay," he said finally, lowering the rifle. "Tell them we're coming down."

As they crossed the field back to the cabin, Alex saw that the agents were sitting on the ground outside it, and grudgingly, he respected the fact that they hadn't invaded their space by waiting inside. The woman was smoking a cigarette, looking pensive; she stubbed it out when she saw them approaching and jumped to her feet. "Mr. Kylar," she said briskly, walking towards them with her hand out. "Sophie Kinney. This is a real pleasure."

He shook her hand, feeling nonplussed. She was gazing at him with an expression akin to wonder.

She seemed to catch herself. "Sorry, it's just that you were something of a legend in the office...over two hundred angels, single-handed. And you must be Willow Fields," she said, offering her hand to Willow.

"Hi," said Willow shyly, shaking it.

The man came forward; he was taller than Alex, with broad shoulders. His blue eyes had the odd intensity of all angels, piercing into Alex's own. "Nate Anderson," he said, holding out his hand.

After a beat, Alex took it. "So what made you change sides?" he asked brusquely.

The angel's expression didn't change. "I was never on the other side," he said. "Not all of us feel that we have a divine right to use humans as cattle."

"We have so much that we need to discuss with you

both," broke in Agent Kinney. "Please, could we go inside?"

Alex glanced at Willow. "Okay?"

She nodded, and Alex opened the door. With the four of them inside, the cabin seemed even smaller than usual; he saw Agent Kinney noticing the narrow bed with its joined-together sleeping bags.

Willow looked at the two chairs. "Here, um – why don't the two of you sit at the table, and we'll take the bed?" she suggested to the agents. Smoothing her hair back, she quickly tied it into a knot.

"Call us Sophie and Nate, please," said Agent Kinney as she took a seat.

Alex didn't respond. He had no intention of getting chummy with these two until he knew what was going on. Propping his rifle against the wall, he grabbed the unpacked T-shirt he'd left out for the day and pulled it on. He sat beside Willow on the bed, leaning back against the wall and tapping his fingers on his knee.

"How did you find us?" he asked.

"Remote viewing," said Nate. "I've been trying to get a psychic fix on you for weeks; its not easy when there's no personal attachment. Finally I saw that you were up in the mountains somewhere. I kept thinking it was the Rockies; I wasted several days scanning them before moving further west."

Willow looked nervous. "But if you can do that, then the other angels can, too," she said.

He nodded. "It's a specialized skill, but I'm sure they're trying. You're just lucky that we found you first."

"*We're* lucky," said Sophie. "Though it would have saved a lot of time if we hadn't lost you outside of Phoenix."

"That was you following us on the interstate?" asked Willow.

Nate nodded. "I've got contacts in the Church of Angels; I heard through the grapevine that a couple of devotees almost got you in Texas – for a while after that, we were only a few steps behind you."

"Kudos to both of you, by the way, for keeping alive so far," put in Sophie. "It's quite an achievement."

Willow shook her head. "It's all been Alex," she said. "I'd have been dead the first day if it wasn't for him."

"You saved me, too," said Alex quietly, thinking of their battle with the angels in New Mexico. Their gaze met briefly, and then he turned back to the agents. "How long has Project Angel been infiltrated?"

"About four months," said Nate. "Some of the agents in the field had already died or been subject to angel burn by that point – afterwards, most of the remaining ones were dispatched by the angels, or are now missing, presumed dead."

Alex had already known it, but it was like a hard kick to the chest anyway. His muscles tensed; he saw Willow dart him a worried look, her eyes full of sympathy. "Right," he said finally. "So how come I wasn't dispatched?"

Nate gave a sad smile. "Because you were the best. So the angels decided to use you for their own purposes — doing away with traitors like me."

Alex's spine straightened as he came away from the wall. "*What?*"

Sophie nodded. "For the past four months, every hit you've done has been an angel sympathetic to humans, who was working to help save them."

"You're insane," he said shortly. "I *watch* them, remember? Every single one was about to feed."

Nate shook his head. "No, they were going to do something called marshalling, where they place psychic resistance into a human's aura. It can act as a protection against angels who are feeding. In the right conditions, it can also be passed on to other humans through auric contact — almost like a virus, but with positive effects."

Alex's mind was spinning. He thought back to his last hit before he'd received the order for Willow: T. Goodman, approaching the drunken businessman on the sidewalk. *Don't be afraid. I have something to give to you.*

He swore. Distantly, he felt Willow take his hand; he gripped her fingers.

113

Sophie crossed her legs. "You had no way of knowing, of course; you were just doing your job – excellently as always, I might add."

He felt like throwing something at her. "Right, so there's this thing called marshalling, and no one even bothered to *tell* me about it? So that I could maybe *not* kill angels who are on our side? Great, that's just great. How did you guys manage to lose control of things so badly? No, scratch that – how did you even get your jobs in the first place?"

She sat impassively. "The angel spotters were aware of this information for the past year, which is how long Nate's been with us. None of the hits authorized by us since that time were against sympathetic angels. And probably very few prior to that; there just aren't that many of them."

Alex let out a breath. Willow was still holding his hand; the steady warmth of her touch calmed him somewhat. "Okay," he said after a pause. He squeezed Willow's hand and released it, scraping his face. "Sorry."

Sophie inclined her head. "If this news didn't bother you, then you wouldn't have been fit for the job in the first place."

Nate leaned forward, resting his forearms on his knees. "Look, it's actually the current situation that we need to deal with, not what happened four months ago. If we don't act quickly, things are about to get a whole lot worse.

Which brings us to the next point." He paused for a moment as his gaze went to Willow, taking her in. "So, it really is true that you're a half-angel," he said.

"Yes, it is." Her voice was quiet, steady. Remembering her anguish in the desert the month before, Alex felt a rush of love and admiration for her.

Nate nodded. "I knew it already, but actually seeing it for myself is…" He trailed off, shaking his head. "You should be impossible, you know."

Willow smiled slightly. "Here I am anyway."

"Do you know why the angels think you can destroy them?"

"No. I don't have any idea. Before all of this, I didn't even know that there *were* angels, much less that I was a half one."

"Well, I know a bit more than you, then," said Nate. "Among the angel community, the consensus is that Paschar's vision had something to do with the gate."

"Start at the beginning," interrupted Sophie.

"Right," said Nate. "The first thing you have to understand is that most angels in this world are here because of something called the Crisis. Our world is similar to your own, except that there, we can feed off the ether itself. Being a predator isn't our natural state."

"Yeah? You give a great imitation of it," said Alex before he could stop himself. Willow gave him a quick glance.

Nate shrugged a broad shoulder. "It's true, there have always been angels who liked to come across here and feed off humans. They liked the buzz, the excitement of it. But their numbers were relatively few, overall. You'll just have to trust me when I say that most angels had no interest in it. However, then the Crisis came – though no one knows why, our ether began to fade, and it's getting worse. Currently there's no longer enough energy left to support all of us. Soon our world won't be able to sustain any of us at all."

Alex listened intently. They'd been right, then – something had gone wrong in the angels' world, bringing them to this one.

"The Seraphic Council decided that our only hope was to start an evacuation." Nate's eyes flicked to Alex's. "To here."

"The Invasion," said Alex.

"The Invasion," agreed Nate. He took a breath, tapping his fingers together. When he spoke again, he sounded as if he was choosing his words carefully. "The evacuation has been planned in waves. What you call the Invasion was the first one; there are still several more to come."

For a moment Alex didn't take it in, and then suddenly what the angel was saying slammed through him like a tsunami. Coldness gripped his chest as he stared at Nate. Beside him on the bed, Willow had gone very still, her lips white.

"The First Wave was primarily to see if it could be done," said Nate quietly. "Could angels survive in this way? And the answer seems to be yes. Most angels have… taken to feeding off humans with alacrity. Enjoyment, even." His face twisted in disgust. "So, it's been deemed a success. The news came through about six weeks ago; the Second Wave has now been authorized. When it occurs, it will roughly double the number of angels currently here."

"When?" asked Alex. His throat was dry.

Nate's eyes met his. "Tomorrow," he said.

"*Tomorrow?*"

Nate nodded. "The plans have been in place for over two years; once the decision was made six weeks ago, things happened quickly."

"Here, look at this," said Sophie, reaching for her briefcase. Stretching across to the bed, she handed them a white flyer with silver and blue lettering. It had the Church of Angels logo of an angel with outstretched wings and arms on it, and read:

THE ANGELS ARE COMING!
October 31st is usually All Hallow's Eve…
this year it's All Angels' Eve.
We have prayed, and the angels have answered.
By their loving grace, our world is about to be blessed
with an even stronger angelic presence. The angels have

heard our pleas, our hopes and dreams…and they are
coming to us. Be there to help herald in a new,
better world with the angels.
SPECIAL SERVICE AND CELEBRATION
CHURCH OF ANGELS MAIN CATHEDRAL,
DENVER CO, SUNDAY OCTOBER 31st, 4 P.M.

Alex stared at it, lost for words. The Invasion had been bad enough. He tried to imagine the number of angels on earth doubling, and then more arriving after that, and even more after that. It would be wholesale slaughter of humans when it got to that point. And from the sounds of things, he was the only Angel Killer left in the country.

"How can they…do this so publicly?" whispered Willow, touching the flier.

Sophie shrugged. "It's the usual thing, hiding in plain view. Those who don't believe will just think there's nothing to it, that the Church of Angels is full of loonies."

Willow hugged her elbows. "So all these people are going to come, to celebrate the angels – and they're going to be *fed* off?" Her voice sounded harsh with sorrow and revulsion.

Nate shook his head. "The arriving angels won't be feeding just yet; this world will be totally new to them. It'll take them some time to get settled, get acclimated…then it will start. But yes, it's still obscene, the thought of the crowds being so thrilled to see the angels arrive, without any idea of what lies in store for them."

Alex frowned tensely, trying to picture the scene. "How are they supposed to see them, if the angels aren't feeding yet?"

Nate snorted. "It's a special occasion," he said. "The angels are going to lower their frequency on the ethereal plane as they fly through the cathedral – it'll mean that the audience will be able to see them as they arrive. They're looking forward to all the cheers."

Cheers. Alex tossed the flier onto the table, feeling sick.

"This wave, and the ones planned for after it, can't be allowed to happen," said Sophie. "We were struggling to fight the angels already. If even more arrive on this scale, we won't have much of a chance – society as we currently know it will probably be gone in ten years."

Willow made a small noise. Alex gripped her hand briefly, and glanced back at Nate. "Right, so fill me in on the angels' grand plan, then," he said in a rough voice. "If you infect all the humans with angel burn, how are you supposed to feed once they're all dead?"

The angel looked reluctant. "As long as humans have children, angels will have fresh energy sources. I believe there are plans afoot to begin encouraging larger families among followers."

It figured. Alex grimaced, unsurprised. At his side, Willow had gone pale, her green eyes wide with horror.

"As I said, this can't happen," put in Sophie. "We absolutely have to stop it; it's our only hope."

"How?" said Alex after a pause. "Is there any way?"

There was a slight shift in the room as Nate and Sophie glanced at each other. Suddenly Alex knew, without a doubt, that he wasn't going to like whatever they suggested.

Slowly, Nate said, "There's a thin…wall, let's call it, of energy that separates our two worlds. When it was only small numbers of angels coming across on their own, the wall remained fairly stable – its energy was briefly disturbed by being passed through, but it could reform itself. However, an exodus of this scale is very different. A special opening – a gate – has to be generated, so that hundreds of thousands of angels can pass through the wall in a short time without destroying it altogether. The wall will be extremely unstable for the twenty minutes or so that it'll take for them all to fly through – it's a very delicate operation."

"It's planned that the gate will open in the main Church of Angels cathedral at 6 p.m. tomorrow night, two hours after the service starts," said Sophie, indicating the flier. "We've got someone inside the Church who's helping us – we know all the details, including the exact place inside the cathedral."

"Right," said Nate. "And what we think is…if the gate is disrupted just as it's starting to open, it will set off a chain reaction that will damage it enough to make it unusable. Effectively, it will slam shut, keeping the remaining angels in their own world, away from this one."

Alex sat listening, rapping his fist against his knee. "So how exactly do you disrupt it?"

Instead of answering, Nate reached his hand out to Willow. "May I?" he asked.

She hesitated, and then put her hand in his. Nate closed his eyes briefly; Alex could see faint movement behind his lids, as if Nate were watching unseen images. When he finally let go of Willow's hand, he sat and gazed at her for a few moments without speaking.

"Paschar was right," he said finally.

"Paschar?" asked Willow. "Was that – Beth's angel?"

Nate nodded. "He saw that your very existence is a danger to the angels; you have the means to destroy us all. I've just seen the same thing. Some of the images are unclear, but…" He turned to Sophie. "It's our best chance."

"What is?" said Alex sharply.

Reaching into her briefcase again, Sophie pulled out a small stone and placed it on the table. It looked almost like molten lead, gleaming with silvery lights. Nate picked it up. "This is a piece of angelica," he said, turning it over.

It was oval in shape; just small enough to be hidden in his hand if he closed his fingers over it. "It's from my own world. It has several unique properties; one is that on the ethereal plane, it has a sort of…consciousness. If communicated with, its physical form will emit short, rapid bursts of energy at a very high frequency – more than enough to disrupt the gate when it's in such a vulnerable state."

His eyes rose to Willow's. "You're as unique as the angelica," he told her. "Your angel form exists at the same time as your human one. That means you could communicate with the angelica, activating it at the same time as you place it within the opening gate – none of the rest of us could do that."

Alex stiffened as he realized. "Wait a minute," he said, his voice hardening. "You want *Willow* to be the one to do this?"

"She's the only one," said Nate heavily.

The angel handed the stone to Willow; looking stunned, she took it in slow motion, turning it over in her hand. Finally she swallowed and glanced at Alex. "If I did do this, then, what…what would happen?"

Sophie's expression was anxious, tight with tension. "We hope the gate would be destroyed, closing it for good."

"You *hope*?" said Alex. His words came out like razor blades. "So you're not exactly positive, are you?" Their silence was assent. "And what would happen to Willow? Would she be destroyed, too?"

Sophie hesitated. "We don't know that," she said finally. "The wall will become extremely unstable; we don't know exactly what form that will take. But Willow, with you standing right beside it…" She trailed off.

Fear leaped through Alex, along with an anger so raging that it was all he could do not to start punching things. "And how would she even get into the cathedral in the first place? It's going to be a madhouse – tens of thousands of Church of Angels fanatics, who all want her dead anyway! Just so she can do this thing that might kill her, that you *hope* will work?"

"We can get her in," said Nate. "Our person in the Church will help. We've got a plan in place that will put her close to the gate without being noticed."

"Yeah, great," said Alex harshly. "And even if it all works, what happens if standing next to the gate *doesn't* kill her? The angels don't arrive, and everyone's seen that she's the reason why – are they all just going to say, '*Oh, well,*' and go home?"

The agents didn't answer. Alex glared at them. "They'd kill her, and you know it," he said in a low voice. "A small army couldn't keep her safe in that situation." Then he saw the truth on their faces, and his jaw hardened. "Right, except that you don't think that's going to happen, do you?

You think the gate's going to blow her to pieces, no matter what."

There was a long silence. Finally Sophie let out a breath. "Willow, he's right, it's tremendously dangerous. The gate's reaction when the angelica touches it is likely to be…quite violent."

"No way is she doing this," said Alex. "Seriously. No way in hell."

"There's more though," said Sophie. She glanced at Nate, who nodded.

"We angels are creatures of energy," he said. "We all come from the same original source, so that even though we're individuals, we're also linked – whenever an angel dies, we all feel it. If the gate is closed, then those left in our own world would perish soon. With casualties on such a massive scale, it's only a matter of time before the angels here would perish as well. We couldn't survive for long with so many of us gone."

Willow looked up at Nate. "But – if that happened, then you wouldn't survive, either."

"No, I wouldn't," said Nate. He was silent for a long moment, tapping his fingers together. "The…betrayal of my own kind isn't a thing I take lightly," he said finally. "But what's happening is abhorrent. Even if it's to save ourselves, we angels can't cause such death and destruction to another race; we simply don't have that right."

Another time, Alex might have been impressed at Nate's selflessness; as it was, he just wanted to strike him. "Well, that's really noble, but you're not the one taking the risk here, are you? You're asking Willow to do that, when nothing's even certain."

Sophie's voice took on an edge. "The thing that's certain is that if we do nothing, more angels will invade our world. If we act, we at least have a chance to destroy them all."

Willow was silent, turning the silvery-grey stone over in her hand. Finally she said, "You...you really think it has to be me, don't you?"

Alex felt his stomach go into icy knots as he looked at her.

Nate nodded. "With the way your dual nature works, you're the only one who can physically move the stone, and communicate with it in its ethereal form at the same time. Plus, it's written all through your psyche – you're the one who can destroy us."

Willow swallowed, still gazing at the stone. "And...how likely is it that the gate would close?"

"I can't give you odds," said Nate levelly. "We can't really know what will happen until you actually try."

Sophie leaned forward, watching her intently. "Willow, time is already extremely short," she said. "If – if you agree to this, then we need to leave immediately, so that we can brief you and get things ready."

"Willow, no," said Alex. He gripped her arms. "*No.* There is no way that you can do this. Just no way."

She looked up at him, and he saw that she was close to tears. She took a deep breath. "Um – could you excuse us, please?" she said to Sophie and Nate. Leaning over, she placed the angelica back on the table.

"Yes, of course." Sophie put the rock in her briefcase and snapped it shut; she and Nate stood up, scraping their chairs back. "We'll be outside."

A moment later, the door had shut behind them. Alex hardly heard it. He stared at Willow, still clutching her arms. "You can't do this," he said. "You can't. Tell me that you're not serious."

She was pale. "Alex, I…I just don't see that I have a choice."

"Weren't you *listening*? Willow, they think the gate will blow you apart; they don't even have any idea whether you can close it or not!"

Very slowly, she nodded. "I know," she said.

Sudden fury gripped him; his voice rose, ringing around the tiny cabin. "You cannot seriously be considering this! Have you gone completely insane? Do you want to just throw your life away, is that your plan?"

A tear darted onto her cheek, but when she spoke, her tone was almost steady. "What else can I do – go to Mexico with you, and ignore all of this? How could I live with myself, knowing that maybe I could have stopped the angels for ever, and I didn't even try?"

"Willow, this *isn't the way.* All this is going to do is kill you! Look, we'll find a way to fight them, we'll—"

He was gripping her arms too tightly; she pulled away from him, her expression agonized. "Of course this is the way! This is what it all *means,* don't you see? My premonition last night, and Paschar's vision – I'm the only one who can stop them, this is how I have to do it!"

Terror that she was right jolted through him; his breath felt like it had turned to ice in his chest. "No. You are not doing this; I'm not letting you."

Her expression was so torn, so full of sorrow and love for him. "Alex, if there's even just a chance that I can stop the angels, then I have to try. You've fought them your whole life, you must understand—"

"*Not like this!*" he shouted. "This is suicide; they can't even tell you if it's going to work or not! Does throwing your life away really sound that good to you?"

"It's not like I *want* to do it!" she cried, her eyes bright with tears. "All I want is to be with you, and for things to be like they have been!"

"Then *do* that," he said. He gripped her hands hard. "Willow, please – you don't have to do this—"

She ducked her head down, her mouth twisting against tears. The pendant that he'd given her had worked its way out from under her sweater. Letting go of his hand, she reached up and touched the crystal, stroking its facets. "I'm sorry," she whispered.

Without looking at him, she rose from the bed and moved stiffly to the table. She started to tuck the clothes that she'd left out for the day's journey into her bag.

"*No!*" Alex leaped up, grabbed them away from her. "No. Willow, no – you are *not* doing this—"

"*I have to!*" she burst out, spinning towards him. "I don't have a choice! Do you think I can just turn my back on this, like it never happened? I can't!"

She was actually going to do it – this thing that would kill her.

The world pounded in Alex's ears as he stared at her. All at once his chest felt tight; he could hardly breathe. Oh god, no. Not again, not someone else he loved. Why had he allowed himself to believe that this time might be different? How could he have been so *stupid*?

"Right, so I guess you've decided," he said finally.

"Alex, I – I could never live with myself otherwise," she said in a tiny voice. "I'd see my mother's face every day for the rest of my life, and – and Beth, and your family—" She stopped abruptly, covering her face with her hand.

He wanted so badly to comfort her. Instead he found himself glaring at her, almost trembling with anger. "Don't bring my family into this. If you're going to kill yourself, do it for your own reasons." He shoved the clothes at her.

Willow's cheeks were wet with tears. Slowly, she put the clothes away in her bag, her hands unsteady. "Alex, *please* understand. How could you and I ever have anything good together, if I walked away from this? I feel like it would – would poison things between us; we'd always know that—"

He wouldn't have thought it possible that he could hate her, but right then it felt close to it. "Don't you dare, don't you *dare* say that you're doing this for us," he broke in, his voice shaking. "There won't even be any us after you do this." Her bag wasn't fastened; roughly, he reached across and tied it shut, thrusting it at her. "Just – go," he said. "Go on, they're waiting for you."

Swallowing hard, she clutched the bag to her chest. "Will – will you come?" she asked faintly.

Her eyes. Her face.

The words felt like ground glass in his throat. "No, thanks. I've seen enough people I care about die."

Her face crumpled. She looked away, her mouth trembling. "I – I guess I'd better go, then."

"Yeah, I guess you'd better."

Slowly, Willow started for the door, then stopped and flew back to him, hugging him tightly. "I love you," she said as she started to sob. "Alex, please, please don't let it end like this. I love you."

He ached to hold her. He couldn't do it; he was frozen. "Just go," he said through clenched teeth.

Willow pulled away, gazing up into his face. Her green eyes were stricken. "I know you don't mean this," she whispered. "I love you, Alex. I'll always love you." He stood unmoving as she kissed him; he could taste her tears. Turning quickly away, she ran for the door.

Then she was gone.

As if from a great distance, Alex heard the sound of voices from outside, then footsteps moving away. Silence. He stood alone in the centre of the room, his muscles quivering. Abruptly, he picked up one of the chairs and hurled it across the cabin, sending it crashing against the wall. Sinking down onto the edge of the table, he scraped his hands through his hair, breathing hard. Around him were the still-rumpled sleeping bags where they'd slept the night before; his black nylon bag, packed with both their clothes. Willow's purple Converse sneakers still lay in the corner, one of them on its side. What had happened? What had just happened? For several minutes Alex sat clutching his head, his emotions crashing through him so violently that it felt like they'd tear him apart.

He heard the helicopter start up.

His head jerked up as the sound roared through him, spiking his pulse with sudden clarity. Willow was in the helicopter. She was about to fly away from him – he'd probably never see her again. Panic leaped through him; he was on his feet so fast that the table scraped against the floor. Lunging out of the cabin, he ran across the small clearing, skidded his way down the deer path.

"Willow!" he shouted. "*Willow!*"

The blades pounded in his ears as he burst out into the open. The helicopter had already taken off; it was swinging away over the valley. Alex sprinted after it, jogging to a stop as the wind stirred his hair. It was growing smaller; he couldn't even see its occupants through the tinted windows. Knowing it was hopeless, he put his hands to his mouth anyway. "WILLOW!"

The helicopter kept going. As he watched, it moved away over the mountains, until it became a small, dark flyspeck and then vanished from sight, taking his heart with it.

Alex stared after it, shaking. What had he done? Willow had most likely gone off to her death – and he'd actually told her to *leave*? He hadn't held her. He hadn't told her how much he loved her.

He had let her go alone.

"No," he said out loud. No, this wasn't going to happen. This seriously wasn't going to happen; it wasn't going to end like this. If she had to do this thing, fine, but she wasn't going to do it alone, thinking that he hated her. He'd be there – to either help her or die with her, he didn't much care which, as long as he didn't have to live the rest of his life without her.

Denver by six o'clock tomorrow night. He could make it if he drove non-stop.

Running back to the cabin, Alex hurriedly changed from his sweatpants into jeans; threw on his jacket. He grabbed his wallet, the keys to the truck, his pistol and fresh cartridges. He was back in the rocky valley minutes later, flinging himself into the driver's seat of the truck and starting up the engine. Spinning the wheel, he lurched out of the valley and started down the slope.

This wasn't going to be like with Jake. He wasn't going to let down someone else he loved.

CHAPTER *Seventeen*

FOR A LONG TIME IN the helicopter, nobody said anything. Nate sat up front with the pilot, a man wearing sunglasses whose name I didn't catch, and Sophie sat in the back with me. I was still clutching my bag, staring down at it, my throat so tight that I couldn't have spoken if I tried. The look on Alex's face as he told me to leave... My muscles clenched as I held back a sob. When we'd first flown away I could actually feel my heart breaking, splintering to pieces inside my chest. I couldn't even be angry with him for not understanding – I *knew* what this was doing to him, and the thought of it was like knives slicing through me. I wanted so badly to tell Sophie and Nate to turn the helicopter around, so that I could go running back to Alex – throw my arms around him, tell him that I'd changed my mind; I wasn't going to do this after all.

But I couldn't.

Dimly, I was aware that the mountains were slowly flattening out below us, turning to desert plains. "I'm sorry," said Sophie finally, leaning towards me to be heard above the blades. "The two of you are…together, aren't you?" I nodded, wondering if it was still true, and felt tears spilling over. Rummaging quickly in her bag, Sophie handed me a tissue. "You're doing the right thing, Willow," she said. "This is our only chance to stop the angels – we're incredibly grateful to you. I know that it must be awful for you."

I swiped my face with the tissue. "I don't have a choice," I got out. "If I had a choice…" I couldn't finish. Alex and I would be together right now, on our way down to Mexico. My pendant flashed against my sweater; it hurt to even look at it. Sophie stopped talking then, and I was glad of it. Dropping my head back on the seat, I stared down at the blurred, watery plains.

A few hours later, we were landing in Colorado, at a small, private airport outside of Denver. My legs were stiff as I climbed out of the helicopter; my ears still thudding from the incessant noise. I could see the Rocky Mountains in the distance, their peaks capped with snow. I looked away. I didn't think I could ever look at a mountain again without it hurting.

Nate and Sophie walked me across the pavement, where a car with tinted windows sat waiting for us. I felt like I might fly into little pieces at any moment, but I knew that I had to at least try to act normal, or else I would just collapse. I cleared my throat. "I, um – I thought you were the only two left on Project Angel."

Nate nodded. "We're being sheltered by another department. They don't know the details; just that we have high security clearance and our mission's been compromised."

He opened the door for me as we reached the car, and I slid into the back, onto soft black leather seats. It reminded me of Alex's Porsche. Everything around me reminded me of Alex. Nate got in the front with the driver; there was a glass panel that separated the front from the back. I sat tensely with Sophie beside me, hugging my bag and watching as the airport glided away. Soon we were on a highway with green fields to either side of us, the mountains rising up beyond.

Suddenly I thought of something, and I looked across at Sophie. "Do you know what's been happening back in Pawntucket? Is my mom okay?"

I could sense her relief at being able to tell me something

good. "Your mom's fine," she said. "So's your aunt."

My shoulders sagged. "Really, they're okay?"

"Really. I promise."

I let out a deep breath, and felt the aching tightness in my chest ease slightly. My mom was all right. She was really all right. "What happened after I left?" I asked.

Sophie took out a pack of cigarettes; rolling the window down a few inches, she lit one. "The Church of Angels influenced the police investigation about your disappearance," she said, blowing out a puff of smoke. "It was closed after only a day or two. Basically, there were a hundred witnesses who said that you ran off with a boyfriend – that you were seen loading a suitcase into his car and kissing him."

I stared at her as her words sunk in. No wonder Aunt Jo's vibes had seemed so irritated every time I'd tried to pick up on them. "But – my friend Nina knew that wasn't true. Didn't she tell them?"

Sophie smiled. Taking an iPhone out of her bag, she tapped something into it and then handed it to me. I gazed down at the small screen. It had Twitter on it, with a post from Nina: *WILLOW FIELDS DID NOT HAVE A BOYFRIEND, END OF! Doesn't anyone actually CARE that my friend has vanished?*

Oh, Nina. I touched the phone as sadness swept through me.

"No one's listening to her," said Sophie, taking it back. "From what I've heard, your classmates back at Pawntucket High prefer the secret boyfriend story – and there are enough Church members in the Schenectady police force to ensure that no one's going to look into things further." She put the phone back into her bag. "It's probably what's saved her life so far, to be honest."

"Alex said that there would be," I said after a pause. "Church of Angels members on the police force, I mean."

Sophie's face was thoughtful as she flicked ash out the window. "He's quite extraordinary," she said. "For someone so young, to do the things he's done…"

"He's never really been young," I said softly, looking away. "He never had the chance." No, but when it was just the two of us, alone together – I swallowed hard, seeing his grin; his laughing eyes. And then his face when he had realized I was leaving.

He hadn't even told me goodbye.

I wrapped my arms tightly around myself, aching for us both. Glancing at me, Sophie went silent; neither of us spoke for a long time. Finally the car took a turn-off, and a few minutes later we were heading down an unmarked drive. A low, tan building rose up from a manicured lawn. There were no signs. Sophie sat up, unfastening her seatbelt. "A CIA satellite office," she said, though I hadn't asked. "We can brief you here, and there's showers, beds…"

I nodded dully as I gazed at the stark, featureless building. I was so far away from Alex, almost a thousand miles. It felt like every one of them was crushing my heart like a stone.

Getting out of the car, we walked up a short flight of cement stairs and then through a pair of gleaming glass doors. Sophie and Nate showed ID at a desk and then ushered me down a carpetless hallway. It was so polished that I could see our reflections as we walked; our footsteps echoed around us.

"Here we go," said Nate finally, opening a door. We stepped into a small apartment, with sofas and chairs. A kitchenette sat at one end, with a breakfast counter and bar stools.

Sophie put her briefcase onto the coffee table. "Would you like to get freshened up?" she asked me. "There's a shower, if you feel like it." She indicated the hallway past the kitchen.

I was still wearing the sweatpants and T-shirt I had slept in; the red sweater Alex had given me. An irrational part of me never wanted to take it off, as if doing so would break the last link that I had with him. But it didn't make any difference, did it? I'd probably never see him again no matter what I wore. The thought lashed through me like a whip. Then I realized that Sophie and Nate were both looking at me, waiting for an answer. "I guess," I said.

My voice was barely audible, even to me. "I don't, um — have any shampoo, though, or—" Memories of the motel room in Tennessee swarmed over me, and I broke off, closing my eyes against the sudden pain. "Sorry," I said, trying to regain myself. "I don't have any shampoo."

Sophie's brown eyes looked troubled, but she tried to smile. "Don't worry, there's everything you need in there."

In the bathroom, I slowly stripped off my clothes, folding them carefully. As I glanced in the mirror, the pendant gleamed on my chest. I stared at myself, trying to comprehend how quickly things had changed. Just hours ago, I'd been standing in front of the cabin with Alex's arms around me — his mouth warm as he kissed my neck, the two of us about to leave together.

Suddenly I couldn't hold it in any longer. Turning on the shower so that I couldn't be heard, I got in and sobbed, holding myself tightly as the hot water rained down around me. Oh, Alex. Please don't hate me, please don't. I miss you so much already. I wanted it all with you, everything — I want you here with me now, to hold me and tell me it's going to be okay, that maybe I won't actually die when I do this thing…

I cried until there were no tears left. Finally, feeling worse than I had before, I washed my hair and climbed stiffly out of the shower. My face in the steamy mirror looked sore and swollen, like someone had been using it as a punching bag. I stared drearily at myself, not caring. Mechanically, I took the clothes from my bag and got dressed. Underwear, jeans and the pale blue T-shirt. Over it, I pulled on the red sweater again. It hurt, seeing it, but it would have hurt ten times worse not to wear it. Finally I combed out my wet hair, twisting it up into a knot.

When I went back into the living room, Nate and Sophie were sitting on one of the sofas talking. They looked up, their faces creasing in concern as they saw me. Nate went over to the kitchenette and got out some mugs. "Coffee?"

I sat on the edge of the armchair. My head was pounding. "No – thank you. Just water, please."

"How about some food?" asked Sophie. She leaned forward with her arms on her knees, watching me. "We've got sandwiches, or we could order something else in if you wanted it."

"I'm not really hungry. Thanks," I added faintly, as Nate filled a glass with ice water and brought it to me. It was a hexagonal shape, and felt cool and slightly damp against my fingers. I rubbed it against my throbbing eyes and forehead.

Nate leaned against the sofa. "You should eat something. You need to keep your strength up."

I stared down at the glass, swirling the water. "Maybe later."

Sophie hesitated, and then said, "Look, Willow, we're concerned about you. Believe me, I know what you must be going through, but…well, to put it bluntly, we need you to be able to function tomorrow."

Pain kicked through me. I saw the cabin; falling asleep in the warmth of Alex's arms. The feel of his lips, kissing me awake in the morning. I closed my eyes, longing to say, *I don't want to do this, I've changed my mind.* But it had to be me – I was the only one. Somehow, I had to pull myself together enough to do this, or else leaving Alex and breaking both of our hearts had been for nothing.

With a deep, shaking breath, I opened my eyes. I took a sip of water and placed the glass on the table, carefully lining it up with the edge.

"I know," I said in a small voice. "I'll be able to."

We spent the rest of the day going over the plan. "The celebration will be massive," said Sophie, spreading out a map of the cathedral onto the table. "They've got a musical programme lined up, a special service – the works. None of that really concerns you, though. You won't be arriving until just before the gate opens."

I gazed down at the map. There were hundreds of rows of pews, and then thousands of other seats behind them, stretching up towards the ceiling. At the very front of everything, near the pulpit, was a long, wide space. "Is that where the gate's going to be?" I asked, pointing.

"That's right," said Nate, his blue eyes narrowed as he studied the plans. "And there'll be a plexiglass barrier between the front row of pews and the gate area, across here." He sketched a line with his finger. "They were going to have one anyway for crowd control, but it's a help to us – if people suspect you and get unruly, it'll at least slow them down a bit."

Sophie was holding a pen; she twiddled it in her hands. "The others in the front area with you will be the acolytes from each state – you're going to pretend to be one, too – and the preacher. The choir will be up on a second-floor balcony, so they shouldn't be a problem. But unfortunately, there will also be two angels there."

"At least it's only two," said Nate before I could react. He glanced at me. "Raziel is the angel who runs the cathedral. He's decided that the celebration will be for humans only, and that the angels already in this world will greet the new arrivals later. Really, though, he just wants to be one of the only angels present when the Second Wavers first arrive – he's making a statement about his position here."

"Him and his sidekick, an angel named Lailah," said Sophie. "They're pretty certain to be in the gate area along with you and the others, but hopefully, you'll be able to move fast enough so that no one has time to react anyway."

My throat had gone as dry as sand as I stared at them. "But...won't one of them notice my aura as I go in?" I asked. I knew that angels in their human form could scan things just like Alex if they tried, and with its silver and lavender lights, my aura looked exactly like what I was: half-angel, half-human.

Grimacing, Sophie tucked a strand of her brown hair back. "Unfortunately, that's a variable we can't really control," she said. "We've done our best, though – our contact is going to report your death tomorrow, so hopefully neither of them will be scanning for you."

I swallowed hard, imagining what Alex would say about all of this. "Okay," I said finally. "What happens next?"

"The gate's scheduled to open at six o'clock sharp," went on Nate. "The energy needed to do so is all being generated from the other side. At about two minutes to six, a line of acolytes from every state in the country is going to file in, entering from this door here." He pointed it out on the map.

"You're Wisconsin," said Sophie. Getting up, she went to a small closet and took out a silvery-blue robe with a hood. "We didn't know whether we'd be able to find you or not, but we had one made in your size just in case.

Would you try it on to check?" She held it out to me.

The thought of the robe already being made, sitting in a closet in Colorado waiting for me, sent goosebumps up my arms. Biting my lip, I went across and took it from Sophie; it swung slightly on its padded hanger. When I pulled it on its material was silky-slippery, whispering its way down my body.

Sophie took a step back, her eyes narrowed as she scrutinized me. "Not bad, given that I had to guess at the measurements. A little too long, but I think it'll be all right once we get some heels on you."

I stood gazing down at myself. The robe had long sleeves and a high neck; it covered every inch of me. I smoothed my hands down the front of it. It felt awful, like a costume I wasn't ever going to be able to take off. A chill swept over me as I realized that was pretty much the case. It was likely that I'd die in it.

"The hood was a last-minute addition, once our Church of Angels person agreed to the plan," said Nate. "It should help stop people from recognizing you."

"We'll need to pull your hair back, though," added Sophie. "I've got some bobby pins."

"All right," I said. All I wanted to do was get the thing off me. I started to pull it over my head.

"Wait a second, let's test the angelica," said Nate. He opened the briefcase, taking out the greyish stone.

"Yes, look," said Sophie. Reaching inside my left sleeve, she showed me a hidden pouch with an elastic top. Nate came over and handed her the angelica; she tucked it in. I could feel the weight of it, heavy against my arm. "Can you take a few steps, so that we can see what it looks like?" asked Sophie.

I hated this, really hated it. But I'd agreed; I was here of my own free choice – and now I had a job to do. Taking a deep breath, I walked across the room and back. The robe billowed about my feet.

"Good," said Sophie, watching. "The sleeve's full enough so that you can't see the outline of the angelica at all."

"Right, the plan is that you'll enter with the other acolytes, right before six o'clock," said Nate. He sat on the back of the sofa, one foot still resting on the ground. "There's a dress rehearsal tonight, but you won't be going to it; we can't risk someone recognizing you. But what's going to happen is simple: the acolytes will enter single file, face the wall and kneel."

Sophie nodded. "At that point the giant TV screen is going to be turned off," she said. "The official reason is that no one would be able to view the screen with the angels flying past, but really it's just to give you a bit of added security while you make the attempt, so that no one in the audience will notice your face."

I shook my head slightly, feeling dazed; they seemed to have thought of every detail. "And…what happens then?" I asked finally.

Sophie's voice was businesslike, almost brisk. "When you kneel with the others, you're going to be front and centre: right in front of where the gate will start to open. The acolytes will all have their hands in the prayer position, so as you kneel, slip the angelica out of the pouch and hold it between your palms." She demonstrated with her hands.

"Then keep watching the air in front of you," said Nate. "The moment you see a faint ripple begin, that's your signal. Materialize your angel, contact the angelica, and run forward. The gate will be twenty feet away; you'll only have a few seconds to get to it in time."

Dizziness washed over me. This was real; it was actually going to happen. "Maybe – maybe I'd better practise contacting the stone," I said weakly, fingering the pouch inside my sleeve.

"Yes, we were going to suggest that," said Sophie. "Try getting it out of the pocket, too, and hiding it between your palms."

It was harder than I'd thought it would be. I had to do it over and over, my fingers fumbling with the elastic, before I finally got the hang of twisting my left hand upwards into the sleeve and snagging the angelica in a single motion. At last I had done it smoothly a few times in a row.

"Good, now pretend that you've seen the ripple," said Nate. He was sitting on the sofa, watching with his forearms propped on his knees. "Ready to try contacting the stone?"

I nodded. Closing my eyes, I found my angel. She was there immediately this time, waiting for me; in a matter of seconds I'd merged with her and lifted up out of myself, hovering with wings spread. The moment I did, I was aware of the stone between my human hands: it gave off a silvery aura, throbbing with life. I reached towards it with my angel-hand, stroking its energy with my own and sending it a wordless greeting.

As our two energies made contact, the angelica began to pulse. I could actually feel it beating between my palms, like a living heart.

"And that's when you'd start to run forward," said Nate, nodding. "Good work, Willow."

In my angel form, I drifted downwards, folding my wings and gently merging with my human one. Alone again, I stared at the stone, turning it over in my hands. It looked so ordinary, almost like a piece of granite.

But it could destroy a wall between worlds.

Feeling cold, I tucked it back into its elastic pouch. "I think I'll, um – go practise on my own for a while, and then go to bed," I said. It was almost six o'clock by then. "Is the bedroom mine?"

Nate nodded. "I'll be sleeping on the sofa bed tonight; Sophie's got another apartment down the hall."

"Don't you want anything to eat?" asked Sophie. "We could order in some food."

I shook my head. Suddenly I was desperate to be alone. "No, thanks."

"Willow, you've hardly had anything all day."

"I'm really not hungry."

"Well, will you at least take a sandwich in with you?" she pressed. Going into the kitchenette, she got the plate of sandwiches from the fridge and put a roast beef sandwich onto a saucer for me. "Please?" she said, holding it out.

I sighed as I took it, wondering what possible difference it made if I ate anything or not. "Okay. Goodnight."

The bedroom was small, functional. I did practise for a while, until I could snag the stone smoothly in just seconds. Then, with relief, I pulled the robe off and draped it over a chair. When I got dressed in my sweatpants and T-shirt again, I could feel the detachment that I'd somehow managed to find begin to shatter as I thought, *The last time I put these on, it was to sleep with Alex.*

I curled up in bed with the sandwich untouched on the bedside table, hugging the pillow tightly. Was he still at the cabin, now that there was no reason to run any more?

Or had he started for Mexico on his own? I stared into the darkness, my eyes prickling with tears. Not knowing where Alex was felt so wrong; so unnatural. I wanted him there beside me so badly that it felt like some vital part of me had been ripped away. Oh god, the look in his eyes when he told me to leave...

Holding my pendant, I lay on my side without moving, slow, noiseless tears streaming down my face until the pillow grew damp beneath my cheek. I didn't want to die. I wanted to live, to be with Alex, to experience so much more than I had so far. But just then, it was Alex I was crying for. All that he'd gone through, all those deaths of people he loved – and now he was having to go through it again, with me. Thinking of what he was going through was like being beaten up inside; it was even worse than imagining whatever might happen the next day. Part of me hoped that he really did hate me now – maybe it would help; maybe it would make it not hurt so much.

And more than that, I guess I was crying for both of us...that it hadn't turned out to be always, after all.

The next day seemed endless. I practised a bit more. We watched some TV, none of us really talking much. Had lunch. All three of us were watching the clock, I think. The plan was for us to leave for the private airfield at a quarter to five, and then take the helicopter to the Church of Angels' cathedral. Their contact was going to let me in by a back door, and add me to the line-up of acolytes just before they went on. Everyone had already been told that the Wisconsin acolyte had been delayed, so hopefully no one would think anything of it.

Now that the time was actually approaching, I just wanted to get it over with; for whatever was going to happen, to happen. I sat curled up on the sofa, staring unseeingly at the TV. Sophie was perched tensely in the armchair, smoking a cigarette and looking like she wasn't paying any more attention to the show than I was. In the kitchenette, Nate stood making more coffee.

Suddenly the Church of Angels cathedral with its soaring domed roof came onto the screen. I sat up slowly, my heart thumping. A reporter was standing in the parking lot in front of it, his brown hair looking stiff and hairsprayed. "*In Denver, Colorado, the angels are coming! Hundreds of thousands of devotees are currently flocking to Colorado's capital city, to be present for what they believe will be a second coming of the angels to our world...*"

All three of us had gone very still, watching; in the kitchen, Nate's hands had slowed, the coffee forgotten. The camera panned back, showing a solid sea of people standing in front of the cathedral. I stared at the image, dumbfounded. There were *thousands* of them. Some were wearing angel's wings; others were waving signs: *Praise be to angels!* And *Angels, we love you!*

The reporter went on, gazing intently into the camera: *"Though no one really understands it, in the past two years the angel phenomenon has swept the nation, with the Church of Angels the fastest-growing religion in history. Devotees strongly denounce accusations of a cult...they say that the answer's simple. To know true love, you must know the angels."*

A shining-eyed woman came onto the screen. *"I paid two hundred dollars for a ticket to be here today, and that was cheap, as far as I'm concerned...the angels saved my life. To have more of them here, helping others, is just a dream come true."*

Another shot appeared: long lines of traffic sitting unmoving on the freeway, like gleaming metallic snakes. The reporter's voice said: *"Heartless scam, or divine intervention? Whatever the truth is, with so many people arriving, roads around Denver are currently experiencing severe gridlock – so if you can't fly like an angel, consider staying home this Halloween!"*

As the news changed to a different story, Sophie glanced at me. "That's why we're taking the helicopter," she said. "It's going to be pretty insane."

"Yeah," I murmured, still staring at the screen. I swallowed hard. "Will the two of you be there, too?" I asked suddenly. "When – when I do it, I mean."

There was a slight pause. "I'll be," said Nate. "You won't see me, but I'll be hidden in the audience, close to the gate. If things don't go to plan, I might be able to do something to help."

The thought made me feel slightly better. I glanced at Sophie. Without meeting my eyes, she leaned forward and tapped her cigarette ash off in a saucer. She cleared her throat. "And I'll, um – be leaving in the helicopter for a safe location after we drop you off."

"Oh," I said faintly.

She gave me a quick, apologetic grimace. "Look, Willow, I know you understand. Nate and I are the only two agents left from Project Angel; we just can't take a chance on something happening to both of us."

I nodded slowly, feeling more alone than ever. Of course, it made sense. It made perfect, logical sense. I opened my mouth to ask how Nate and I were supposed to get away in that case, if she was taking the helicopter… and then I closed it again as I realized. Alex had been right. We wouldn't be getting away, and they both knew it. If the gate didn't kill me, then the Church of Angels people would. Nate would die soon anyway if the gate closed, so he was staying on to help – but it wasn't very likely that he'd live out the day either, once the two angels in the cathedral got hold of him. Neither of us was expected to survive for longer than a few more hours.

I had known it already; I don't know why this made it seem so much more real. I sat hugging myself, not speaking. Nate sat down again, putting coffees in front of me and Sophie. Mine grew cold in its cup. On the TV, the game show turned to a soap opera, and then the afternoon news.

Finally Nate looked at his watch. "I guess we'd better start getting ready," he said.

Sophie and I went into the bathroom, where she coiled my hair into a firm bun. "You've got such beautiful hair," she said, pinning it back at the sides.

No, I love it; it's so soft. I stared at myself in the mirror, hearing Alex's voice, feeling his hand as he stroked my hair across his chest. I couldn't speak.

When Sophie had finished, my head felt tight and strange. Back out in the living room, she brought out a few pairs of black wedge-heeled shoes that she'd gone out to get for me that morning. One pair fitted perfectly.

"All right?" she said, peering down at them.

"Yes, fine."

"Do you need a pair of hose?"

I shook my head. I was starting to feel detached, almost dreamy, like a ghost of myself. And at the same time, my heart was beating so hard that I wasn't sure how it was managing to stay in my chest. I kept noticing the strangest little details: the painting on the wall was crooked; Sophie's coffee cup on the table had lipstick on it; Nate's bulky grey sweater had a small hole near the cuff.

"Okay, I think we're ready," said Nate finally.

I picked up my bag. "All right." How was it that I sounded so normal?

Sophie took the robe and folded it over her arm; it fell in shining silvery-blue folds. "We'll get this on you in the helicopter," she said. With her other hand, she picked up her briefcase with the angelica in it.

Nate put his hand on my back as we left the apartment. We walked down the hallway. My legs felt like they belonged to someone else, propelling me around with no input from me. Closing my eyes, I briefly went within myself and found my angel, sensing her bright, loving presence; seeing the pure white flash of her wings. My arms tightened around my bag as sadness rushed through me. I had barely even gotten to know this part of myself, and now it was going to be too late.

As we climbed into the car, it was exactly four forty-five. In just over an hour, I'd be kneeling in front of the gate. I touched my sweater, stroking the slight shape of the crystal pendant as it nestled there beneath it, against my skin. *I love you, Alex,* I thought. *I'm sorry. I'm so sorry.*

I didn't cry as we drove away.

I felt as if I'd never cry again.

CHAPTER *Eighteen*

IT TOOK HOURS TO GET out of the Sierra Nevadas, with their winding mountain roads and hairpin turns. Each minute that passed felt like an hour too long, pounding at Alex's temples. Even so, he grimly resisted the urge to gun the accelerator and take the sharp turns at a hundred miles an hour. He had to actually get there, not go hurtling off the side of a mountain. He drove with his hands tight on the wheel, taking it as fast as he dared. Finally he reached the highway and floored it, relief washing through him to be moving quickly at last.

For the next twenty hours he just drove, stopping twice

for gas. Catching sight of himself in a men's room mirror, he hardly recognized his own image – his eyes looked dark, haunted. The thought barely registered before he was out the door again, heading back for the truck. Evening turned to night and then day again as he crossed Nevada and Utah, finally heading into Colorado. He was making good time, and very, very marginally, Alex felt the sick tension in his gut recede a notch. He still had to cross the Rockies, but it should be okay; he should make it with time to spare.

Half an hour into the Rockies, the truck got a flat.

Pulling over to the hard shoulder, Alex got out and stared in dull disbelief at the left front tyre. He checked the trunk; the space that should have contained a spare was empty. *No.* He slammed the trunk shut; the temptation to just keep driving on the rim was nearly overwhelming. He took a deep breath, trying to calm himself. Right. Don't panic. He'd still get there, he had time for this.

Soon a truck appeared; Alex lunged to the side of the road and waved him down. For a moment he thought the guy wasn't going to stop, and then he slowed, pulling over to the hard shoulder a few hundred yards down the highway. Alex jogged up to the cab. The trucker had rolled his window down and had his elbow propped on the sill, gazing back at him.

The words came out in a rush. "Hi, I've got a flat, and

my cell's not working – do you think you could call a garage for me?"

The man was heavyset, with bright blue eyes that reminded Alex of Cully. He glanced back at the truck. "You might have a hard time finding one open on a Sunday, up here. But I'll give you a lift, if you want – there's a restaurant about ten miles away; you can make some calls."

Sunday. He'd forgotten it was Sunday. Alex swallowed, looking back at the truck himself. It sat leaning to one side, obviously undrivable. "Yeah – yeah, thanks," he said hurriedly.

The restaurant was brightly-lit, with piped-in music that throbbed at his skull. It took Alex almost an hour on the payphone to find someone who could come out, and then almost two hours more of waiting, his muscles stiff with tension, until they arrived. By the time the tyre was finally changed and he was behind the wheel again, the digital clock read *2.46.* The Church of Angels' service would begin in just over an hour; Willow would be attempting to disrupt the gate in just over three. The thought clutched at Alex's stomach; he still had to get over the rest of the Rockies. *I'll make it,* he told himself grimly, pulling back onto the road and accelerating hard. *I'll make it or die trying.*

Soon he was deep in the mountains, on a twisting

highway. The route was familiar to him; he'd been to Colorado many times. Alex blew out a breath. He should be in Denver by around four-thirty – he'd have time to spare.

But then the traffic stopped.

He was about twenty miles outside of Denver when it happened. For the last hour or so, the stream of cars on the highway had been steadily increasing, slowing him down. His hands tight on the wheel, Alex had kept glancing at the clock, trying to reassure himself that he still had time, even with the traffic.

The flow of movement became slower and slower, until finally he was hemmed in on all sides with cars, all of them creeping along in fits and starts, no faster than about five miles an hour. Finally they just ground to a halt altogether. Alex sat staring at the unmoving cars, his heart thudding wildly as the minutes passed. Ten minutes. Then fifteen, with no movement at all. What the hell was going on? And then it hit him, like a drench of arctic water.

Everyone was going to the Church of Angels. Tens of thousands of them, all heading in the exact same direction he was.

Getting out of the truck, Alex jumped up onto the hood. His blood froze. He was on a slight rise; he could see miles of unmoving cars stretched out before him, glinting in the sun. Far ahead, people were standing outside their vehicles with the doors open, looking as if they'd already been there for hours. He was still over fifteen miles away; it was a quarter past four now.

He wasn't going to make it. Willow would die alone, thinking that he hated her.

No. *No.*

Leaping off the truck again, Alex flung open the passenger-side door. Grabbing his gun from the glove compartment, he shoved it under his T-shirt and started to run.

Dimly, he was aware of cars and people moving past his vision. He kept his eyes on the road ahead, feet thudding rhythmically on the hard shoulder. At the gym, he could run almost eight miles in an hour. This was a lot harder – he was on a hilly road; the mountain air was thin. It didn't matter. Setting his jaw, Alex ran faster, pushing himself. After a few miles he abandoned his jacket, throwing it to the side of the road.

He lost track of the time. There was only the endless concrete, and running, and the frantic beating of his heart. Finally he came up over a rise and saw two motorcycles parked on the grass to the side of the hard shoulder. A man and a woman were standing beside them, looking like they'd stopped to rest and were now pulling on their helmets. On the freeway, the line of cars stretched out, as unmoving as ever.

The couple stopped mid-motion, gazing at Alex in amazement as he jogged up to them. He put his hands on his thighs, gasping for breath; he could feel the sweat coursing down his face. "What – what time is it?" he panted.

The man had long brown hair in a ponytail; a braided goatee and sunglasses. He took a cellphone from the pocket of his jeans. "Five twenty-seven," he said, glancing at it.

Alex's heart lurched. "How – how far to the Church of Angels?"

The man made a face. "Ah, dude, you're not one of those, are you? I don't know, five or six miles?"

His blood pounded in his brain. Half an hour. Willow might die in just over half an hour, and he wasn't going to make it in time; he wasn't going to be there for her.

"Here," said the woman, handing him a bottle of water. She was short, with a round face and long black hair, and was staring at him in concern. "You look like you need it."

His hands were unsteady; he gulped down half of the water at once. Wiping his mouth with the back of his hand, he handed the bottle back and said, "I've got to get to the cathedral by six o'clock – I've got to. Do you think you could give me a lift?"

The man shook his head with a grin. "Sorry, we're

heading down to Colorado Springs; we'll be taking the next exit off. I can give you a tip, though – the angels aren't really coming, so you don't need to bother."

"No!" Alex struggled to sound halfway calm; knew he wasn't managing it. "It's my girlfriend, I've got to get to her – she's in trouble. Please, I've got to be there – it's life or death, I mean it."

The smile faded from the man's face. "Well – I sure wish we could help you, dude, but—"

"What do you mean, life or death?" broke in the woman, her eyes wide.

Oh, *Jesus,* Willow might die and he was actually standing here *talking* to these people? "I can't explain," he said tightly. "I've just got to be there." He glanced at their bikes; one was a vintage Harley; the other an aging Honda Shadow. "Could I buy your bike?" he burst out.

The man's eyebrows shot up over his sunglasses. "Are you serious?"

Alex felt like punching him. "*Yes.* Look, I'll give you a grand for the Honda, cash – please, just let me have it." It would only leave him with a few hundred; he knew it didn't matter. If Willow died, he didn't want to live anyway.

The woman's mouth had dropped open. Slowly, she closed it and looked at her boyfriend, who shrugged. "You were thinking of getting a new one," he said to her.

She shook her head. "Well – yeah, but I only paid eight hundred for it, and that was two years ago—"

"Great, you've made a profit." Grabbing his wallet, Alex counted out the bills, thrust them at her.

She stared down at the money. Finally she took it, tucking it into a leather bag across her chest. "Um – well, okay." She shrugged, laughing in surprise. "Here, I guess you'd better take this." She handed him the blue helmet she'd been about to put on.

"You do know how to ride, right?" said the guy as the woman took her things out of the motorcycle's side storage compartment.

Strapping on the helmet, Alex nodded as he straddled the bike. It had been a few years, but Juan had had a motorcycle back at the camp; he and Jake used to take turns on it. The woman handed him the keys. "Here," she said. "And – good luck. I hope you get to your girlfriend in time."

"Yeah, me too," muttered Alex. Starting the engine, he twisted the throttle in short bursts, manoeuvring the bike past a car and out into the centre of the freeway, where there was space between the lines of traffic. Then he kicked the clutch and gunned it.

Even with having to manoeuvre around cars and stragglers, it was far faster than running, and relief drenched through Alex – along with terror that he still wasn't going to make it in time. The final few miles went past quickly as he wove in and out of the traffic. Finding the cathedral was easy – there were huge signs every mile or so. He took the exit, leaning into the turn. Dimly, he noticed that the cars he was passing now were abandoned; the devotees had apparently decided to just give up and start walking.

Another mile and he was up on a hill with the cathedral below him at last, its huge domed roof glinting golden in the late afternoon sun. He could tell at a glance that he wasn't going to get in through the front doors. There were tens, maybe hundreds of thousands of people outside the building: a dark, solid carpet of humanity that covered every inch of the cathedral's steps, its lawn, the parking lot. People were sitting up on their cars, watching and waiting. Stopping briefly as he stared down at the scene, Alex could just hear a choir singing, their voices broadcast outdoors through speakers.

There had to be a way in; there had to be. Forcing himself to stay calm, Alex scanned the cathedral; it was laid out below him like a postcard. Suddenly his pulse leaped as he saw a black helicopter slowly rise up from the rear of building and fly off to the east, looking exactly like the helicopter that had taken Willow away yesterday. Of course, there was a rear entrance – that must be where Willow had entered. Peering down, he could see a service road leading to the back of the cathedral; the door would probably be near there.

On his left was a large field that ran alongside the church complex, solid with parked cars; a space for access had been left up the centre of them. The field looked like it would lead to the road, if he was lucky. Seconds later, Alex was roaring through it, the motorcycle kicking up clumps of earth as he went, and the same words beating over and over again through his skull:

Please, please let this get me to her. Please let me be there in time.

The helicopter landed behind the cathedral at exactly twenty minutes to six. Nate and Sophie took me to a rear entrance, a grey door set into the back of the building. The robe's silky fabric whispered around my ankles as we started towards it, the angelica hanging heavily in my sleeve. The hood lay draped over my head like I was a monk, showing only my face. Everything seemed so quiet. I'd seen the massive crowds out front as we flew in, not to mention the miles of stopped cars on the freeway – but back here, it was as if there was a sort of hush falling over everything, even with the amplified echo of the service going on inside.

Or maybe the hush was just within myself. I stared

down at my feet as we walked, looking at the shiny black flash of the new shoes, and thinking of my jeans rolled up under the robe. In my pocket, I could just feel the slight bulk of the photo of myself and the willow tree. I hadn't wanted to leave it in my bag, which was back in the helicopter – Sophie had said she'd "keep it safe" for me. I knew I'd never see it again. I felt very distant, but I was aware that if I thought too hard, everything would come crashing down. It was as if I had to carry myself very carefully, like a hollow eggshell, so that I wouldn't break.

A guard stood beside the door in a brown security uniform. "Hi, we've got the Wisconsin acolyte here," said Sophie with a smile. "Could we see Jonah Fisk, please? He's expecting us."

The man spoke briefly into a walkie-talkie; a moment later a young guy with a mop of curly dark hair came to the door. I gazed at him in faint surprise. I don't know what I'd been expecting the contact to be like, but this wasn't it. Jonah looked about twenty-two, with worried brown eyes. He was wearing a grey suit; his tie was the same silvery-blue as my robe.

"Um – good, Wisconsin, you finally made it," he said, licking his lips nervously. From somewhere outside of myself, I almost laughed at what an awful liar he was. The security guard didn't seem to notice; he was leaning against the outside wall with a bored expression on his face.

Jonah ushered us in, and a moment later the four of us were walking down a long, quiet corridor. The floor, walls and ceiling were all gleaming white. He took us into an empty room about halfway down it, closing the door behind us. "So you're Willow," he said, staring at me.

I nodded, my throat too dry to speak.

"Is everything ready?" asked Nate.

Jonah was still looking at me like he couldn't quite believe his eyes. Shaking his head slightly, he turned to Nate. "I hope so. As ready as I can make it, anyway."

"And are they scanning for her?" put in Sophie anxiously.

"No, I don't think so. Raziel believed the news of her death. Um – your death," he added awkwardly, looking at me.

I managed a thin smile. All I could think was, *It'll be true, pretty soon.*

Sophie let out a breath. "Thank goodness for that, at least." She glanced at her watch. "Right, I guess I'd better go now." She turned to me, looking conflicted as she touched my arm. "Good luck, Willow. And whatever happens, thank you. That sounds so inadequate, but…" She trailed off.

I tried not to hate her for leaving. "I'll – I'll do my best," I said. "I mean it."

"We know you will." Suddenly she gave me a quick

hug; she smelled of perfume and cigarette smoke. She turned to Nate. "Good luck to you, too," she said, shaking his hand. "It's been a real honour working with you."

"And you," said Nate with a faint smile. Bending down, he kissed her cheek. I turned away, not really wanting to hear the finality in their goodbyes.

After Sophie was gone, Nate looked at his watch, too. "I'd better get to my seat – we don't have much time." He gazed at me for a second, and I could see how desperately he wanted me to succeed. "I'll do anything I can to help," he said finally. "Good luck, Willow. And thank you for trying, no matter what."

"Thanks," I said. It wasn't really the right answer, but it was the best I could do right then. Squeezing my shoulder briefly, Nate left, shutting the door behind him.

Jonah's face was pasty-pale. "I'd, uh…better take you to where the other acolytes are now," he said, shoving a nervous hand through his curls. "He's right, we don't have much time. And before I forget, your name in the line-up is Carrie Singer, okay? I'll be checking everyone off the list in a few minutes; don't forget that that's you."

"I won't," I said. Amazingly, my voice sounded almost normal. I could hear the noise from the cathedral growing louder from behind a pair of double doors: a sort of muffled booming, throbbing all around us. It took me a second to realize it was a choir singing. Swallowing hard,

I fingered the angelica in my sleeve, reassuring myself that it was still there.

"Um – this way," said Jonah, putting his hand on my arm before we got to the doors. At his touch, a cold jolt of fear leaped through me; I didn't know whether it was mine or his. He took me down another short corridor. "They're all in here," he said in a low voice, stopping in front of a door. "You'd better keep your head sort of down – I'm sure they've all seen your photo."

I nodded, and ducked my head. The hood swayed obediently forward. As we went into the room, the excited chatter of girls rose up to meet us; all I could see from under my draped hood was a flurry of silvery-blue robes everywhere. Jonah cleared his throat and called, "It's almost time, everyone – let's get into the line-up from yesterday."

Immediately, the chattering stilled; a sense of deep excitement pulsed through the air. A rustling noise, as the robes adjusted themselves into a single long line. Feeling conspicuous, I stayed where I was, scared to look up too much and not knowing where to go, anyway. Thankfully, Jonah took my arm again. "Right, Wisconsin, we've got you in the middle…here you go."

He guided me to a spot in the line; two girls moved aside to make room for me. As I got into place I had a sudden sense of the minutes racing past, hurtling me towards whatever was going to happen. My hands felt like I was holding ice.

Jonah was walking down the line, checking off names on a clipboard. Soon he was almost halfway down.

"Jessie King?"

"Here."

"Latitia Ellis?"

"Here."

"Carrie Singer?"

It took me a second, and then I remembered. "Here," I said.

Checking me off, Jonah moved away without looking at me. "Kate Gefter?"

"Here."

The drone of names and replies continued. I stood stiffly. I could sense the eggshell inside of me trembling, straining to crack. We were all standing facing a wall; there was a poster on it that said *The Angels Save!* I stared at it, taking in the angel, trying to memorize its every feature.

"Susan Bousso?"

"Here. Or – actually, I'm not, I'm Beth Hartley. I'm taking Susan's place."

Terror flinched through me. Beth was *here*? I couldn't help glancing down the line; she was only four girls away from me. Her features under her hood were tired, but as beautiful as ever. I looked quickly forward again before she could see me, my heart battering in my chest.

Jonah stood frozen. I could sense his confusion, his fear. "Beth," he repeated.

She nodded. "Susan was sick, so they asked me to come instead; they were supposed to let you know. It's okay, isn't it? I meant to mention it to you yesterday, but there wasn't a chance."

As clearly as if I was thinking it myself, I knew that Jonah was frantically wondering if he could shift the line-up, so that Beth was further away from me. But there was no time. "No, um – that's fine. Glad you're here," he said finally.

He moved on down the line. A few minutes later, he said, "Right, this is it, girls." Even out of the corner of my eyes, I could see that he was sickly pale. He went and opened the door. "Let's go."

He led us down the short passageway. Numbness swept over me as I watched the double doors growing closer. This was it. This was really it. Jonah stopped the first girl just in front of the doors; the long line of us stretched down the corridor, identical in our silvery-blue robes. "It's time," he said, glancing at his watch. "The – the angels be with you, everyone."

He swung open one of the doors, and the girls started filing into the cathedral. My legs were trembling; I ignored it and moved forward with the others. I could sense the massive hush from the audience, feel the deep sense of expectation and yearning pouring from them. Fleetingly, my eyes met Jonah's as I walked through the door. He was staring anxiously at me. Fear. He hoped that this worked; there was nothing left for him any more.

The thought flashed past, and then Jonah was behind me and I was moving out into the cathedral with the rest of them. First passing through dim shadows at the side, we then entered a brightly-lit area like a stage, where it was suddenly so dazzling that I couldn't see the audience at all; just a deep, waiting blackness to my right. Our footsteps sounded around us, amplified by the microphones like a heartbeat. Details, all of them so clear: an angel-winged pulpit up ahead with a white-haired preacher behind it; just beside him were a dark-haired man and a voluptuous woman with auburn hair – the two angels, I realized. Raziel and Lailah. A giant TV screen was just sliding up into the ceiling, revealing towering stained-glass windows of angels, with the sunset shining through. And at the front of everything there stretched a space half the width of a football field, with massive floral arrangements to either side.

The gate.

My heart thudded, pushing away all thought. Silently, the other girls and I stopped directly in front of the gate. I dipped my hand inside my sleeve, touching the angelica. And as everyone moved, I moved with them.

Turn. Snag the stone and kneel. Hands in prayer position.

I kneeled on the floor with the others with the angelica cupped in my hands, watching carefully for the ripple in the air that would signal the gate was starting to open. Somewhere under the surface, the eggshell had cracked. A deep, aching sorrow; a flash of blinding fear. I didn't want to die. Not yet, not like this; I was too young. It felt like a cold chasm had wrenched open inside of me. I kneeled there quietly, shaking slightly, trying to ignore it as I focused on the gate. *Don't think. You are not here to think. You are here to act.*

As I crouched there with the others, Raziel paced in front of the gate, gazing up at it with his hands behind his back. I caught a glimpse of his face, and even through my fear, it teased at me, distracting me. Where had I seen it before? Then he turned and strolled away again – and I saw him full-on.

A tidal wave of shock crashed through me. The angel's handsome, dark-haired face was the same one I'd seen in my mother's mind, so long ago.

It was my father.

I couldn't help it; my head jerked up as I gaped across at him, my concentration shattered. *No.* Focus. I tore my attention away and stared back at the wall, my pulse slamming at my temples. At the same moment, I was

172

aware of a shifting a few girls down from me; a sideways, frowning glance. And then a quick breath, and a widening of eyes.

"Oh, blessed angels," I heard Beth whisper. "That's – that's Willow."

There was a shuffling in the line as nearby girls glanced at her, and then at me. I kneeled rigidly, staring straight ahead.

"That's *Willow*," said Beth, louder. Her voice rose to a panicked shout; I heard it picked up by the sound system. "Somebody, do something! That's Willow Fields! She's here, she's here, somebody stop her!"

Oh, my god; oh, my god. I crouched there trembling, unable to move. Dimly, I saw Raziel start striding forward, frowning in shock; the girls around me gaping with open mouths. And then suddenly there was a faint swirling in the air, like water stirred gently with a hand. *Don't think, just* move, *do it!*

I contacted my angel and ran, scrabbling up from the line and hurling myself forward. I lifted up out of myself. I was flying, I was running. Swooping downwards on my wings, I stroked the angelica's energy with my own, and felt it start pulsing in my hands.

About halfway through the field, the cars had started parking in the access lane, so that Alex had to slow down to manoeuvre around them, his blood pounding in an agony of frustration. Finally, he reached the end of it. As he'd hoped, the field backed onto the road, separated by a wide ditch. It was a matter of seconds to wheel the bike across, and then he was back on it and roaring down the road, his back tyre slipping slightly as he leaned into a turn. The Church of Angels lay just ahead. From this angle, the massive building looked like the sports stadium it had once been – a plain, curved exterior, rising up from the ground in a solid white wall. As he got closer, he could see that the road led to a small parking lot beside the service entrance.

Skidding to a stop in the parking lot, Alex flipped down the kickstand; tearing his helmet off, he flung it onto the seat and ran for the door. A guard in a brown uniform stood outside it. Alex hardly noticed him. There was a latch on the door; he turned it and shoved, throwing his weight against it.

"Hey!" said the guy, grabbing his arm as the door started to open. "You can't go in there!"

Alex jerked away from him and lunged inside. He was in a long, gleaming white corridor. He had only gone a few steps before the guard was on him, gripping his arm again. "Get out right now, sir," he panted. "You're trespassing."

All Alex could see were the double doors, far away at the end of the corridor. Willow was in there; he knew it.

Red exploded through him. He slammed the guy off him, heard the startled gasp as he hit the wall, and then he was running again, his footsteps echoing against the polished floor.

As he neared the doors, he heard frantic shouts, amplified through the cathedral sound system:

"Somebody, do something! That's Willow Fields! She's here, she's here, somebody stop her!"

I had nearly reached the gate, where the air was swirling in front of me like a whirlpool – and then above me, I felt my angel balk as another angel swooped harshly under her, breaking her connection with the angelica. The stone's pulsing ceased in my hands, like a dying heart. *No!* I stopped in despair, staring upwards.

It was Raziel. My father.

Dimly, I was aware of someone bellowing, "Let go of me!" and of Jonah's voice shouting, "It's all right! Everybody stay back, keep away from the barrier, the angels are handling this!" In my angel form, I darted this way and that, my wings beating frantically as I tried to dodge Raziel, to get past and touch the stone again. He cut in front of me at every move, his powerful wings glinting a bright, pure white. I could see the gate's ripples growing stronger. Any moment, and it would burst wide open.

"You will *not* get away with this," hissed Raziel. Briefly, our eyes met. His widened in sudden recognition, and I knew that he'd seen my mother's face in my own. For a split second, he hesitated – and then another angel appeared, diving in and attacking him from the side. Nate. With a cry of fury, Raziel spun on him.

The two angels fought, their wings in a frenzy. At the same moment, a burst of white light came from above. There was no time to wonder what it was; in my angel form I swooped down and touched the stone in my human hands. It came to life again, and I lunged the final few steps.

Behind me, I could still hear Jonah shouting frantically; a battering noise; people screaming, "Stop her! Stop them both, he's on her side!" The gate was starting to spiral open before me, like an old-fashioned camera shutter. I caught a glimpse of thousands of angels waiting to come through – shining, white, beautiful.

Dropping to my knees, I thrust the pulsing stone into the gate. The wall of energy leaped like a wave, seething and warping as it fought with itself. I gasped in pain as it pummelled at me; I could hardly see my hand in the midst of it. The wall bucked and shuddered as the gate struggled to open; the angels disappeared and then appeared again. A deep rumbling noise, a vibration. With a splintering crack, the floor suddenly heaved up under me. I shrieked, lurching sideways. The angelica started to crumble to pieces in my hand as the floor surged again; something fell behind me with a crash. Oh god, the wall was tearing me apart; I could feel it happening. I gritted my teeth, struggling to hang on. Distantly, I thought I heard someone call my name – and then, with a roar of white noise, everything exploded.

I was tumbling, falling. Pain, so much pain. I tried to cry out and couldn't.

As everything slowly faded, I thought, *Alex.*

CHAPTER *Nineteen*

BURSTING INTO THE CATHEDRAL, ALEX had seen a blue-robed girl that had to be Willow running towards the gate, while another girl screamed. He pounded forward; his only thought was to get next to her as she reached the gate, to put his arms around her and hold her so that she wouldn't die alone. Dimly, he was aware of a commotion going on to one side – two men struggling, one holding the other back; a cluster of shrieking robed girls.

Before he reached the lighted area, Willow suddenly stopped short, staring upwards. Angels. Stopping too, Alex quickly drew his gun with the silencer on it and sped through his chakra points. Three angels swam into view: Willow's own, dodging around a male angel, and higher up, a female angel with a hard, beautiful face, diving straight at Willow's human form. Dropping to one knee, Alex tracked the female, aimed and shot. She vanished into scattered pieces of light.

In the audience, people were shouting Willow's name, thumping against the plastic barrier as they tried to break it down. As Alex burst into the lighted area Nate appeared in his angel form, his wings beating strongly as he attacked the first angel. At the same time Willow's angel dove towards her physical form and Willow lunged the final few steps; reaching the gate she shoved her hands in it. The energy warped, leaping wildly – he could see glimpses of angels waiting to come through. The floor near the gate lurched upwards, sending her slipping sideways. Nearing Willow, Alex almost lost his footing as the floor seethed under his feet; he regained himself and sprinted towards her.

"*Willow!*" he shouted.

The gate exploded open. A wave of energy slammed past in a blinding flash of light. Crying out, Alex shielded his eyes with his forearm. A confused blur: the two angels tumbling, fragmenting into pieces – and Willow, thrown with the blast. There was a wrenching, groaning noise; a crash of dust and cement as a section of the ceiling fell, shattering only a few feet from the huddle of robed girls.

Screams. With a spray of spitting sparks, the lights went out. The entire front area fell into shadow, lit only by the dying sunset through the stained-glass windows. At that moment, as if on cue, hordes of angels began soaring through the open gate and out over the pews, wings and halos shining, glimpses of their own world's fading sunset just visible through the open gate behind them. A solid wall of sound cracked through the cathedral as the audience began cheering. The people in the first few pews were all staring upwards, jumping up and down, Willow completely forgotten as they took in the celestial river flying overhead.

It had all happened in a moment. Willow. Where was Willow? Alex's consciousness was still hovering above his crown chakra, and in the sudden gloom around him he could see people's auras come sharply into view, the coloured energy fields pulsing with excitement as everyone stared upwards. He scanned the front area hurriedly, fear building in him as he couldn't spot Willow's aura.

And then, faintly, he saw it – a silver and lavender flutter off to one side, away from the others. Alex plunged through the shadows; stumbled and almost fell on the uneven floor. Finally he reached her. He could just see that she was lying on her back, her head facing sideways. Frantic, he dropped to his knees and gathered her up in his arms. "Willow! Willow, please be all right – please, please—"

Her head dropped back. She lay unmoving against him, her aura dim, growing dimmer. Alex felt his heart die in his chest as he stared down at her familiar features. No. Oh, god, *no*.

With a weak shimmer, Willow's angel appeared over her, so pale and ghostly that she could hardly be seen. She motioned to Willow and then to Alex, her eyes pleading… and then she faded from view. What had she been trying to tell him? Swallowing hard, Alex stared down at the prone girl in his arms. Willow's aura was scarcely visible now, the barest flicker of light. Alex hesitated…and then, not quite knowing why he was doing it, he placed his hand over her heart and closed his eyes.

Please, take my strength, he thought. *Whatever I have, take it…just please live, please, please live…*

Desperately, Alex tried to picture his strength and his love for Willow flowing into her, helping her, finding her and bringing her back from wherever she was going. He wasn't sure how much time went past – he could hear the angels still flying overhead; the cheers still sounding. Willow's body in his arms remained unmoving. Finally, dreading what he might see, Alex opened his eyes.

Willow's aura was gone.

Pain punched him like a blow. "No!" he choked out. "Please, no…" Willow blurred in his vision as he clutched her to him, burying his face against her shoulder. The softness of her skin, the smell of her hair. Alex began to shake as he held her. He'd been too late. She'd gone to her death alone, without ever even knowing he was there. He kissed her unmoving lips, fighting tears. "I'm sorry," he whispered, stroking her still-warm face. "Oh, Willow, I'm so sorry…"

Dimly, Alex became aware that a deadening weakness was slumping through his muscles, draining them so that it was all he could do to keep his arms around Willow. There was a quick, wrenching pain, like something being torn away from him. His head reeled; he wondered vaguely if an angel had ripped his life force away. For he could feel that his own life was fading now, slipping away like water down a drain. As he held Willow's still form, dull relief filled him at the thought.

A swirling of light above them; faint silver and lavender mixed with vibrant blue and gold.

Alex looked up in confusion as the lights moved together over him and Willow, like twin plumes of smoke. The silver light was barely visible. As he watched, the blue light wrapped itself around it, stroking it, caressing it. Slowly, the blue and gold brightness faded as the silver and lavender began to glow more brightly; Alex had an impression of strength pouring from one aura to the other.

Finally the silver light was softly steady, its lavender hues gleaming. Alex's aura drew itself back to him, faint but already starting to recover. He felt his life force return in a rush. The silver and lavender aura settled gently around Willow – dim at first, but unwavering, and growing brighter by the second.

An agony of hope roared through Alex as he stared down at her in his arms. He touched her cheek again, hardly daring to breathe. "Willow?"

At first there was nothing…and then her green eyes came slowly open. She stared up at him, looking dazed.

"Alex?" she whispered. "Is it really you?"

He felt a jolt of joy so great that it was almost pain. He cradled her to him, weak with relief. "It's me, baby," he said hoarsely, his lips moving against her hair. "It's me."

Her arms came up feebly around him; she pressed her face into his shoulder with a sob. "Alex…you're here, you're really here…"

Pulling back, he stroked a stray strand of hair from her temple, scanning her face in the shadowy light. "Are you all right?"

She gulped, nodded. "I think so. I'm just so tired…"

Thankfulness drenched through him like water. He held her tightly, kissing her hair, her cheek. "I'm sorry," he whispered. "I love you, I didn't mean it – I didn't mean any of it—"

Her embrace tightened around his neck; he could feel her lips moving against his skin as she spoke. "I know…

Alex, I know, I love you, too…"

For a moment he savoured just holding her, warm and alive in his arms. Urgency followed sharply; they had to get out of here. He glanced back over his shoulder. Angels still hadn't stopped soaring from the gate; the entire length of the cathedral was a winged river as they flew out over the pews and then finally out through the massive doors at the far end.

The crowds' cheers had become somewhat ragged, but were still going strong. Nate had said that it would take around twenty minutes for all the angels to arrive. How much time had already passed?

Quickly, he kissed Willow's lips. "I love you," he said again. "Come on, we've got to hurry." He scooped her into his arms and stood up, feverishly grateful that the front area was still cloaked in shadow. He started towards the double doors he'd come through, picking his way as fast as he could across the uneven floor.

When the doors were only a few dozen steps away, Willow tensed against his shoulder. "Alex, an angel!"

He whirled around; one of the angels he'd seen fighting earlier was diving through the air towards them, wings outspread, his beautiful face set in a snarl. Grabbing his gun, Alex set Willow's feet on the floor in almost the same motion, keeping one arm around her. The angel landed, and with a dark ripple changed to his human form: a handsome, slender man with pale skin and coal-black hair. He stood about ten feet away, gazing at Willow.

"The half-angel and her assassin," he said in a low, deadly voice that somehow carried over the noise. "And it appears that I was the culprit, somehow. *Miranda,* correct?" Alex stiffened at his English accent. It was the same angel who'd ordered Willow's death. At his side he felt her take a quick breath, and suddenly remembered that her mother's name was Miranda.

It was him. Willow's father.

"Don't say her name," said Willow faintly, staring at the angel. "You have no right..."

"Oh, I beg to differ," said the angel. "Why, this is quite *historic,* isn't it? The first half-angel in existence...now, how did I manage that, I wonder?" He stared hard at Willow. Behind him, now almost half the length of the cathedral away, the stream of arriving angels still flew overhead, bright and shining.

Holding Willow close, Alex kept his gun pointed on the angel. "I thought you died in the blast," he said roughly.

"Wouldn't that have been convenient?" replied the angel with a sneer. "But no, it was only the traitor who died – I was merely a bit dazed." Eyes narrowing, he took a step forward.

"Get back or you'll regret it," said Alex.

The angel curled his lip. "I think not, actually. It's time

now for you both to die, the way you were supposed to in the first place." Shifting back into his angel form, he surged straight towards them, wings flashing.

Alex shot. The angel dodged at the last moment, his wings slicing the air, and the bullet caught the very edge of his halo. Its blue-white energy rippled, hesitated. Hovering above them, the angel writhed as tremors shook through him, his wings flapping like a giant trapped bird. Before Alex could shoot again, he went still and collapsed to the floor, in his human form once more. He lay unmoving.

Willow stared down at him; she seemed almost ready to drop. "Alex, he…that was…"

"Shh, I know," he said, picking her up again. She slumped against his shoulder, her arms tight around his neck.

Fleetingly, Alex wished that the creature really was human; he thought he'd have no compunction at all about peppering his prone body with bullets. But there was no point; the only way to kill an angel was to shoot it through its halo heart. At least this one would be out of action for a while. Glancing back at the arriving angels, Alex headed quickly for the doors with Willow cradled in his arms. Please, just a few more minutes and they'd be out of here.

Just a few more minutes, that's all they needed.

* * *

When the Second Wave of angels had begun pouring out of the gate, Jonah had simply stood frozen, gaping above him. It hadn't worked. After all of their planning, after everything he'd risked – he'd lost it all, and the angels had arrived anyway. Beautiful face after beautiful face flashed past – and soon they would all be hungry, and feeding. Jonah shuddered, feeling dizzy with dismay. His cheekbone throbbed where the preacher had punched him.

From somewhere behind them in the cathedral, there was still light; in this front section all was in shadow. Jonah could just see the preacher a few steps away, applauding loudly as he beamed up at the arriving angels. The acolytes were jumping up and down, cheering; Beth and another acolyte had their arms around each other's shoulders, their faces alight. Behind them all, the crowd had forgotten about crashing through the barrier – people were throwing their hats in the air; calling out to the angels to bless them; laughing and crying.

Jonah didn't know how long he simply stared upwards in a daze, wondering what he was supposed to do now. Then, at the corner of his vision, he saw a brief flash of light. Glancing over, he saw a dark-haired figure disappear through the double doors carrying a girl.

Jonah stared as he recognized her. Willow. Was she still alive – or not? And then all at once he realized that he had to get out, as well. Raziel knew now that Jonah had betrayed him – not only had he lied about Willow's death, but the angel must have noticed him shouting at the crowd, and holding the preacher back from stopping her. During all the confusion Jonah had seen Raziel vanish, obviously turning to his divine form; so far the angel hadn't reappeared.

What would he do to Jonah when he did? For that matter, what would the Church members do, when all of this was over with?

Panic slammed through Jonah, and he started running through the darkness, stumbling across the uneven floor. Near the barrier he saw the security guard gaping upwards, and veered sharply away from him. As he finally neared the doors he jerked back with a gasp, his brown eyes widening. There was a dark shape lying in the shadows: Raziel, sprawled unmoving in his human form. Shock reeled through Jonah, along with a sick relief. Could Raziel actually be dead? He couldn't tell; he wasn't about to touch him to find out. Edging cautiously around the prone figure, he sprinted the final few steps.

He pushed through the doors; the lights here were making a humming noise, flickering on and off. The person carrying Willow was already halfway down the long corridor, disappearing fast. Jonah ran after him, suddenly desperate to know whether the girl was all right or not. He caught up with them just as they reached the outside door.

"Hey—" he started. And then sucked in his breath as the dark-haired youth whirled on him, clutching Willow to his chest with one arm and holding a gun on Jonah with the other.

"I seriously don't think you want to try and stop me," he said in a low voice.

Jonah felt the blood leave his face. "No, I – I'm sorry, I just—" In a daze, he saw that the guy was younger than he was – and at the same moment realized that age had nothing to do with it; he was older than Jonah would ever be.

Willow had her arms around his neck, her head against his shoulder. At the sound of voices, she tiredly opened her eyes; her gaze and Jonah's met briefly. "Alex, he helped," she said softly.

Alex? Jonah gaped at him. Of course, it was the assassin. He was here.

At Willow's words, Alex seemed to relax a fraction. He lowered the gun, and Jonah let out a breath. "You're the contact," stated Alex.

Jonah nodded. "You're – um – the assassin."

Alex didn't respond; his eyes flicked down the long corridor behind Jonah. "You'd better get out of here, too; they'll kill you when this is over." Putting his other arm under Willow, he shoved through the door and was gone.

Jonah glanced nervously behind him. He could still

hear the sound of distant cheers, but for how long? Pushing the door open, he stepped out into the dying sunset. At the edge of the nearby parking lot, Alex and Willow were standing beside a motorcycle. Alex had just helped Willow off with her silvery-blue robe; as Jonah watched he dropped it to the ground. He seemed to be asking her something; she nodded as she glanced at the motorcycle. Abruptly, he bent down and kissed her, gripping her face in his hands.

Jonah ducked his head away, not wanting to pry on their private moment. When he looked back again, Alex was helping Willow put on a helmet; then he quickly straddled the bike and she got on behind him, wrapping her arms around his chest. All at once Jonah remembered something, and fear surged through him.

"Wait!" he called, running over to them. Alex was already revving the engine; he glanced back over his shoulder.

"Raziel," panted Jonah, reaching them. "Is he dead?"

"The angel?" Alex shook his head. "No, he's just knocked out. He'll be out of commission for a few days, but he'll be fine. Unfortunately."

Willow's face was pale and drawn. "Thank you for helping, Jonah," she said softly. "I – I wish…" She trailed off.

"Yeah," mumbled Jonah. He'd been stunned to see Willow face-to-face at last – in his mind he'd built her up to be some kind of supergirl. Instead she was diminutive, and had been so gravely frightened and self-composed that he'd just felt ashamed of his own terror.

Now he looked back at the door, swallowing hard. "Um – what will you do now?" He meant, *What will I do now?* but he couldn't say the words.

Alex lifted a muscular shoulder; Jonah could sense his impatience to leave. "Getting away sounds like a pretty good plan. What about you, have you got a car or something?"

Jonah nodded. "In the employee parking lot, just around the side."

A humourless smile crossed Alex's tired features. "You'd better use it," he said. "I don't think you're going to be working for the angels any more."

"Take care, Jonah," said Willow weakly, and then Alex kicked the clutch and they were gone, roaring off down the road. Jonah stood watching them for a moment, until they had vanished from sight and he couldn't even hear the engine any more.

Or anything else. The sound of cheering had stopped.

Jonah licked his lips, frozen where he stood. He hadn't expected this; he had thought that the destruction of the gate would kill him along with everyone else who stood near it, and on some level, he had preferred it that way. What was his life going to be like now, without the one shining, beautiful thing that had been his – the knowledge of the angels, and how they were here to help humanity? Miserably, he thought that if he had any courage he'd go back inside, and let the crowd do to him what they would. But he didn't have courage; he never had. That had always been the problem.

Then, softly, a memory came to him: his angel, the first he had ever seen, flying towards him on the campus in a glory of wings and light. *Don't be afraid. I have something to give you.* She had been helping him, he hadn't imagined it. He *had* had courage because of her; he had managed to change his whole life. If he could just hold onto that – that there really were angels who were good and kind, regardless of what the rest of them were like – then maybe that would give him the courage he needed now, to somehow go on living.

Glancing anxiously at the doors, Jonah took off at a run, heading for the employee parking lot.

The service road led them back to the freeway, where Alex could see the long lines of cars creeping along on the other side, still caught in gridlock. Heading away from the cathedral, there was hardly any traffic at all. As dusk fell, he switched on the headlight and headed south, feeling the wind lashing at his hair and T-shirt. Occasionally he put his hand on Willow's arms around his chest, just to reassure himself that she was really there.

He would have preferred to put a thousand miles between them and the cathedral, but it wasn't happening tonight – he could feel the tiredness fighting to catch up with him, like a dark undertow lapping at his skull. He drove for as long as he dared, taking them to a town called Trinidad, in the Sangre de Cristo mountains in the southern part of the state. He stopped at the first hotel he came to, sweeping into the parking lot and idling to a stop. His muscles stiff from the cold mountain air, he helped Willow off the bike. In the glow of the streetlights she was pale and wide-eyed as she pulled the helmet off, clearly as exhausted as he was.

She had never been more beautiful.

For a moment, they just stood in the parking lot gazing at each other, drinking each other in. Alex thought that he'd never get enough of simply looking at Willow from now on, not if they both lived to be a hundred. The dark bulk of the mountains rose up in the background, and a single car passed by on the quiet, late-night street. He touched her face; she put her hand over his, rubbing her cheek against his palm. Bending his head, he kissed her slowly, savouring the softness of her lips, the warmth of her. She was alive. Somehow, somehow, he still had her. With a soft sigh, Willow wrapped her arms around his waist and leaned against him. Alex held her, dropping his cheek to her hair and stroking her back.

He kept his arm around her shoulders as they went inside, and she almost fell asleep as he was checking in, slumped wearily against his chest. He wasn't much more awake himself. On the way to their room Willow staggered, and he picked her up, carrying her the final way down the hallway. Shifting her in his arms, he managed to unlock the door and got them both inside, leaning against it to shut it behind him. He turned on the lights with his shoulder.

Laying Willow down on the bed, Alex stretched out beside her. She cuddled against him and he drew her close, shaping his body around hers. He hadn't meant to fall asleep just yet – the lights were still on; they were both fully dressed – but when he opened his eyes again, it felt like several hours might have passed. Forcing himself to rouse, he gently undid Willow's hair, taking the pins out and uncoiling it so that it fell freely around her shoulders. She blinked drowsily, only half-waking. He helped her off with her shoes and sweater; her jeans. Stripping off his own jeans and T-shirt, he turned the lights out and got them both under the covers.

Willow nestled against him. He smoothed her long hair down the back of her T-shirt, feeling the softness of its strands. In a few moments she'd fallen asleep again, her breathing warm and regular against his chest. Alex kissed her head, his arms tightening around her. As he drifted back to sleep himself, he saw a brief flash of the thousands of angels streaming in, but right then it seemed distant, almost unimportant. The only thing that mattered was that he was lying in a bed holding Willow, their bare legs entwined.

It was all he wanted to do for the rest of his life.

I woke up in a soft bed, hearing Alex's voice. I opened my eyes slowly. We were in a hotel room, shadowy with the curtains drawn, and he was sitting on the edge of the bed talking to someone on the phone. I lay gazing at the firm lines of his back, feeling a joy so deep that there weren't any words for it. It hadn't been a dream; he had really come. We were really together again.

He hung up and slid back under the covers, his arms wrapping around me, drawing me close. "You're awake," he murmured, kissing my temple.

I nodded and snuggled tightly against him. "Who was that?" I whispered against his shoulder.

"I got the room for another night," he said, rubbing my arm. His head was on the pillow, his eyes closed. "I don't even want to move today; I just want to lie here and hold you."

We both nodded off again. When we woke up once more it was mid-afternoon, and the sunshine angling in around the curtains was bright and strong.

For a long time, we just lay in bed talking, telling each other what had happened while we were apart. I described what had happened to me first, and Alex's expression hardened as I told him about Sophie leaving. "Right, so she's in a safe location now, and she just left you there."

I sighed. "I understand it, I guess… It just made me realize how much they really expected me to die." And Nate *had* died. I shuddered as I remembered Raziel's sneering reference to "the traitor" dying, and felt a pang for the angel who'd believed so strongly that his kind didn't have the right to destroy humanity.

Alex touched my hair, as if he knew what I was thinking. I played with the edge of the sheet, looking down. "Alex, I can't believe that Raziel is my…" I swallowed; I couldn't say the word.

"Only biologically," he said. "Willow, he's nothing to do with you. He never was; it doesn't matter who he is."

"I know," I said. "It's just – strange, now that I've seen him with my own eyes. And to know that he knows, too. I really wish he didn't."

"Yeah," said Alex curtly. "And I wish I hadn't missed his halo."

I swallowed. I couldn't actually wish for Raziel's death,

no matter how much I hated him – but I knew that I wouldn't have been sorry if Alex had succeeded. I sat up against my pillows, hugging my knees as I remembered the thousands of angels I'd seen behind Alex when I first opened my eyes.

"I – I wonder what went wrong?" I said. "Whether it's that the angelica would never have worked after all, or if I just got to the gate too late once Beth started screaming?"

"I don't know," said Alex. There was a long pause as he glided his hand up and down my arm. Finally he said, "Pretty soon, I know that I'm really going to hate the fact that there are more angels in the world...but right now, all I feel is so incredibly glad that you're still alive."

I gave a small nod. "I know. I wish I'd been able to stop it, but I can't be sorry to still be alive – and to still have this with you." I gazed into his blue-grey eyes, so startling under their black lashes. "Alex, it's all I ever want – just to be with you."

"Don't worry, you will be," he said softly. Pulling me against him, he kissed me, and for a few minutes there was just the warmth of our mouths together. A shiver ran through me as I ran my hands through his hair, feeling the muscles of his neck move as we kissed. I had been so afraid that I'd never have this again.

When we started talking once more, Alex described how he'd got to Denver, and then what had happened when he arrived at the cathedral. He kept it short, his tone almost terse, but I got the idea clearly enough.

"Oh, Alex..." I whispered, touching his cheek. The thought of him holding me, believing I was dead, felt like my heart was being pummelled. "I can't – I can't believe that you went through that..."

Letting out a breath, Alex reached up and squeezed my hand, his eyes never leaving mine. "All that matters is that you're alive," he said. "I'd go through it a hundred times again, to have you."

A dim, dreamlike memory came back. I shook my head in wonder. "I – I remember it. I could feel myself going; I was sort of – drifting down a long hallway. And then you were there, bringing me back. It was like you were pulling on me, tugging me..."

Wordlessly, Alex kissed my palm. I gazed at him, remembering the incredulous joy that had flooded through me when I first opened my eyes and saw him. That was still flooding through me now. "I thought I'd never see you again," I whispered.

He traced his fingers across my face as if he was memorizing it. "Five minutes after you left, I was in the truck," he said roughly. "I knew that I'd made the biggest mistake of my life. Willow, I'm sorry. I'm so sorry. Everything I said; the way I acted – letting you go alone—" His jaw tensed. "Can you forgive me?"

I felt tears come to my eyes. "You don't even have to ask me that."

"Yes, I do," he said shortly. "I should be down on my knees, asking."

"No! I know what you were going through…" His eyes stayed on mine, unwavering. My throat constricted. Gently, I stroked my hand down his neck. "Of course I forgive you. Alex, don't even mention it again. The moment I opened my eyes and saw you there…" I stared at him; I couldn't even begin to express what I felt for him. "I love you," I said.

Closing his eyes with a sigh, he drew me tightly into his arms. "I love you, too," he said, his lips moving in my hair. "From the second you left, all I could think of was getting to Denver in time, so I could be there with you, holding you… Willow, if you had died, I wouldn't have wanted to live, either."

"I know," I murmured against his shoulder. "I feel the same way. Flying away from you was – awful, so awful. Alex, I'm sorry, too, but I had to do it, I had to at least try—"

He leaned back. "Don't apologize! You had to try – I *knew* that; I just couldn't stand the thought of anything happening to you. And then, when I got to the cathedral and thought I was too late…" He shook his head, his eyes haunted. "If you hadn't lived, I would never have forgiven myself for letting you down."

I linked my fingers through his. "No, you were there – Alex, you didn't let me down, you brought me back."

"Thank god," he said, touching my hair. "It was your angel who told me what to do, though – I wouldn't have known." He fell silent, and I could feel his tension; it was coming off him in great waves. Finally he swallowed and said, "I thought – I thought you were going to die, and that it would be like Jake."

The muscles in his arms were rigid. I hesitated, not sure whether to ask – but it was something that had been bothering him for so, so long. "Alex...how did he die?"

At first I thought he wasn't going to answer; then he looked down and cleared his throat. "We, um – we were on a hunt in Los Angeles," he said. "Jake and I would – play this game sometimes, where one of us would lure an angel in and the other one would shoot it. We weren't supposed to put ourselves at risk like that; Cully would have killed us if he'd known. We just – we were both such good shots that it never seemed like that big a deal. Anyway, we were right beside one of the canyons above the city, and Jake was the one luring. And...the angel went for him, and I shot her – and then I went over to Jake, and we sort of – high-fived, you know..."

He stopped abruptly. Still holding his hand, I had another flash of the dark-haired boy with Alex's eyes, sitting on a wall beside a canyon. He was grinning, lifting his hand in a high-five. *Good one, bro, she didn't even see it coming.* I could feel Alex's dread just remembering this, and regret that I'd even asked him swept over me. I pressed myself close, kissing his cheek.

"It's okay," I whispered. "I'm sorry; you don't have to tell me."

"No, it's all right." Pulling away slightly, he scraped an unsteady hand through his hair. "Um…so basically, there was another angel – they'd been hunting in a pair. I didn't do another scan before I put my gun away; I didn't even see it. He came – flying out of nowhere at us, and Jake jerked backwards – and I managed to get the angel, but Jake had fallen into the canyon…"

Alex trailed off, and my heart twisted; I'd never seen him look so young, so vulnerable. Fighting tears, I hugged him as hard as I could, and felt his arms tighten around me. "It was my fault," he choked out. "He trusted me, and I let him down. We got him to the hospital, but it was too late; he was too—" He stopped.

"It *wasn't* your fault," I said against his neck. "Alex, the same thing might have happened if Jake had been holding the gun. It was just a mistake; it could have happened to anyone."

When he spoke his voice sounded flat, weary. "You can't make mistakes on a hunt. Not like that."

I drew back, looking into his eyes. "All right," I said. "But if it *had* happened that way, if it had been Jake who'd made the mistake – would you forgive him?"

He stared at me without answering. I saw his throat move.

"Alex, you know you would," I said, running my hand over his tattoo. "So please, forgive yourself, okay? Please." I kissed his cheeks, his brow, his mouth.

He sat very still as I peppered him with kisses, as if he was hardly breathing. Slowly, I felt the tension in him ease. Catching my head in his hands, he gazed at me; neither of us moved for a moment. "I love you," he said.

The words didn't feel like enough, but they were all I had. "I love you, too. I love you so much, Alex."

He kissed me, softly at first – a tender, gentle kiss that left me weak – and then more strongly, pulling me close against him. Twining my arms around his neck I kissed him back, sinking into his warmth, his strength. I could feel his love for me wrapping around me, could feel mine flowing out towards him.

He had brought me back. I had died, and he brought me back.

Finally we drew apart, lying on the pillows facing each other. And then slowly, we both started to smile. Alex traced a line from my temple to my chin. Under the covers, my foot was against his bare leg; I rubbed it gently, tickling my toes up his calf. From outside I could hear the faint drone of traffic; a bird singing.

"It's worth it, you know," said Alex, smiling into my eyes.

"What is?" I said.

His thumb moved slowly over my cheek. "All of this. Having you. It's worth – anything."

Minutes passed as we just lay there, drinking each other in. Suddenly, aware of our bare legs, I thought of something and almost began to laugh – except that actually, it wasn't funny. "So…I guess we don't really have any clothes, do we? Except what we had on yesterday. Or – anything else, either."

Alex shook his head and sat up a bit. "No, the truck's probably been towed by now – we wouldn't be able to get it back anyway, without our names on the registration. And it had most of our stuff in it. My bag's still at the cabin with all our clothes – we could try going up there on the bike, I guess, but…"

"It doesn't really feel safe there now," I finished, sitting up too.

"No. It doesn't to me, either."

I felt a pang as I thought of the cabin – our first kiss; the realization that we felt the same way about each other. All the hours that we'd spent talking there, playing cards, holding each other. But it was only a place; it wasn't important. The only important thing was being together.

"So…what now?" I said finally. I adjusted my pillows, lying facing him.

He smoothed my hair away from my face. "Well, the first thing – the main thing – is that I'm not letting you out of my sight again. Whatever happens from now on, it's together."

I reached out and touched my pendant, feeling its smooth facets. "Always," I said. And felt joy flood through me, that we still had a chance at it.

He kissed me gently. "And as for a plan…" Sitting back, he rested his forearms on his knees, his eyebrows drawing together as he thought. "Well, we know that Project Angel still exists – barely. I guess that Sophie will be trying to start it up again, once she gets tired of her safe location."

I pulled my own knees to my chest as I watched him. "Would you want to be involved with them again?"

He snorted slightly. "No. I don't trust them; I don't like how they work. What about you?"

I shook my head. I supposed it wasn't her fault, but I didn't really want to see Sophie, ever again. With a shudder, I realized that she hadn't given me any contact details anyway. She'd been that certain that I was going to die.

Alex tapped his fingers on his knee. "To be honest, Mexico still sounds good to me," he said finally. "We're going to need a safe base, and I don't think we'll find one in this country any more. Plus, it's pretty cheap; I've only got about six hundred dollars left. I'll need to try to get a new training camp going as soon as I can, but for now we could just find someplace safe and I could try to get some new AKs together, and get things started." He looked at me, linking his fingers through mine. "How does that sound to you?"

I hadn't wanted to think about this, but I knew that I had to say it. Gazing down at his hand in mine, I said slowly, "Alex, do you think that – I might still be the one to destroy the angels? I mean, it could still be something that's going to happen, even though it didn't this time." I tried to smile. "Not that I'm really all that eager to try again anytime soon, but…" I stopped, knowing that as unspeakably horrible as the last few days had been, I would do it again, if it really meant that the angels would all be destroyed. I didn't want to; I hated the thought of it. But I would.

Alex rubbed his thumb against my fingers. "I don't know," he said finally. "But Willow, if it's something that happens, then I'm going to be right there with you."

Alarm jolted through me. "I don't want that! Alex, I'd want you to be safe—"

He touched my cheek. "Forget it," he said. "I will never, ever, let you face anything like that alone again."

I couldn't speak. Moving closer, I leaned against him, hugging his waist. He wrapped his arms around me and I nestled against his solid warmth, feeling so incredibly glad that I had him, and that somehow, we were together again. Clearing my throat, I trailed a finger along his forearm. "Mexico sounds…pretty good, actually," I said.

He pulled away, peering into my face. "Are you sure? We wouldn't have anything great there, but we should have enough to survive for a couple of months – long enough to get things going, hopefully."

"Yeah, I'm sure," I said, nodding. I started to smile. "Very sure, in fact." Even knowing what lay ahead, with new angels in the world and Alex one of the few people who could fight them…after these last two days, the thought of just being together – loving each other, spending time together – was like sunshine after rain.

I sat up. "So what will I be doing, while you're finding new AKs?"

His eyebrows rose in surprise. "Helping me, I hope. Willow, I really need you – you get feelings about things; you can tell just by touching someone what they're like." He grinned suddenly. "Plus you get to be the one to fix the bike, if it breaks down."

I laughed. "Psychic-consultant-slash-mechanic…yeah, okay, I accept." My smile faded as I looked down at the bedspread. "I just wish – I wish I could go home and say goodbye to Mom, somehow. I mean – not that she'd realize, probably, but…" I trailed off.

Alex squeezed my hand. "I'd take you there in a second, if it was safe," he said softly.

"I know." I sighed, and shook the thought away. Mom was all right, that was the main thing. And at least I'd be doing something to fight the beings that had hurt her. "Hey, you can teach me how to speak Spanish," I said after a pause.

He smiled, and kissed my nose. "What do you want to learn how to say?"

"How about..." Suddenly I almost couldn't speak. I gazed at Alex, taking in his dark hair, the firm lines of his face, and remembered the first time I'd ever seen him – the way his blue-grey eyes had caught and held me, so that I was barely able to look away from them.

I could barely look away from them now.

Swallowing hard, I touched his lips with my finger, carefully tracing their outline. "How about, you make me so incredibly happy, and – and all I want is to be with you for the rest of my life?"

The look in Alex's eyes was so warm that I felt myself falling. "I've already taught you that one, remember?" he said. Leaning his head down, he kissed me, his lips lingering on mine. "*Te amo,* Willow."

And somewhere inside of me, I knew that my angel was smiling.

ACKNOWLEDGEMENTS

Every story is a journey, for its author no less than for its readers. This particular story has been a longer journey than most; I've known and loved Alex and Willow for many years now, and am thrilled that their tale is finally being told. A lot of people have helped me along the way, and it's only right that I take the time to thank them now.

Liz Kessler and Isobel Gahan, whose staunch belief in the story helped keep its fires burning over the years (even though it eventually turned out to be very different from what I'd first envisioned!); Linda Chapman and Julie Sykes, who keep me sane on a daily basis, and who read early drafts of *Angel* and reassured me that it wasn't rubbish – huge thanks to both of you; your enthusiasm as the first readers meant more than I can say; my agent, Caroline Sheldon, for her steadfast support and guidance, and for loving the story right from the start; my editor, Megan Larkin, for her wonderfully insightful input, and for being so completely in tune with the story and its characters (it's been such a pleasure working with you on *Angel,* and we're still not finished yet!); my editor, Stephanie King, for all of her help, and for being so lovely and calm when I was having panic moments; the publicity and marketing teams at Usborne, who have done such a stellar job at putting *Angel* out into the world – I really couldn't have asked for anything more from them, even if I had handed them a personalized wish list; Katie Beat, for her help with the Spanish translations in the text; Neil Chowney for his advice on car engines and useful suggestions in the breakdown scene; all of the early readers of *Angel* who wrote such glowing reviews – there's no greater lift for a writer than realizing that other people love something you've written as much as you do; the musicians Sarah Class and Karl Jenkins, whose work I listened to over and over during the writing of *Angel;* and finally, my husband Peter, who has been there on this journey with me from the very beginning, and whose practical support during the writing of *Angel* will be forever appreciated. Because of him, I was able to concentrate solely on writing for weeks at a time – a luxury that very few writers enjoy! Thank you for being there, Pete. I love you.

www.angelfever.com